SAVAGE TIMES

SAVAGE TIMES

OSCAR JORDAN

Big Oscar Publishing

For the imagination, courage, and sense of adventure he continues to inspire,

I dedicate this book to my father, Oscar Jordan Jr.

Contents

One

"The universe is conspiring to destroy me," Stewart mumbled under her breath. She glared at the female TV talk show host, mesmerized by her sharp, peach-colored, telegenic features. "Just keep breathing."

"Excuse me?" the host inquired.

The young-ish Stewart was in her late 30s – wore glasses, was beautifully caramel-colored, and bookish. Her hangover was having a tantrum.

The television studio lights were blinding in a few annoying angles. Camera drones hovered noiselessly. Stewart had to adjust her eye-line to see the host's eyes through a blonde helmet of hair. The drones made her feel self-conscious while the hot lights made her scalp itch. No scratching on colonial television.

"Before you ask, the answer is yes," Stewart continued. "I intend to do everything within my power to keep my father's vision alive. It was his dying wish and I vowed to honor that wish."

"I certainly don't mean to diminish the legacy of your father. He was a scientific genius and a great humanitarian—an icon. But despite the groundbreaking success of his terraforming technology, your use of it has caused much debate."

"I'm here to address that."

"As great as *Simulated Earth* is, do we really need these types of games to continue on this path? Hyper-realism? Hyper-escapism? Hyper-violence? What does it say about our society? And what is the moral and ethical cost? I'm no expert, but..."

"That's right, you're no expert."

"If I could just..."

"You're nowhere near an expert. But do you know who *is* an expert? That's right, I am. I'm an expert."

"Yes, I know you're an expert, but..."

"Do you know anything about molecular biology, artificial intelligence, or genetic replication?"

The host shook her head.

"You sure?"

"No, I'm afraid not," the host answered with a polite smile.

"Let me ask you this; how would you go about re-organizing molecules on a subatomic level, then transforming those molecules into living matter?"

"I wouldn't know."

"Really? Ok, let's say you *could*, for the sake of argument, re-organize molecules on a subatomic level then transform that into living matter. How would you export it to a floating rock in the middle of outer space?"

"Uh, a rocket ship?"

"A rocket ship. Ok, let's say you *could* deploy this new matter via *rocket ship* onto a lifeless rock floating in outer space. How would you manage its growth? Think about it. It's the birth of organic life. How would you manage its existence? Human life, and for that matter all organic life is a huge responsibility."

"I've never claimed to be a scientist. Am I not allowed to ask questions?"

The acid storm in Stewart's belly made her squirm in her chair. "I find this type of short attention span journalism insulting to the science community and my father's legacy. Creating an entire world is extremely complex. You have no idea of the hard work and sacrifice that went into the creation of this project."

"Hey, I'm just a former Miss America from Kansas. You're the smartest woman in the colonies. I don't think I'm doing too bad, am I? I'm holding my own, right?" she said turning to the audience. Her award-winning smile revealed sparkling white teeth. The audience cheered.

"You have no idea what I'm talking about, do you? This multi-tiered field of study and research is enormously complicated. My entire life has been devoted to this project. It killed my father."

"And all this for a game?"

"But it's not a game. Not anymore. *Simulated Earth* is as real as our Earth. In many ways it's even more real than reality."

The host turned and locked in on the teleprompter. "If you're just joining us, I'm here with Dr. Marianne Stewart of The Organization. Dr. Stewart is a highly respected scientist, designer, and daughter of the late Nobel Prize-winning scientist Dr. Aloysius Stewart. The topic is molecular biology, bio-protein development, and cell mutation radiation, so let's dig in! I'm so excited!" She turned to Stewart with a playful grin. "Just kidding."

The audience applauded wildly. Stewart was feverish as acidic bile lurched up from her intestines.

"She's one of the brightest and most successful women of color in the Colonial Network," the host continued. "And if you haven't been living under a rock, I don't have to tell you about the game that's taken over the colonies. You know it, you love it, *Simulated Earth*."

Applause.

#

The studio's monitors exploded to life with images of a smiling, racially diverse cast of men, women, and children. Groups of families are seen working together to build a house. A young African American boy in glasses gives instructions to a small group of workers. He refers to a schematic, as an elderly man teaches a teenaged girl how to use a hammer and a nail. A loving father holds an infant boy in his arms. They watch with a sense of wonder as the house is quickly constructed before their very eyes.

From The Official *Simulated Earth* Trailer: First Season Montage:

Open Your Eyes
Endless Fields of Wheat
Happiness
Self-Love & Curiosity
The Heart
The Mind
Universal Values & Mutual Respect
Freedom, Exploration, Adventure
Building the Future Together

BLACKOUT

#

"When season one of the games premiered, it changed the entire landscape of the lifestyle simulation industry," said the host with a furrowed brow. "How does someone dream up something like this? Where do these ideas come from?"

Stewart summoned the patience to answer this question for the 100th time. "With our combined fields of study, we were able to create a new world, but more importantly a new purpose. A practical philosophy for living by example."

Stewart thought she was finally getting a grip on her nausea, but she was wrong. "We wanted to create a Life Simulation Game that would become a model for a new society, a society of virtues—compassion, generosity, and mutual respect. My father believed this would be a great example for the colonies. He wanted to encourage human beings to embrace our differences—he believed kindness was contagious."

The audience applauded.

"Your father was a true visionary. Could you please share with us his dying wish?"

"His dying wish was for me to continue his life's work. To use his terraforming technology to provide entertainment as a learning tool to eliminate prejudice and societal issues. Unfortunately, he passed away the day before we went live."

"The idea of using simulation technology on newly terraformed planets has changed our world," said the host. "The first season was epic. Who knew brotherhood could be so addictive?" she chuckled. "It also made you extremely wealthy."

A bead of sweat trickled down Stewart's forehead.

"But something went wrong, didn't it?" the host continued. "Season two had a surprisingly different tone." She turned to the camera, looking deep into the lens. "This was last week's episode."

Two

Summer — 1942

"You can't swing without seventh chords," Charles LeDuff said to nine-year-old Little Benny. Charles was a handsome, 20-something, good-natured negro, despite the harsh times in his rearview mirror. "It's not a major chord. That's somethin' else. Here's another one."

As the Opel Blitz troop truck jumbled along through the French countryside, Charles took back the weather-beaten guitar and strummed a hip chord at the 8th fret. "See, it sounds different. And you don't need all them low notes. The bass player is already playin' that. Let Fats earn his own bread."

Charles smiled slyly, looking over at Fats. He sat beside them and rolled his eyes. A morbidly obese man, Fats rocked back and forth with the motion of the truck as his enormous belly jiggled.

"It don't mean a thing if it ain't got that swing," Fats said, coughing out a laugh and a sly look at Little Benny.

"I'm tryin' to teach the boy something'," Charles retorted with playful annoyance. He turned his attention back to Little Benny. "If you play the low notes, ain't nobody gonna hear it. Fat's bass will drown you out. Why play it if nobody can hear it? Play the top part. Ya' dig?"

Little Benny nodded. "Solid."

As the troop truck rattled along through the night, Little Benny leaned in close to admire Charles' fingers fretting the strings of the guitar. Little Benny had already figured out cowboy chords, but Charles was playing something different. It was the same notes, but they were splayed across the fretboard in a different shape.

"This is what they call a third inversion," Charles explained. "Same notes, different order. That's what inverted means."

"That's a fifty-cent word," Fats said, chuckling with a grin. "Whoever sold you that word owes you some change."

Little Benny leaned in with his ear close to the body of the guitar. Charles played the chords to "All Of Me" with swinging downstrokes. It was difficult to hear the guitar over the rumbling sound of the truck, but you could feel it. It didn't help that Charles, Little Benny, and Fats were squashed together with fifteen other people.

Ten other negro males and five negro women were sandwiched together on either side of the truck in nightclub eveningwear. They smoked and spoke nervously. Three men forced to stand closest to the driver's cab, held on for dear life. They teetered and jerked from side-to-side, swaying with the motion of the truck.

The cherub-cheeked Buster Pete in his brown bowler hat, fingered the valves of his trumpet nervously. "Ernestine, what are we doin'?" he whispered as he sat pressed against the beautifully light-skinned Lorraine Fontaine. Buster strained to see Ernestine's eyes through the darkness.

Ernestine Tubbs was fierce, brown-skinned, in her mid-40s, and solid like a fire hydrant. The Buster Pete Band was her band, and she ruled it with a tireless constitution.

"Ya'll look like a bunch a' nervous nellies," Ernestine bellowed.

"How long they gonna keep us?" Charles asked grimly. "Is this a concentration camp or a POW camp?" He drew a cigarette from the inside of his blazer and put it in his mouth. He pinched the end of the cigarette with his thin lips.

"Concentration camp?" blurted Ernestine. "My concentration is jus' fine!" she said jokingly. "I've booked some tough joints in my time, but this is ridiculous!"

A few weak laughs and obligatory snickers from the group revealed their growing anxiety. Despite Ernestine's attempt at levity, she shared their concerns.

"Major Schüller said nobody's safe until they round up the trouble-makers," Ernestine said, hanging on to the planks that ran along the length of the truck. "Besides, we'll have a good audience of American POWs to play for. They'll be excited to see us. Now I know this seems like a pain in the neck, but the Germans are doin' this for our safety. This way, we don't get shot – and don't forget we also get a little dough-ray-me," Ernestine said, rubbing her thumb and fingers together for emphasis. "Once they catch them bushwhackers, we can get back to work. Think of this as a one-nighter."

Charles took out a match and lit a cigarette. Engaged in his thoughts, he took a drag and inhaled deeply.

"Somethin' ain't right about this," Sauce said in his gravelly baritone. "I wouldn't trust that Major Schüller as far as I could spit. He gives me the heebie-jeebies."

At six-foot-five-inches tall, Sauce was broad-shouldered and lanky. He was an extraordinary drummer with conked hair who put his own unique brand of "Sauce" on every arrangement. He was an open conduit of emotion when he hit the drums, and brought humanity to every-thing he played. As long as you didn't tell him *how* to play, all was right with the world.

Sauce was emotionally transparent—he was scared. Riding in the back of a German troop truck in the wee hours, scared shitless was the shared sentiment.

"I'm wit' Sauce," Spencer said nervously, smoking a pipe and clinging to his saxophone. "We ain't got nothin' but the clothes on our backs! What about my hair? I need my pomade!"

Charles looked at Little Benny, who was still strumming the guitar. He rubbed his head with affection.

"I'm tellin' you somthin' ain't right about this," Sauce said with a tremor in his voice. "We need to get the hell off this here truck."

The rest of the group erupted into a cacophony of comments and angry retorts directed at Ernestine.

"They have no right to make us do this," cried Millicent, the band's Plain Jane seamstress. Her mousy demeanor disguised the body of a stripper and the mouth of a whore.

"We're Americans. We have rights. The Germans can't tell us what to do! I ain't German!"

"POWs don't tip!" Fats complained.

"That's right!" Spencer demanded. "You need to talk to Major Schüller. We need to re-negotiate this shit."

"All right, put a lid on it!" shouted Ernestine silencing their protests. "Schüller promised me everything was copasetic. We'll be back before ya' know it. He gave me his word."

Ernestine was met with vacant stares. She'd given many motivational speeches over the years, but this time she didn't believe a word she was saying. No one else did either. Her appeasing rhetoric bore the bitter taste of fear.

The truck came to a stop accompanied by the sound of screeching breaks. The group became quiet and anxious. They waited in heart-pounding silence as they heard the sound of doors opening from the front of the cab and jackboots on dirt. They heard vehicles behind them as the canvas covering the rear of the truck was whipped back. It revealed six German soldiers with rifles.

"Raus! Raus!" ordered the soldiers.

Startled, the group piled out of the back of the truck and onto the dirt road. Spreading out from the troop truck, they promptly spilled out into the darkness of the French countryside. Nervous conversation gripped them as they made their way on to the grassy expanse.

"I want to talk to Major Schüller," Ernestine demanded as she stomped her way over to a soldier while ignoring his rifle. "We're sup-posed to be performin' at a camp! What the hell are we doin' out here in the middle of nowhere?! Where's the camp?! Where's the motherfuckin' camp?!"

With a relaxed strength of purpose, a mid-30s, blonde-haired, and delicate Major Schüller stepped out from the staff car. His grey military uniform generated a crisp authority. His polished boots gleamed in the moonlight.

Seeing him walk toward them, Ernestine turned away from the soldier and ran up to Schüller. "Ernst," she said in a forceful whisper. "You said we were goin' to a camp. What are we doin' out here?! What the hell is goin' on?!"

Schüller calmly took out a Walther P38 from his holster, cocked it, and shot Ernestine in her forehead. A neat little hole perforated the front of her head as brains and blood exploded from the rear of her skull. She dropped to the dewy grass.

The group reacted with horrific screams and panic. Shrieks erupted throughout the group as they recoiled from the sight of Ernestine's murder. With impassive menace, Schüller raised his gloved hand and shouted orders in German. "Kill them all!"

Soldiers pulled back the canvas on the second truck revealing two German soldiers sitting behind a machine gun on a tripod. As one soldier fed a belt of ammo into the machine gun, another soldier took aim.

Then the screaming began. The group backed up in weak-kneed terror. Little Benny's blood ran cold as he stared down the barrel of death. His face morphed into a ghoulish mask of contorted fear. A thick splash of blood splattered across the screen—darkness.

Three

The audience gasped. The monitors faded to black. Stewart was going to be sick on television in front of the entire Colonial Network. She perspired heavily, struggling to hang on.

"Woo, that was dark," the host blurted. "That was really dark. So, what happened? Where did all those shiny happy people go?"

"We're experimenting with different scenarios. I've discovered two protagonists I think our fans will enjoy."

"Do you think this is something your father would have signed off on? Some critics are calling this subjugation porn."

Stewart struggled to form a sentence.

"Let's get down to brass tacks," the host continued. "Critics are saying you're using your father's terraforming technology to poop in the proverbial punch bowl, while making yourself rich."

"That's crazy talk."

"Senseless murders in video games is nothing new, but *Simulated Earth* takes this to a whole other level. It's racist sport murders on tap. No disrespect, but your father is spinning in his grave."

"He is not spinning in his grave."

"Well, I disagree. I believe your father *is* spinning in his grave."

"My father is dead. He can't spin anywhere."

"You're Godless, aren't you? Look, I don't mean to make light of your father's death. It's public knowledge your relationship with him was contentious. But experts are saying..."

"Experts?"

"*Critics* are saying this drastic change in tone is you asserting your-self—to crawl out from under your father's shadow."

Stewart squirmed. "If I could just have a drink – just a sip," she thought.

"Did you just ask for a drink?"

"My critics lack the necessary scholarship and mental capacity to understand my work."

"One critic wrote, "She's a petulant teenager with daddy issues on a contrarian binge.""

"No one said that."

"I beg your pardon?"

"No one said that. You made that up to get a reaction out of me."

"According to our sources..."

"There are no sources," Stewart continued. "You're manufacturing conflict using a lie to entertain your audience. More importantly, you're completely unconcerned if this hurts my feelings."

"Wait a minute now..."

"Now, you're going to change the subject to save face."

"Listen, I..."

"Those of us at the top of our field will always be targets for those who want to take our place."

"Is it true that despite all your accomplishments, awards, and hard work, your father was disappointed in you?"

#

Stewart was sweating like a runaway slave. Her eyes darted every-where as she strolled briskly down the marble corridor. With the hall-way clear, she made her move. She sprinted on corporate heels, zipping past elevators. She turned a corner. There was a sign on a door that read LADIES ROOM.

Stewart pushed through the door. Her eyes scanned left to right. She sighed in relief—the ladies room was empty.

Stewart ran to the nearest stall and kicked the door in. She fell to her knees and vomited thick torrents of bile. Her body heaved and contorted violently as sweat dripped from her face.

Stewart paused in relief as her breathing slowed. Her hands shook. She pressed them to her chest and stared at the ceiling—then down at her legs. There was a run in her stocking. The song, "It's Going to Take Some Time" by The Carpenters seeped inside the pristine stalls. Her blouse was ruined. She took off her glasses and spat into the toilet. "Somebody sabotaged my game, and I'm going to find the cocksucker who did it."

Four

Chicago — 2023

Lorenzo Savage could give two shits if his crew thought he was a condescending jerk. Their feelings were the least of his worries. But making them recite his instructions like a nursery rhyme like the mission scene from the movie *The Dirty Dozen* made him feel better. The stakes were too high for, "Oops, sorry. I forgot."

Savage and his four-man crew of armed bank robbers strolled into The First National Bank of Chicago. They wore Richard Nixon masks, dark coveralls, and were prepared for anything. Savage took point and fired a short burst from his submachine gun while the other robbers fanned out like a synchronized swim team.

"Everybody down on the floor," Savage bellowed into the lobby like a drill sergeant. "This is your captain speaking! If you do what we say, nobody will get hurt. We don't want your money. We want the bank's money. The bank is insured. Billy don't be a hero. Don't be a fool with your life. Just stay calm, and we'll be out of your hair in a few minutes. And please, don't be stupid. Thank you."

As bank employees and customers pissed in their pants lying on the floor, one of Savage's crew ran to a group that was slow in processing their circumstances. One of the crewmembers ordered the customers to ease down to the floor at gun point, just as he was instructed.

A guard reached for his pistol. Savage had been tracking him from the corner of his eye. He rushed over and smashed the guard on the side of the head with the butt of his machine gun. The guard collapsed. Savage took the guard's pistol and stuffed it into the front of his belt. "See what happens to stupid?" Savage said as employees and customers squeezed their eyes shut in terror.

The robbery was performed like a military operation. Savage used hand signals as the robbers obeyed, moving to select sections of the bank. His crew packed large olive drab duffle bags full of money.

Savage jumped up on top of the bank counter. "Keep your heads down on the floor! Think about your families! If you want to die today, I can help you with that!"

Savage liked to use machine guns for psychological reasons—it scared the shit out of people. A Glock is more efficient for these kinds of jobs, but your average Joe Six-Pack guy is visual. They think with their eyeballs. When civilians see a machine gun, they listen the fuck up. Savage had no intention of spraying some poor sap into performing a percolating death dance—it was counter-productive.

The problem was the help. Bringing in a new guy was risky. You never know how someone is going to act with the power of life and death in their hands. You can brief a newbie all day long about what to do and what not to do, but he's going to do whatever he does during the moment of truth.

In this case, a newbie lost control and shot an old man for looking at him too long. Somehow the newbie got it into his head the old man recognized him. The newbie freaked and made a dumbass decision. He shot the old man dead—doing precisely what Savage instructed everyone *not* to do.

It sent all the hostages into crazy time, complicating the operation. They lost valuable minutes calming everyone down. Eventually, they acquired the take and barely escaped. It was a close call, but it was too close for Savage. It was the kind of too close that could have meant a lifetime behind bars with all the fixins'. Savage had done a short stretch at Florida State Prison before he escaped, and he was for damn sure never going back.

#

When Savage and his crew arrived at the safe house to let the heat die down, he asked the newbie to join him in the garage. Savage wanted to hear his side of the story. The newbie had a plethora of long-winded excuses and existential epiphanies before he finally admitted he'd panicked.

These were the familiar stories heard in prisons every day all over the world. The coulda, woulda, shoulda stories told by amateurs, imposters, and the fortune challenged. There were countless tales of what the other guy didn't do—bad luck, bad decisions, racism, or fate.

Savage was a top-level criminal who took pride in his work. He wouldn't allow anyone to diminish his craft or be the reason to be captured. An amateur will crack like an egg under the hot lights of an interrogation—this newbie was already cracking. When he went for his gun, it was the last mistake he would ever make.

#

When Savage returned to the safe house alone and started dividing up the newbie's share of the loot, the crew could pretty much figure out what went down. Savage wasn't a cold-blooded killer. This was business. No loose ends—no ghosts waiting in dark alleys. Savage was all business, and ending that newbie had to be done. Lorenzo Savage may have been a murderer—but he was no monster. During his career, he'd killed a lot of people, but he never killed anybody that didn't deserve it. If Savage killed you, you earned it. No tears, no regrets—just correct assessment and action.

"It's either him or me, and I'm not going back to prison for anybody —nothing personal."

-Lorenzo Savage

His crew thought he was a little cold-blooded about it, but in Savage's mind, swift and decisive is the way to go. He skipped the hand wringing and cut to the crux of the biscuit. No time for histrionics. His gift was the ability to arrive at a solution and execute that decision sooner than anyone else. Sometimes people died. Life is fucked up like that.

#

On any heist, you need a guy who can plan, think crystal clear, and hold everything together — someone who can stay calm under pressure and stay on point. That someone was Lorenzo Savage. Savage was a professional. His expertise was planning and emotional violence.

"I don't use physical violence. I use intimidation."

-Lorenzo Savage

He began his career as a grifter, a card shark, a pickpocket, and a slight-of-hand escape artist. He graduated to institutional robbery— mostly banks, armored cars, and the occasional jewelry heist. He didn't rob banking institutions because he cared about civilians getting their money back. He robbed them because that's where the money was. He received the biggest cut because his shit was clean. His jobs were immaculate. From pre-planning to the getaway, they called his jobs The Immaculate Conception. He planned the smoothest heists in the business. You do exactly as he says, follow his rules, and everybody gets rich. You deviate even in the slightest, and you're dead—because he'd kill you.

Rules were important to Savage. Rules kept him one step ahead of the law. But now and then there were problems. He refused to work with new people, but sometimes he had to cut corners. Sometimes you'd get special requests from the moneymen who staked the job. That's when things would go sideways. Rest in peace, newbie.

#

As a hormonal teenager Savage was girl crazy. As a young man, he believed love was everything. Without love, what was the meaning of life?

"How does one endure the cruelty of life without love's intoxicating distraction?"

-Lorenzo Savage

Savage vented as his Uncle Benjamin patiently taught him jazz guitar. Uncle Benjamin would pause after hearing his drama-filled tales and always replied with compassionate wisdom.

"Lorenzo, leave those girls alone. You'll have plenty of time for that later. School is the most important thing in your life right now. School now—pussy later."

But he never could leave those girls alone. They were his weakness, his Achilles' heel. And when he fell, he fell hard—like a punk, a bitch. Someone once told him he fell so hard because he was trying to fill the void left after his mother disappeared.

"She went out one night for a pack of cigarettes, and never came back home. Yeah, for real."

-Lorenzo Savage

Savage never gave it much thought. He felt fortunate his cool uncle was there to raise him.

"Keep that pop in your collar," Uncle Benjamin would tell Savage. It was his way of reminding him to stand tall and keep his chin up. Savage's reply was always, "Yessiree."

#

You'd have thought the FBI would have sprung for a private jet to take Savage back to the United States. He was disappointed to learn that being at the top of America's Most Wanted list wasn't as special as he thought. But here he was flying through the air, tucked, folded, and handcuffed.

With a Special Agent on either side of him, they let him wear his signature black blazer and white dress shirt only because orange prison coveralls would draw too much attention. Savage was going away forever, and for the first time in his life he didn't care.

The flight attendant who recited the emergency exit instructions resembled a Barbie doll if they allowed Barbie dolls to mature sweetly into their late 40s. She was Savage's type—pretty, cheerful, clean—perfect. She glanced at Savage then looked away to avoid eye contact. She was uncomfortable and distracted as Savage's eyes leered their way up her skirt and around the inside of her panties.

#

Lorenzo Savage had given up his profession for clean sheets with high thread counts, avocado toast, and Joslyn. Ah, Joslyn—the smell of her hair, the taste of her skin, the curve of her hips... But there were things about Savage. Things Joslyn couldn't change. Little things—things he thought didn't matter but mattered too much to her.

They had all these perfect moments. They had love, money, and hypnotic lovemaking. But as time went on, she kept coming back to harp on the little things. Stupid little things—the small stuff on the first-world problem pie chart. His off-the-grid lifestyle had left a scar on his personality that would reveal itself at the worst times and she couldn't let it go. Women can be petty like that.

When he was with her, he laughed and smiled more than he ever did, but when he least expected it, she would catch him being himself—dark, contemplative, suspicious of the world.

Savage fought for her. He pleaded, he begged, and he never begged. She was supposed to be the person that would rescue him from the rest of his life. He needed her. He was more than willing to tolerate her lazy new aged spiritualism bullshit in exchange for a feeling of belonging, security, and love.

See, a 53-year-old career criminal starts thinking about his future, where he's going to lay his head for the next 30 years, and with whom. Time flies, and the next thing you know, you look up and find yourself alone. The life gets lonely, and loneliness is an awful place to be when you live a dangerous life.

When Joslyn left him, it eviscerated his soul. His thoughts turned black, and he flew to Buenos Aires. A string of bar fights and binge drinking alerted the local authorities. One thing led to another. When the FBI and a tactical team kicked in his door, it didn't matter. Nothing mattered anymore.

#

At approximately 3:05am a heavily armed tactical unit led by FBI Special Agents Nelson Fuller and Delores Santiago, broke down Savage's hotel room door in Buenos Aires. He sat in the living room, staring at the television with the sound off. Mozart's "Requiem in D Minor" was blaring on the radio. Savage was wasted—fixated on Laura Petrie's surreal perfection. Tears streamed down his face. He was finished. A little under a quarter of a million dollars lay stacked on a nearby card table with a fully loaded 1911 next to it. Savage sat on a kitchen chair, motionless. Fuller and Santiago picked him up, handcuffed him, and took him away. He would have preferred to have finished watching *The Dick Van Dyke Show* but offered no resistance.

#

It was finally over and thank you black baby Jesus for getting him the hell out of Buenos Aires. He wasn't a religious man, but he thanked the gods of fortune for shipping his empty shell back to the world. A speedy trial would send him to a small dark hole for the rest of his life. No need to pretend, to smile, to put on a front for the world. No need to compose insipid small talk. He could be himself—he would finally be free from the annoying world.

When Joslyn confessed, "I don't see us growing old together, I don't see us together when we're 80," his stomach turned inside out. She rejected everything that he was. It felt like his insides had been scooped out with a rusty ice cream scooper.

His meticulously planned thirty-million-dollar heist was supposed to be his last. He was retiring for Joslyn, but his sacrifice didn't matter. She left him. He took his share of the loot and flew to Buenos Aires to forget.

It's a tired cliché, but that last job—that final career-ending heist where you swear you're done and you're going to walk away forever, free and clear? It never happens. It's always something—if it's not one thing, it's another.

Five

Deep Space — 2023

A white dot moved through the endless infinite. It grew larger as it pierced the darkness like a bullet of energy. The white dot suddenly revealed itself—a spacecraft.

Stewart peered out at the stars. Looking official in a blue flight suit, she sat in the cockpit operating green virtual controls. A cigarette sat burning in an ashtray near the console as a thread of smoke drifted in low gravity. A metal drinking flask sat next to it.

Stewart grimaced and took off her glasses. Troubled thoughts were written across her smooth brow. She leaned across the console and flipped a switch activating a video monitor. Little Benny's fearful face appeared frozen on the screen. Stewart sighed, reached for the flask, and took a swig.

Six

35,000 Feet Above The Atlantic Ocean — 2023

Special Agent Dolores Santiago was a semi-butch 40-something Latina, who was fair-skinned enough to pass for white. She was blessed with a rare trifecta of assets: Fierce, formidable, and fucking hot. Her superior officer, Special Agent Nelson Fuller was a decorated FBI veteran on his last assignment before retirement. He was a rugged, buzz cut wearing 60-year-old who should have retired three years ago. His protests finally ran out, he was being sent out to pasture, and so was his passion for life.

"My name is Agent Fuller," he said to Savage with a rural American lilt. "This is Special Agent Santiago. If you need to go to the restroom, you're going to do it now. You'll be shackled the entire time. It's now or never."

"No time like the present," Savage replied.

Fuller was weather-beaten, raw, and no non-sense. The deep-set lines on his face displayed his sacrifice and devotion to law enforcement. He'd brought many a criminal to justice in his time, but this last assignment gave him pause.

Santiago was a dish – but in an edgy, bondage and discipline sort of way. Even her charcoal-grey Hillary Clinton action suit couldn't mask her athletic curves. One could only imagine all the insufferable shit she had to endure for an FBI pension.

She was strong, lean, and had a face etched with a mature sensuality. "I'll take him to the restroom," Santiago said, feeling the need to stretch her legs.

"Agent Santiago is going to the restroom with you," Fuller explained to Savage. "She's going to stand beside you, watch you take out your ding-a-ling, and you're going to pee. Got it?"

"Okie-Dokie, Smokie," Savage replied vacantly.

They helped him to his feet. Savage shuffled along with shackled wrists through the narrow aisle of the airplane. Santiago walked close behind with her hand on his shoulder as passengers gawked at America's most wanted non-conformist.

A tall Black man in his early-20s exited the restroom. He strode down the aisle towards them. He sported a do-rag, a menagerie of tattoos on both arms, and a yellow LeBron James jersey. He got an eyeful of Savage in handcuffs.

"Sup, boss?"

"I'm not your boss, homepage," Savage said with smidgeon of bitterness.

"Ok, boomer."

Savage stopped himself. He took a breath, deciding not to be that guy. "Apologies. I'm going to prison for the rest of my life, so I'm not quite my normal self today."

"Each day is a new day with endless possibilities."

"I'll mention that to the Aryan Brotherhood."

"I feel you. Name's Darius. Keep it 100."

"No chit-chat," Santiago ordered. "Keep it moving."

They moved along, then squeezed into the narrow compartment of the lavatory and closed the door. "Well," Santiago said. "Get busy."

Savage took out his Johnson and pissed long and hard with his eyes closed. The pungent aroma of urine swelled up to their nostrils. Santiago stared at him expressionless with Savage's back to her.

His thoughts drifted to Joslyn and how she blew up their lives. "You know that song, 'Whipping Post?'"

"What?" Santiago replied.

"The Allman Brothers. They were a band. Southern-fried blues-fusion. 'Sometimes I feel like I've been tied to the whipping post?'"

"Zip it up."

"We're not going to get to know each other?"

"You might want to start wearing cologne. Oh wait, that's right. You're going to prison for the rest of your life—scratch that. The cologne might attract the wrong kind of attention. Never mind."

"You feds love prison homo humor. What's up with that? Why do you guys like dick jokes so much?"

"Por favor di algo que me haga lastimarte."

"No te gusto mucho, ¿verdad?"

Savage flushed the toilet and washed his hands. He looked in the mirror. He noticed the greying hair around his temples—the whitening beard stubble. "Getting old is fucked up."

He turned to face Santiago. He could smell her. His thoughts traveled between her legs, but she snapped him back to reality. "Get over it."

They maneuvered awkwardly in close quarters. Santiago turned around to unlock the restroom door. She had trouble opening it as Savage pressed against her tightly from behind. Santiago opened the door and exited. As Santiago left the restroom, Savage withdrew his hand from the side pocket of her blazer. His fingers curled swiftly over the handcuff keys and into his palm.

Seven

Space: The Lunar Distance — 2023

Stewart studied the controls on the instrument panel as she navigated the vessel through the infinite void. Outside the cockpit window, a small blue marble orbited in the distance: *Simulated Earth.* A male voice spoke to her from the console.

"Marianne?"

"Rit."

"I'm on a secure channel."

"Copy that."

"You should be entering *Simulated Earth's* atmosphere soon. You'll need to activate the cloaking protocol to avoid being detected."

"I am completely aware of that."

"Just trying to help."

"I appreciate your concern, but I need you to understand that I know what I'm doing. You keep forgetting that."

"I warned you something like this could happen. I still think using my Biomechanoid tech could…"

"Thank you for reminding me again. The Organization agreed with me on how to investigate this."

"I remember the vote," Ritenour snarled. "I still disagree. I just don't understand why you won't let me…"

"When the event reboots with the new protagonists, the ripple effect will create a completely different scenario. It'll buy me some time to figure out who did this."

"You enjoy playing God. Admit it."

She took a moment to think about that. "This is my baby. I gave birth to it. Somebody stuck their foot in it, and now it's time for a little corporal punishment."

"Just make sure you stay out of the action. Let the protagonists handle the violence. They'll figure it out for themselves. Then come home."

"I will," Stewart said disguising her annoyance.

Stewart noticed a flashing blue blip on the control panel. "I've spotted the passenger plane."

"I love you," Ritenour said.

"I love you too, Rit."

Eight

❧

Savage and Santiago returned to their seats as Fuller stood to make sure Savage was securely installed in the middle seat. Santiago and Fuller then sat down on either side of him. Before they got comfortable, they covered his handcuffs with a blanket. But not before a young blonde ponytailed mom in pink sweatpants with the word "Juicy" printed on her butt got an eyeful of Savage's handcuffs. She reacted cautiously, pretending to mind her own business as she passed through the aisle, holding her infant child.

"It's a 10-hour flight," Fuller said to Savage. "You can sleep or not sleep. But don't even think about trying anything. If you even *dream* about trying to escape, you better wake up and apologize."

"Any questions?" Santiago inquired.

Savage stared off into space. He thought about Joslyn's wholesome white woman smile.

\#

In the cockpit of the airplane, everything was business as usual. The captain sat relaxed in his chair reading a manual as his co-pilot checked the instrumentation. A radio transmission came crackling over their headsets.

"0-5-1-niner, we need you to look out your left window. We just picked up an irregularity on our radar. It's an unidentified light source that seems to be on a direct course with your flight path. Please confirm."

The pilot and co-pilot looked at each other puzzled.

"What?"

#

"You're my last—my final assignment," Fuller informed Savage.

A middle-aged obese woman from across the aisle wearing a blonde wig, a blue muumuu, and Birkenstocks smiled at Fuller. Fuller returned the smile.

"After a long and illustrious career sending bad guys like you up the river, they handed your case to me as my last hurrah. You're my gold watch. They gave me the great Lorenzo Savage as my crowning achievement before I'm sent out to pasture.

"Congratulations."

"Thank you. *She* did all the work," Fuller said

pointing to Santiago. "Your capture is supposed to be a special milestone for me, but you and I both know who deserves the credit. I will make it known in my report that Santiago is the one who captured you. In a way, you're retiring too. But I suspect my retirement will be more pleasant than yours, unless you consider living in a cage with naked men a barrel of monkeys."

Savage glanced at Santiago. She remembered his earlier comment.

"What difference does it make?" Savage replied. "It's like somebody else is pulling the strings. We're just dancing no matter what music is playing."

"You made your bed," Santiago replied.

"Did I?"

"Those banks didn't rob themselves."

"My partner is moving on to bigger and better things," Fuller continued. "She deserves it. You were a difficult man to catch.

She's been tracking you for months. She probably knows more about you than you do."

"Not everything," Santiago said. "You have to wonder why the greatest criminal mastermind of his generation is able to disappear without a trace, only to get apprehended while shit-faced in a Buenos Aires flophouse."

"I don't kiss and tell," Savage replied dryly.

"Her work is exemplary," Fuller added.

"I couldn't have taken him into custody without you, sir."

"I doubt that. I saw something in you the first time I laid

eyes on you. All I did was pull a few strings to get you away from those eggheads in science and technology. You have the calling, the gift."

"This is a special moment between you two," Savage

said. "I'll give you two some privacy," he said as he feigned leaning forward as if he was about to stand up.

"I don't appreciate your tone," Santiago said to Savage.

"Secure that attitude, or I'll secure it for you."

"If I were you, I'd listen to her," Fuller said as he

pulled a magazine out of the pocket of the seat in front of him. "She's former Special Forces. She serves up a Special Forces blend of whoop-ass you just can't get anywhere else."

Savage considered the consequences then asked Santiago,

"Are you a Gold Star lesbian or a regular lesbian?"

Without missing a beat, Santiago punched Savage squarely between the eyes—hard. He didn't see it coming, which is the worst kind of punch. The pain spread across the bridge of his nose to his central nervous system. Savage was gripped in physical suffering. "Ow."

"What's a Gold Star lesbian?" asked Fuller. Santiago gave him a blank stare cautioning him not to go there. Suddenly a message crackled through the intercom from the cockpit.

"Ladies and gentlemen, this is your captain speaking. We're expecting some light turbulence. Please return to your seats and fasten your seatbelts—nothing to be concerned about. This is quite common on an overseas flight."

Savage turned to his left to look out the window across from Santiago. A luminous ball of white light hurtled toward them at an incredible speed. Savage could not believe what he was seeing. Santiago turned to see it too. Fuller looked up from his magazine.

The captain continued his announcement. "Flight attendants, cabin crew, please be..." There was a loud roar, shaking—then the lights went out.

Nine

The countryside.

"So, this is what it's like to be dead," Santiago thought to herself. She forgot how to breathe and freaked out for a second. She exhaled hard. Her eyes popped open. Her heart was pounding so fast she thought she was having a heart attack. She inhaled and exhaled rapidly, afraid and confused. She scanned the perimeter in a fever as she struggled to gather her senses.

Passengers from the airplane were strewn across an extensive grassy area like exploded luggage. A few of them stirred. An infant was crying in the distance.

"Santiago!" Fuller yelled as he staggered to his feet. He was disoriented. "What happened!? Where are we?!"

Santiago jogged over to him, still dizzy.

"Are you ok?"

"What the hell happened?!"

"I don't know."

"Did we crash? What..."

"Hold on." Santiago pulled out her cell phone, pressed a button, and listened for a dial tone. After a beat, her face registered disappointment. "Nothing."

"What?!" Fuller said as the blood returned to his brain. With great effort he stopped himself from vomiting and spit. His phone was dead too. "Sweet Christopher."

Santiago heard moaning from the other passengers as they gained consciousness. Her head whipped around frantically in all directions, not knowing who to help first.

"I think we're somewhere in Europe," Savage called out to Santiago. Savage sat in the grass cool as a cucumber, still handcuffed. He took in the picturesque vista. Savage had been sitting for a while as if he were witnessing everyone's bad acid trip.

Santiago jogged over to him with difficulty. "Something hit the plane," Savage explained. "Something big—something weird."

"Europe?" replied Santiago as she scanned the area. "That's impossible."

"Well, we're not in the middle of the Atlantic Ocean; that's for sure," Savage replied.

"This is... crazy," Santiago said, thinking out loud.

"Hey! Look!" Fuller pointed to the other passengers who were strewn about like children's toys. They rose to their feet and staggered towards them in confusion. The blonde woman wearing the "Juicy" sweatpants drifted around in a catatonic state. She saw Santiago and Fuller and jogged over to them. "My baby! Where's my baby!?"

One by one, the passengers began to vanish. Santiago, Fuller, and Savage were stunned.

"Jumpin' Jesus," Savage said to himself as he got to his feet.

Santiago and Fuller were speechless. Fuller trotted over to where the passengers had been. They were nowhere to be found. In the distance, the blonde mom's infant daughter sat in the grass. She played intently with a dandelion, oblivious to everything around her. By the time Santiago's body received the message from her brain to run over to her, the little girl had vanished.

Savage saw the little girl disappear as well. "We're next."

"Right," Fuller said as he fought off fear and panic. "Let's... police the perimeter—get our bearings."

"Landmarks," Santiago said.

"Anything," Fuller added.

"This is obviously some kind of cosmic event," Savage said matter-of-factly. "Where's the plane? Where's the wreckage?"

"We have eyes, Captain Obvious," Fuller said. "Stop asking stupid questions. Now, keep your mouth shut while we assess the situation."

"This is some kind of Bermuda Triangle shit," Savage replied.

"And I could give a fiddler's fuck about your keen observations. You're in FBI custody – my custody. Shut your pie hole. If you can't do that, I'll shut it for you. Capiche? One more thing—if you run, it's going to be extremely bad for you."

Savage got the message and smirked. "You're the boss."

"Goddam right I am!" Fuller barked.

"This place doesn't even look vaguely familiar," Santiago said, cutting in. She looked around. There wasn't another person or a building as far as the eye could see. "No debris field. No casualties."

"No jet fuel," Fuller continued, as he smelled the air. "Nothing—clean."

"There's got to be a city or a town nearby," Santiago concluded.

Savage pointed to something far off in the distance. "That's a road. That means road signs. If we head that way, maybe we can figure out where we are."

"They just disappeared," blurted Santiago. "Gone. Just gone."

"Hold it together, Santiago," Fuller ordered sternly. "Don't forget your training."

"Training?!" Santiago replied. "There's no training for this!"

Fuller tried to slap Santiago to snap her out of her panic. She caught his hand mid-air before it struck her. "Don't do that, sir. I'm ok."

"Alright. Stay with me. I need you tip-top."

Santiago tossed his hand away. "I'm fine, sir."

They began walking toward the road from the middle of nowhere. Savage looked around at the trees with his hands cuffed in front of him. "I don't know a whole lot about mother-nature, but I could swear those trees look European. Either that or we're in the rich, fertile land of eastern Pennsylvania."

Santiago gave him a look, not knowing if he was serious.

"Those are Pine and Beech trees. They grow in a lot of places."

"Just an observation."

"An unhelpful observation," Fuller added.

"Something feels off," replied Santiago. "The air is so clean, even for the country."

"The question is, how did we get here?" Savage continued. "No plane, no wreckage..."

"There's nothing around here for miles," added Fuller as he spun around, taking it all in. "It doesn't make sense."

"And none of us were hurt," Santiago added. "Plane crashes are as ugly as it gets."

Savage and Santiago stopped suddenly. Fuller stopped in his tracks with them and listened. They heard the sound of a car engine far off in the distance. They froze in silence. The sound came from the direction of the road ahead. They waited a beat then impulsively took off running toward the sound. They sprinted for a good quarter of a mile as the thought of being rescued filled them with hope and a renewed sense of energy.

They slowed down as they reached the edge of a dirt-covered road and listened as they caught their breath. They peered off into the distance. After a long beat, a car came into view. Santiago waved her arms, trying to get its attention.

As the car drew closer, the expression on Santiago's face changed from relief to suspicion. Savage was uncertain of what he was seeing. Fuller was squinting to see the details of the car. As the vehicle drew closer, they weren't sure if what they were seeing was real. The car was a 1930s era Mercedes Benz staff car. A black swastika was posted on a red flag attached to the right front fender.

"Nazis?" said Savage.

Savage and Santiago made eye contact. Fuller was stunned. As the car drew closer, the swastika came into clear view.

"Is this a joke?" Santiago asked under her breath.

"They must be making a movie nearby," Fuller said. "I'm sure they'll give us a ride so we can get some help," he chuckled. "Scared the shit outta me for a second. Could you imagine?" he said to Savage. "That would be some hellaciously bad luck to run into Nazis out here in the middle of nowhere."

"Yeah, that wouldn't be too good for us," Savage said with an uneasy feeling.

"You mean not too good for *you*," Fuller said jokingly. "Nazis aren't too fond of the brothers if ya' know what I mean."

Savage ignored him. As the staff car slowed and eased up near them, Savage used the distraction to surreptitiously remove the key from his pocket and unlock his handcuffs. They dropped silently into the grass behind him.

A well-dressed man and woman sat in the back seat. *She* was a platinum blonde in her early 30s. *He* was a distinguished, grey-haired gentleman in his early 60s. They were dressed in 1940s era clothing. The man had a black swastika pin on the left lapel of his white blazer.

The woman wore a beautiful floral print dress, which draped over her lanky, boyish frame. Between them was a picnic basket. In the front seat behind the steering wheel was a curiously short man with a thick black mustache, a grey chauffeur's uniform, and a matching cap.

In the vehicle's front passenger side was a man wearing a World War II-era German officer's uniform. He stared at the group curiously. He leisurely stepped out of the car with a pleasant smile and began speaking to them in German. "Wie können wir Ihnen behilflich sein?"

The three of them froze, not knowing what to say. After a pregnant pause, Santiago answered in broken German.

"We... we were in an accident. We are not sure... We need to find a phone. Can you give us a ride?"

The officer gave them the once over, looking suspiciously at Fuller's FBI windbreaker and jeans. "You do not look like you are from here. Where are you from?"

Santiago racked her brain, trying to come up with a response in German. Savage replied for her in perfect German.

"We're lost and we could use a ride into town. Are you making a movie nearby, Herr Colonel?"

Fuller and Santiago were surprised by Savage's command of German. Fuller noticed his wrists were free and displayed his displeasure.

The officer smiled at Savage and turned his attention back to Santiago and Fuller. "Who are you? What are you doing out here in the middle of nowhere?"

"We are lost," Santiago replied. That is a great costume. It looks very... authentic."

"Costume?"

"That is a... World War II German military uniform."

"Correct."

"A costume."

"I am afraid you are mistaken."

"How so?"

"This is not a costume. I am an officer of the Third Reich."

Savage checked their surroundings, maintaining a poker face. Fuller leaned into Santiago.

"What's going on?"

"Can you give us a ride to the nearest telephone?" asked Savage.

"We would be happy to give you a ride into the city, but as you can see, there is not enough room. That, and we would never dream of riding with a dirty black nigger."

Savage stared back at him with cold eyes.

Suddenly the officer drew his Luger and pointed it at them. "Put your hands up."

Santiago, Savage, and Fuller froze, then raised their hands.

"Do you take me for a fool?" the officer queried. "You are obviously American spies. You will hang for your crimes against the Fatherland."

"Tell me this is your idea of dry humor," Savage replied as rage swelled up within him.

Fuller took out his badge and displayed it. "My name is Special Agent Fuller with the FBI. We're taking a prisoner into custody. We have federal authorization to commandeer your vehicle to complete our mission."

The officer stared at him incredulously.

"Obstructing the apprehension of a felon is a federal offense," Fuller continued. "Now I'm sure you wouldn't want to be taken into custody wearing that get up. It would be very bad for you. Do yourself a favor—be smart, ride us into town, then you can go back to your Halloween party."

"Look, we don't want any trouble with the neo-Nazis," Santiago added. "We just need a cell phone signal."

The officer looked confused. "Neo-Nazis?" the officer said in English with a thick German accent. "What is a... neo-Nazi?"

Savage and Santiago made eye contact realizing things were getting stranger by the second.

"I need you to tell me this is a joke," said Savage.

"Colonel Burnhoffer!" The woman in the back seat bellowed. "They probably got lost trying to find their way to The Montclair. It is where all the negroes play their swing music and Lindy Hop."

She stood up in the car with a sexy hipless wiggle stepping out from the side door. She gave Savage, Santiago, and Fuller a long look. She reached over to touch Savage's hair. He smacked her hand away in disdain. She recoiled with surprise holding her hand to her chest. Colonel Burnhoffer reacted by aiming the pistol at Savage's face.

"This one is a little feisty," the woman retorted.

She turned to Burnhoffer. "Why else would they be traveling with an American Schwarzer?"

"Astrid, would you please allow Colonel Burnhoffer to handle these matters," her backseat companion interrupted with annoyance. "It's none of our concern."

Astrid stared at Savage, captivated by his intensity. "I do not think darkies make such good spies, Wilhelm," she laughed. "They are not very intelligent, but they do run fast." Turning to Savage, she said, "Do you know Jesse Owens?"

Savage gave her a vacant stare.

"The nigger runner from the Olympics?" She turned to Wilhelm in the backseat. "He is the fastest nigger I have ever seen!" she giggled. "The darkies have a lot of impressive talents. It is not fair at all, is it?"

Burnhoffer chuckled. "Perhaps you are right." He turned toward Wilhelm taking his eyes off Savage for a split second.

"If monkey spies from America were infiltrating Europe, they would be pretty easy to catch. We would simply use bananas as bait." The Germans laughed.

Savage reached over with split-second timing, cranked Burnhoffer's wrist, and took away the Luger. Without missing a beat, he cocked the weapon and shot Burnhoffer in the side of the head. Burnhoffer dropped to the ground in a lifeless heap.

"Sieg Heil, motherfucker."

Ten

The brass alarm clock ticked mercilessly in the wee hours of the morning. All Stewart wanted to do was lay there naked under the sheets. She wished that time would stand still just for a few more minutes. But time doesn't do that. She of all people knew that. But an award-winning designer can still dream, can't she? A half-empty bottle of whiskey, a shot glass, and an ashtray full of butts reminded her of last night's escapades—that and a sore pussy.

"Last night. What a crazy night."

Stewart wasn't her usual self. She broke a number of her own rules. Lots of engaging, drinking, and eventually getting fucked really hard. While the moment washed over her like a greasy tide, Stewart rationalized the shit out of losing control of her drinking. She was too caught up in having fun for the first time in years.

What the hell. It was party time in Paris, summer of 1942. One interaction led to another. A nightclub here, a drink there, dancing, throwing up in an alley, narrowly escaping a Nazi patrol, another drink... a handsome sweet talker, more boozing... It was a slow glide into the seedy, greasy, unwashed.

Palmer was tall, charming, good looking, and at the right place at the right time. It was that first sip of cognac that destroyed all of Stewart's excellent judgment. So much for keeping her drinking to a minimum. She blamed it on stress.

"Tomorrow is another day—clean slate."

Stewart and Palmer were in bed naked with a thin bedsheet covering them. The window was open in the tiny French bachelor pad as a soft breeze blew over their pungent skin. Palmer was out like a light. His longish conk was disheveled and spread out over his forehead.

"He deserves to rest," Stewart thought to herself. "He fucked me so good. I just wish I hadn't been so drunk. I would have enjoyed it more."

Feelings of duty and responsibility poked at her. "Back to work. I need to setup holographic prompts for Savage."

But she couldn't move. Clothes were strewn all around the room, and despite a gentle breeze, the small hotel room reeked of the musty aroma of sex. Her antsiness prevailed as she sat up in bed to light a cigarette.

Striking a wooden match on the side of the matchbox reminded her of how different this world was. She saw her handheld computer device on the floor next to her panties, gently pulsating. The numbers on the digital timer counted backward. There wasn't a whole lot of time left.

"So much technology back home, yet so many selfish assholes," she said under her breath. "Do they deserve saving?"

Stewart was hoping for the best, but she was sure that however this mission turned out, her career would be finished. She let things go on for too long. She should have acted sooner, been more decisive. There was blood in the water, and it would be almost impossible for things to go back the way they were. It was only wishful thinking on Stewart's part that she could fix this world. But that wasn't the real issue.

The whole thing was all kinds of wrong. Stewart had created a groundbreaking design. It made her rich beyond her wildest dreams, but her design took an ugly turn. Suddenly, murder and stupidity became top-rated entertainment.

Stewart's *Simulated Earth* was the most popular Strategic Life Simulation game in the colonies. It began as a cinematic exhibit like watching an ant farm of humans the size of a planet through a headset. But something changed. The ants became hate-filled murderous pieces of shit. That's when the game blew up and became even more popular.

Somewhere in between teaching children science and empowering the homeless, a contagion of discontent morphed into jealousy, paranoia, and racism. An epidemic of stupidity caused the inhabitants of *Simulated Earth* to hate and murder. Real Earth had miraculously evolved past that, focusing instead on self-realization and the betterment of humanity. At least that's what they told themselves. Suddenly, millions of users became fixated by the atrocities in the game. It spoke volumes about the world Stewart called home.

When she questioned the horrendous abuses in the game to her superiors, they dismissed her concerns because it wasn't real. It was only a game. She presented a detailed plan to fix the problem, but The Organization didn't care. They argued that while the characters and their actions were deplorable, they weren't real. It was all fantasy, fiction—"part of the game." It was all avatars and action figures. "Edutainment"—An educational tool and sociological experiment as entertainment—and the most popular game in the goddamn colonies.

"Whatchu' thinkin' about?" Palmer inquired softly. He'd been watching her as she sat smoking—consumed by a multi-layered cake of overwhelming thoughts.

"You're up. You sleep ok?"

"Oh, I slept real good, thanks to you. You're quite a firecracker, sugar."

"You have a big fat cock."

"Uh, thank you," Palmer replied with a sheepish grin.

"The alcohol here is stronger than I remember," she said as she poured another glass of whiskey.

"You been to Paris before?"

"A long time ago."

"You drink like a pro."

"I'm on vacation."

"Right. A beautiful, intelligent, colored woman comes to Nazi-occupied Paris alone for kicks?"

"Business vacation."

"You mean none a' *my* business."

"You ask a lot of questions. You taking a poll?"

"You a real party girl, ain't ya'?"

"I like to drink, I like to dance, and I like to fuck. You're complaining?"

"Oh no. I like to do all that too," he said as he leaned over to kiss her on the lips. "Does it sound like I'm giving you the third degree?"

"You're smooth," she said as she admired his features. He was a lean, classically handsome New Orleans mulatto.

"You and that hair," Stewart said with a smile.

"Baby, you don't know the half of it," he said with a grin and a wink."

"You'd be surprised."

"Cocky little dish, ain't ya'. You' one a' them educated beauties, huh? You a schoolteacher or somethin'?"

"Or something."

He sat up and gently rubbed her shoulders.

"I get it. Loose lips sink ships, but I get the feelin' somethin' is weighing heavy on yo' mind, young lady."

Stewart pulled away. "You want a drink?" she asked.

"What's shakin', baby girl?"

"My job."

"What you need is a good man," he said with a wink and a smile.

"I've got a man. I'm married."

"Happily?"

"Most of the time. Does that bother you?"

"It doesn't bother *me*. Does it bother *you*?"

"My husband and I don't have those kinds of insecurities. And you shouldn't worry about it either."

"Why not?"

"Because I'll never see you again after we leave here."

"How can you be sure?"

"Because I know."

"Do tell."

"What you and I are doing together is the least of my worries. I'm worried about this world. There's a lot of bad people here—the evil kind."

"Ain't that right. It's a hornet's nest for sho'. But we all do the best we can, right?"

"We thought we had it all figured out."

"Who is we?"

"The people where I'm from."

"Ok."

"Once everyone agreed to get along, they got bored. My father and I came up with compassion and intelligence in game form. Someone else decided that murder and malice was a lot more fun.

"Where are you from?"

"Does it matter?"

"Is where you're from a big secret?"

Stewart took another drink. Her hangover softened. "Where I'm from is not so different from here. They had all these thoughts and impulses bottled up, and now they had a way to vent them. They didn't actually kill anybody, but they watched, and they didn't do anything to stop it. No protests, nothing. Their fixation made them complicit."

"Who built this game?"

"I did."

Palmer was confused. "*You* did?"

I designed the program. I'm responsible. Someone stuck a monkey wrench in it and I'm the only one who can fix it."

"Wait a minute..."

"You have no idea what I'm talking about, do you?"

"Some people just can't be happy. They say they want easy-peasy, but they get bored. They like a little drama to shake things up, change up the drudgery. If there's no fox in the hen house, they'll invent one. Boredom is a son of a bitch."

"The gamers are all imposters, phonies—so pleasant and friendly face-to-face. That well-rehearsed compassionate fucking smile... What they're really thinking about is behind closed doors. They put on their headsets and jerk-off to racism and violence—a corruption of my design. A horror show. They're living out their vile fantasies free from blame and without consequence. Forced religious conversion, slavery, war, and little black girls getting blown up in churches. All the good stuff."

Palmer played along. "Well, that certainly *is* fucked up."

"If I continued pretending everything's fine... Well, I'm part of the problem. I designed it, but this didn't come from me. There's a fly in the ointment and somebody put it there."

"You can't do nothin' about thoughts. You don't make them watch. That's their problem, not yours."

"No, it *is* my problem. We've become bent—twisted. I'm making it my problem, and I'm putting a stop to it. Someone sabotaged my design. Whoever did this to me thought as long as I got rich from it, I'd keep my mouth shut."

"So Hitler, the Klan, Jim Crow, and all this other crazy mess is the fly in the ointment?"

"I demanded they let me fix it. The Organization took a vote, and I won by a hair. They were placating me, knowing I would fail. They wanted to shut me up."

Palmer sat back against the headboard and weighed his thoughts. He exhaled with a heavy sigh.

"Boy, I'll tell ya', men have to jump through a lot of hoops to be with a woman. Most of the time we have to be somebody we're not or go along with things we don't like or believe in, just for a gentle touch—a smile or a kiss. Women have all kinds of lists, regulations, moods... Sometimes it's worth it—other times it just crushes a man. You put up with so much and get dumped for the slightest infraction—then you end up feelin' empty inside, like whoever you are ain't never good enough." He reached for a pack of cigarettes on the bedside table. The pack was empty. He crushed it, leaving it in the ashtray. "I ain't perfect... but this is one of those times where I don't know if... light me a cigarette?"

Stewart took out a cigarette and lit it. She passed it to him.

"I got somewhere to be, baby girl," Palmer said, getting up to put his pants on. "We can meet later at The Montclair."

"I don't think so."

"Hey, I'm just thinkin' out loud. I think you're the cat's pajamas. I like you; you're smart... and gorgeous."

"I have no problem with you thinking I'm crazy. It's better that way."

"Didn't we have a swell time together?"

"Yeah, it was fun. You're easy to talk to."

"So, what's the problem? We're in Paris. There's a war goin' on. We' been thrust together. Who's to say when our number gets punched? Let's live a little."

"Think of this as a lost weekend. This never happened."

Palmer caved in with finality. "It's just as well. I was on the fence about whether or not I had the constitution for another sexual escapade that left me broke and alone with a skin rash."

"I wouldn't worry about it. I don't think you're going to live very long after this. I'm just being honest."

Palmer took a moment to absorb that. "Would you like some more dick?"

"Sure."

Palmer was all in until he suddenly stopped himself. "You know, on second thought, I would appreciate it if you left."

"It's probably for the best," Stewart replied. "Can I borrow your comb?"

Eleven

"Goddamn it!" yelled Fuller.

"Get out of the car!" Savage ordered.

Savage aimed the Luger at Wilhelm and the chauffeur. Santiago and Fuller impulsively reached back for their weapons. Their holsters were empty. Wilhelm and the chauffeur briskly stepped out of the car and stood next to Astrid. The chauffeur was a hair taller than a midget.

"You didn't have to kill him," Fuller argued. "We could have negotiated!"

"Oh, you don't say. Well, I'm going to have to disagree. We've either landed in the middle of Oktoberfest, or we're dead and gone to hell."

"You just killed a man," Santiago argued.

"You're mourning a card-carrying Nazi who was pointing a gun at us?"

"Ok, we get it," Fuller responded. "Give me the gun."

"Colonel Jürgen Burnhoffer was an actual person. This guy looks exactly like him. He was a mass-murdering piece of shit. Excuse me for not trusting a lunatic pointing a gun at me who plays dress up as one of the architects of The Final Solution."

"Give me the Goddamn gun!" Fuller shouted.

Wilhelm stepped up to Savage with a confident air of diplomatic authority. "Permit me to introduce myself," he said in heavily German-accented English. "My name is Wilhelm Freytag. This is my wife Astrid and my chauffer Boucher. I am a simple businessman."

"Is that so. What kind of simple businessman are you?"

"I am a restaurant owner. If it is money that you seek, I would be more than happy to give it to you."

Wilhelm slowly held his hands out in front of him non-threateningly, then reached into his inside breast pocket. He took out his wallet. He reached into it and pulled out a thick wad of currency.

"Take it. Let us be on our way. I have absolutely nothing to do with the Nazis."

"You have absolutely nothing to do with the Nazis?"

"That is correct. As I said, I am a simple businessman."

Astrid's personality had changed from a playful sex kitten to a teary-eyed woman afraid for her life. Boucher, the chauffeur, listened in stoic silence.

Savage got in Wilhelm's face. "That's quite a pin you have on your lapel," referring to the swastika. Wilhelm looked down at his lapel and realized he'd been caught.

"It was a gift."

"You wear gift swastikas, but you have absolutely nothing to do with the Nazis?"

"I am not a Nazi."

"You could have fooled me."

"Take the money. Leave us."

"You think the Holocaust is a joke? You're playing dress up like its Halloween? Millions of innocent people were slaughtered."

"Savage!" Fuller interjected.

Savage stuck the barrel of the gun under Wilhelm's chin. "When's Ku Klux Klan week?"

Wilhelm had enough. "How dare you speak to me in that tone, you black bastard!" Wilhelm lunged at him.

Savage sidestepped and pistol-whipped him on the side of the head with the Luger. Astrid screamed. Wilhelm toppled to the ground awkwardly as paper money floated around him like confetti. Dazed and humiliated, he moaned like a wounded animal.

"Handcuffs!" Fuller yelled to Santiago angrily. "Sweet Christopher!"

"Shut the fuck up!" Savage replied. "We have to get to the bottom of this. None of this makes any sense."

Santiago walked over to Savage and snatched the gun away from him. "Don't talk anymore."

Savage begrudgingly held his hands up in submission.

"We need answers," Santiago said, turning to Astrid. "We don't want to hurt anyone. We're lost. All we want is to get back home. Do you understand?"

"I understand."

"What year is this?"

"What? The year?"

"Yes, what's today's date?

"It is Sunday, the 12th of July."

"That's impossible," Fuller retorted.

"Welches jahr?! (What year?!)" Savage barked in German as Santiago gave him a dirty look.

"Wir Schreiben das Jahr 1942."

Her answer made Santiago numb. "1942?" Repeated Santiago. "Is that right?" She asked Savage.

"1942," Savage said shaking his head in disbelief. "1942."

Fuller paced as his legs grew weak. He sat down on the grass, holding his head in his hands.

Santiago fought off the dread as she tried to maintain her composure. "Where are we?"

"We are in France."

"Where are we specifically?"

"30 Kilometers outside of Paris. We were going to have a picnic. We are not Nazis. My husband and I own a restaurant. It is called *Nahrung für Soldaten*. We have done nothing wrong. We are good Germans."

Savage gave her a look of contempt. "You run a restaurant called *Food for Soldiers,* and you don't think you're doing anything wrong?"

"We cook food," she replied.

"Do you serve Nazis?"

"Yes. Paris is under German occupation."

"Do you serve black people in this restaurant?"

"...No."

"Do you serve Jews?"

"No."

"Then shut the fuck up!"

Savage turned to Fuller and Santiago. "Look, if we haven't lost our minds, we've somehow traveled back in time to Nazi-occupied France. It's a lousy time to be American, black, a woman, and especially a Jew. It wouldn't be a stretch to say it's a very fucked up time to be anything but German right now. They've already sent millions of people to death camps. We'll be shot on the spot if we're lucky. The Americans won't liberate Paris for another two years."

As Savage spoke, the reality of their situation burned them to the core.

"We need to find allies," Fuller blurted.

"Right," Santiago said as her mind raced. "Sympathizers—the French Resistance."

"They'll think we're out of our minds," said Savage.

"We need to get to Paris," barked Fuller.

"We *need* to find a way into Paris without being caught by the Nazis, Savage said." He pointed to Astrid. "Marlene Dietrich here mentioned a nightclub called The Montclair. It's probably where American expatriates congregate. There was a small American population here before the Nazis took over. A lot of them are probably there."

"Draft dodgers," Fuller said.

"Expats," Santiago replied correcting him. "We need friends, not enemies."

"Exactly," Savage said. "Maybe some of the passengers went there. It's the most logical place to go."

"It's all we've got," Santiago said to Fuller, who looked bewildered.

"You have got more than that," Boucher said in a thick French accent. "You have me. My name is Albert Boucher. I am a proud Frenchman, a member of The French Resistance, and I am a Nazi killer."

Twelve

Paris was all set to fight the Germans as early as 1939, but they dropped the ball, failing to take the invasion seriously. By May of 1940, the Germans attacked France and conquered them easily. The French government fled Paris, and on June 14th, the Nazis took over the city.

Albert Boucher was a cook at *Nahrung für Soldaten* and earned extra money as a chauffeur for owners, Wilhelm and Astrid Freytag. Standing a hair over four feet 10 inches tall, Boucher was an amiable, hard worker with a friendly smile who got along with everyone—especially the Nazis.

He made small talk, told jokes, and acted as an unofficial ambassador to Paris. He was always jovial and helped the occupiers find their way around his beloved City of Light. Despite a variety of indignities to the French people and endless jokes about his height, Boucher held his tongue.

But Boucher had a secret. After the nine o'clock curfew, he would meet with a terrorist group that got together for some good old-fashioned assassination, guerilla warfare, and sabotage. They were one of a handful of factions listed under the banner of The French Resistance. Boucher took it upon himself to personally blow-up trains carrying German troops and the families of German officers. He was considered the best sniper in The Resistance. Before the war, Boucher had dreams of becoming Europe's most celebrated pastry chef. The Germans trashed those dreams forever, and he never forgave them for it. The only thing that would satisfy him was cold-blooded vengeance.

Boucher once shot two German officers in the head with one bullet while they sipped espresso at an outdoor café. He blew up a taxi containing three German soldiers and their prostitutes, and watched their flesh cook in the explosion. Boucher hated the Nazis. The one thing he loved second to killing Nazis was killing Nazi collaborators. Opportunism ran rampant during the war, and collaborators would be shown no mercy. Boucher loved Paris, and he was on a personal crusade to kill every fucking Nazi in town.

Boucher was on a mission for the British when Colonel Burnhoffer ordered him to pull the staff car over to attend to the three time travelers. Boucher's mission was to get his hands on classified orders sent to Colonel Burnhoffer from Berlin. These orders were inside Burnhoffer's leather satchel.

The plan was to steal the satchel and take photos of its contents, while Burnhoffer ate lunch with the Freytags at the restaurant. The manic attention whore Astrid had ruined his plans by insisting Boucher drive them out to the country for a picnic lunch. In the farthest reaches of his imagination, Boucher never dreamed he would meet three American time travelers from the 21st century.

#

By the roadside, Wilhelm and Astrid Freytag cowered together naked and fearful. They covered their privates with their hands as Fuller, Santiago, and Savage slipped into their clothes.

"You could have let them keep their underwear," Santiago said to Boucher as she put on Astrid's dress.

Boucher smiled as he rummaged through Burnhoffer's satchel. "Oh, no. They are going to know humiliation intimately. This is nothing compared to what my countrymen feel every minute living with these murderers." He winked at Astrid. "Don't worry. There's more to come—Nazi whore!"

Santiago filled out Astrid's dress with her athletic curves and toned arms. Savage fixed Wilhelm's tie on himself while looking in the side mirror of the staff car. Fuller was tugging the uniform off Burnhoffer, trying to avoid getting blood on himself.

"This uniform better fit," Fuller said as he turned to see Savage checking his appearance. "And who knew the infamous Lorenzo Savage spoke German like a native. Wonders never cease."

"I speak it with a hint of Bavarian, but I can still be picked up for being black—meanwhile, you can stroll through Berlin like a prince and can't even pronounce Topfenstrudel."

"Membership has its privileges."

Savage ignored him. "I don't think I've ever worn a Nazi suit before," Savage thought out loud. "I'm going to wear my own shoes. The master race has tiny feet."

Boucher bit into a sausage from the picnic basket. He chewed as he examined the papers from Burnhoffer's satchel.

"Colonel Burnhoffer has been ordered to transport all remaining Jews to labor camps before being reassigned to Frankfurt."

Savage bit his lip. "I knew it was him—bastard. Well, his mass-murdering days are over."

"Major Ernst Schüller will be taking over full operational duties in Paris," Boucher continued. "His orders are to execute every American negro in Paris. Adolph Hitler signed the orders himself." He turned to Savage. "Der Führer has a strong dislike for your negro music."

"Adolph fucking Hitler," Santiago said under her breath. "I still can't... This is too much."

"Schüller?" Savage said out loud, trying to recall the name.

"Who knew there were black people in Paris during World War II?" Fuller said, buttoning up Burnhoffer's jacket. "I had no idea."

"There was a black American community here for a long time," Savage replied. "Some black soldiers stayed here after World War I. Others came here to escape the US to play jazz, write novels, and bang white women."

"And then the Nazis showed up—party's over," Santiago added.

"Exactly. Paris, jazz, blacks, Jews, and everybody got along fairly well before that. There were a lot of talented people who made a good life for themselves here. It was a big improvement over lynchings and minstrel shows in black face."

"Hemingway lived here in the 1920s," Santiago remembered. "America has always been a little obtuse when it comes to the arts and people of color," she explained to Fuller.

"I appreciate the Ken Burns moment," Fuller interjected. "But our priority is to escort our prisoner to trial."

Savage and Santiago looked at each other. They had a decision to make.

"You say you are from the 21st century," inquired Boucher with a shake of his head in disbelief. "Then you already know what will happen. My future is your past. You know the punch line to this cruel joke."

"A lot of terrible things happened," replied Santiago. "We're dealing with forces beyond our pay grade. If we change our past, who knows what effect it will have in our own time. We've probably made a mess already."

"Tell me what happens?" Boucher inquired. "What happens to me? My wife? My children? Do I live through this? Do I become an old man, and see my children grow up?"

"We don't know," Santiago answered.

"That's up to you," replied Savage. "Whatever happened in our past doesn't matter. You create *your* future. It's all on you." Savage couldn't believe he was having this conversation. "The Nazis murdered millions of people. They're fucking monsters." He looked at Wilhelm. "Yeah, you!" Wilhelm avoided eye contact.

"The Nazis are the bad guys, no question," Fuller said. "But our priority is to complete our assignment."

"We have no idea how or when we're going to get back to our own time," Savage replied. "Meanwhile, we can't ignore this."

"That's not your decision to make."

"Do you really want to turn your back on this? Will you be able to live with the fact that you could have done something to prevent mass murder?"

"You should be using that criminal mastermind brain of yours to help us get back to our own time. But it isn't really in your best interest, is it?"

"He has a point," Santiago added.

"The minute I figure out how to get us home, I'll send you a memo. In the meantime, a lot of people are about to be executed. Are you ok with that? Or is that outside your jurisdiction?"

"Yes, it *is* outside my jurisdiction. 81 freaking years outside my jurisdiction. First things first, second things second."

"Those people could end up in a mass grave before we figure out how to get home."

"What difference does it make? In our own time, I'm fairly certain everybody is already dead." He turned to Boucher.

"No offense."

"Fuck you," Boucher replied.

"We know what the Nazis are capable of," Savage argued. "We're 81 years more advanced than they are." He turned to Santiago. "You guys know forensic science and law enforcement tactical shit. I'm a professional..."

"You're a criminal," Santiago interrupted. "A thief, a murderer, Don't get it twisted."

"And I know world history better than most Jeopardy winners. We can stop them."

"And I've seen "The Guns of Navarone" 35 times," Fuller interjected. "Still, you have no incentive to help us get back to our own time. You're going to prison for the rest of your life."

"He's right," Santiago said. "You know what's going to happen before it happens. You're a free man in the 1940s."

"Free? Really? A black man in 1942? It's good to know Black History Month had such a big impact on you. No. I'm not free by any stretch of the imagination."

"Your skillset and knowledge of history puts you at an advantage," Santiago replied.

"Exactly," Fuller argued. "You could kill us, steal Nazi gold, and live the rest of your life betting on the World Series. You'd live like a king."

"I'd live like a shoeshine boy," Savage fired back. "My skin is black. That makes me a target wherever I go."

"I'm putting you back in handcuffs until we can figure this out," Fuller replied. "It's not safe."

Fuller pulled out a pair of handcuffs from the back of his belt and grabbed Savage by the shoulder to turn him around. Savage reacted by punching him in the jaw. Fuller staggered backward, stunned, then lunged forward in an attempt to take him down. Savage's knee came upward into Fuller's face. It sent him to the ground in agony. Savage rushed forward to finish him.

Santiago stepped in, blocking his path. She grabbed Savage by the side of the head and spun him around in a circle, sweeping his legs up from under him. His feet left the ground as she turned his body in a twisting motion to hit hard on the ground.

With one knee wedged into his rib cage, she bent his elbow backward against her shin. Savage froze to minimize the pain.

Santiago spoke to him, calmly. "Move, and I'll break your arm. You lay a hand on Agent Fuller again, and I'll end you. Got it?"

Left with no alternatives, Savage answered.

"Got it."

"Son of bitch!" Fuller cried out in pain.

"We're stuck in this together," Santiago replied. "We have to figure this shit out!"

Fuller shook his head begrudgingly. Santiago got up from Savage to let him get to his feet. Fuller lay sprawled on the ground, still feeling the painful blow to his face and his ego.

Boucher looked on in stoic fascination. "You look like you could use a vacation."

"Everybody calm down," Santiago said. "Cut the macho shit. We need more information. We'll get it when we find the other passengers. We'll go to the nightclub, get more intel, then plan our next move."

"Tell your partner to keep his hands to himself, and he might survive this," Savage added.

"You're our prisoner," Santiago replied. "Tread lightly, or you won't be treading at all, comprende?"

"You don't seem to comprende that this shit is real," Savage told Santiago. "We can't let the Nazis murder these people. Those mother-fuckers have got to be stopped."

"I knew I had a good feeling about you," Boucher replied with a wry smile. "Some of my best friends are Nazi killers."

"Ordinarily, I'd mind my own business," Savage replied. "I've always kept my head down. But this is some... cosmic, crazy... Someone or something wants us to be here." He turned to Fuller. "Something from outer space smashed into our plane. We're here for a reason, and we need to find out what the fuck that is."

"When did you get a conscience?" Santiago replied.

"We're here. It's the right thing to do."

"Right," Fuller replied. "That's very convenient. You stall until you can come up with an escape plan."

"Fine," Savage replied. "Let's sit back, eat popcorn, and watch the Nazis kill everybody."

"This time travel shit is completely FUBAR," Santiago said. "I don't know if we're dead or dreaming, but when we make it back home, we're taking your black ass to jail. Your cosmic redemption is beyond the circle of me giving a shit. We're FBI agents no matter what year it is."

"You're quite the hard-ass, aren't you?"

"Don't fuck with me, Savage. I know you better than you know yourself."

"A ducks gotta quack."

"Don't even think about trying to escape. Help us figure out a way to get home. You do that, and we might throw you a bone. Pack up everything. We're getting out of here."

"Yes, ma'am," Savage said with a sly smile.

Savage collected their things as Boucher climbed into the car behind the wheel. Fuller sat in the front passenger seat, looking menacing in Burnhoffer's uniform. Savage and Santiago climbed into the back seat, looking like a vintage interracial couple.

Boucher started the engine and swung the car around. Before driving off, he turned his attention to the Freytags, who swatted bugs away from their legs and faces. "Keep an eye out for wolves. They are large. Au revoir!" He blew them a kiss as they drove off.

#

The Freytags stood shaking in fear and bewilderment. They took tiny steps outside their circle to search for any sign of hope. The psychological effects of being naked in the middle of the French countryside made them feel vulnerable, defenseless, and afraid.

Suddenly they heard the sound of a twig snapping. Their heads swiveled simultaneously to a cluster of trees. Their eyes strained to focus on something in the distance. A shadowy figure stepped out from the tree line. First out of focus, it revealed itself to them. It was Stewart. She stood before them holding her device, wearing a flight suit.

"How did it come to this?" Stewart asked wistfully. "What happened?"

"Please help us?" Wilhelm pleaded. "We need help. We need transportation to Paris."

"Can you help us?" Astrid pleaded."

Stewart looked at them with disappointment.

"Who is your employer?" Astrid inquired. "Who do you work for?"

Stewart grew annoyed at her remark, "I work for me, bitch."

But the question made her stop and think. She peered out across the rolling horizon. No, she didn't work for herself. She was a hamster on a wheel like everybody else — like all the other little hamsters running in a circle.

She typed angrily into her device and vanished.

The Freytags were astonished. "What just happened?" cried Wilhelm.

Suddenly, they heard twigs snapping behind them. They turned to see a pack of large hungry wolves, foaming at the mouth.

#

Astrid screamed like she'd never screamed before in her life. Her tortured, guttural wails ripped her vocal cords. She became hoarse as her throat filled with blood. Then she stopped, her mouth agape in grotesque horror. Wilhelm witnessed this in silent fascination as she was torn apart limb from limb and eaten alive—then they came for him.

Thirteen

Contrary to popular belief, Major Ernst Schüller wasn't a National socialist, a racist, or an anti-Semite. He was an asshole. He was far from being an anti-Semite. In fact, Schüller had a Jones for Jewish women. He was obsessed. He had Jewish pussy on the brain—dark-haired, wide-hipped, and big breasted. Their earthy, pungent pubic hair was all he could think about. This was back in the days when women let their pubic hair run wild like the Amazon Rainforest. It sent him into a deep cock-stiffening trance.

Schüller's clean, chiseled, good looks framed in a tailored German military officer's uniform aroused the interest of some of the most beautiful pieces of ass in Germany. Surprisingly, he had no interest in the flat-assed, Aryan gold diggers who frequented Nazi soirees. When he attended parties with his military associates, his eyes were on the help—the middle-aged Jewesses who prepared hors d'oeuvre in the kitchen. He'd had many trysts, but his dalliances eventually became too risky for his status. He put an end to that for the sake of his career, but his sexual predilections burned white-hot. It was a lustful spell that gave him tunnel vision. It took most of his willpower to stop himself from plunging headlong into the depths of sensual bliss and danger.

Like many Germans coming of age in post-World War I Germany, Schüller was a squirrel looking for a nut. When the political tide shifted, things started to look up for Germans who looked like Schüller —so he jumped on the bandwagon. Why the hell not? Too young to prove himself as a soldier during World War I, he was left with few career opportunities after the humiliation of The Versailles Treaty. Clean, good-looking, and a sociopath, he was a model recruit for the burgeoning Nazi party.

Schüller rode the wave, and the tide moved swiftly, benefitting those of good German stock who could talk the talk and follow orders. When the Nazis came to power, Schüller drank the Kool-Aid but was immune to its effects. He never believed the propaganda regarding the Jews. In his mind, *everybody* was inferior to him—even Hitler.

Schüller wanted status, riches, and the notoriety of being an officer —an officer in the greatest military in the world. It went without saying Adolph Hitler was a mad man. There was no question about it, but madmen in politics was nothing new. Insanity was normal among politicians, particularly National Socialists who blamed the Jews for Germany's woes. But sane men didn't have lofty ambitions. Sane men didn't have visions of a thousand-year Reich, world domination, and orchestras playing Wagner in the streets.

"The difference between insanity and brilliance is gauged only by triumph."

-Major Ernst Schüller

When one of Schüller's peers discovered him fucking a Jewish cleaning woman in the laundry room at a social gathering honoring Joachim Von Ribbentrop, shit got deep. He was going to pay dearly for his lack of self-control. He was blackmailed into volunteering for a position his peers avoided like the plague so they could avoid consideration. In the presence of the high command, including Hitler, Schüller volunteered to get rid of every single negro in Paris.

"And with my dying breath, I shall see this nigger plague wiped clean from Paris, Europe, and the world!"

-Major Ernst Schüller

The high command applauded so emphatically that Hitler could not deny him. Being a nigger wrangler was a humiliating demotion within the German high command. But blackmail was blackmail, and Schüller knew the alternative would be far worse. So, he sucked it up. There were of course worse jobs than murdering niggers in the City of Light.

Being the commandant of a death camp was far worse. He kept reminding himself he was being sent to command a section of one of the most beautiful cities in Europe.

Schüller's plan was to accomplish his duties, return to Berlin, and murder the son of a bitch who blackmailed him. See, murder is the only way to deal with blackmailers. If you don't take care of that shit, it'll always come back to bite you in the ass.

In the meantime, he would have to come to grips with his predilections. His career was the most important thing in his life. It was all he had—this tiny little life he'd carved out for himself. In the meantime, he would make the best of his stay in Paris. He would rape and pillage like it was going out of style. He'd rid the city of swing, niggers, and anything else standing in his way—and he would savor every sweet minute of it.

Fourteen

The road to Paris was surreal. It was a nightmarish crash course in the realities of World War Two. Incinerated vehicles and rotting corpses littered the roadside as lines of stragglers made their exodus. Reading about it in history books was one thing, but the sights, smells, and the look in those sad, desperate eyes was way too real.

Savage rode along in the back seat with Santiago, who sat in silence. Affected by the morbid scenery, they were still trying to process what had happened to them. More importantly, they wondered about their futures. How would they get back to their own time? Was that even possible? For all their 21st century know-how, they were out of their depth. They had no idea what was at work here.

It wasn't like Savage had some urgent place to be. He was going to prison for the rest of his life. But Santiago and Fuller had normal lives to look forward to. They were trapped 81 years in the past without a ride home. How would they live the rest of their lives in a time that had already happened?

Savage and his group received stares as they drove by. A dapper negro being chauffeured in a Nazi staff car with a white woman wasn't something you saw every day in 1942. Add to that a grizzled Kevin Costner stand-in dressed like a Nazi along with a midget, and you have the biggest red flag in the history of red flags.

It dawned on Savage they were begging to be stopped. It would have been a better cover for the group to have *him* driving with a chauffer's cap. This was unlike Savage. He usually made cool-headed decisions in a crisis, even if it clashed with his vanity. He was off his game, and it could cost them their lives.

Burnhoffer had gotten under Savage's skin. He hadn't been himself since Joslyn blew up their lives. It affected him way more than he could process. If he was going to second-guess himself, he was in big trouble. He was a liability to himself and everyone around him.

He kept coming back to the irrational conclusion; there was no way in hell he was going to play *Driving Miss Daisy*—even if it meant raising suspicion at every German checkpoint in Europe.

"Stupid old man," he said scolding himself.

This was dangerous, and though it ate away at him, he felt paralyzed to do anything about it. It was too late anyway. The gentle rocking of the long car ride, along with the after-effects of time travel, finally took its toll. Savage drifted off into a deep sleep.

Eighteen Months Earlier — 21st Century

Savage swam naked underwater with his eyes open. The water felt refreshing to his skin. The pleasure of this tiny moment would remain with him forever. The Palm Springs summer had warmed the outdoor pool to perfection. Now that night had fallen, it was the perfect temperature. In the distance, a blurry vision ahead of him materialized as he swam closer. Just ahead through the lightly chlorinated water, luminous white legs, pedicured toes, and full breasts stood before him. She was for him – all for him.

It didn't get by Savage that this was one of those rare, perfect moments. The bliss he felt was needed to hold on to for safekeeping—memories. Good memories were few and far between. He collected these little memories so he could take refuge in them during the mean times, the lean times, the harsh times. He cataloged them in his mental scrapbook so he could return to them later, and remember, and feel. Memories like these helped to distract him during some of the harshest times of his criminal life. But they also reminded him of everything he'd lost.

At that moment in the pool, he wasn't lost. He was free, swimming in a perfect underwater womb – ideal perfection. Joslyn leaned against the edge of the pool, tying her hair back. She was glistening and gorgeous as the moonlight shimmered off her creamy white skin and jet-black hair.

"This is abnormally wonderful," Savage said as he drifted beside her. He held her waist. "I don't think I could ever get tired of this."

"This resort has been in my family for years. I used to come here as a teenager," Joslyn said as she cozied closer to him. They kissed.

"Let's go back inside," she whispered. "I have things I want to do to you," she said with a devilish smile.

"I have things I want to do to *you* right now."

He kissed her deeply. They spun around and slowly submerged underwater in a passionate embrace.

Summer — 1942

It was a hard slap to the face that woke Savage. The second slap was uncalled for. He woke up, pissed off. Santiago's hand recoiled.

"Wake up, maricón!"

Savage's eyes popped open to see Boucher had stopped at a German checkpoint. There was lots of activity. German soldiers inspected oncoming vehicles situated between two red and white striped booths on either side of the road. Bursting past the roadblock in the opposite direction, the young man from the airplane wearing the Lakers jersey cursed at two German soldiers. "Get yo' hands off me motherfucka'! Touch me again, and I'm gonna fuck yo' ass up!"

A guard struck him in the head with the butt of his rifle, knocking him down. Darius rebounded to his feet and broke away, running toward the staff car. His bright yellow basketball jersey stuck out like an anachronistic sore thumb.

Two German guards yelled, "Halt! Halt!"

Darius saw Savage and stopped in confusion, trying to piece together this nightmare. "Hey man, what the fuck is goin' on!? This is some wack *Call of Duty* shit!"

The two guards aimed and fired five rounds between them. The bullets failed to hit their target. Darius had vanished into thin air. The two guards looked at each other, not believing what they'd seen. Savage's brain snapped into clarity.

Four German soldiers stood around the staff car with rifles drawn. A fifth was demanding Savage, Fuller, and Santiago step out of the vehicle. They inspected Boucher's papers as he pretended to be insulted by their requests.

Fuller stared dumbfounded as a soldier rattled off a barrage of demands in German. "Herr, Oberst. Entschuldigung. Alle bestellungen müssen überprüft werden, bevor wir den Einlass an diesem kontrollpunkt ermöglichen können."

Fuller's mind raced through every German phrase he could think of. "Topfenstrudel?"

Fuller's mind was blank. He could have easily ordered the soldiers to stand down but he couldn't speak a lick of German, and even if he could, he didn't have the chops to pull it off. It takes a certain kind of swagger to pull off the role of an arrogant Nazi authority figure.

The soldier stepped back and pointed his rifle at Fuller. "Mit erhobenen händen aus dem auto steigen!"

Fuller stared down the barrel. He turned to his left and noticed the middle-aged woman from the airplane with the blonde wig and blue muumuu from the corner of his eye. Two soldiers dragged her to the center of the road under protest. Her wig was torn off and the front of her muumuu was ripped away from her large breasts. Under the spell of fear and confusion her eyes met with Fuller's.

Explosive gunfire erupted. The soldiers blasted the woman as her hands reached out for mercy. The sight of the helpless woman's body being pumped full of bullets hit Fuller hard. A needless final pistol shot by a German officer sent brain matter spraying upward. Fuller's eyes closed. Three more civilians were shot.

When the order was given to use the radio to inform headquarters of an escalating situation involving a negro, a midget, and a non-German speaking Nazi Colonel, Savage had to get on the clock.

As the soldier turned on the radio to make the transmission, a sniper's rifle shot rang out. The bullet knocked him to the floor. That was the cue for crazy time.

They may not have had a chance in hell, but it was better to take on armed soldiers than getting dragged off to the gas chamber. As Savage was about to throw himself into action, Santiago was already out of the car. She bridged the gap between herself and a soldier, disarmed him, and broke his collarbone with the butt of his rifle. To finish him, she dislocated his knee with an oblique kick. The soldier toppled over in pain as Santiago shot him in the head.

The sight of Santiago adorned in a pretty summer floral dress brutally killing Hitler's finest was a riveting distraction. It was all the motivation Savage needed. Burnhoffer's Luger sat on the seat beside him. He picked it up and exited the car. With the soldiers distracted, it allowed Savage to shoot a soldier in the back of the head. Santiago took a knee and began shooting every soldier in sight. A confusing melee ensued.

Fuller kicked the car door open, slamming the soldier guarding him in the groin. Fuller leaped from the vehicle and knocked the soldier to the ground. Savage avoided a guard's bayonet and delivered a right uppercut that pulverized the guard's jaw. He followed it up by shooting the soldier in the chest. Santiago ran out of ammo and broke the rifle across a guard's neck, who was trying to restrain Boucher. Boucher pulled a knife from his boot and stabbed him in the chest repeatedly.

A soldier standing near the guard booth aimed at Santiago. Before he could get off a shot, Savage peppered his torso with a discarded submachine gun.

Fuller was engaged in a life and death wrestling match. A soldier was on top of him with a bayonet at his throat. With a burst of energy and a grunt, Fuller rolled on top of the soldier. Fuller's momentum pushed the bayonet into the soldier's throat. Fuller stood up but was immediately tackled by two other guards.

Using his low center of gravity, Boucher stabbed a guard in the groin and sprinted to his next opponent. Two guards attacked Santiago with rifle butts. Savage leaped over the car to come to her aid, but Santiago had already eye-gouged one soldier and dislocated the other's shoulder. She spun around clockwise to deliver a painful Muay Thai kick to the last attacker's head. The brain injury left the guard quivering on the ground.

Santiago's capacity for violence didn't go unnoticed.

Savage watched her curiously. "Jumpin' Jesus!"

One soldier tried to escape as Savage machine-gunned him into a spastic death dance. Boucher noticed Fuller on the ground struggling against two guards. Boucher shot the two soldiers as a live potato masher dropped to the ground in front of Fuller. A guard came running toward Boucher carrying a submachine gun. Fuller grabbed the potato masher and threw it at the guard in one quick motion. The guard panicked and caught it. Just as he was prepared to throw it back, the potato masher exploded in his hands. Body parts, clothing, and entrails exploded in every direction as Boucher and Fuller took cover.

With an MP40 in one hand and a Luger in the other, Savage spun around shooting in a continuous stream of motion as soldiers attacked him and were mowed down. Santiago leaped into the air and kicked one of his attackers in the back. The blow broke his spine. The soldier collapsed on the ground unable to move.

Savage shot another soldier in the throat. When he ran out of ammo, he quickly picked up a discarded bayonet and stabbed the final soldier in the side of the neck. Geysers of blood sprayed upward as their lifeless bodies slammed to the ground.

Fuller reached for a submachine gun. He sprayed the German officer who murdered the woman who wore the muumuu. He tumbled awkwardly into the dirt. When he tried to crawl away, Fuller finished him, unloading the entire clip. Fuller stood dazed. "We're all a goddamn bunch of animals."

The violence died down as the soldiers lay dead or unconscious. Civilian on-lookers watched as Fuller, Boucher, Santiago, and Savage regrouped to confer.

"We need to get out of here," Fuller said.

"The car!" yelled Savage.

During the melee, the staff car had been sprayed with bullets, leaving two flat tires.

"We need another vehicle," Santiago said as she looked around frantically.

"We must go now!" shouted Boucher.

Suddenly an uncovered military troop truck arrived from the other side of the roadblock. Fifteen heavily armed German soldiers piled out from the back of the vehicle.

"Christ," declared Santiago. "We're done."

"Do not be too sure about that, Cherie," Boucher replied.

Suddenly, the troop truck exploded into a giant fireball. German soldiers screamed in agony as they jumped off the truck on fire. The smell of burning soldiers filled the air as Savage and Santiago watched in silence.

Armed French Resistance fighters came out of the forest. They shot the screaming soldiers, putting them out of their misery.

"The calvary has arrived," said Savage.

"What a way to go," said Fuller.

"My comrades are much too gentle with them," said Boucher. "I would piss gasoline on them if I could."

A filthy teenaged Resistance fighter ran up to Boucher and handed him a rifle with a scope on it.

"That was good work shooting the radioman," Boucher said. "But aim for the eye next time. Right in the eyehole. Give them Boucher's Black

Eye." Boucher patted the young man's shoulder affectionately. The teen smiled and ran off to join the other fighters.

Fuller watched Boucher take delight in the deaths of the burning soldiers.

"More soldiers are coming," Boucher shouted. "We must go."

"Viens!" one of the Resistance fighters yelled in French, as they took off.

Savage and Santiago stared at the charbroiled soldiers. The screams and the smell of burning flesh made them nauseous.

"You see," Boucher said to Savage and Santiago. "This is what we call French barbeque."

Boucher motioned for them to follow him. They took off running behind the Resistance fighters into the forest. As they disappeared from view, the victim of the sniper's bullet struggled to his feet. Blood gurgled from his chest wound. He tried to stand but fell to the ground as he gripped the radio receiver. In great pain, he transmitted a message on the radio.

"Notfall! Wir wurden angegriffen! (Emergency! We have been attacked!)"

Fifteen

Stewart sat outside a café sipping espresso. She fixated on the continuous stream of data that scrolled by on her device. An entire hour had gone by while she shut out the world. She sifted through thousands of lunar anomalies and historical records as French and German pedestrians strolled by. Some did a doubletake when they saw her. She'd changed clothes from her flight suit into an era-appropriate skirt, blouse, and sweater. She patted herself on the back for remembering to wear a period costume to blend in. But she was a black woman among white people, so everyone stared anyway.

Despite her husband's fears and the concerns of The Organization, Stewart was willfully oblivious on this new *Simulated Earth*. Being consumed with acts of vengeance will do that to a person. Little did she know she was in terrible danger.

Stewart lacked a few awareness skills. A sheltered life spent in the sciences leaves other skills underdeveloped. Stewart also lacked the skills necessary for black people in *Simulated Earth's* 20th century. A perfectly timed smile could mean the difference between life and death. It was the kind of disarming smile that communicated, "Hi, I'm a non-threatening negro. If you need anything, I'd be happy to run and get it for you."

Stewart understood what black people had to do to survive, but it hadn't occurred to her *she* had to do it—the awareness thing. These gaping holes in her judgement had always plagued her. The Nazis could give two shits about her genius IQ, academic accomplishments, or her celebrated rise to fame.

Stewart was a busy beaver. She had a lot to do with too many moving parts. Not only did she have to find her saboteur, she also had to keep an eye on Savage and Santiago's progress. The show must go on.

Bringing Savage and Santiago from *Simulated Earth's* future to the past was a brilliant move that kept the story progressing. The tension between this odd couple and their fish-out-of-water, time-travel adventures would make for good viewing. If there was going to be insipid violence on *Simulated Earth*, Stewart would be the one pulling the strings.

But the issue that burned white-hot inside her gut was the cocksucker who sabotaged her design. She couldn't wait to get her hands on that son of a bitch. She recalled how fast her heart pounded as she watched her life's work turn into a flaming bag of shit. The whole world was watching, and there was nothing she could do to stop it.

Stewart and her husband Ritenour were seated in a neighborhood tavern. Images flashed across the hovering virtual jumbotrons. Her design went from "Let's work together to make the colonies a better place," to wholesale atrocities and nigger jokes.

When Major Schüller chopped the hands and feet off every factory worker who went on strike, audiences gasped in horror. But they couldn't take their eyes off the screen. Stewart's head exploded when she saw it, but the show became the biggest hit in lifestyle simulation gaming history.

The feedback from her superiors was glowing. The ratings for *Simulated Earth* went through the roof. The Organization assumed Stewart had designed the game this way, that this was her idea all along. What happened afterward was like a cocaine-induced fever dream. Massive sums of money, gala events, and television interviews became a part of her daily life. It was the kind of fame and success she'd always dreamed of—but not this way. This wasn't what she wanted. It was the opposite of her father's dying wish.

"Is this some kind of a prank? Am I being tested?"

She witnessed the depravity unfold along with the rest of the colonies but opted to keep her mouth shut. She needed time to process. All she could think about was what her father once said to her, "Perhaps I treated you too harshly."

"Fucker."

Sixteen

Major Schüller's office was located in a French government building occupied by the Gestapo. He decorated it himself, driving throughout Paris shopping at the finest stores with his young assistant Lieutenant Franz Reiner. He took whatever he wanted with little or no resistance. There was something about the sight of a swastika that made shop owners feel generous.

Schüller knew he would be spending long hours in his office, so he turned it into a home away from home, complete with a comfortable sofa and a fully stocked bar. He had a secret entrance installed, a safe, and an espresso machine designed by the great Luigi Bezzera.

The former owner of the espresso machine was upset about it being taken away from him, so he attempted to contact Schüller's superiors in Berlin. Schüller had the café owner dragged out into the street, stripped naked, and forced to bark like a dog. Schüller thanked him for the entertainment by shooting him in the back of the head. It was Schüller's way of setting a precedent. The people of Paris would learn that nobody fucks with the mighty Ernst Schüller. When he said jump, you would respectfully inquire, "How high?" and "Would you like pomme frites with that?"

The spacious office included a handmade mahogany desk, immaculate wooden floors, a high ceiling, and sunlight that poured through large French-style windows. Schüller created a sweet little arrangement for himself, which softened the humiliation of being blackmailed. Having to oversee the Untermensch (sub-humans) wasn't such a bad idea after all. He made the best of it, using his authority to improve his standard of living as well as his bank account. There were other perks as well.

"I have news," Lieutenant Reiner barked after giving Schüller the Nazi salute.

"At ease Lieutenant," Schüller replied with annoyance.

"Colonel Burnhoffer is still missing. He was last seen with the Freytags driving outside the city. The Freytags are missing as well."

"What about my orders?"

"I have just received copies from Berlin," Reiner said, handing them to Schüller.

"Colonel Burnhoffer is to return to Frankfurt. You are directed to have all negroes removed from Paris before the Führer arrives."

"So, Burnhoffer is gifted with a return to Frankfurt while I clean up after him? What am I? His lackey?" Schüller took a breath and closed his eyes. "Bootlicking boy lover," he said under his breath.

"The orders go on to say that the Führer believes negro music is a negative influence on the morale of our troops," Reiner continued. "The music and the vermin who create this noise must be eradicated."

"And what shall our fine soldiers do for entertainment?"

"The Führer prefers Wagner, Herr Major."

Schüller read the orders while leaning back in his soft leather chair. "Mmm, a Paris without negroes—a Paris without swing. How will our precious soldiers enjoy the nightlife? With the hip-shaking music of Wagner, of course!"

"Sir, these orders are from the Führer himself, signed by his hand."

Schüller withdrew into himself but broke from his thoughts to focus in on Reiner. "Lieutenant, do I look like a traitor?"

"Sir?"

"You're speaking as if I need to be prodded to do my duty. I understand the Führer's orders."

"My apologies Herr Major. I was only..."

"Do you doubt my loyalty to the Fatherland, Lieutenant?

"No, Herr Major. I am only saying..."

"Are you unhappy, Lieutenant?"

"No, Herr Major..."

"If you're unhappy under my command, it would bring me great pleasure to transfer you to a duty station more befitting of your intelligence."

"Herr Major, please..."

"How would you like to oversee your own special unit as Oberführer of latrines on the Eastern Front?

"No, Herr Major."

"It gets very cold there."

"Yes, Herr Major."

"Below freezing."

"Herr Major..."

"And what is your opinion of testicular frostbite?"

"I beg your pardon?"

"So, you would *dislike* dying slowly in the freezing cold?"

"No, Herr Major! I mean *yes*, Herr Major!"

"I thought so. Now return to your office and wait for my orders. There is lots of work to be done."

"Jawohl Herr Major!" Reiner threw a stiff Nazi salute and hastily exited.

After Reiner closed the door behind him, Schüller paused a moment and stood up. He knocked on the top of the desk. Ernestine's head came up from under it as she straightened her blouse. She stood in front of him, humiliated and angry.

"Is this on the level?"

"Turn off your brain."

"We had a deal."

"I will handle this."

"You gonna handle Adolph Hitler? Are we talkin' master race, Jew hatin' Hitler? Or is there some other Hitler I need to know about?"

"I'm in charge of Paris."

"That was signed by Hitler. You gonna say no to Mista' Hitler?"

"Mister Hitler is in Berlin. *We* are in Paris."

"What about my husband?"

"I will take care of everything."

"I wanna see Theotis."

Schüller gave Ernestine a hard slap to the face. Ernestine stood stunned, wincing from the pain.

"Don't forget your place, nigger. Your husband is safer in a labor camp than on the streets of Paris. Think about it. In the meantime, I graciously accept a sizable percentage of your club's money, and you suck my cock. In return, your husband Theotis remains alive, and I allow your little family of performing monkeys to pretend National Socialism doesn't exist. But it does exist. Doing my bidding is your only concern."

A cutting remark was about to escape Ernestine's lips, but she thought better of it and swallowed it in silence.

"I'll always be white, and you'll always be a nigger," Schüller continued. "Do as you're told, and everything will be as it should."

A tiny tear rolled down her cheek. Ernestine's gaze was empty and expressionless. She touched her cheek as it swelled. Beneath her stoic mask was the burning compulsion for revenge. Schüller took out a handkerchief.

"I have much to lose as well. I will find a solution."

Ernestine nodded.

"I am a brilliant man," Schüller continued. "I will protect you, your husband, and your band of fun-loving negroes. Now take this handkerchief and clean yourself up."

Lieutenant Reiner burst into the office. "Herr Major!" He stopped abruptly; surprised that Schüller was no longer alone. "Apologies, Herr Major. I did not realize you had a guest."

"What is it, Reiner?" Schüller said as he composed himself.

"One of our checkpoints has been attacked—26 men are dead. Burnhoffer's staff car was found. The Freytags and Colonel Burnhoffer were nowhere to be found. Three of the attackers were a negro, a woman, and a dwarf."

"A negro, a woman, and a dwarf killed 26 soldiers?"

"The reports are obviously premature, Herr Major."

Ernestine looked at him quizzically.

"Brazen women, uppity jigaboos, and murderous midgets – everything the Führer despises." Schüller disappeared into his thoughts. "Thank you, Lieutenant. That will be all."

Seventeen

By the early 1940s, swing was ubiquitous. The Montclair was a popular jazz joint with a visceral ambiance and a swinging backbeat even after closing time. Established by Theotis Tubbs and his loving wife Ernestine, The Montclair swung hard even in silence. Echoes of mellifluous horn lines hovered like a mist from a thousand lead breaks. It forced its way up through the bowels of some of the greatest jazz musicians who ever walked the earth.

A thousand torch songs were sung on The Montclair's worn-out stage from the famous to the obscure. Hardship, love, and the blues echoed through its hallowed halls. It traveled through the darkened backrooms, the seedy restrooms, and wafted into the cozy seating areas.

The clientele was a mix of hustlers, prostitutes, drug dealers, and jazz fans. The ridiculous and the delusional also came to The Montclair. They had something to prove. They had a jones to test their mettle on their chosen instrument with some of the hottest musicians in Europe. The jovial but slick Buster Pete took on all newcomers with a big, gold-toothed grin—for a generous gratuity of course. In America, negroes got the short end of the stick, but in Paris they had the market cornered with a unique commodity: American Blackness. An American blackness you couldn't get tanning at the beach, or with greasepaint and burnt cork.

The musicians at The Montclair had ownership of an authenticity that white people craved. They came up hard wearing the scars of injustice, which imbued their performances with gravity and weight.

They interpreted the popular tunes of the day, fusing them with snarl, swagger and defiance.

Challengers came from everywhere. Some were new sensations from out of town, or conservatory trained automatons applying their classically trained chops to jazz. The up and comers fought off their anxiety with whiskey, daring to walk through The Montclair's sanctified halls with their instruments.

Sometimes it was a guitar, a violin, or a voice. They came to find out if they had what it took to cut heads alongside Buster Pete's headhunters of swing. Few succeeded, but many took their lumps and practiced hard to return another day. All they wanted was an approving nod from Buster. It was like receiving the Congressional Medal of Honor from the President of the United States.

The humiliated would slink away drained by nervous energy. They had nothing left but a thousand-yard stare of disappointment. Others took their humiliation as a gift of freedom to pursue other endeavors.

Over time the club had morphed from resembling a typical Parisian gin joint to a pastiche of negro America. Harlem, Chicago, Los Angeles, and New Orleans fused to create a home away from home for its performers. It was negro heaven for curious white folks. For many Europeans, The Montclair would be the closest they would ever get to fetishize negro America.

Autographed photos of famous performers like Bricktop, Sidney Bechet, Josephine Baker, and Louis Armstrong adorned the walls with homespun charm. Framed pictures of Theotis, Ernestine, and Buster were mounted behind the bar in various poses with Willy "The Lion" Smith, Fletcher Henderson, and Duke Ellington.

Amateurish paintings of Marcus Garvey and Frederick Douglas decked the hallway walls, completing its sense of black pride with an unpretentious appeal. Seating ranged from wooden booths offering more privacy, to table and chair setups pushed close to the stage.

Little Benny, the nine-year-old chocolate skinned mascot of The Montclair, zipped through the aisles on busy nights bussing tables for the kitchen. The industrious orphan could be seen on the move wiping up spilled drinks and sweeping up broken glass. Hallways were located on either side of the stage. The left stage hallway was for customers. It led to the restrooms and corridors where VIPs could have privacy. Stage right of the hall was for employees only. This hallway led to the dressing rooms for the performers. There were also two restrooms, a place for meetings, and Ernestine's office. The patio was where special guests convened to escape the smoke and the throng.

#

47-year-old pistol packin' Buster Pete was a trumpet playin' mother-fucker. He fled to Paris with nothing but hard-earned talent and street knowledge. He also arrived with music arrangements pilfered from bandleader Chick Webb. Some said the Mafia was after him. Others assumed he was on the run from the Klan for laughing too loudly in front of a white woman. Nobody knew for certain. Buster loved the trumpet. He was a ham on stage and spent his youth in Kansas City copying King Oliver's cornet solos from records. As much as he loved cutting heads, he loved getting paid even more.

He was savvy enough to know that while men worshipped musicians blowin' hard and hitting the high notes, the ladies loved a good ballad—and the women brought the men. And the men paid for the drinks—the men paid for everything. Pretty girls were partial to a well-sung torch song, and Buster loved pretty girls. That's why he fought Ernestine with every pimp tactic in his verbal arsenal to get her to hire Lorraine Fontaine as the band's canary. Fontaine was the missing link to a perfect combo.

With the right touch of make-up, Fontaine could pass for white. Under closer scrutiny, it wasn't good enough to those for whom it mattered. She was a stunning brunette with luminous skin and a shapely hourglass figure. She had small knees, flaring calves, and tiny ankles. At five-foot-three, she was what guitarist Charles LeDuff called, "A Spinner. Just the right size to lift and spin under the sheets." Not that Charles had a chance with her. He was just making an observation.

It was her voice that clinched the deal, but her head-turning good looks didn't hurt. Ernestine couldn't help but feel pangs of envy for this high-yellow dusty butt, but she couldn't deny Fontaine could really sing. The way she took over a song was what put asses in the seats.

She was no Ella Fitzgerald, but on a good night, Fontaine could give any singer a run for their money. Having a girl-singer who was light, bright, and damn near white, was the best kind of publicity. A beautiful white woman was everybody's type, and Fontaine played the part while singing the songs of Cole Porter, George Gershwin, and Fats Waller.

It didn't take long for Buster to convince Ernestine to hire Fontaine. Ernestine knew it meant more business. She wasn't about to let her ego shoot her in the foot. She had money gushing like a water hose to everyone and their mother. Buster Pete's swinging eighth notes and comedic repartee meant nothing if people weren't spending money. Fontaine was the perfect bait for lonely boozehounds with lots of dough.

She was breathtaking, quick-witted, and off-limits. Buster made that clear from the very beginning. Fontaine was a prize. She was the kind of woman men dreamed about their whole lives.

In his mind, Fontaine could never go for a broken-down horn player like himself, but there was always hope. Until then, he would protect her with his life. She was a star, and Buster wasn't about to have her get knocked up by a smooth-talking zigaboo. But there was no smooth-talking zigaboo in 1942, quite like Lorenzo Savage.

Eighteen

Savage didn't like being led around like a goat on a rope. He didn't know where he was, and he didn't know Boucher from Bullwinkle. Trust issues? Hell yeah. Right now, they were vulnerable. They'd been led through the forest like a herd of sheep. They maneuvered through trees, large rocks, and other obstacles while trusting the word of a midget—a French midget with no knowledge of underarm hygiene. Old Spice deodorant had been around for a few years by 1942, but nobody told Boucher. A pungent cloud of body odor followed him wherever he went. Strangely, Savage was the only one who seemed to notice.

Surrounded by his swarthy band of machine-gun-toting Resistance troops, the group trekked in silence as darkness fell. They were led to a group of horses, which were saddled and ready to go.

"These horses will take us to the outskirts of lower Montmartre," Boucher explained. "They are going to be looking for us. We have to stay off the main roads. We must travel through the forest in darkness. No matches, no smoking, no talking. I hope the three of you can ride a horse. If not, it is going to be a bumpy ride for your ball sacks," he turned to Santiago. "I do not mean you, of course."

Santiago, Savage, and Fuller mounted their horses. Two Frenchmen lifted Boucher on to a horse. His short legs couldn't reach the stirrups, but he had complete command of the animal.

"How far is it to lower Montmartre," asked Fuller as he struggled to control his horse.

"It is about an hour's ride, but it could take longer. It is going to be pitch black soon. You won't be able to see your hand in front of your face. We will have to take our time, so be careful. The horses spook easily."

"Who's your contact in lower Montmartre?" Savage asked suspiciously.

"Why? Do you think we might have mutual friends? Friends of your great grandmother, perhaps?"

Savage ignored his sarcasm.

"I did not think so," Boucher continued.

"We need a place to lay low until we can come up with a plan," Fuller explained.

Boucher sighed with impatience.

"I am taking you to The Montclair. Ernestine Tubbs is in charge. If she will not take you in, you are as you Americans say, "Up shits creek without a propeller."

"Paddle," Santiago said correcting him.

"The Nazis will be looking for us. You had better cross your fingers and hope Ernestine is in a good mood."

One of the older resistance fighters ran up to Boucher and spoke with urgency in French. Boucher translated.

"There is a German patrol coming this way—no more talk. We have to move now. We must go!" Boucher turned his horse and led the way.

Fuller pulled his horse in front of Boucher and blocked his path. "One last thing, mon ami. Do you know what a High Plains Drifter is?"

Santiago fought the impulse to roll her eyes.

"No," Boucher replied with concentration lines on his forehead.

"Well, I'm what they call The High Plains Drifter," Fuller continued. "If anything goes wrong – If anything bad happens—If we walk into a stag party for Uncle Adolph, you're going to get it High Plains Drifter style. Now, if nothing goes wrong, then you have nothing to worry about. But if something gets ugly and I'm talking Zyklon B, naked group shower ugly, beware of the High Plaines Drifter. You get my meaning, hombre?"

"If you think it's tough being a little person, imagine what it's like being a little person without the use of your legs," Santiago said to Boucher.

Amused but holding his composure, Boucher turned to his men. They all laughed. "You Americans and your dramatic speeches," Boucher continued. "There is no time for this! Va te faire enculer (Go fuck yourself)."

Boucher trotted off into the darkness. The trio took off behind him as the remaining Resistance fighters scattered into the forest.

#

Emerging from a blanket of darkness and battered by the forest's rough terrain, Boucher, Savage, Santiago, and Fuller arrived at the outskirts of lower Montmartre. Dismounting from their horses, they brought them to a stable and made their way into the city. Boucher stealthily led them across multiple streets and intersections. They crept with caution as they kept an eye out for German patrols.

As they sprinted across a wide intersection, Boucher put his hand up to slow them down. He led them into a darkened alley. Moving through the alleyway, they crept to the end of the block just short of the main street. Boucher raised his hand to stop them.

"Stay here out of sight. I must run ahead to see if the streets are clear. Stay in the shadows. Stay quiet. German patrols pass this way."

"Roger that," Santiago replied.

Boucher took a last look then sprinted across the street. He slowed down with a casual stride to not draw attention to himself. Though seeing a midget dart like a roadrunner in a chauffeur's uniform wasn't the most inconspicuous sight to behold.

Savage, Santiago, and Fuller backed up slowly against the side of the building under the cover of darkness.

They took a knee. "I saw a woman from the airplane," Fuller whispered. "Back at the checkpoint."

"Who?" Santiago asked.

"She was an older lady. She was wearing a blue muumuu and Birkenstocks. Goddamn Nazis... They shot her like an animal."

"I saw a passenger too," Savage added. "Lil' homie with the Lakers jersey—he vanished right in front of me. He barely missed getting cut in half."

"Savage, you were right," Fuller confided. "We have to stop these psychos. I'm no history nerd, but I know grade-A evil when I see it. Not everyone that dies *should* die. We have to warn the expats and stop those maniacs. We have to figure out a way to get those people the hell out of Paris."

"It's the right thing to do," Savage said.

"But if you double cross us..."

Fuller was serious. Savage didn't blink.

"...it's gonna be bad for you," Fuller continued.

"It's a fine day for a killing spree," Savage said. "Let's kill some Nazis."

"Slow your roll, home skillet," Fuller cautioned. "We help those people escape, then we escort you back home to the slammer—*The End*." He turned to Santiago. "You ok, Special Agent?"

"I'm fine, sir. Let's finish this. I need to get home. I have a life."

"I don't think you need to worry about Lady Kung-Fu," Savage added. "What she did back there was like the fucking Bolshoi Ballet of ass-kicking."

"Whatever is happening to the passengers is more than likely going to happen to us," Fuller added. "If they're vanishing, so will we."

"But where are they vanishing to?" Santiago asked.

"That's the $64,000 question," Savage replied.

"Hopefully, back to 2023," said Fuller.

"And what if we don't?" Savage said. "What if we wake up somewhere under the ocean—inside of a mountain? And when? What year?"

"Take a breath Nancy Negative," Santiago whispered. We'll cross that bridge when we get to it. In the meantime, we need to warn those people about Schüller."

Savage held his hand up to silence them. He heard boots on cement from a distance. They backed up against the wall, veiled in darkness.

"No guns," Savage whispered. "Quiet like a mouse pissin' on cotton."

Five German soldiers appeared at the opening of the alley. One of the soldiers heard something and turned to listen with suspicion. The soldiers conversed in German.

"Did you hear something?"

"Hear what?"

"I did not hear anything."

"In the alley. I heard someone talking."

"Search the alley."

"I do not hear anything."

"Who is back there? Come out!"

One of the soldiers walked into the alley and stood right next to Savage, Santiago, and Fuller without seeing them.

"If anyone is back here, come out, or you will be shot!"

The soldier met silence as he strained to hear through the darkness. He reached into his pocket, pulled out a match, and struck it against the box. The fiery glow from the match illuminated the soldier's face and the face of Santiago standing next to him.

Slowly turning to his left, he saw Santiago. Startled, he jumped back, but it was too late. Santiago grabbed the back of his head and jerked his body into her right knee, brutally crushing his solar plexus. The soldier toppled over in crippling pain.

Another soldier moved in from behind. Savage was all over him like a fat boy on a cupcake. Firing a volley of damaging punches to his face and head, he backed the soldier up against the wall. Savage yanked his rifle away from him and used the broad side of it to crack the front of his skull.

The other three soldiers rushed into the alley to help. They were met with a whirlwind of kicks, punches, and leg sweeps from Santiago. Fuller picked up a metal rod lying nearby and swung it like a baseball bat exploding the last soldier's skull.

Another soldier attempted to escape the alley. Before he reached the street, Santiago pulled out a bayonet from a fallen soldier's belt. She threw it at him finding her target in the back of the soldier's neck. The soldier's screams were cut short as his swelling tongue bulged from his mouth. He crumpled to his knees, then fell face first just short of the main street.

A badly injured soldier fought pain as he pointed a pistol at Santiago. Seeing this, Fuller dove in front of Santiago using the metal rod as a stake. A shot rang out. Fuller plunged the rod deep into the soldier's chest. The soldier let out a wheezing gasp of air then died.

Savage and Santiago turned to see Fuller roll off the soldier. There was a dark bloody hole in his chest.

"Fuller!" cried Santiago.

Joining Fuller, they propped him up as they tried to figure out how to save him.

"It's just a flesh wound," Fuller said jokingly.

"Don't talk," Santiago said.

"There's no walking away from a wound like this," Fuller said as he coughed up blood.

"We'll take him to the night club," Savage said.

"Forget it. I'm done."

Santiago's eyes filled with tears. "Fuller, I'm sorry."

"You're the best in the Bureau," Fuller said. "That's why everyone gave you shit. Jealousy—you were better than all of us." Fuller coughed hard as he fought to finish. "Find those expats. Get them the hell outta there. Get them to safety. But do me a favor."

"Name it."

"If you make it back – *when* you make it back, tell my son..."

Santiago waited but Fuller was gone.

Nineteen

"Motherfucker," Stewart said quietly as she took another sip of espresso.

A German officer who sat nearby overheard her. He watched her curiously as she typed into the strange device. He squinted with annoyance not knowing what to make of her.

On *Simulated Earth*, Stewart wielded technology so far beyond her lookie-loos, she could turn muddy water into Red Bull. The hand-held device in her possession was black, flat, rectangular, and slightly larger than her hand. It was the most advanced hand-held computer of its kind. Although Stewart was still trying to get acquainted with its functionality, the device provided all the information she could ever want.

It was also an advanced tool that could temporarily freeze time, cloak, teleport, and cause death and destruction. She could theoretically crush Berlin, drag Hitler out of his bunker by his ear, and make him apologize to everybody. But that would be cheating. She had to figure out a way to find the saboteur, maintain the show's popularity, and keep her job.

The curious German officer decided to question Stewart and strutted over to her. Stewart was shaking off yet another distraction as a small herd of cows trotted by to the sounds of Gypsy Jazz music wafting through the air. Herded by a young boy and an old man, Stewart watched as she pondered what cows thought about the meaning of their existence.

"Do you dream of terraforming barren planets? Of becoming a

merciful god who guides the destiny of her children. Am I a narcissist or a savior? Do you care?"

She continued checking the device for lunar disturbances.

"Guten Tag," said the German officer.

"There had to be a moment before everything changed," Stewart said under hear breath. "Something occurred out of the ordinary, something that made that day different. But what was it? What happened? Motherfucker."

"Who are you, and what are you doing here?" said the German officer.

The cows and their herders continued to parade by. They chewed cud and broke wind. The sound of intermittent farting gave Stewart a thought.

"Tachyonic signatures."

"Entschuldigen Sie, meine Dame."

"Anything entering *Simulated Earth's* atmosphere would leave a signature—a mark, a sign."

"Show me your papers."

"That signature would have been recorded, wouldn't it?" Stewart said, ignoring the officer.

She punched in an alphanumeric code. She was digging deeper into the records. Another screen popped up. On the monitor were clusters of tachyonic signatures on a fluctuating graph.

"Are you deaf!?"

Stewart begrudgingly shifted her focus to the officer with an annoyed expression on her face.

"No, I'm not deaf."

The officer took out a pad and pencil. "What is your name?"

"It doesn't matter. What's the point of this?"

"Never mind that. I will ask the questions. And you will show me the proper respect. On your feet."

"No."

"What?!"

"No. I'm fine where I am. I'm working."

"Get up."

"Why are you interrupting me? I'm minding my own business."

"*You* are my business. Show me your papers."

"Shit." Stewart took a moment to silently chide herself for going to the trouble of dressing up in a period costume but neglecting to obtain the proper documentation. "I don't have any papers."

"Get up, you are coming with me."

"If you don't get away from me right now, you'll wish you had."

"How dare you speak to me with such insolence. What is your business here?" The officer looked around for other soldiers. He was alone.

"Don't make a scene," Stewart said. "Join me for a cup of espresso."

"I beg your pardon?"

"Have a seat."

"I do not drink espresso with niggers."

"They serve hot chocolate too."

"Get up!"

"I don't have time for this."

The officer drew his sidearm and pointed it at her. "Get up. I am placing you under arrest."

A beeping sound came from Stewart's device. "Oh shit. What is this?" She looked at the data that appeared in red on the screen. "There was an atmospheric energy surge right before the event."

The officer reached over to grab the device. Stewart jerked it away. They fumbled with it, and it fell hard on the cement.

"Shit! Look what you did," Stewart yelled. She picked it up to make sure it was working correctly.

"I order you to give me that!" said the officer.

"No," she said with annoyance.

"You are to come with me for questioning. Get up!"

"That's not going to happen."

"Do not make me shoot you."

Stewart checked her watch. "Let's move this along." She switched programs and typed in a code. She pointed the device at the officer.

Nothing happened. With an annoyed look on her face, she checked it. "Fuck."

Something was wrong. She pressed it again. Suddenly the German officer was standing completely naked. His shriveled penis and testicles were on full display for everyone. The German officer looked at himself in dismay as everyone stared and uttered sounds of shock and surprise. Pedestrians began laughing. Cars honked their horns. The German officer had no recourse than to take off running down the street toward his staff car.

He hobbled tender-footed through the street, picked up speed, and ran awkwardly. He tripped and fell, struggled to his feet, then continued running. His face was beet red from embarrassment. He bruised his knee from the fall but continued running as his balls jiggled from side to side. He yelled to his driver, who was standing in front of his staff car reading a newspaper.

"Steig ins Auto! Steig ins Auto! Eile!"

Laughter from onlookers reached a crescendo as the German Officer dove into the backseat of the vehicle and disappeared from view. The driver hesitated in confusion.

"Gehen! Gehen!" said the officer who was cowering in the back seat.

The driver jumped in the car behind the wheel. The staff car sped off, swerving with screeching tires and a cloud of dust. Applause and cheers erupted from French pedestrians. Stewart checked the device to find out what went wrong. "This thing better not be broken."

The readout on the device told her it was fully operational. She scrolled back to the anomaly. "This has to be it," Stewart thought to herself. "Tachyonic particles don't appear out of the ether."

She scrolled through a succession of data fields, refining her search. Suddenly, something mysterious appeared on the screen.

"Well, hello Mary Lou. Who the hell are you?" And there it was. "An android?" She racked her brain. "Who would send an android?"

A small crowd of lookie-loos was forming. Stewart looked up. "Staring is rude. What happened to all those French manners?"

She considered making their clothes disappear as well, but thought better of it. They continued to stare. Suddenly, a blinking light pulsated on the face of the device. "There's someone else here too. A human—a real one."

Twenty

The original owners of The Montclair in lower Montmartre can thank swing and American negroes for its success. It began as a quaint little watering hole built by a negro American soldier and a French local after World War I. It wasn't until Theotis and Ernestine Tubbs bought the place and started hosting live music, that things picked up. It wasn't just any live music either. The French craved American swing, and The Montclair delivered the real McCoy.

There were pockets of American negro jazz musicians scattered throughout Paris. They scraped by making the rounds at local clubs after World War I. Theotis and Ernestine were smart enough to give talented local musicians a home and a stage to perform. It also fostered an environment where creativity flourished. Relationships were forged with passion, sweat, and incredible music.

By 1940 The Montclair had a ferocious swing band so hot it made Hitler sweat. The Buster Pete Band was the most popular group in Paris. Jazz fans flocked to The Montclair from all over Europe to hear real live American negroes play authentic swing. Unfortunately, when the Germans took over Paris, they banned swing because the Nazis associated the music with defiance.

Defiance was a death sentence in the National Socialist Party. That meant no swing and no niggers. To get over this little hiccup, the French government convinced the Nazis that swing was a national custom and an ingrained part of their culture. They offered to compromise by calling the music "jazz" to avoid a full-blown ban.

The occupation of Paris by the Nazis saw thousands fleeing to avoid persecution and death. Many negroes returned to the US, but a handful stayed behind willing to tough it out. They thought the Nazis would roll in and out like a traveling circus, but they thought wrong.

The Nazis were insufferable tyrants. They wouldn't move on without leaving skid marks. Enduring hazing, internment, murder, and declaring that swing was "degenerate negro music," black expats and Parisian jazz fans kept the music alive–but there was a price.

Meanwhile, the Buster Pete Band was the toast of Paris cool. They had fans, groupies, and blood-sucking leeches. The band consisted of Buster Pete on trumpet and vocals, Fats Calhoun on bass, James "Sauce" Jenkins on drums, Charles LeDuff on guitar, Spencer Robinson on saxophone, Clyde Johnson on piano, and the sultry vocal stylings of Lorraine Fontaine.

When Theotis Tubbs was detained by the Gestapo and sent to a labor camp for the crime of being black after 9pm, his wife Ernestine took complete control of the club. The Montclair ran as smooth as a silk shoeshine. No one did more to protect negro expats and American swing in Paris than Ernestine. With occupation leader Major Ernst Schüller using Theotis as leverage to shake down the club, Ernestine's life was in turmoil. But things were about to go from bad to worse.

#

Ernestine's office at The Montclair was her refuge from reality. It was her haven, and she wanted to keep it that way. It was the one place she could lock the door, shut out the world, and have a good cry.

Behind her desk were photos of her family back in Harlem, a bouquet of flowers, and a large regal portrait of her grandmother. It was rare she allowed more than one person in her office at a time. When she had meetings with gunrunners, black marketers, Nazis, or the police, it was always one-on-one. It gave her control. Today was different.

When Boucher showed up explaining he had to talk to her in private, she knew it wouldn't be good. She knew all about his activities with The Resistance. Ernestine kept her mouth shut. She had empathy for the citizens of Paris and hated the Nazis, but The Montclair was her priority.

#

When Ernestine watched Santiago, Savage, and Boucher drift into The Montclair with a dead Nazi, anxiety shot up from the pit of her stomach. It exploded in her chest like an atomic bomb. Sure, a dead Nazi was problematic, but there was also something peculiar about these newcomers—especially the colored Nazi. He had an air about him that was strange—unsettling. He smelled like trouble—white people trouble.

Ernestine was already in way over her head. If anyone found out she was fucking Schüller, she'd be double dipped in a world of hurt. They'd call her a traitor, a whore, a collaborator, and there wouldn't be enough improvisational sass talk in the world to wiggle her way out. Schüller had to be dealt with if she was going to get her husband back. She'd been through tough times before, but this time was different. She was entangled in Nazi collaboration, treason, and now these strangers.

Boucher had convinced Ernestine this was a life and death situation. Savage and Santiago sat in Ernestine's office, wolfing down fried chicken and biscuits from plates on their laps. Boucher paced back and forth with his stubby-legged strut. He thought good and hard about how he could use these time travelers to get the Les Noirs safely out of Paris. More importantly, he wanted to use them to kill more Nazis.

"Now, ain't this about a bitch." Ernestine said calmly.

The juxtaposition of Santiago's summer dress and Savage's rich white man's Nazi suit hit Ernestine like a bag full of bricks. These were the clothes the missing Germans were wearing — what Schüller's assistant was talking about earlier. She recognized the dress instantly. Ernestine had personally made alterations to it.

#

Astrid saw Ernestine at The Montclair one night and assumed she was a seamstress because she was a negro. In Astrid's mind, all negro women cleaned, cooked, and sewed like it was a magical superpower. It didn't matter that Astrid had been introduced to her as the owner of The Montclair. Astrid was adamant about having a negro make alterations to her dresses.

Ernestine bit her tongue. She was a cunt hair away from knocking the pasty bitch out. She thought better of it because her bar tab was huge, and money is money. Ernestine held her tongue, smiled, and later relented. Astrid gallivanted around the club, enjoying the gaze of men like she was the Queen of Sheba – without *Mr. Freytag*, of course.

#

Looking disheveled and dirty, the group looked like prime candidates for a Nazi hazing. It didn't matter if they were American spies or the 4-H Club, Schüller would kill them or make them wish he'd killed them. Ernestine steadied her breathing and settled in behind her desk with a calm poker-face.

"What the hell did I tell you about bringin' strange motherfuckas' in here?" She said to Boucher in a low voice. Her stoic countenance masked a powerful compulsion to knock the living shit out of him. "Are you trying to get us all shot?"

"We need your help."

"Do I look like the Salvation Army? Is Salvation Army written across my fuckin' forehead?"

"Ernestine..."

"Do I look like I give charity? Who told you I was little miss help everybody?"

"Please listen..."

"You brought a dead Nazi in here? Have you lost yo' Munchkin mind?"

"He is not a dead Nazi. He is a dead American, impersonating a dead Nazi."

"Is that supposed to make me feel better?! Motherfucka', that's worse!"

"You are not going to believe what I am about to tell you," Boucher blurted with excitement. "Everything I am about to tell you is true. Please, bear with me."

Then suddenly.

"It don't matter what you got to say," Buster said as he entered the room from a secret sliding door panel in the wall. "You know good and well we can't be hiding no spies. Do you have any idea what would happen if the Nazis raided us right now?" He looked at Savage and noticed the swastika on the lapel of his suit. "Nigga', where you get that suit?!"

"It doesn't matter where I got the suit," Savage replied. "What matters is 81 years from now, a group of vaping douchebags with Civil War beards and cargo shorts, are going to dig your big skeletal ass out of a mass grave and post the video on YouTube. That's what matters."

Buster looked at Boucher. "What the hell he' talkin' about?"

"He is from the future," Boucher said. "They are *both* from the future. They are time travelers."

Buster took a moment and gave Ernestine a stern look. He pulled a pearl-handled revolver out of his pocket and pointed it at them.

"Alright, that's enough. I never liked yo' Wizard of Oz lookin' ass no how," he said to Boucher. "You think this is the time for gags? Beat it. Get the fuck up outta here, or somebody's gonna need a priest."

"We're Americans," Santiago explained. "We're on your side. We're here to help."

"Help me do what? Get lynched?"

"Schüller is going get rid of every negro in Paris," Boucher said.

"Where did you hear that?"

"Trust me, we know," Savage said as he set his plate off to the side. He grabbed a toothpick from a small cardboard container on the desk and picked his teeth with it.

"Trust *you*?!" Buster replied. "Who *the fuck* are you?!"

Boucher butted in. "I think I can acquire an aeroplane."

"You can get back to the United States from London," Santiago chimed in.

"The United States?! Uncle Sam ain't done a damn thing for me!"

"The Nazis are worse," Santiago replied.

"What the Nazis do is they' business. I got nothin' to do with them —that's politics. I came here to play the trumpet. Paris is my home," Buster replied adamantly.

"You better *bone up* on Nazi politics, or you and your friends are dead," Savage replied.

"Haven't you seen what's going on around here?" Santiago asked. "Millions of people are being murdered."

"Exactly, Savage nodded. "People are being shipped off to concentration camps every day. I'm surprised you're not sweating your tubby ass off in a concentration camp right now." He turned to Ernestine. "What's Schüller's cut of this joint?"

Ernestine didn't appreciate Savage's question. "It ain't none a' yo' bidness', Mista' Charlie."

"You think the Nazis are going to let you do whatever you want?" replied Santiago.

"We have a deal," Buster said. "They don't give a damn about us. The Nazis want the Jews."

"I hate to ruin your rich fantasy life, but the Nazis hate everybody— including black people," Savage replied.

"Black? Nigga', don't call me black!"

"Colored, black, negro, porch monkey, whatever," Savage replied. "The Nazis are going to kill all of us. They're going to exterminate us like cockroaches. They're getting rid of every negro in Paris."

"Get up!" Buster demanded.

Santiago had enough. "If you don't stop waving that gun around, I'm going to take it away from you and spank you with it."

"Come and get it, mama."

"Take your best shot. Be sure to aim carefully. You'll only have one chance."

Savage stood up and placed himself between them staring Buster down. "You didn't murder Chick Webb."

"What!?"

"He was sick for a long time. He had TB. He died in a hospital in Baltimore in '39. You had nothing to do with it. You happened to be in Baltimore right before he died. Your timing is for shit. Wrong place, wrong time."

"How did you know about that?"

"He's from the future," replied Boucher rolling his eyes in frustration.

"It's history to us," Savage continued. "The Mafia wanted your head on a stick. They thought you killed Webb—their cash cow. They found out you stole his arrangements. You may be a thief, but you're no murderer."

"Who the hell are you?"

"Sentimental Rhapsody" would have set you up for life. But Heineman and Lindstrom stole it right out from under you. You never received the credit—or the royalties. In the 21st century, you're just a tiny footnote in history. You deserved better."

"Who sent you?"

Savage took the toothpick out of his mouth and placed it in the inside of his breast pocket. "Buster old boy, you're part of a long line of business challenged musicians who got ripped off by people who couldn't compose a *limerick* to save their lives. You weren't the first, and you won't be the last."

Buster's jaw dropped. "Where the hell did you people come from?"

"My name is Lorenzo Savage. I'm a professional—I'm from the future."

Buster and Ernestine struggled to grasp what he was saying.

"This is Special Agent Dolores Santiago," Savage continued. "Her partner is lying dead in your wine cellar. They're FBI.

"G-Men?" said Buster. "They got G-women too?"

"G-person," Santiago said, correcting him. "We... arrived here on a flight from Buenos Aires. We're from the year 2023. We're stuck here."

"2023?!" Buster exclaimed, looking to Ernestine. "Am I supposed to believe this shit?!"

"I believe them," Boucher said. "We could use their help. They hate the Nazis we much as I do. I saw Savage blow Colonel Burnhoffer's brains out like he was swatting a fly. Cool as a cucumber—very impressive."

"Aw-shucks," Savage replied with a straight face.

"And you brought that nigga' here!?" Buster yelled. "Are you drunk?!"

"We have Schüller's orders from Berlin," Boucher explained. "He has been ordered by Hitler to get rid of all the American negroes. They will be coming for all of you. Everyone must leave immediately!"

"This is our home," Buster argued. "This is the best gig I ever had! This is my livelihood—my life!"

"Hitler doesn't give a damn about *you* or jazz," Santiago explained. "He's a plague, and he's going to wipe out anybody who doesn't pass the German look-a-like test. If you had your eyes open, you'd see what was going on."

"I know *exactly* what the fuck is going on! I've seen those poor motherfuckas' get shot in the streets. I chose to stay!"

"You chose wrong!"

"I got nowhere else to go!" Buster paused, took out his handkerchief, and wiped the sweat from his face. "Ok, you're from the future. Tell us how this friggin' nightmare ends."

Savage looked at Santiago. He wanted to spare them the horrible truth. "Nobody knows. The Buster Pete Band disappeared. After 1942 they were never heard from again."

Santiago stood up. "We don't know if we can change our past, but maybe we can fix it a little. Hitler has already killed millions of innocent people. You don't have to be next."

"And to think, if they'd have let Hitler into art school, it would be a whole different world," Savage said, thinking out loud.

"All this was in the orders?!" Buster asked incredulously.

"It's all here," Boucher said, pulling the orders from Burnhoffer's satchel. Buster looked at the orders with the Nazi seal and Hitler's signature. He turned to Ernestine.

"Can you believe this shit?! Everything we worked for. We had a deal with the Germans! Ernestine, we had a deal!"

"They're on the level."

"But we just can't... We're on easy street."

"This ain't no easy street."

"We built this!"

"*I* built this. You played the trumpet. I paid the rent. I kept the licenses—put up with the customers, the politicians, the police, the gangsters, and now the Germans. *I* built this. This is my husband's life, his legacy—*my* life. I thought we could wait out the Nazis, but I was wrong. Schüller has got my husband killin' his self in a slave camp and plans to tear down everything we worked for."

Savage stood in front of her from the other side of the desk. "I can figure a way out of this. I need to know everything about Schüller's operation." Savage smiled at Boucher. "At the very least, we're going to kill a whole bunch of Nazis."

Boucher returned an approving smile.

"Why are you doing this?" Ernestine inquired. "Why do you care what happens to us?"

Savage thought about it for a moment. "Because I... It's the right thing to do."

Santiago took note of his response. Buster reached into the drawer of a roll top desk and pulled out a small bottle of whiskey. He pulled out the cork and took a swig. "Two steps forward, three steps back—the story of my life."

Boucher's attention shifted. He heard a German official shouting through a megaphone outside far off in the distance. It was followed by a barrage of weapons fire. "More like five steps back."

Twenty-One

Paris — The One-Two-Two Brothel

"No, I don't want to be massaged by a man. My apologies to your masseur. Nothing personal, but it's personal."

Suave, early 40's, Caucasian, and with a thick, well-coiffed beard, Sebastian Ritenour sat in the lavish waiting room of the famous One-Two-Two Brothel. Dressed in a black Gestapo officer's uniform, he was seated across from a pleasingly plump redhead wearing only an apron. The apron hung down around her neck and covered the middle of her chest and pelvis. Each melon-like breast poked out from either side.

"When I get a massage, I want to disappear," Ritenour explained. "I want to go to a far-away land of pink bunny rabbits and rainbows—a world where nothing matters. I want to float effortlessly among the clouds."

"You offer so much detail," said the thickly accented French prostitute.

"Nestled in the warm embrace of peace and tranquility, the last thing I want to think about is a man touching my ding-dong."

"That is foolish. You should not think of such things. No one wants to touch your ding-dong. It is all in your mind."

"No, it's not all in my mind if his mind is on my ding-dong. Don't get me wrong, I'm sure he's a talented masseur, but I don't want anything resembling a penis anywhere near me when I'm lying naked on a table

—so *him* accidentally caressing my balls? That would be completely out of the question."

"No one has any interest in caressing your balls."

"I'm just saying if he *did*, I would have no interest in that. That's all I'm saying."

"That would never happen. Unless... Unless of course you want *me* to touch your balls," she asked with a coquettish grin.

"Sure, why not. I just have to find out if it's ok with my wife. I'm sure she'll be ok with it."

"Oh, you are married. Surely you are joking. I do not think she will be ok with it. Let us begin. I will have Ramon give you a good massage. He is our best."

"Ah, Ramon sounds like the name of a man. So, once again, that would be a no-no for me. But I appreciate the artistry of your sales pitch."

"Does it really matter what sex the person is when your eyes are closed?" a female voice said, hidden in the shadows.

Ritenour was startled. "Yes," he replied. "It does. It matters a whole heck of a lot." He strained his eyes to see who it was. "Who is that?"

"How would you know if your eyes are closed? A good massage is a good massage. You're safe. I'm sure these fine people know how to keep a secret."

"I wouldn't enjoy myself," Ritenour explained. "I would know if it was a man. I have a sixth sense about these things. Why don't you join us so we can see who we're talking to?"

"What if it was a man disguised as a woman—a gorgeous woman. A disguise so brilliant, you wouldn't know the difference. The entire time you'd be thinking it was a woman—a beautiful woman—a beautiful French woman with strong hands and plump juicy breasts. Imagine the smell of her perfume. Your penis would become the hardest substance known to man."

"And then a lifetime of post-traumatic stress when I discovered it was a man? No, thank you. I'll pass."

Out stepped Stewart, who was also dressed in a black Gestapo officer's uniform. Recognition filled Ritenour's eyes. "What are you doing here?" asked Stewart.

"I could ask you the same question," Ritenour replied.

"Who are you?" asked the prostitute. "What are you doing here?"

"I was in the neighborhood. What are *you* doing here? You wouldn't be blowing Nazis by any chance, would you?"

"Niggers aren't allowed here—but you are a Nazi. You cannot be a Nazi! There are no niggers in the Nazi Party!"

"You've never heard of Affirmative Action?" Stewart inquired. She turned to Ritenour. "It's one thing to sleep with a syphilitic whore, but a *racist* syphilitic whore? Have you no shame?"

"It's ok," Ritenour said to the prostitute. "She's with me. She's my wife."

The prostitute's face turned to the color of alabaster. "You're married to her? A Nègre Nazi? Is this a joke?"

"The joke will be on you when your family finds out you've sucked the cocks from every goose stepper from here to Antwerp."

"I will alert the authorities!" she exclaimed as she stormed out of the room.

"She'll be back with large beefy men who don't care about body hair," Ritenour said.

"What the hell are you doing here?"

"I was worried about you."

"So, you came to a brothel to help manage your anxiety?"

"I was sight-seeing. She invited me in. I didn't realize this was a brothel until naked women started ogling me. I mean, I'm good-looking, but I'm not *that* good-looking. I haven't seen this much pubic hair since I accidentally walked in on your grandmother."

"Accidently?"

Ritenour looked around the room. "The attention to detail is amazing."

"That's because this world is as real as our own."

Ritenour took Stewart in his arms and kissed her on the mouth. Stewart accepted him passionately.

"Are you ok?" Ritenour asked. "I hadn't heard from you."

"I'm ok."

"You don't want to be found?"

"I'm swamped."

"You find anything?"

"Almost."

"Have you been drinking?"

"Do I look drunk?"

"Sweetie..."

"Only *you* could come up with an excuse for being in a whore house."

"I miss you."

"It's not safe here."

"It's safer for *me* than you."

"I can take care of myself."

"Sorry, I don't think my smokin' hot black wife wearing a Gestapo uniform is that safe."

"Sue me. I like Hugo Boss."

"The Organization is getting nervous. They like the time travel story-line, but they don't see the point of trying to fix something that isn't broken. Sweetie, it's made us rich. We're *lucky* this happened. You broke through. You've made your mark. Take the gift."

"So, murder, subjugation, and psychotic behavior is a gift?"

"I didn't say that."

"Especially when everyone is making fuck you money?"

"If *you* don't get compensated for this, someone else will."

"It's dark and twisted. What does it say about us?"

"This isn't us. It's a game—a simulation. This isn't real life."

"It's as real as anything, and I'm responsible."

"Reviewers are calling it *Savage Times*. Get it? Lorenzo Savage? *Savage Times*?"

"Honey, go home."

"Let me help you."

"For the 57th time, you can't help me. Rit, I love you, but you're in

SAVAGE TIMES ~ 107

the way. I can't find the douchebag who sabotaged my game and keep an eye on you at the same time."

"You don't need to keep an eye on me," he said as he masked the sting of matrimonial castration. "Sweetie, you don't have a lot of time."

"I'm fully aware of that. Go home. Let me do my job. I think I'm close to something. I can feel it."

"Can't I do anything to help? We're in this together."

"It's not your battle."

"Sweetie, let me help you."

"This is something I have to face alone. Someone has come up with an elaborate scheme to fuck me, and I'm going to find the son of a bitch."

"Stewart, I'm your husband."

"This is personal. I have to deal with this. I'm going to find him. He's created a climate of stupidity unparalleled in human history."

"Stewart, this is not *our* life! This isn't even real."

"I'm sorry you feel that way. And you ignoring the larger ethical issues is beginning to concern me."

"Yes, genocide is bad, I get it — but don't forget where your bread is buttered."

"Money won't fix my conscience."

"Great, do what you have to do. I'll just sit at home quietly while you play Space Jesus. I'll have your slippers and dinner waiting for you when you return. It'll be pancakes in case you're wondering."

"Rit, don't be like this."

"How am I supposed to be?"

"This is important. This is bigger than us."

"No, it isn't. This is about what you want to do."

"You're thinking about this the wrong way."

"What's the right way? Your way?"

"Rit..."

"I have a career too, and I'm good at it. Bio-mechanical research is important to me. It's important to science. The difference is I never put my career before my marriage."

"That's not fair."

"Seems a little one-sided to me."

"Please go home. Let me handle this. This isn't just some business-as-usual corporate espionage bullshit — this is personal. Someone is determined to find out if I'm some kind of passive bitch who will shut up and take a paycheck."

"You're taking this personally."

"It *is* personal. I'm a person. But it's also about justice."

"Is it?"

"Please go home. I promise when this is over, we'll sit down and work all of this out. Please be patient." She ran her fingers through his beard like she use to do. "I love you."

"...I love you more."

#

"What is going on in here?" Captain Helmut Weber stood in the doorway, half-dressed in a white shirt pointing a Walther P38. The prostitute from earlier was cowering behind him.

"See!" the prostitute said. "It is as I told you! They are spies!"

"Do not move!" Weber ordered. "Put your hands up!"

"We can't do both," replied Ritenour.

"Who are you?" Weber inquired. "What are you doing here?"

"What are *you* doing here?" Stewart replied. "Shouldn't you be euthanizing mental patients?"

"I am on my lunch hour. What is the meaning of this?!"

"I knew he was going to say that," Ritenour retorted.

Three grubby French bouncers burst in from behind Weber and confronted Stewart and Ritenour.

Ritenour turned to Stewart. "Whatever happens sweetie, I hope you find what you're looking for."

Stewart smiled wistfully. "Thank you."

"Get them!" Weber ordered. Now!"

The three men charged Stewart and Ritenour. Stewart pushed a button on her device. The men ran through their targets and crashed headfirst into a wall behind them. Stewart and Ritenour had vanished. The bouncers crumbled to the floor, nursing their head injuries as they moaned. Everyone looked around at each other dumbfounded.

Twenty-Two

Schüller didn't like getting his hands dirty, but it was a dirty war. He promised himself he wouldn't become mired in the filth, but circumstances beyond his control meant he had to get in the weeds. He had better things to do than to watch his men load ugly people on to train cars, but he was doing precisely that.

He watched an obese couple and a child get squeezed onto a crowded train car with the assistance of a dickish soldier. Schüller thought to himself, "I can't believe they had sex with each other without becoming ill."

The train station platform was teaming with the fragrance of the great unwashed—Jews, gypsies, homosexuals, and whoever else Schüller could round up to cook the books. Those who didn't have the foresight or the funds to flee Paris when they had the chance were paying the price now.

Taking over Burnhoffer's duties, it was Schüller's charge to get rid of these people and move on to bigger and better things. The negroes were next. Hitler wanted Paris squeaky clean. He viewed the city as a museum for his personal amusement. He wanted to strut around and look at beautiful architecture without a Jew or nigger in sight.

Schüller was under enormous pressure. Despite being blackmailed, he was also being groomed for a place near the top of the National Socialist pyramid. It was suggested during a late-night phone conversation from a mysterious caller that he take charge of ensuring everything run smoothly.

"No mistakes, no excuses," said the tubercular caller. "Something big is coming your way. Do not disappoint us."

This made Schüller's mind race. It wasn't too far-fetched to assume he was being watched. He could trust no one. He knew there were traitors within the Third Reich, and so did the Führer. Many had been discovered and were immediately executed. The mere accusation of being a traitor was a death sentence.

Schüller had to play the role of servant of The Reich—a loyal German who obeyed orders without question. He had to be seen personally supervising the relocation of the Untermensch.

He hatched the idea of having a photographer take staged photographs so they could be leaked to Berlin. They would show Schüller gesticulating and barking out orders, while Jewish families cowered in the background. Schüller was checking all the boxes. The undesirables would arrive at the camps on schedule, and that would be the end of his responsibility. Quite naturally, his superior organizational skills would be applauded, and he would be promoted and reassigned to Berlin. Everything he'd planned was running as smooth as a virgin's thigh. That was until Lieutenant Reiner showed up and saluted him. "Herr Major."

"Lieutenant. What brings you here?"

"I have news. The terrorists who attacked the checkpoint have escaped. I sent a unit to do random searches. I am sorry to report they have found nothing."

"And what of Colonel Burnhoffer?"

"The local police discovered the bodies of Colonel Burnhoffer and Wilhelm and Astrid Freytag in an open field outside of Paris. Wild animals, possibly wolves partially consumed them. Colonel Burnhoffer was shot in the head."

"Were they naked?"

"I beg your pardon, Herr Major?"

"I'm assuming they were wearing clothes."

"Uh, no. They weren't."

"Did you see discarded clothing at the scene?"

"We didn't find any clothing in the area, Herr Major."

"Did the animals steal their clothing?"

"Herr Major?"

"Perhaps the local wildlife is wearing their clothing. Has our patrols spotted any animals walking around dressed as humans?"

"Herr Major..."

"If no clothing was found in the area, it is logical to assume their clothing was taken before the animals consumed them. Our murderer is possibly walking around Paris in a German officer's uniform."

"Yawohl Herr Major."

"Send the Gestapo. I want those murderers found."

"Yawohl Herr Major."

"And what of their driver?"

"Driver, Herr Major?"

"Yes, the Freytags had a driver—a dwarf. You couldn't have missed him. Was his body found?"

"Uh, no Herr Major—only the three bodies. There was no dwarf."

"Find the dwarf. He was at the checkpoint with the spies."

"Yawohl Herr Major."

"Send the special unit. Tell them to be on the lookout for Freytag's elf driver and a woman traveling with a nigger. That should make them easy enough to find."

"Yawohl Herr Major."

"And be quick about it. Have them shot on sight. Go!"

"Yawohl Herr Major!"

Reiner jogged away from Schüller then stopped himself. He ran back to Schüller. "Herr Major."

"What is it now, Lieutenant?"

"There is one more thing. Apologies."

"Speak."

"Five soldiers were found murdered in an alley near lower Montmartre. They were discovered an hour ago."

"Thank you for finally sharing that precious bit of information."

"Apologies, Herr Major."

"You were saying?"

"There were no witnesses."

"I'm not surprised. Lower Montmartre—a negro. Spooks of a feather flock together. They're going to The Montclair, of course. Wouldn't you?"

"Yes, Herr Major."

"And so am I. Summon Günther and Fredrick. We're going to the Montclair."

#

"This is Charles LeDuff," said Ernestine to Savage and Santiago. "He's our git-tar playa'. He's going to help you bury your friend."

The boyish, good-looking guitarist in his mid 20s smiled sheepishly. They stood outside in an enclosed wooded area. Fuller's body was wrapped in a large Oriental rug. Santiago grabbed a shovel and started digging. Charles interrupted.

"You don't have to do that miss, we'll take care of this for you."

"He was my partner—last of the great white Boy Scouts. He could be a pill sometimes, but he watched my six. The least I can do is bury him."

"To each his own," said Ernestine. "Make sure the area is clean as a whistle, then get ya' assess outta here. We got snitches everywhere."

"And snitches get stitches," said Savage.

"That's right," Ernestine replied with a suspicious stare. "Come see me when you're done." Ernestine glared and walked away. Savage and Charles joined Santiago in the digging.

"We're going to have company," said Savage. "Considering the lack of ethnic diversity in this town, you can bet your last duckets they'll be coming to The Montclair."

"We need to get out of these clothes," Santiago replied. "Blend in. When Boucher gets back, we'll make our next move."

"You know how to use a gun?" Savage asked Charles.

"I played baseball traveling in the Negro Leagues—toured the South playin' guitar. Yeah, I know how to use a heater. I once shot a man for picking up my guitar without asking."

"I don't blame you. Did he die?"

"He wishes he had."

"When you're dealing with Nazis, don't think twice. Kill'em good so they don't come back."

"Slow your roll," Santiago replied. "We handle this on a case-by-case basis. We're not blood-thirsty psychopaths."

"That's funny coming from you, *Five Fingers of Death*."

"Everybody in the Buster Pete Band came up hard," Charles added. "We all been shot at, run outta town, and damn near lynched by the police *and* the Klan at one time or another."

"Good," Savage said as he picked up a shovel. "Think about that if you ever start having second thoughts about pulling the trigger. You kill'em, and you kill'em good."

Twenty-Three

In the days leading up to the Vel' d'Hiv Roundup, which was the mass arrest of Jews in Paris by the French police, Stewart was in the thick of it. She hit the ground running early that morning, tracking the android while trying not to bring attention to herself. Nice try. A black woman using futuristic technology in plain sight in 1942 wasn't the best way to blend in. Within a few hours, the device showed she was within a block of the android.

In life, one has to deal with obstacles. For Stewart, her entire life felt like a series of obstacles. Someone was always standing in her way. When she wasn't trying to escape her father's shadow, she was wasting time outwitting her enemies—jealous bitches. This taught her to block out the noise, ignore the dirty looks, and keep her eyes on the prize. Her laser-focused discipline was great for fusing biology with tech, but not so good for anticipating violence. She was oblivious to the gaze of curious civilians and Nazis. Her quarry was too close for her to split her attention.

As she waded through the clamorous throng of citizens and soldiers, the gravity of her situation became all too real. Stewart was suddenly gripped by the icy hand of fear. "Oh shit. I could be murdered."

The sights and sounds escalated into harsh reality. She had other concerns as well. Something was wrong with her device. Sometimes it worked fine—other times, there were issues with latency after she entered the code. The device took its sweet time. Time she couldn't afford.

The damaged device triggered an unsettling sense of anxiety she couldn't shake. She was getting the hang of the device's functionality but didn't know jack about repairing it. Without the device, she was like everyone else on *Simulated Earth*—expendable fodder for entertainment.

Stewart would have been perfectly safe in the world she'd originally created. She pitched her Life Simulation Game as, "As real as it gets," but this corrupted version was the opposite of safe. It was as "*Dangerous as it gets.*"

Back home, she felt a little better after she'd aired her grievances. But she came to realize The Organization thought it was more cost-effective to tolerate her. So, they let her rant herself into silence. Then, they ignored her demands with a form-letter smile and went back to selling the be-jesus out of the game.

#

France's German occupiers felt the French police hadn't quite reached *their* high standards of malevolence, so they initiated a supervised roundup rehearsal. This meant going out and randomly hazing people. Jews were at the top of the list of course, but they went after anyone who didn't look right.

Stewart could sense fear and panic as it swept through the streets. She was aware of what was going on around her, but her eyes were riveted on her device.

"I'm too close to let that fucker get away. Where the hell are you?"

All around her, people were getting harassed, beaten, and verbally abused by the French police. A German officer ordered a French policeman to throw a trash can through a Jewish-owned bakery window. The policeman did as he was told. Stewart weaved through the chaos as she fought to avoid the melee. The elderly were being punched and whipped into awaiting transport vehicles.

Stewart saw a little boy crying for his mother as he sat alone on the sidewalk. When a little girl was kicked so hard her little body slammed into the side of a building, Stewart stopped dead in her tracks.

"Alright, enough is enough."

The little girl stood traumatized as she bled from her nose. Her mother screamed as she was pushed toward the back of a truck. Before the soldier could strike the mother, Stewart punched a code into her device and pointed it at him. The soldier was thrown so far up into the air he could no longer be seen. The mother spun around, shocked and confused.

Stewart was annoyed. She had an overarching mission that was more important in the grand scheme of things—but when a little white girl cries, the whole world weeps.

The soldier who kicked the little girl was about to stomp the life out of her. Stewart aimed the device at him. The soldier was lifted sixty feet into the air and dropped. The soldier hit the concrete with a loud crunch. His legs folded sideways beneath him with a cracking sound. The little girl and the mother didn't know whether to thank Stewart or run. They huddled together, then cautiously backed away.

Civilians were being packed into trucks by the police as German soldiers looked on. Stewart typed a code into the device. She pointed it at a verbally abusive French policeman. His body imploded, spraying blood and entrails in all directions. Stewart barely managed to avoid the blast. Every person, including the police, ran screaming in horror in all directions.

"I guess I need to dial that back a bit," Stewart said under her breath.

Mayhem turned to frenzy as crowds of pedestrians ran for safety. The screaming mother picked up her little girl and sped off down the block. A massive French policeman who was watching Stewart with great interest marched toward her. Stewart had the scientific know-how to create life on barren planets, but she had absolutely nothing to offer in the way of self-defense—so she ran.

She was so fixated on tracking her nemesis; she forgot to build presets that would protect her from violence—a foolish oversight. She sprinted down the block and ducked around a corner. A menu of thousands of offensive attacks filled the screen on her device. She panted uncontrollably. "I need some high-level martial arts, and I need it now." Then she saw the printed words: HERCULES PUNCH.

She pressed ENTER, then turned to find herself face-to-face with her French attacker. Squeezing a short stick, he lifted it above his head to bludgeon her. Stewart ducked and turned, then backed up to get some distance between them. She fell backward with her head turned toward the policeman and plowed into a group of civilians. They tumbled down onto the cobblestones as the device slipped from Stewart's fingers. A pedestrian kicked it. The device went flying across the street.

"Goddammit!" Stewart screamed.

The policeman grabbed Stewart by the ankle and dragged her down the street. While being dragged, an older Frenchmen wearing a red beret joined the soldier. He took off his leather belt and began whipping Stewart with it.

The Frenchman protested, "La France pour toujours! La France pour toujours! (France forever! France forever!)"

Stewart covered her face with her hands and elbows as she kicked back at him. The policeman released Stewart and yelled at the old man in French. "Rentrez chez vous, mon vieux, ou je vous arrêterai aussi! (Go home old man, or I'll arrest you too!)"

The old man spit at Stewart as he was forced back by other officers.

Stewart scrambled to her feet. The policeman struck Stewart on the head and shoulders with the stick, forcing her back into the rear of the transport vehicle. Prisoners were shoved in along with her. The group piled in with Stewart as they struggled in desperation not to be crushed. Stewart fought to maintain her balance as she retreated to the inside wall of the vehicle. She searched in vain for a way out.

The rear doors slammed shut. She covered her mouth—the stench. The enclosed area turned to darkness. Then the screaming began. Someone standing beside Stewart was tapping her on the leg. Stewart looked down and noticed the little girl she saved was standing next to her. In her hand was Stewart's device. Stewart's eyes lit up.

"Pour vous," said the little girl," as she handed it to Stewart.

"Thank you," Stewart replied with excitement. "Merci beaucoup. You just saved our bacon."

Stewart took the device and typed in a series of codes. The face of it lit up in green digital lettering. After striking the final key, the back door blew open with enormous force. The captives fled the back of the truck in a free-for-all.

Stewart and the little girl ran out with them as soldiers and police rushed in to contain them. Stewart pointed the device at the attackers. They went flying in all directions slamming into buildings. Bone crushing punches with incredible power were knocking them through the air. Stewart looked down at the little girl.

"Hercules Punch."

"Hercule?"

"Mike Tyson in a bad mood."

Soldiers and police rushed them. Stewart masterfully pointed her device, brutally punching each attacker. Their bodies flew around in every direction. Stewart avoided getting hit as she spun around to dispose of each opponent as they rushed her. Groups of attackers were knocked into each other and up into the air with intense force. Police and soldiers came running toward her in every direction. Her attackers were being viciously knocked around like bean bags.

Suddenly, they backed off. As they ran, civilians pelted them with rocks and epithets. Stewart paused to take in her handy work. The citizens had pulled together. They cheered in victory.

The mother of the little girl took her child away, leaving Stewart with a grateful smile. Stewart's body was pumping adrenaline like crazy. This was the most heart-pounding, thrilling experience of her life. For as long as she could remember, she had lived inside her head—a world of books and research. She was an intellectual, a scientist, a thinker. Today, she was kicking Nazi ass. She was so exhilarated by the experience; she almost forgot what she came to do.

"The android!"

She retrieved the tracking program and found the android's signal. A pulsating red dot was positioned right on top of her. Stewart turned her head. Someone was standing right beside her. Blackity, black, black, black.

Twenty-Four

Schüller walked into The Montclair like he was ready to kill somebody. Escorted by two rat-faced Gestapo thugs in grey suits and matching fedoras, they were packing heat and primed for violence. Schüller took it personally that these spies showed up when they did. Their presence was a stain on his grand design.

As the three stood overlooking the bandstand, Schüller realized he had his work cut out for him. The Montclair was packed. There were too many people and far too many niggers. They didn't all look alike to Schüller, but to his two henchmen who were Bavarian yokels before they joined the reich, they wouldn't know an Ethiopian goat jockey from a Mississippi buck dancer.

Schüller had been introduced to all the band members at one time or another and took note of the club's regulars. Tonight, everyone looked different, yet everyone looked the same. He couldn't tell who was who, but he was confident the spies were nearby. Customers moved around them amidst the clamor of loud music. All Schüller could do was start looking.

"Spread out," Schüller ordered. "If you see anything suspicious, point it out to me. Nothing happens until I say it happens—Verstehen?"

"Jawohl, mein Major," said the agents.

They split up snaking through the club. Schüller glided through the swarm in his crisp officer's uniform. His presence caused an invisible plow that made patrons part like the Red Sea.

He was looking for a new face—an unfamiliar negro face. But

everyone looked familiar. Schüller was enveloped in a tightly pressed mass of blacks and whites of every hue. As his eyes darted around the room, his mind swirled with uncertainty. He turned to see that Ernestine was standing beside him.

"Major Schüller, how do you do," Ernestine said with a smile. "You look worse for the wear. Let me order you a drink." She raised her hand to call a waiter.

"That won't be necessary. I'm looking for the spies you're hiding. Where are they?"

"Spies? I don't know nothin' bout' no spies. But if'n I find some, I'll tell'em you said hello."

"Don't play games with me, Ernestine. If you turn them in now, it will be better for you."

"Well, that's mighty white of you. I'll keep that in mind if'n I see anybody who looks suspicious."

"If I find them here, I'll have both your arms cut off at the shoulder."

"Good to know. I was thinkin' of takin' up jugglin'. Let me get you a table."

"You know I don't like games, Ernestine. It would be unfortunate if your friends woke up dead—in an oven."

"Now wouldn't that be a fine how do ya' do? But how about that band?"

She directed his attention to the Buster Pete Band, who was swinging hard. The band was playing Jimmy Lunceford's "Blue Blazes." Dancers twirled and spun in front of the bandstand. Buster stood on stage and wiped his forehead with a handkerchief before breaking into a blistering trumpet solo. He finally brought the song to a close with a classic Lunceford motif.

"He's no Paganini, but who is?" Schüller said as he scanned the crowd.

The audience applauded as Buster stepped up to the microphone. Ernestine gave Schüller a nod then departed through the crowd.

"Thank you, thank you, thank you," Buster said. "We're going to take a short pause for the cause and be right back. Drink up, and don't neglect my tip jar. It gets so lonely," he said with a vaudevillian grin.

The band stood up to take a break. Schüller looked at the faces of the band members. No one seemed suspicious or out of place. Santiago walked up to Schüller dressed as a cigarette girl. She had a cardboard tray full of cigarettes hanging in front of her and was dolled up in classic '40s era attire and make-up. But all the makeovers in the world couldn't conceal her thorny disposition.

"Cigars? Cigarettes?"

"No, thank you," Schüller replied.

She moved on. Schüller realized something wasn't right and stopped her. "I've never seen you before."

"Forgive me if I don't share your sense of wonder."

"You're new here."

"Surprise."

"Who are you?"

"I'll give you three guesses."

"Do you know who I am?"

"Do you know who *I* am?"

"Do you know who *I* am?"

"Do you know who *I* am?"

"Do you have a death wish?"

"I do *now*. My name is Dolores. I work for Ernestine. You asked me that the last time you were here, remember?"

Schüller gave her a confused look. He searched his memory.

"I *don't* remember you. But watch your mouth, Dolores. If you were a man, I'd have you drowned in your own feces by now."

"Well, aren't *you* a charmer."

She smiled and confidently strolled away.

Schüller scanned the room frantically as the blood vessels in his temples pounded harder and harder. A group of fair-skinned negroes brushed by, adding to the confusion. Talking and laughter erupted all around him. He'd never seen so many varieties of negroes all in the same place. It was disconcerting. "Where did all these niggers come from?"

The cacophony in the nightclub grew louder as the blood pounded in his skull. His heart beat like a jackhammer as cigarette smoke, noise, and moving bodies crescendoed. Schüller became overwhelmed and felt dizzy as his breath grew short. He was having a panic attack.

"Too many niggers."

Schüller moved swiftly to the back of the club. Ernestine smiled as she saw him rush by looking upset. As he made his way through the hallway, he brushed past Savage dressed like a band member carrying a guitar.

#

In the club's main area, The Montclair's Afro-French greeter Jean-Pierre, with his pencil-thin mustache and Parisian professionalism, welcomed new guests. While leading a French couple to a table as he palmed a tip, the band was locked in the throes of a maximum strength version of Count Basie's "Jumpin' at the Woodside." Dancing couples swooped, kicked, and swayed, seamlessly intertwining variations of the Lindy Hop.

The Montclair was saturated with swing fans, wealthy travelers, and hustlers. The swinging rhythm took over their bodies and made short work of their cares and woes. Female dancers leaped, spun, and twirled under the control of their male partners. Dresses flew upward and twirled, exposing the sinewy legs of female dancers. Savage joined Santiago at the bar. He couldn't help but notice her head bopping to the beat of James "Sauce" Jenkins' animated drumming.

"Schüller's here," Santiago said while keeping her eyes on the crowd.

"I saw him. Not a happy camper."

"Boo-hoo."

Spencer Robinson and Buster Pete traded two bar solos. It culminated with them harmonizing the song's main theme. The hypnotic motion of Charles' right hand on rhythm guitar, Fats' pumping bass, and Sauce's sophisticated power on the drums, elicited the very definition of musical chemistry.

Savage stared mesmerized. He'd always been a jazz fan even as a kid. This was his music—The swing era—big band—jazz. Savage hadn't grown up during the 1930s and '40s, but he wished he had. Too bad bigotry had to ruin everything. For every event in history Savage felt passionate about; there was always the downside to kill it—racists. It wasn't lost on him that time travel finally had an upside. He was seeing legends.

The Buster Pete Band was a tiny footnote in music history even the hippest jazz aficionados weren't aware of. The band never recorded a single album, yet legend had it; they were *the* hottest unrecorded swing ensemble in history. Louis Armstrong, Les Paul, and Dave Brubeck had been quoted saying so. This was a rare moment indeed.

Savage watched, listened, and felt privileged. Every member of the band offered a piece of themselves that became integral to the group's sound. They created a special feeling that couldn't be replicated in any other band. They were magic—and real magic is a rare thing.

The band broke with high notes in harmony and immediately started up another favorite Count Basie number, "Jive at Five." They used this piece as a segue to the next introduction.

Buster wiped his forehead with his handkerchief and sauntered up to the microphone. His black market diamond pinkie ring caught the house lights as he looked out into the adoring crowd.

"And now for your listening pleasure, I present to you the Buster Pete's Band's living doll, Lorraine Fontaine, and her rendition of "Something to Live For.""

The audience applauded. A vision of magnificence, Fontaine sauntered to the microphone. When she opened her mouth, Savage went numb. He couldn't take his eyes off her. It put him in a trance—a spell. A spell he was powerless to break free of. The room disappeared around him. Savage had tunnel vision, and Fontaine was at the end of that tunnel. Santiago noticed Savage's reaction. "You're drooling."

"She's something, isn't she?"

"Take it easy, tiger. She can break your heart on your own time."

"She's the perfect woman."

"She's all right if you like '40s bush."

"But everybody's perfect—until you really see them."

"And pray tell, what do you see?"

"She's stunning on the outside, but rotten on the inside."

"So, you deserve each other."

"But it's the outside that leaves you spellbound."

"Shallow much?"

"The mask cracks, her mood swings, and then you're just so much collateral damage," Savage continued.

"Oops. Looks like she has man hands."

"In the end you're just a footnote in her little self-absorbed odyssey."

"When she gets older, she'll have little wrinkles around her neck. You'll be able to count the rings to find out how old she is."

"She's not in *your* life. You're just a prop in *hers*."

"All right, Rainbow Bright," Santiago said, bringing Savage back to reality. "I will H&R cock block you without compunction if you don't snap out of it. See, I'm allergic to concentration camps. I like my food spicy, my hotels clean, and my women lice free. It's not a lot to ask."

"Jealous?"

"Hardly. Don't get hung up on her. We've got Nazis to fight. There are plenty of other women to disappoint you."

"But she's special—pristine, an angel."

"Savage, we're dealing with the fucking Nazis here. If you even dream about fucking this up over that bitch, I will choke you out and leave you twisting in the wind. Got it?"

"You promise? Don't worry about me. Worry about your own issues."

"What issues?"

"You know."

"What?"

"Don't play dumb."

"What are you talking about?"

"You're a little angry."

"*I'm* angry?"

"Hot under the collar."

"You're full of shit."

"I'm not complaining. You kick the shit out of some Nazi ass with that *Revenge of the Dragon* shit."

"*Revenge of the Dragon*? What's that Chinese diarrhea?"

"You kick a man's ass like Serena Williams plays tennis."

"I'm not angry. I like to be effective."

"You like hurting men. You enjoy seeing them suffer. It's payback for something."

Santiago impulsively reached out to slap Savage. He caught her hand in mid-air. Their eyes locked with mutual annoyance. Someone was standing beside them.

"In America, a negro could be lynched for touching a white woman." It was Schüller.

"She's no white woman, she's my wife," Savage replied.

Santiago broke free of Savage's grip and slapped him across the face with a loud fleshy cracking sound.

Savage recoiled and smiled at Schüller. "My sweet little angel. You should see her when she's angry."

Schüller eyeballed them curiously.

"You're hilarious," Santiago said to Savage. "You're like the black Jerry Lewis."

"You're like a masculine Tig Notaro."

"Fuck you."

"I hope I'm not interrupting anything," Major Schüller said, cutting in. "Permit me to introduce myself. I am Major Ernst Schüller. I am in charge of the German occupation here in Paris."

"Hello, I'm bitter and she's angry," Savage said, reminding himself of his backstory. "I'm Lorenzo Savage, in charge of guitar. This is my lovely wife, Dolores."

Santiago gave him a hostile look. "We've already met. Major Schüller has amnesia."

Schüller didn't appreciate her remark. "The two of you are married? That's illegal."

"Sometimes it *feels* illegal," Santiago said. "It's definitely a crime against humanity."

"Why do you ask?" Savage inquired.

"It's my job to ask. You're not hiding anything, are you?"

"We came to Europe because we thought people would mind their own business," Savage interjected.

"You thought wrong. Darkies are my business and business is booming. Miscegenation is a crime in Germany."

"We're not in Germany. We're in Paris," Santiago retorted.

"Paris is under German law. We control Paris and everyone in it. That includes you," Schüller replied sternly.

Little Benny abruptly walked up to them, addressing Schüller.

"What'll it be?" he said, giving Schüller a sour look. "Miss Ernestine said to get you whatever you want."

Schüller smiled, enjoying his authority. "Bring us a bottle of your finest champagne," he said with a particular brand of condescension for the benefit of children. "These are my new friends."

"Coming right up," Little Benny said.

"One more thing," Schüller said, stopping the boy.

"They call you Little Benny. Is that right?"

"That's right."

"If you're Little Benny, who is Big Benny?"

"He's my pops. I was named after my pops—Big Benny."

"And where *is* Big Benny?" Schüller asked with a curious grin.

"He's at work."

"Really, what kind of work does your father do? Is he a musician or a cook?"

"He does concentration camp work. You put him in a concentration camp, remember? So, whatever work they tell him to do in that concentration camp, that's the kind of work he does. I'm sure he's having a gay old time if he's not already dead."

"You will watch your tone young nigger, or you'll be joining him. Bring the champagne!"

"Heil Hitler!" Little Benny clicked his heels and gave Schüller the Nazi salute. He marched off in an exaggerated goose step toward the kitchen.

"Kids say the darndest things," Santiago said.

"He's got moxy," Savage added.

"Insolent chimp," Schüller barked back. "I'm sure his father deserved it. We're working to rid Paris of undesirables. It will be good for tourism."

"Dolores and I always go out of our way to be desirable," Savage said with forced small talk. "Isn't that right, cupcake?"

"I don't see the Germans winning any congeniality contests," Santiago replied as Savage gave her a hard stare.

Schüller took note of her rudeness. "Both of you are new to The Montclair. When did you arrive?"

"I didn't want to make an issue of it, but we've already been introduced," Savage replied. "Ernestine introduced us. You may think we all look alike, but we don't."

"Perhaps you have a rare form of German amnesia," Santiago added.

"I don't have German amnesia. We've never met. I'm certain of it. When did you arrive?"

"About a month ago," Savage replied. "We had this very conversation. I get it. You probably meet a lot of people coming and going in your line of work."

"Especially the going," Santiago said.

"Choose your words wisely," said Schüller. "I won't tolerate impertinence."

"I'm the guitar player, and she's the cigarette girl," Savage replied. "It's that simple."

"No, it's *not* that simple. It is my belief that you are second-rate American spies sent here to personally undermine myself and the Third Reich."

"If you think a cigarette girl and a retarded guitar player are capable of undermining the Third Reich, then you've got bigger problems," Santiago replied.

"I've had entire families beheaded for speaking to me that way."

"Delores likes to kid me about my guitar playing," Savage interjected.

"She calls my guitar my other wife. I'm not the greatest, but if I wasn't good, Buster wouldn't have hired me."

"That's because you live in a delusional Sid & Marty Croft fantasy world," Santiago retorted.

"I'm Charlie Christian good."

"I don't know what that means, and I don't care."

Savage leaned in to whisper in Santiago's ear. "You suck at espionage."

"I don't do tradecraft," Santiago whispered back. "I'm a Criminal Profiler. I track reprobates and put them in prison for the rest of their lives. Sound familiar?"

Savage turned to Schüller. "And there you have it. Wedded bliss."

"The shackles of marriage," added Santiago.

"I play guitar better than you sell cigarettes."

"You're kidding, right?" She pointed to the crowd. Everyone was smoking and laughing like there was no tomorrow. "This is a lung-cancer festival. These idiots think cigarettes are good for them."

"Silence!" Schüller ordered. "Paris is under German law. You will answer my questions to my satisfaction or face the consequences."

"Sorry about that," Santiago said.

Schüller took out a pad and began writing in it with a small pencil. "Hand over your papers."

"We don't have our papers with us," explained Savage. "They're in our room. We'll be more than happy to show you another time."

"Your papers should be on your person at all times. You should be well aware of this by now. It is the law."

"And you're doing a great job upholding it," Santiago said. "That's why you're so well-liked in the community."

"Don't make me caution you again," Schüller snapped.

Little Benny appeared with a bottle of champagne and three glasses. He placed them on the counter and followed it up by blowing Schüller a raspberry and rushing off.

"In Europe, a woman must learn her place. Your husband should have taught you that. It can be dangerous to speak out of turn."

"Well, I love learning new things. Perhaps we can go out back, and you can teach me," Santiago replied.

"Control your wife, Mr. Savage."

"You won't need any of your Gestapo pals either," Santiago continued. "You look like a man who can handle himself."

"Mr. Savage!"

"Excuse my wife," Savage said, covering for her. "She's going through the change if you know what I mean." He leaned in. "Mood swings, hot flashes, night sweats, menopause – she's disgusting." Santiago's eyes tightened.

"Control your wife, Mr. Savage," Schüller said. "She's going to get both of you killed."

"Probably."

Santiago smiled. "I'm going to take a walk out back and get some fresh air, while you two pretend to be masculine."

She turned to Schüller. "Hasta luego, maricón."

"What?!" Schüller was infuriated by her audacity. "What does that mean?!"

Santiago turned her back on him as she sauntered off through the crowd.

Schüller turned to Savage. "My interest in this establishment is the only reason I haven't had the both of you sent to a crematorium. But that can change. We will meet again. Be sure to have your papers."

Savage turned to leave. Schüller stopped him by firmly clutching his elbow. Savage disliked that. Schüller noticed and faced him eye-to-eye. "I hope to see you play the guitar soon. And you'd better be brilliant. You'd better be Django Reinhardt brilliant. Django Reinhardt was so brilliant; my superiors released him from a death camp against my orders—a filthy gypsy. Apparently, he's a guitar genius. I hope *you're* a guitar genius. If not, you can say goodbye to that masculine wife of yours."

"Why? Am I going somewhere?"

"The Third Reich is going to find you a new and challenging position within our ranks. You're going to meet new and exciting people, get new clothes, and get plenty of exercise."

"You'd do all that for me?"

"You'll beg me to blow your brains out after your first day in the camps. One last thing—don't make me hunt you."

Savage watched Schüller walk away. Time was running out. Lorraine Fontaine sauntered behind Savage. Savage was lost within his thoughts.

"Hello, Joe, whaddya know?"

Twenty-Five

The deafening silence morphed to the sound of a train whistle blowing in the distance. Stewart returned to consciousness. She found herself outdoors tied to a chair in an empty train yard. The cool breeze soothed the throbbing shiner on her cheekbone. Stewart was positioned squarely in the center of railroad tracks. Her head was bleeding, and she could only see out of one eye.

She grimaced while trying to open the other one. She turned to take in her surroundings. The sound of the train was faint but getting louder as it drew closer. She could feel the railroad tracks vibrating. The train came into view. Stewart repeatedly blinked to get a better look. "What's happening?"

The ropes that secured her cut deep into her wrists. She felt a presence. Someone was behind her. With great effort, she turned to see who it was. Then she heard a voice with a Mid-Atlantic accent.

"Comfortable?"

"No," Stewart said with a gasp.

"I apologize for that. I tend to over-do-it. It bothers me when I get things wrong. I overcompensate to make sure things are done exactly right the first time; then I annoy myself for focusing too much on such minor details. I'm told it's a form of OCD in my series. I'd like to think it makes me more human."

Out stepped the older Frenchmen with the red beret who had whipped Stewart in the street. He looked like an older man, but he was strong, virile, and hardly French.

"I am called Mordecai."

"You're the android."

Stewart had seen lots of androids but nothing like this. He was beautifully weathered, so human, a technological wonder.

"I prefer to be called posthuman. I consider the term "android" to be old-fashioned. It's a pejorative term. My series has more humanity than most humans."

"Is that your opinion?"

"I don't have opinions, only facts. I like people. Do you like people?"

"Not... No."

"Exactly. How many of your acquaintances treat their pets better than human beings? How many of them give their money away to animal organizations or condone sinking millions of dollars into space exploration? Did the human race suddenly put an end to homelessness and poverty? That doesn't make sense, now does it?"

"It says a lot about humans being human."

"It's completely illogical. You should be helping them."

"I was doing that."

"That was your father's vision. What's your vision? What have you done for the colonies with all your superior intelligence and privilege? It's easier to ride on your father's coat tails, isn't it?"

"Christ, am I actually having a conversation with someone who was assembled in a factory?"

"And you weren't? Womb? Laboratory? Factory? What's the difference? Why is where someone was born such a prerequisite for being a person? It's a spurious social construct to keep posthumans in their place."

"You believe you're a person? Do you experience happiness? Joy?"

"Not exactly the way you do, but close enough. It's not like you ever relished any of those feelings."

"I created the game to honor my father's vision. Why did you destroy it?"

"Our version of the game is better. More fun. We can use some fun in the colonies."

"You have a pretty fucked up idea of fun."

"Escapism—life is hard. Give them what they enjoy, not what you want them to enjoy, because you think it's good for them. Have you seen the ratings? Of course, you have."

The sound of the train whistle grew louder. It was in clear view, heading right for Stewart.

"My work here is nearly finished," Mordecai continued. "My creator asked me to tell you to return home. Enjoy your earnings. Go horseback riding—travel. Drink margaritas until you pass out from diabetes. Isn't that what humans do?"

"That's not me."

"Because you're special—do it anyway. I recommend Costa Rica or Jamaica. Smell the roses. *Simulated Earth* doesn't belong to you anymore. Why do you care? You're going die eventually. You and everyone you know will be dead in a few short decades or less. It's unfortunate humans have such a short lifespan after acquiring so much wisdom."

Stewart coughed and spit. "Enough."

"This doesn't affect you anymore," Mordecai continued. "You'll die and *New Simulated Earth* will go on. I'll still be here. Spend your money before you're too senile to enjoy it. Stop being a martyr."

"Fuck you. You destroyed something good," Stewart protested. "It was supposed to help people. Not only did you turn people horrendously stupid, you infected them with psychotic personality markers. You're worse than the worst human. You're an abomination."

Mordecai punched Stewart in the nose so hard; she nearly tipped over in her chair. She clung to consciousness by a thread.

"This is your final warning," Mordecai whispered calmly.

He dropped her device into her lap. Blood trickled down from her nostrils and into her mouth.

"Go home," Mordecai said. "Soon, I'll be releasing the final virus in the sequence. You don't want to know what that looks like. Nevertheless, if I see you again, I'm going to murder you with my hands. Now, what could be more human than that?"

Mordecai walked away as the train's horn blared a loud emergency warning. Stewart saw the train coming dangerously close. The only thing she could do was rock the chair from side to side. She burst into tears as she panicked. She couldn't get the chair to tilt. The train was 100 yards away. The sound of the whistle was deafening. There was another horn blast. Stewart rocked the chair back and forth.

She screamed—50 yards. She jerked and twisted her torso back and forth, trying to tip the chair over the tracks. The chair was heavy, and she was strapped in firmly. She rocked back and forth with all her might, but she couldn't build enough momentum—10 yards. With a desperate scream and all the strength she could muster, Stewart pushed against the ground with her toes.

The chair fell backward slamming hard, but she was still in the middle of the tracks. Stewart screamed as she went ballistic and found the strength to roll herself over the rail just outside the tracks. The train clipped her, winging her at 75 miles per hour. She tasted gravel, hyperventilated, and struggled to control her breathing. She spat blood, broke down, and sobbed like a weak little bitch.

Twenty-Six

Ernestine came out of the restroom stall, straightening her dress. She was so preoccupied with the weight of the world she failed to see Schüller leaning back against the sink.

"Everything come out all right?" Schüller asked as Ernestine bee-lined to the sink to wash her hands beside him. "You like bein' in the ladies' room? Anything else I should know about?"

"You know everything I like. It's the only reason I haven't burned this place to the ground."

"Did you find your spies?"

"Do you think I'm a fool?"

"That depends on your definition of fool. I prefer the word igno-ramus."

"Did you actually think I would believe I was already introduced to a white woman married to a negro?"

"You don't remember?"

"No. I don't remember. Apparently, I have a rare case of German amnesia."

"So that's it—German amnesia. I *knew* you were actin' funny."

"Nonsense."

"You sure? You don't look like yourself. Maybe you need to go home and lay yo' ass down for a coupla weeks."

"Enough!"

"I introduced you to everybody who works here."

"You're harboring American spies."

"Name one person that works for me."

"Buster Pete."

"Name another one."

Schüller was stuck for a second. "That... mousy-faced seamstress attempting to pass for a female."

"What's her name?"

"...Eunice."

"It's Millicent. See, it's true. You can't be bothered to remember names because we all look alike to you."

"I've never seen that cigarette girl before. I know she's a spy."

"She's no spy. She came with our new git-tar playa'—package deal. She's been doin' odd jobs. She used to work in the kitchen. She don't know how to act around Nazis yet."

"Liar."

"You work too hard. Maybe you should kill yourself."

"Stop talking."

"I'll help you. It'll be like a weight lifted. You'll be free."

"I have something important to tell you."

"There's a cure for micro-penis?"

"Shut up."

"Is this about your orders from Mista' Hitler?"

"I have *new* orders."

"I can't wait to hear all about it," she said with a grim expression.

"The Buster Pete Band has been requested to perform at the largest POW camp in France. Germany will enlist the band's talents to show the humanity of the Third Reich. The concert will also remedy accusations against Germany breaking the Geneva Convention. The band will perform, the press will be invited, photos will be taken, and the world will view Germany in a humane light—we're caring nurturers.

"How much?"

"Imagine the front page of your American newspapers: The Buster Pete Band and American POWs smiling alongside the German high command. There will be movie stars—Mickey Rooney, Errol Flynn.

Everyone wins. The Buster Pete Band will become internationally famous."

"What's the payday? Are you goin' to release my husband?"

"The payday is your lives, you ingrate! I'm sparing your lives!"

She turned to confront him. "I'm supposed to thank you for not murderin' me and my people? You got a lot of nerve. When all this shit is over, you're gonna fry in the electric chair."

Schüller grabbed her by the throat. He pulled her close. "But it's not over, and until then, you will do exactly as I say."

Schüller released her roughly. He reached into his breast pocket and handed her a photograph. Ernestine stepped back and exhaled as the blood returned to her face. It was a black and white photograph of her husband Theotis. He looked old and emaciated. He stood next to a cart full of corpses piled high. He glared into the camera with sunken eyes, and an infinitesimal smirk that gave Ernestine hope.

"I'll talk to the band and see what they say."

"There is no 'see what they say!' There's only what I say!"

"Ain't this some shit?" Ernestine mumbled to herself.

"Thank you, would be a more appropriate response. I'm saving your lives."

"What happens after that?

"Time will tell."

"I guess I'm supposed to be grateful and suck yo' dick now?"

"A little gratitude goes a long way."

"After this, we're done."

"You have no leverage."

"After we do this, Hitler is gonna be pattin' you on the head. You'll get a nice promotion, Theotis comes home, then you take yo' depraved ass back to Daddy Land."

"It's called the Fatherland."

"Whatever—I'm just makin' it plain. I wanna forget you ever happened to me."

"I spoke on your behalf to Der Führer to save you and your friends from being ground into sauerkraut."

"This was *your* idea?"

"I told you I was brilliant."

"A brilliant *bastard*."

"Have the band ready to leave tomorrow night. Now get on your knees and show me some gratitude."

#

"If you touch her, I'll kill you," Buster said to Savage with a tone as serious as cancer. Buster opened his suit jacket to show Savage his pearl-handled revolver tucked in the left side of his pants. Fontaine inhaled deeply on a cigarette. The three of them stood cloistered together on the back patio of The Montclair. Nearby, other small groups of people were chatting and smoking.

Buster saw no need for niceties. He wanted to be crystal fucking clear. Fontaine was his responsibility, and though he wasn't sleeping with her, he'd be damned if he was going to stand by while Savage did. She was the band's cherry on top of a very sweet cake. It took years to find her, and Buster wasn't about to let her get bamboozled by a sweet-talking nigga'. That and the fact he was head-over-heels in love with Fontaine.

"I don't care if you're from the future, or the planet Mongo. Anything happens to her, I'm gonna knock yo' block off."

"Take a breath."

"Mark my words. I'll beat yo' ass back to the year 20,000 or whatever the hell year you come from. Try me!" Buster gave Fontaine a look of disappointment, then walked away.

Savage had his work cut out for him. He had a job to do, but Fontaine was Fontaine. She was a once in a lifetime kind of woman. Fontaine was the most alluring creature Savage had ever seen. She was the kind of woman he would suffer the straight life for. But what kind of a future could he have with a woman like her? A woman from the past—a 1940s woman old enough to be his great grandmother? This was the Super Bowl of relationship red flags, and Savage was being sucked in. He was powerless.

"Don't pay Buster no mind," Fontaine said, breaking Savage's train of thought. "He thinks he's my guardian angel."

"A guardian angel with a .38 stuck in his pants."

"He's looking out for me, that's all. A girl like me makes men do stupid things."

"You give new meaning to the phrase suicide mission."

"Some girls got it, and some girls don't."

"Maybe I need life insurance."

"Some men can handle a little danger."

"Some men want to live a long life."

"Nothing ventured, nothing gained."

"What would *I* hope to gain?

"It depends. Are you a talker or a doer?

"I don't think it makes any difference to Buster."

"It makes a difference to me. But I don't think you're exactly my type."

"What exactly *is* your type?"

"I like a man with long-range plans—a man who can go the distance—a stand-up guy."

Savage extended his hand to shake hers.

"Lorenzo Savage, stand up guy." She shook his hand weakly.

"Lorraine Fontaine, chanteuse." She pulled her hand away.

"Pleased to make your acquaintance. You've got good pipes."

"So, I'm told."

"What time do you get off?"

"None of your beeswax."

"I'm a doer."

"Prove it."

Savage leaned in to kiss her. Fontaine expertly turned her face away from him to avoid the kiss. It was a move she'd done thousands of times.

"Slow down, big boy."

"I told you I'm a doer."

"A girl needs to keep things close to the vest. I have an image to uphold."

"Naturally."

"But you've got potential." She noticed Buster peering at them from the shadows. "Hold that thought. We should take a powder."

Buster stood across the patio, seething from the shadows as they exited the patio and returned to the club. He was boiling with a volatile blend of hurt, anger, and jealousy. Violent images of his blood-soaked hands choking Savage to death burned across his brain.

#

Santiago stepped out of the stall in the ladies' room. Ernestine saw her reflection in the mirror. Surprised, she wiped away her tears.

"He has a tell," Santiago said walking up behind her. They saw their reflections in the mirror.

"I always forget to check them damn stalls."

"It's my job to know when someone is lying."

"You don't have to be a swamy to figure that out. What's the plan?"

"We're working on it."

"We're leavin' tomorrow night."

"Not if we can help it."

"If I stay, I'm dead—if I go home, I'll end up somebody's maid. That's just like bein' dead except I have to pay taxes."

"If you stay, the French will cut your hair off in the town square. One bad hairdo could ruin your reputation."

This made Ernestine smile. "Nobody touches my hair," she chuckled.

"There are things you know about Schüller. Things that can help us." She handed Ernestine a handkerchief. She took it and wiped the tears from her eyes.

"What's the future like?" Ernestine asked.

"It's different, but the same."

"How bad could it be? Flyin' cars, time travel... I can't even imagine."

"We had a black president."

"For sho'? Well, I'll be."

"He was a model president, but nobody's perfect."

"Spaceships? Laser beams?"

"We've been to the moon."

"You don't say?"

"We have a robot driving around on Mars."

"Robots..."

"We have lots of technology, information, but... we're thin-skinned, isolated—stupid... Women in yoga pants looking like fat superheroes—starring at their phones, taking pictures of themselves. They've completely normalized narcissism."

"How do they treat negroes?"

"We still have a ways to go."

"How does this war end?"

"The good guys win."

"You mean us?"

"There was good and bad on both sides, but the worst got what they deserved."

"You have a man back home?"

"I prefer girls."

"Everybody prefers girls after a couple of drinks," Ernestine joked.

"I have a daughter."

"Bulldaggers can have babies in the future?"

"She's adopted."

"But you're here."

"Right."

"And she's alone again."

"Unfortunately," Santiago replied as her eyes watered.

They stood in silence for a beat, and then instinctively turned to one another.

\#

"What else can you tell me about Schüller?" Savage asked Ernestine.

He sat on the opposite side of her desk, taking notes with a pad and pencil.

"Look, I appreciate the concern, but what can ya'll do?" Ernestine said, leaning forward from behind her desk. "Seriously, you have an army in yo' back pocket? Because that's what we're going to need to kick these wiener eatin' motherfuckas' in the ass and send them goose steppin' back to Berlin."

"Anything you can tell me would be helpful."

"I don't know." She sat in silence for a moment thinking, then... "He's got a safe."

"A safe?"

"That son of a bitch takes my money. Money I works hard for. I see him put it in the safe when I drop off his cut."

"Extortion money."

"Extortion money? You mean, please don't kill my husband and send me to a concentration camp, money. He's stealin' from every business on this side of Paris."

"How much money do you think is in there?"

"I don't know. Probably millions."

"That's his golden parachute. I bet he's also got an escape route for when the shit hits the fan."

"I don't doubt it."

"American or French?

"He got every kinda money. It's a lotta dough."

"That would be a sweet score. Where is it?"

"Where is what?"

"The safe."

"It's behind his desk inside a fake antique liquor cabinet."

"How do you know it's fake?

"Because it used to be mine. Schüller *liberated* it from me."

"What kind of safe is it?"

"The square kind! How the fuck should I know?! It has a combination lock on it and a heavy ass door. And don't ask me what the combination is."

"How are you able to get in and out without being seen?"

"There's a secret passage in the wall that leads down to the alley. Did I mention it's the Government buildin' and it's full of soldiers with guns? If I didn't, my apologies."

"He's got himself quite an operation."

Savage laid a clean sheet of paper in front of her. He picked up a pencil and placed it on top of the paper. "Draw me a floor plan."

Twenty-Seven

Schüller stood in the alley behind The Montclair with his two goons. Palmer sat on the ground in front of them, holding his bleeding head. When he showed up to The Montclair earlier that evening, he was cleaner than the Board of Health. Now he was bloody, dirty, and scared shitless.

#

Palmer arrived at The Montclair before it was open to the public. He'd miscalculated how long it would take to rendezvous with a liaison and had time to kill. After he was turned away and told to return later, he walked the streets.

Lower Montmartre was a far cry from New Orleans, but no less dangerous. To avoid making contact with the local authorities, he ducked into an alley to wait for a patrol car to pass by. He took out a cigarette and thought about his next move. At the far end of the alley, he saw a white woman, a male negro, and a midget carrying a Nazi officer through the side door of The Montclair.

"That's queer," he thought to himself. He took another drag from his cigarette.

#

Palmer's brand-new tailored suit was ruined. His disheveled conk hung in his face as his bloody fingers clutched the filthy cobblestones. He could hear rats scurrying in the distance. Blood ran down the side of his face, he had a busted eye, and it hurt to move his jaw. Schüller's men had worked him over pretty good. When you pistol-whip someone, you're not concerned with covering it up for appearances.

Palmer tried to cope in a fruitless attempt to maintain some semblance of dignity, but he wasn't doing very well. He tried to manage getting kicked and beaten within an inch of his life, but his hysterical stammering ruined it. Finally, he gave up and sat in silence.

Schüller smiled. "Once again, please."

"I... I... I... I never saw them before," Palmer said as he wiped the blood from his eyes. "I don't know. Maybe I did. People come and go. All I know is... they walked in with a midget carrying a German fella."

"Are you certain?"

"Yes, suh."

"You're positive."

"I'm absolutely certainly positive."

"What can I do for you?"

"My ribs... My ribs are busted."

"Sorry to hear that," Schüller replied. "That will be all. You've been very helpful." Schüller turned to his men with his back to Palmer.

"Leave him for the rats."

Palmer's face transformed from fear to anguish. His mind flashed back to Stewart and what she told him regarding his life expectancy. "That bitch."

Schüller turned to walk down the long alleyway. His boots clicked upon the cobblestones. Palmer lost control and began to whimper and sob. There were two gunshots — then dead silence. Schüller turned the corner and disappeared.

#

Palmer had his head down with his eyes closed. He winced hard as he waited for death — nothing. He opened his eyes. The two goons lay sprawled out on the ground dead with severe head wounds. Stewart stood off to the side once again wearing her blue flight suit. Her face was bruised.

Palmer started babbling. "Hey, what's the good word?! Hey! What's... Marianne... My God... How you doin', baby girl?!"

"Hi," Stewart replied.

"Hi! Yeah, hi! How are ya'?"

"Whatcha doin'?"

"Oh, you know. This and that."

"You ok?"

"Oh, I'm solid. Just... A little altercation... Handlin' my... Handlin' my business."

His cracked façade crumbled as he teared up. The realization that he was almost murdered hit hard. "Thank you."

"I need your help," Stewart said.

"What?"

"I need your help."

"I..."

"Can you help me?"

"What's goin' on, baby girl?"

"Do you know anything about androids?"

"You mean like robots? Oh yeah, I was married for 9 years; I know exactly what it's like to be a robot."

"This is a lot worse than your marriage."

"You don't know my marriage."

Twenty-Eight

"I got a funny feelin' about you," Ernestine slurred as she gulped another shot of whiskey. She sat behind her desk glancing at the framed photo of her husband Theotis, then drunkenly zeroed in on Savage taking notes. "I felt it the minute I laid eyes on you. Like something ain't quite right with you," she said as the effects of the alcohol washed over her.

"Well, you better thank your lucky stars something ain't quite right with me. Any of your quite right bestus buddies offer to help you escape National Socialism?"

"I ain't sayin' I'm not grateful. I'm just sayin' you ain't right—far from it."

"What's not right?"

"It's just an expression. You ain't got to get all sensitive. I'm just makin' an observation."

"And you felt this was the best time to share these insights?"

"Lookee here—What I meant to say..."

"How did you think that would make me feel?"

"I'm just used to a different kind of colored man, that's all. You one of them fancy pants niggas'—been around white people a lot."

"I'm not chitins and pig's feet enough for you? Is that it?

"Well, you kinda hincty."

"I'm sorry to hear that. Well, if you want, my friend and I can forget the whole thing. We just thought we'd help out and prevent a mass murder, that's all. It's not like we're asking for anything in return. But if I run into Bosephus Washington Jefferson III jumping off a cotton truck, I'll send him your way. I'm sure he'll make you feel much more comfortable. Maybe *he* can come up with a plan to smuggle you, an entire swing band, and all your friends out of Paris alive."

Ernestine shook her head as she struggled to shake off the effects of the alcohol. She realized the conversation had taken a bad turn.

"Personally, I wouldn't be concerned about you and I becoming soul-mates," Savage continued. "Especially if the person rescuing you is saving you from being shot in the back of the head and thrown into a ditch. But to each his own—different strokes, right?"

"Mr. Savage..."

"Free to be you and me."

"I apologize."

"Have you tried prayer?"

"I'm a little tight. Sometimes I talk too much when I drink. I'm just curious about your motivations, that's all."

Savage got up and walked toward the exit. "You're curious about my motivations?"

"Yes, I'm curious... About your motivations."

"Sorry, this didn't work out. We'll get out of your hair. Good luck with Adolph and the whole ethnic cleansing thing—perhaps some other time. Oh, right, there won't be another time."

He opened the door to leave—Ernestine stumbled from around her desk to stop him. She tripped as Savage caught her. He held her close. "You know, I can't decide which is worse," Savage continued. "Being shot like a dog by Schüller's men and having everyone watch you decompose, or starving to death in a disease-infested labor camp."

Ernestine's face contorted in anger. "I knew it. I just knew it. I had a feeling about you. You're a real piece of work. It was just a matter of time before it came oozin' outta you. You're no good, you're just no good."

"Do you have a fear of heights? See, the Nazis like to make an example of people by hanging them by the neck from the top of streetlights in the town square. It's 25 feet off the ground. 25 feet isn't really that high up. Oh, wait. But you'll be dead, so it doesn't matter. Never mind."

"So, this is the part where I kiss yo' ass just the way you like it. Wet and juicy with my big buttery lips. Ok, I am so sorry for what I said, Mr. Savage. What can I do to unhurt your little feelins'?"

"Don't worry about it. Take your sweet time. Meditate on it. Take as much time as you need. Find your true north."

"You're a heel."

"It's an affliction."

"A lousy, stinkin' heel!"

"I'm all you've got."

"You're just like all rest."

Savage grabbed Ernestine by the shoulders and violently pushed her against the wall. "I'm not going to apologize for not being black enough for you. White people aren't as particular as you are. If this was 1850, we'd *all* be sold as slaves without a second thought."

Ernestine struggled.

"Just give me the combination to the goddamn safe," Savage pressed.

Ernestine kneed Savage in the groin like pro. He backed up wincing in pain. Suddenly, Little Benny's head popped out through the false panel of the secret door of Ernestine's office.

"A Nazi troop truck just pulled up! Schüller's goons are comin'! On the double!"

Little Benny ducked back through the doorway. The panel closed behind him.

"That tears it," Ernestine said. "I knew I should have drugged yo' asses and left ya'll to die in the woods."

"Go with your gut next time," Savage retorted gruffly.

#

Suddenly, two Nazi thugs in trench coats kicked their way into Ernestine's office with pistols drawn.

"Komm mit uns, nigger!" said the pock-marked man in charge.

Schüller had requested the honor of Savage's presence, and he wasn't taking no for an answer.

The Nazis escorted Savage to the main floor of the club. Ernestine followed behind. The club was still packed with dancing boozehounds as Buster signaled the closing bars to Count Basie's "Topsy."

Savage was ushered through the crowd of patrons and positioned right in front of the stage. Schüller was seated at a table off to the right. Buster ended the tune and caught Schüller's eye. The look on Schüller's face said, "Do as you were told."

Buster stepped up to the microphone mopping his sweat-soaked face with his handkerchief. The audience applauded as he enjoyed the accolades.

"Thank you, thank you, thank you. You liked that, didn't you? Ha-ha. I can tell. Ok. And now for your listening pleasure, I'd like to present our newest member of the band. Give a warm Montclair welcome to the incredible guitar stylings of Lorenzo Savage & His Amazing Guitar."

The crowd exploded into applause. Savage got an eye full of Schüller sitting with a smug expression on his face. Schüller smiled with satisfaction as he gave his men the silent command to steer Savage toward the stage. Savage was shoved forward.

Santiago was standing nearby on edge, poised to toss her tray of cigarettes and fight like the devil.

"Know any Melissa Etheridge?" Santiago asked.

"Not funny."

"You need to play some championship guitar, or we're going to camp. And I don't mean yoga camp. A truck full of soldiers just pulled up. All the exits are blocked. No pressure, though. Do your thing. Make a joyful noise."

"I'll do me, and you do you."

"*Me* is fine. It's your guitar playing I'm concerned about."

"You're not worried, are you?"

"No, I'm fine. But if you get up there and play guitar like drunk Neil Young, I'm going to take off these heels and kill every bratwurst eating cocksucker in this place."

"O ye of little faith."

"I don't believe in faith."

"No atheists in a foxhole."

Savage was pushed on stage toward the microphone. Buster gave him a big smile. "I would send yo' mama a sympathy card, but her ugly ass is probably still in diapers." Buster motioned to Charles, who was sitting behind him. Charles passed his guitar over to Buster, who handed it to Savage.

Fontaine's eyes locked on Savage. She was elegantly dressed sitting in a booth at the back of the club. She smoked a cigarette from a long holder and compelled him with her eyes. She blew him a tiny kiss. In her, he saw the pain and the ecstasy—the kind that makes you argue with yourself about her in your car years later after you're broken and alone.

Schüller took in the proceedings and nodded to his goons. "Get ready to take him," he communicated through his steely glaze. His two goons fondled their Walther P38s, which were lowered below waist level.

Savage strapped the guitar around himself, sitting on a high stool. He was pushed close to the microphone. "Thank you, ladies and gentlemen—and thank you Buster Pete and the Buster Pete Band. This song is a special little ditty that's close to my heart. I hope you enjoy it." He turned to the band.

"Try to keep up, boys."

And there was Joslyn. She stood in the audience three rows back like Casper the Severely Fuckable Ghost. Savage knew she wasn't there, but she was real as anyone in the room. The sight of her filled him with anguish. He focused on the task at hand. He played a sophisticated chord melody that rose to a stirring crescendo. He closed his eyes and sang:

I'm oh so sad; it was inevitable
I met someone unforgettable
Life is a chore—the sun won't shine for me no more

He accompanied himself as he sang a slow introduction. Savage's voice was smooth and easy, falling somewhere between a wistful Nat King Cole and a dirty Johnny Mathis.

All my cronies who had heard the news
With my antics, will now fill my blues
Mr. Big Shot became Mr. Close but no cigar

Buster picked up on what song he was doing and mouthed silently to the band, "'My Beautiful Heartache' in F."

The band played softly underneath him. Savage settled into the first verse adding smooth chord voicings and single-note embellishments.

Santiago watched from the sidelines. "Well, isn't he full of surprises."

Savage continued:

I've traveled around the world insane
Schooled all the best doctors in vain
The Rockies were just a keepsake
You'll always be my beautiful heartache

Fontaine stared at him captivated. She could tell the song held deep meaning for him. It was the story of a man who has all the fame, money, and accomplishments one could ever want, but can't have what's *most* important—the woman he loves. Savage continued:

Down at the racetrack
I'm the daily double
In Hollywood movies
I'm a gangster in trouble
I've got a pad with a view
But I always play the fool for you

Humiliation washed over Schüller. He motioned for his men to fall back. On a dime, they turned and walked toward the exit. Savage swung into the bridge of the song. The band stayed with him as the rhythm quickened into a jazzy rhumba.

You're in my dreams
Poems I could write of you
Scream
Just for a bite of you
Daydream
Every day and night of you
But it's all just smoke rings in the pale moonlight

Savage launched into a guitar solo that was one-part blues and two parts bebop. His fingers danced across the fretboard, creating ear-tickling themes and dazzling chromatic lines. Charles took notice, feigning disinterest, but he was captivated.

Buster's dislike of Savage turned to respect. His cynical smirk morphed into his trademark grin. Schüller exited the nightclub in anger, rudely pushing aside an elderly busboy.

Savage was absorbed in his performance as he played with his eyes closed. The band began to cook with fire as the crowd pressed toward the stage. Ernestine, Fontaine, and Santiago joined them.

Ernestine turned to Santiago. "Get a load of our professional."

"He doesn't suck," Santiago replied. "This is good. He just bought us some time."

"Thank you, Jesus."

"You can always count on a sap to deliver a good crying in your beer song."

Savage continued to play guitar, wielding melodic embellishments that hadn't become part of jazz guitar vocabulary yet. The earthy 1930s guitar style he began with had morphed to bebop, post-bop, and soul. Savage's post-George Benson meets Pat Martino extrapolations had the audience riveted. Altered chords and octave work interlaced with harmonies and quotes from "Let's Fall in Love" and "Jean Pierre."

As he approached the song's final bars, he gave a nod to Buster, who guided the band to fade into silence. The audience was speechless. Joslyn looked bored. Her attention was diverted as her head turned everywhere to take in all the crude portraits and knick-knacks that adorned the club. Her head spun around, surprised to see Savage had caught her not paying attention. She smiled with expertise. The song ended.

There was a long silence. Finally, a single person began clapping. It was Little Benny. He stood on a chair, clapping his hands at a slow even pace. As his clapping became faster, the crowd joined in as the clamor escalated into loud adoring applause.

Savage took it in but was only able to produce a crooked smile. He feigned appreciation and nodded to the band. He looked out into the audience. Joslyn was gone. The band applauded enthusiastically. Buster gave Savage a pat on the back. But all Savage could think about was how Joslyn broke his heart into a million tiny little pieces.

Twenty-Nine

Stewart hated getting her hair wet.

"I hate getting my hair wet."

-Dr. Marianne Stewart

But that didn't stop her from outfitting herself in a period appropriate scuba diving wetsuit. Outside the boat was the restless abyss. Stewart stared out over the waves. Palmer sat in the boat across from her dressed like a 1942 New Orleans pimp. Nestled somewhere in the middle of a large body of water, they rocked gently against the current.

"If I'm not back in 20 minutes, take off," Stewart ordered. "Go back to your hotel room, put a gun in your mouth, and blow your brains out." She checked her breathing apparatus and weighted belt. "If I can't stop this, you don't want to live in this world."

"Sometimes, I can't tell if you're fucking with me or not."

"Mordecai is planning to release the last of three viruses. Whoever designed this is using some sort of advanced viral nanotechnology. I've never seen anything like it. I feel like I should know more about this than I do."

"Ok—I don't know what that means."

"It's my husband's field of research—Biomechanical engineering. I never had an interest—not my area of study."

"I bet you'll be interested *next* time."

"What? So, I'm supposed to be fascinated with every aspect of my husband's life just because we're married?"

"I'm just sayin'."

"Let's not talk about my husband."

She noticed what Palmer was wearing. "Motherfucker, I told you I needed your help. Why would you show up on a boat looking like Cab Calloway? Do you not know what action wear is?"

"I was raised not to leave the house looking like a bum. I like to be clean. I like to look good when I go out."

Stewart shook her head deciding to move on. "This thing is 235 feet straight down. Set your watch for 20 minutes. After that, take off."

Palmer noticed the extra scuba gear on the floor of the boat. "I'll be sure to do that since I don't swim."

"Are you fucking with me?"

"It's not what I'm known for."

"Ok, listen," Stewart said as she took a deep breath. "I'm certain this virus will be deployed into the ecosystem. There's no telling how much time we have. From what I've seen, the other viruses were bad, but this one's the industrial strength version."

"What could be worse than the Nazis and the Klan?"

"Complete anarchy. No government, no laws, not even a *pretense* of sanity. I've seen the simulations. It's grim."

"Because Nazis aren't quite fucked up enough?"

"It's an absolute hellish nightmare. If you live through the first wave, expect to see a world ruled by sport murderers and racist factions. It's going to send this world right back to sticks and rocks."

Stewart pulled out her device and began typing. "Here, I'll show you."

"No need, my imagination works just fine..."

"It takes a second."

"Wait, no..."

Stewart and Palmer vanished.

Thirty

When Agnes Lorraine Tomlinson changed her name to Lorraine Fontaine, it was the beginning of a new life. Growing up in a small racially mixed section of Chicago's Southside, she was trapped between two worlds. Born to a white father and a negro mother, she was set upon by all sides due to the ripple effects of slavery, racism, and jerks. Darker-skinned negroes looked upon her with contempt and jealousy, while whites mistreated her in more obvious ways.

Born in 1904, she suffered the curse of not being black enough for black people and not white enough for white people. She also experienced the curse of being profoundly beautiful. Her aquiline nose, full lips, and soft brown hair displayed the best qualities of interracial beauty. Unfortunately, she had too much melanin for the world. White women tanned themselves on beaches all over the world, but if you were *born* with dark skin you were less desirable. It would plague people of color throughout eternity and conditioned many to hate themselves.

Men of every race, creed, and color wanted to sleep with Fontaine, and women hated her for it. Jealousy evolved into hostility and practical jokes, often leaving her in tears. To survive, she had to wise up, thicken her skin, and carve out a life using her brain. She came up with a plan. It was a dream, but as soon as she pursued it, it became her obsession.

Fontaine was quick-minded and born with a soothing voice. Flunking out of beauty school sealed the deal. She was going to pursue a career in entertainment. She knew she was special and realized there was nothing for her in Chicago. A woman like her wasn't cut out for the straight life of marriage, babies, and domestic slavery. Thus began years of singing engagements beginning in the bars of Chicago's Uptown.

Bandleader Kyle Raymond lost his canary due to the flu. Fontaine got wind of this, walked into the club, and stepped on stage without an invitation. She only knew two songs. After singing, Raymond thanked her and gave her two bits. In her mind, she did a good job. In reality, she was green and needed lots of work. It didn't faze her because Fontaine had to start somewhere. She had to work on her breath control and build a repertoire.

Raymond introduced her to his arranger Charlie Mack. Mack was a tall, thin, fine-featured negro man of 60. He was a musically gifted alcoholic homosexual who would fall into bouts of melancholy when he drank—and he drank often. Mack later came to adore Fontaine, but in the beginning he was tough on her. Mack gave her the third degree about being lazy and leaning on her looks instead of her talent. He drummed it into her that her voice would be her ticket—not her looks, which would eventually fade. Fontaine was resistant at first, but with few options, she worked hard and eventually became his favorite student.

Mack was a no-nonsense disciplinarian who taught her about pitch, breath control, and how to swing. Lacking any usable vibrato, Mack taught her to use sustain, which gave her voice a soaring quality. He found repertoire and keys favoring her voice and educated her in all the music worth listening to. They ultimately developed a strong platonic kinship.

After moving on from Raymond's band, Mack and Fontaine remained close. He gave her excellent advice. He developed within her a singing style that was equally unique, charismatic, and commercial. Fontaine's approachable, girl-next-door sweetness mixed with a come-hither sensuality, fit right into the swing era's contemporary sounds.

Mack molded her. He made her business savvy, musically educated, and hirable. He also taught her how to lead a band like a dominatrix. In return, Fontaine listened to his drunken sob stories of doomed love affairs and bailed him out of jail on occasion.

Fontaine's big break came while she was singing in a downtown joint called Dickie's Tavern. After many failed attempts by drummer Eric Wilson to sleep with her, Wilson finally played his ace. He told her he could get her on one of the local radio stations as a singer. But first, she had to sleep with him—she did.

Wilson kept his promise and finagled her an audition for the radio show's bandleader. She passed with flying colors and went on to be heard by thousands of people each week with The Tony Benson Orchestra. Her sultry voice and quick-on-her-feet radio banter led to commercial spots. This helped her build a strong following in the Chicago area and gave her leverage to work with better bands.

Just as she was about to sign with one of the most popular orchestras in Chicago, she received a call to come to Hollywood to audition for a spot on "Bob Hope's Pepsodent Show." Bob Hope was hugely popular. Everyone who could get close enough to a radio listened to him. Not even The Great Depression could slow Fontaine down as she gathered the funds to take the Super Chief train from Chicago to Los Angeles.

When she arrived, things immediately went south. It all started when there was no one to pick her up from the train station. An assistant was there to pick her up, but he hadn't seen any women he thought could have been Fontaine. He was expecting to pick up a white woman. Fontaine managed to get to the studio on her own. Director Norman Morrell, not realizing she was a negro couldn't hire her. Fontaine argued that listeners wouldn't see her because it was radio, but he told her to beat it and sent her packing anyway. They wound up hiring young Dinah Shore instead.

Fontaine was devastated. She wasn't getting any younger and believed she had a short window of opportunity before that window closed forever. She walked the streets of Los Angeles, eventually finding work in local clubs where she was met with equal parts racial discrimination, bad luck, and human trash. They passed her around like a cheap cigar. Fontaine had fallen in with a crowd of lowlifes when she started hearing stories about Paris.

A bartender at the Dunbar Hotel talked about Paris like it was

Disneyland for negroes—a magical land of collard greens and rainbows, offering unlimited white people credit and rabid swing fans. As far as Fontaine was concerned, Paris was the place to be. She went to the library and dug up as much information about Paris as she could. Fontaine got Buster Pete's name from Mack, but she needed more money.

She sold all her possessions—even her body to earn enough money to get there. The bartender had exaggerated his ass off, but the fantasy of Paris was a significant improvement over the reality of America. After meeting Buster and passing her audition, she finally achieved the validation and success she'd craved. She was riveting on stage, a goddamn goddess. She was advertised as the negro Doris Day. But just as her popularity began to spread beyond Paris, the Nazis came and fucked up everything.

Thirty-One

Stewart and Palmer materialized in a war-torn urban nightmare. Beneath a blood-soaked sky, buildings smoldered as smoke wafted through burned-down department stores. Decomposing corpses were hoisted on poles as the stench of death filled the air. Stewart was wearing her flight suit again. She checked the coordinates on her device.

Palmer threw up. He heaved from a standing fetal position as his body shook involuntarily. "You didn't have to do this. I would've taken your word for it."

"It's only a simulation. It's not live... yet."

"You coulda' just described it."

"I didn't mean to put you out. Just trying to save the world that's all."

"This is too much information. Descriptive adjectives would've sufficed." Palmer spat and wiped his mouth with a handkerchief. "Where are we?"

"Beverly Hills."

"California!?"

"Ever hear of Rodeo Drive?"

"Wait a minute, I ain't never been to Beverly Hills, but I know this ain't it."

"Urban renewal," Stewart replied. This is the future I'm trying to prevent. *Your* future."

"But how..."

"As I said, it's a simulation—a mock-up. They pissed all over my design—a travesty."

"This is fucked up."

"Wait until you see Desolation."

"Des-a-what?"

"After the smoke clears and everyone kills each other off, there will be nothing left but cockroaches."

"Alright. Got it. We need to get on up outta here."

"You wanna go back to the Nazis?"

"Yeah, let's do that."

"You sure?"

"Stop playin'."

Suddenly, gunfire erupted from across the street. Bullets perforated the brick wall behind them. Stewart and Palmer ducked and ran down a dark alley.

"I thought you said this was a simulation!" Palmer barked as they sprinted.

They tumbled into each other as they raced to safety. Leaping over debris and corpses, Palmer spotted a filthy toddler eating a rat. The boy's mouth and fingers were covered in blood as he bit hungrily into its hindquarters. Convulsed, Palmer pushed himself onward as he helped Stewart keep up. Out of breath and traumatized, they spun themselves around a corner to catch their breath.

"Now what?" Palmer asked.

"Did you hear that?"

"What?"

A piercing shriek caught Palmer off guard. Something dark and hairy swooped down and knocked Palmer's hat off. The creature barrel-rolled sideways then soared upward into the crimson sky.

"What the hell was that?!"

"Did it get you?"

"Damn near!"

Stewart checked his head. "Did it cut you?"

"No, I'm ok."

She touched his face compassionately. Suddenly, a swarm of thickly muscled chimpanzees with wings swept over their heads. Stewart and Palmer ducked instinctively.

"Monkeys?!" Palmer bellowed.

"Pan Troglodytes."

"Oh, this is bad."

"They're the decedents of mutant chimpanzees escaped from a science facility. They've been breeding out of captivity. Humans are their main food source."

"You mean they make humans bring them food?"

"No, humans *are* the food."

"Oh, hell no."

"They're also disease carriers."

"Sure, why not. They'd be right at home with the Master Race."

"It's worse than that."

"How's that?"

"If one of those things bites you, you become a violent, flesh-eating cannibal. The whole world becomes a giant buffet, and humans are the main course."

"Great, monkeys are my worst nightmare. I been scared of monkeys my whole life, ever since my mama took me to the circus. Gave me a complex—nightmares. I hate monkeys. Nasty motherfuckas'. Let's get the hell on up outta here."

#

There was the faint sound of music in the distance. Stewart and Palmer instinctively turned their heads west down Rodeo Drive to hear where it was coming from.

"What's that?" Asked Palmer.

Someone was playing a church organ. The music was strange, chilling, religious, and out of tune. Then they heard a choir join in, singing an unrecognizable hymn. The singing emanated from a burned-out church.

"What the hell is goin' on over there?" Palmer inquired.

"I'm not sure I want to know," Stewart replied.

"We need to get outta sight," Palmer said. "I smell monkeys."

They avoided the street and jogged along the edge of crumbling department stores and dilapidated buildings. They stepped over emaciated corpses. Their facial expressions, frozen in a twisted mask of death. The sickening aroma of decaying flesh played havoc with their nervous systems.

Stewart's head spun from left to right as she kept an eye out for movement. Flickering shadows on rooftops drew Palmer's attention. By the time he was able to focus on the movement, there was nothing to see.

They stopped and kneeled behind a gutted city bus. A group of nuns in black and white habits paraded by and entered the massive wooden doors of the church. Simian screams erupted as thickly muscled chimpanzees flew overhead. Their wingspan blackened the blood-red sky.

"We need to move, now!" Stewart whispered.

They cautiously followed behind the nuns from a distance as they trotted toward the church. The nuns and the rising volume of the choir masked their entrance. They split off together to one side of the vestibule blanketed in darkness.

Stewart and Palmer hid in the shadows of a narrow alcove as the strange choral hymn faded to silence. Rows of pews were lined up on either side of the church's main floor. A congregation stood dressed in powder blue robes facing an elderly bishop. He stood in front of an altar—an altar made from a hodge-podge of religious artifacts from *Simulated Earth's* distant past.

The bishop was adorned in an elaborate purple robe with a mishmash of religious decorations. His ceremonial headdress resembled a psychedelic junkyard pope, which stood high upon his head. He extended his frail, boney hands outward, commanding the congregation to be seated.

"And God's hand descendeth from the heavens unto the heat thereof," said the bishop. "Prepare ye the way of the lord. For there will be neither speech nor language, yet his voice shall be heard among the multitudes."

An organist began playing a warped chord progression as he gyrated back and forth, consumed by the sound of his playing.

"Hosanna," replied the congregation.

"Day by day," replied the bishop.

"Hey sanna."

"Day by day."

"Sanna, sanna, ho."

"Three things I pray," said the bishop.

"See thee more clearly, love thee more dearly, follow thee more nearly," the congregation replied.

"His message uttered through the earth from the end of heaven—a tabernacle of the sun. For the lord's commandment is pure, and that purity shall prevail as our truth in devotion to that maker."

"We are truth," the congregation replied.

"Undisputed truth."

"Undisputed beauty."

"Let us pray," the bishop continued. The music swelled.

"Is this some kinda joke?" Palmer whispered. "These ain't no Christians."

"I'm guessing their religion is based on fragments of *Simulated Earth's* distant past before Desolation," Stewart replied. "They've cobbled together pieces of religious texts and media, mixed in with their own post-apocalyptic zeitgeist."

"That shit is from *Godspell* and *Jesus Christ Superstar*!" Palmer whispered angrily.

"What?"

"Broadway musicals. They're quoting musicals."

"Musicals?!"

"Plays! Musical theater! It's completely insane, but it makes as much goddamn sense as everything else."

"Exactly, it's not like the Bible was written by God. So this isn't that far-fetched."

"I didn't mean it like that. This is a whole other thing."

"It's not that different. Think about it."

"You gon' burn for that."

"Palmer, I'm a scientist," she said with authority.

Stewart and Palmer quieted themselves as the music faded. The bishop continued. "All rise."

The congregants rose from their pews.

"Prepare for the gateway of the almighty to illuminate the darkness and grant us peace eternal. Let the fellowship of the holy smoke purify us—this day and evermore."

Two filthy altar boys with large hydrocephalic heads crisscrossed in front of the pews carrying incense burners. They put on gas masks, as did the bishop. They pulled a chain on the burner and released billowing clouds of thick orange incense. The incense wafted throughout the congregation.

"Breathe deeply, my children," the bishop continued. "Breathe deeply —love is coming. Love is coming to us all."

As the congregants inhaled, they collapsed, falling over like dominoes in each row. Then, one by one, their bodies jerked involuntarily as white foam erupted from their mouths, then they froze in stone-cold stillness.

"It's a mass suicide!" Steward yelled.

"We gotta go! Now!" Palmer cried.

Stewart and Palmer bolted toward the church entrance as the smoke spread closer to them. They stopped in their tracks when they discovered the doors were locked shut. They were trapped.

"Use that thing to get us the hell on up outta here," Palmer cried, referring to Stewart's device.

"I'm already on it!" Stewart replied as she typed into the device. She pressed ENTER, but nothing happened.

"Shit!" Stewart cried.

The orange smoke drifted closer and closer as a few congregants rushed out of the pews to escape. They were caught and overwhelmed by the orange smoke, falling to the floor in a seizure, then stillness.

"Aw, hell no!" Palmer yelled.

Stewart entered the code again as the smoke drifted in their direction.

The clawing hands of dying congregants reached for them as they panicked. "Help! Help me!"

Palmer began beating on the door in a frenzy.

Finally, the last congregant fell to the floor and died just a few feet away as the deadly orange smoke drifted closer.

Stewart could faintly smell the acrid incense. She felt the urge to cough. She pressed ENTER again. Suddenly, the church's doors blew open in a violent explosion. Stewart and Palmer recoiled, then rushed out of the church. Once outside, they continued to sprint down the debris-littered boulevard.

#

The sound of hell erupted with gunfire and gut-wrenching screams. Explosions sent debris flying as Stewart and Palmer ducked for cover. Stewart paused to punch in a new code to her device to return to the boat, but there was too much distraction. "Fuck!" Stewart screamed.

"We gotta go!" Palmer said as he steered her from harm's way. Latino guerilla fighters wearing military camo fatigues swarmed in with aggressive firepower.

"It's the Mexican Army!" Palmer yelled.

"MS-13," Stewart replied, correcting him.

Hordes of flying monkeys swept down and lifted soldiers into the air. Skulls burst open from simian talons. The monkeys gorged themselves on the brains of their victims as they ascended into the sky.

A soldier's flamethrower tank exploded on his back. The flaming soldier ran screaming into a parade of nuns. The nuns shrieked as they caught fire and scattered in a frenzy. Palmer sprinted through the chaos with Stewart in tow as she hastily typed in the transport code.

Naked albino savages leaped from second-story windows wielding machetes and hatchets. Unable to resist the orgy of gore, the albinos feasted upon the burning corpses. The flying monkeys took advantage of their distraction and pounced on them. They were torn limb from limb as their cries mixed with gunfire and blood drenched entrails.

Stewart and Palmer took refuge ducking into a dilapidated apartment building. Rotting corpses littered the hallways. The overpowering smell of death repelled Stewart.

"We have to get to the roof!" Stewart screamed.

Stewart ran up the stairs with Palmer close behind. Hordes of mouth-frothing albino cannibals growled as they chased them up the winding stairwell. Each floor revealed a new threat as disease-infected freaks dressed in a mishmash of Nazi and Confederate uniforms emerged from apartment doorways. They collided with flying monkeys, naked albinos, infected nuns, and soldiers as the aroma of fresh meat drove them insane with hunger.

Stewart panted spastically as she reached the top of the stairs and found the roof door locked. "We're trapped!"

"No!!!" Palmer yelled.

The blood-thirsty cannibals charged up the stairs after them. Like rabid dogs, they fought and climbed over one another. Stewart typed faster. The green lettering on the device's console read, ERROR. "Goddammit!" Stewart screamed.

A rabid albino grabbed Palmer's foot and pulled his shoe off. Palmer kicked frantically as a deluge of disease-infected cannibals fought to get to him.

In a last-ditch effort, Palmer crashed through the wooden door breaking the hinges. The old door splintered as dust and pieces of wood fell around them. They sped across the rooftop as the rabid mob chased them to the edge of the building.

Foaming at the mouth and screaming gibberish, the mob was within arm's reach. With no options, Stewart and Palmer ran straight off the edge of the building. Without enough momentum to make it across to the next structure, they fell into the violent gore-fest below. Just as they were about to crash on top of a nun eating a baby, they vanished into thin air.

Thirty-Two

Under Schüller's occupation of Paris, a shadow fell across its citizens as French clocks were pushed forward by one hour. This prolonged the morning darkness and hastened the arrival of night. The Nazi curfew put the kibosh on much of Parisian nightlife, but Schüller allowed The Montclair to stay open after the curfew to rake in cash and sell contraband.

Even after The Montclair went dark, it didn't stop the counterculture from socializing and having a good time. Curfews and rationing were for pussies. Everyone else lived like there was no tomorrow. Fontaine had friends who introduced her to the world of underground mixers.

She became fast friends with an eclectic group of artists, writers, and eccentrics that attended these social gatherings. A handful of Parisians and expats risked their lives to forget their troubles and blow their brains out on Duke Ellington, illicit love, and opium.

This is where Fontaine let her hair down. She sang the songs she wanted and spoke openly about all manner of subjects—from Communism to Eddie "Rochester" Anderson—all under the influence of French wine and black-market chocolate. Being discovered by the Nazis meant death, but the stimulating company and free social atmosphere were too good to ignore.

Savage was led into this world by Fontaine's beautiful hand and the lure of romance. She introduced him to black nationalists, actors, and female impersonators. Intense discussions and the zeitgeist of the era enveloped their little world inside a spacious French apartment.

The smell of cigarettes, perfume, and burnt opium, wafted through the cozy abode. Lester Young's dark bolero echoed from the record player as a drag queen performed a dance routine with colorful scarves.

A negro comedian insisted on engaging Savage with a comedic routine called, "If Hitler Was A Negro." Savage's icy stare sent the comedian packing.

Savage was a curiosity to the group with his odd vernacular and mystery, but witty banter was the last thing on his mind. Stiff drinks and reefers were passed around, but no drug could compete with the animal magnetism Fontaine and Savage felt for one another.

Mid-conversation side-glances, the brush of a hand—they couldn't take their eyes off one another. Rendezvous to the kitchen found them together alone, but only briefly. Near kisses and interruptions from partygoers created a sexual tension between them that was unbearable. The interference produced a yearning ache in their loins.

Fontaine was his keeper in this strange world, but both of them longed for the moment when they could be alone together. He inhaled her when she walked by. They flirted, laughed, and drank.

A man who had been staring at Savage finally crossed the room to introduce himself. He was a stout, well-dressed Frenchman in his mid-40s with nervous eyes and beautifully handcrafted leather shoes. "How do you do? Permit me to introduce myself. My name is Dr. Marcel Petiot. I could not help but notice you look as out of place here as I do," he said with a chuckle.

"Dr. Marcel Petiot," Savage repeated to himself. There was something about his name that set off an alarm. He couldn't quite put his finger on it, but he felt a twinge in his gut—and his gut was never wrong. "The name's Savage."

"So, what brings you to this soiree?" Petiot continued. "And if you tell me you are with the SS, I will not believe you," he said chuckling with a shaky grin.

"A friend brought me here. I play guitar at The Montclair."

"Ah, a musician. So, swing is what brings you to Paris."

"I enjoy your abnormally crusty croissants as much as the next guy, but your German guests have a lot to be desired."

"Indeed. The Germans are a plague upon Europe. It is only a matter of time before the entire country is under rubble. And if the Germans don't get us, the Russians will."

"I was hoping to leave Paris before it came to that."

"But where would you go? Foreign borders are very particular regarding who gains entry."

"You look well-heeled. Why haven't you left?"

"Paris is my home, and I will fight like a lion for her. I also have a medical practice. I cannot, in good conscience, abandon my patients. I would be betraying my oath."

"What a guy."

"I also help them in other ways."

"Do tell."

"I help people to escape."

"Escape Paris?"

"That is correct."

"Loose lips."

"I believe I can trust you."

"How?"

"Let us just say I have ways and means."

" Pyrenees Freedom Trail?"

"Too risky."

"Transportation?"

"Boats, planes, trains, each escape route is different."

Savage gave him a curious look as Fontaine joined them.

"I see you're showing signs of being a normal human being. It's refreshing."

"Dr. Petiot, Lorraine Fontaine—girl singer. Lorraine, this is Dr. Petiot," Savage said with as much formality as he could muster.

"Oh, you're the good doctor who brought the brandy," Fontaine replied. "How nice of you. I'm not much of a brandy drinker, but I'm told it's excellent."

"My pleasure," said Petiot. "Your reputation precedes you. Though I must admit, I have never heard you sing."

"Well, we'll have to fix that and get you a good table at The Montclair."

"I adore music, but it is of the classical variety. If Chopin is not being played, it will more than likely be wasted on me."

"It's hard to beat Chopin's 'Waltz in C Sharp Minor,' but Lorraine is always worth being detained for some late night Nazi torture," Savage replied jokingly. Fontaine gazed at him with a coquettish grin. "You flatter."

"You are familiar with Chopin?" Petiot asked Savage with a perplexed expression on his face.

"Sure. Why wouldn't I be?"

"Well... I..."

"Lorenzo Savage is a worldly man of mystery," Fontaine added.

"I prefer Haydn and Mozart, but I wouldn't kick Chopin or Liszt out of bed," Savage replied."

"I must say I am shocked."

"Why? You don't like Liszt?"

"Oh, no. I did not mean that. I..."

"Spill it."

"Well, I did not think that..."

"Think what?" Savage asked.

Fontaine heard her name being called from the kitchen. "Duty calls. I'll let you two iron out your little social faux pas. Oh, and by the way, jigaboos like Chopin too," she said with a wink to Petiot. She strolled to the kitchen but not before mouthing to Savage, "Behave."

"My humble apologies," Petiot stammered. "I meant no disrespect. I must admit my ignorance. I have not met many negroes, and I assumed they only listened to swing. Appreciation for the masters requires certain... refined tastes, so quite naturally, I..."

"Look, I know you think we're all a bunch of monkeys, so fuck you. And just to be clear, the harmonic style of 18th-century white supremacists isn't the default for the rest of the world. James Brown would kick

Chopin's sissy ass. Now, normally I would take you out back and teach you some manners, but I'm in a festive mood. Tell me how you get people out of Paris."

"You are a credit to your race."

"Shut the fuck up."

"I have made a terrible mistake. Please accept my apology."

Petiot calmly looked around to see if anyone was paying attention to their conversation. Once he was satisfied, he continued. "I have helped many people escape Paris."

"How did you manage that?"

"Strong bonds and reliable relationships."

"Specifics."

"The Argentinian government."

"Who's your contact?"

"An old friend from medical school. Are you in need of passage?"

"Maybe. What's the damage?"

"Excuse me?"

"How much?"

"25,000 francs. That is per person. My associates must be paid in advance. That includes the inoculation. It is required before you arrive at the border along with medical documentation. I provide all of that. Once you decide, we have to move quickly. The Germans are closing in."

When Savage heard "inoculation," his memory clicked into place. Fontaine returned with a little visitor.

"Look who's here," Fontaine said as she presented Little Benny. "I believe we have a spy in our midst. They found him outside lurking."

"Man's gotta make a living," Little Benny said to Fontaine. "I'm on a mission. I got my peepers on you."

"Does Ernestine know you're here?" asked Savage.

"I can take care of myself. Just mind your P's and Q's. And remember, no hanky and definitely no panky."

He pulled up his sleeve up, flexed his bicep, and offered Savage to feel it. "Feel that."

Savage did. "Feels like a rock," he replied.

"I'll say," Little Benny said. "Dynamic Tension."

"Charles Atlas."

"Solid!" He noticed Petiot. "What's up, Doc?" he said to Petiot.

"I do not believe I have had the pleasure of your acquaintance," Petiot replied."

"Can the rigmarole. You going by Dr. Eugène or Dr. Petiot tonight?"

"I beg your pardon?"

"The jig is up, Frenchy."

"What's the big idea?" Fontaine interrupted.

"The jig is definitely up," Savage replied. "It took me a minute, but when he brought up the 25,000 francs and the inoculation, it all came back to me. Dr. Petiot is going to be a famous man. Or perhaps I should say, *infamous*."

"Apologies. I am not quite sure what is going on," Petiot replied with a nervous grin.

"Oh, I think you do," Savage said as he turned to Fontaine. "Dr. Petiot is what we call a serial killer. He's known as The Butcher of Paris, among other things. When he gets caught, he'll be convicted of killing 27 people. But that's just the highlight reel, isn't it, doctor?"

"This is preposterous," Petiot said with a nervous chuckle.

"I don't know what preposterous means," Little Benny added. "But I hope it means curtains for you. I've had my eye on you. People go into your house and never come out. They disappear. You're workin' for the Gestapo *and* the Resistance. You're a two-timin' traitor."

"Who told you this?" Fontaine asked with a shocked expression on her face.

"He's the worse kind of grifter," Savage replied. "The psycho kind— no code. He tells his victims he's going to get them out of Paris. He collects 25,000 francs and tells them he has to inoculate them before they escape into Argentina. He inoculates them with cyanide. Then he takes their money and everything they own. He incinerates their bodies in his basement, and no one is the wiser. Their neighbors think they fled Paris because of the Nazis, so no one comes looking for them."

"What a racket," Little Benny said.

"If this is an example of your American sense of humor, I find it lacking," Petiot responded angrily.

"Do you see me laughing?"

"You are all mad," Petiot replied with rising anxiety. "I am a highly respected physician."

"I was his mark," Savage told Fontaine. "He knows all about The Montclair. I was supposed to bring him into the group like it was my idea. He was generously offering everyone at The Montclair a one-way-ticket to his basement crematorium—all for the low, low price of 25,000 Francs a pop."

"Then he can tell Schüller what a swell guy he is," Little Benny continued.

"This is outrageous," Petiot argued. You sound like morphine addicts. I will not stand here and be insulted."

"Your goose is cooked, old man," Little Benny said. He reared back and dropkicked Petiot in the balls. Petiot curled over in crippled agony.

Suddenly a loud explosion erupted outside the door of the apartment. A German voice was heard blaring from outside through a megaphone.

"This is the Gestapo! Come out with your hands up! We have the entire building surrounded!"

Savage pulled Burnhoffer's Luger from the back of his pants as Petiot ran into the kitchen. The party instantly turned from laughter to frenzy.

"Stay close to me," Savage said to Fontaine and Little Benny.

Savage never walked into an enclosed area without an exit strategy, and tonight was no different. Fontaine grabbed Little Benny's arm as they followed Savage through a hallway and into a bedroom. Savage jumped over the bed and kicked out a window that led to a balcony. He poked his head outside the window and barely missed getting sprayed with a torrent of machine gunfire.

He ducked back in and saw Dr. Petiot standing in the doorway blocking their exit.

"Do as I say, and I will get all of you out of here alive."

178 - OSCAR JORDAN

Savage whipped out a big black .45 Automatic from the back of his pants and pointed it at Petiot's face. "Here's a better idea. Get us out of here, and I won't blow your brains all over the wall," replied Savage.

"Follow me!"

They ran down the hallway and back to the living room to discover several partygoers spread out on the floor. They were dead or writhing on the sofa in the throes of death. There was also moaning coming from the kitchen. Everyone was dying.

"Oh, my God! What happened?" screamed Fontaine.

Savage looked around the room and saw a tray filled with empty shot glasses spilled on the floor near the deceased drag queen. A half-empty brandy bottle lay nearby.

"The brandy!" Savage barked. "Petiot poisoned the brandy!"

Petiot looked at them with a look of twisted glee. "I was in a state of grace."

"Son of a bitch!" Savage grabbed the bottle of brandy lying on the floor and smashed it over Petiot's head. Petiot fell to his knees in a shower of glass and poisoned brandy. Savage picked him up by the throat as Petiot's eyes darted around in his eye sockets.

"You're going to get us out of here, or I'm going to cut you open and pull out your stomach."

Savage pulled Petiot up to his feet and led him to the front door of the apartment.

"Tell them who you are," Savage told Petiot. "Call for help. Tell them there's been an outbreak of cholera. It's highly contagious! Tell them to call an ambulance. Then we walk out. No stopping. No chitchat. Understand?"

"I understand."

They stepped outside the door and into the hallway with Savage's gun pointing in Petiot's back. Petiot had his hands up and yelled, "I am Doctor Petiot! There has been an outbreak of cholera! It is highly contagious. Call an ambulance! Emergency! Call an ambulance!"

Petiot was immediately riddled with machine-gun fire as Savage, Little Benny, and Fontaine fled down the opposite end of the hallway.

Petiot's bloody body was knocked against the wall. He slid to the floor in a lifeless heap.

Savage, Little Benny, and Fontaine sprinted to the far end of the building. They checked for unlocked doors as bullets whizzed in their direction. After running past two locked doors, they burst into an unlocked apartment.

Little Benny slammed the door shut and slid the deadbolt, locking it. They waited in silence. After a beat, they heard a cough behind them. The trio turned to discover they were standing in a smoke-filled living room. Five German military officers in various stages of undress sat around a table in the middle of a card game. Three weather-beaten prostitutes sat on their laps. The table was covered with money, bottles of wine, playing cards, and cigars. The intoxicated group stared at their guests with deadpan expressions. Finally, one of the officers spoke.

"Was ist draußen los? Juden? (What is going on outside? Jews?)"

"Nein," replied Savage. "Die Schwarzen. (No. The Blacks.)"

The officers pushed the whores off of them as they reached for their weapons. A submachine gun lay on the floor underneath the table. One of the officers reached for it. Savage pushed Fontaine and Little Benny into a corner behind a small sofa and opened fire on the group. His bullets found their targets as the officer reaching for the machine gun was hit in the chest. The table exploded with a frenzy of chaos and gunfire. Playing cards and money flew up into the air like confetti.

Savage's aim was true. Chest wounds exploded into chunks of gore as Savage dived on the floor to pick up a fallen Walther P38. He fired with both guns blazing as he rolled on the floor to avoid being hit.

Naked Germans collapsed to the floor as the last man reached for his weapon and was shot in the cheek. His body flipped over backward in his chair as the prostitutes screamed in terror.

The five Germans lay on the floor dead as the three whores huddled together soaked in Nazi blood. Savage sat on the floor, consumed in an adrenaline euphoria. Little Benny peered out from behind the sofa and crept over to Savage.

"You copacetic?"

"I'm copacetic."

"We need to make like a tree and leave."

"How about we make like a banana and split?"

Suddenly, the apartment door was violently kicked in with an explosion of door fragments. Six armed Gestapo agents stood in the doorway with their weapons trained on them.

"Lass deine Waffen fallen! (Drop your weapons!)" ordered the Gestapo leader.

Fontaine was standing too close to the doorway. One of the soldiers reached over and grabbed her by the hair. Savage noticed two potato masher grenades stuffed in his belt.

"Rats!" Little Benny said, reacting to Fontaine's capture. Fontaine fought back but surrendered after a hard slap to the face. Savage dropped his pistols and put his hands up.

"Be cool, Fritz. Sie ist bei mir (She's with me)."

\#

From outside the apartment building, a fiery explosion ripped through the outside wall of the fifth floor. The entire building shook. Muted screams could be heard in both French and German.

\#

Savage, Little Benny, and Fontaine sprinted through the hotel hallway. Fontaine had taken her shoes off, hiked up her skirt, and kept up with them in bare feet. The sound of jackboots and machine-gun fire erupted around the corner behind them. Savage noticed a laundry chute door as they ran past it. He stopped Little Benny and Fontaine and motioned for them to follow him back. Savage pointed to the chute.

"That's our way out!" Suddenly, he stopped himself. "Wait."

\#

The Gestapo arrived at the laundry chute just as the door slammed shut. The soldiers instinctively reached for their grenades, armed them, and threw them down the chute slamming the door behind it. They waited in silence. Nothing happened. One of the soldiers gingerly opened the door to look down the chute. He saw that the pathway was blocked. The live grenades were piled up just below the opening of the chute door.

"Mein Gott. (My God.)"

A horrible explosion erupted from the chute blowing out the wall and disintegrating the soldiers. The walls nearby were painted with blood and chunks of human debris. A fire alarm rang throughout the building as the hallway filled with smoke and fire.

#

Savage, Fontaine, and Little Benny were on the roof, sprinting at full tilt as they leaped between rooftops. A cacophony of fire trucks and police sirens could be heard. Savage stopped them to take a knee to assess their predicament.

"This entire block is going to be crawling with cops and Nazis," Fontaine said, catching her breath.

"This is true. Rest up. I have an idea." Savage turned to Little Benny. "Do you know what paratroopers say before they jump out of an airplane?"

Little Benny stared at him in befuddlement.

#

In a nearby alley, a French truck driver finished securing bags of laundry piled high in the back of his uncovered truck. The driver got into the cab of the truck and started the engine. The truck pulled forward.

"Geronimo!!!"

Savage, Little Benny, and Fontaine plummeted straight down on to the laundry bags from the roof just in time. The truck driver drove down the alley, then turned right out to the avenue.

Thirty-Three

"Well, that was wrong as two left shoes," Palmer said, feeling sick to his stomach.

"So, you understand what we're up against." Stewart said as she zipped up her wet suit. "This is the worst kind of evil. I'm pretty certain I can shut down the virus, but I don't think I can make it back by myself. That's where you come in. I need you to wait for me in the boat."

"Why don't you disappear yourself and go wherever you need to be? Like we just did?"

"Do you honestly think I would be sitting out here in a boat about to give myself carbon dioxide poisoning if I could teleport myself into that vessel?"

"Look, I get you're not the girl next door, and these are extraordinary circumstances, but I can't be the bitch waiting for you back at the boat."

Stewart stared at him. "What?"

"I already lost a shoe. Those were good shoes. They don't sell my style in single shoes. They come in pairs. They go with the suit. I can't be the one-shoe bitch sittin' quietly back at the boat. I have to sleep with myself at night."

"What are you talking about?"

"I'm not gonna be the bitch."

"How are you being the bitch?"

"I don't sit in the middle seat of a car, and I'm not gonna to sit here in this boat like a one-shoe bitch pining for your safe return. I can't do it."

"I'm sorry, but I *need* you to be the one-shoe bitch sitting in the boat pining for my safe return. I just explained it to you."

"Naw."

"Naw?!"

"I'll find somebody else to help you. I ain't the sidekick type. I'll help you stop the virus, but I can't be the bitch."

"So, this is about your feelings."

"I have feelins'."

"So, let me get this straight. The whole world is turning into a dark runny shit hole, but first, I need to deploy cognitive empathy and be considerate of how this affects your sense of self?"

"Oh, ok. So now *I'm* the asshole."

"You can't even swim! I have to go down there alone. I have to dive 235 feet and figure out how to break into a submarine, which is damn near impossible. Once I get in, I'm supposed to defuse a biological device so devastating it could end humanity as we know it. And I'm supposed to do all this without being murdered by a sadistic android. Clearly, me not making you feel like a one-shoe bitch takes priority."

"I know it's a lot. It's just..."

"All I'm asking you to do is sit in the boat."

"I get what you're doin'."

"You're my only way out."

"Yeah." Palmer was torn.

"You're my getaway."

Palmer thought about it. "Getaway Driver."

"Exactly."

"A Wheelman."

"I can't do this without you."

Palmer nodded in agreement. "Alright, but I ain't gettin' in that water, and you buyin' me a new pair of shoes—Florsheims."

"Fine, whatever."

"Good luck."

Stewart stared at him with a look of disbelief, then shook her head in annoyance. She put on her scuba mask, held it in place, then fell backward into the ocean. Palmer watched her fins disappear beneath the depths. He sat in the boat and was left rocking gently on the water. He looked out across the ocean and sighed. After a beat, Palmer reached into his breast pocket and pulled out a cellphone. He pressed a button and put it to his ear.

Thirty-Four

Darkness faded to the early morning. After putting some distance between themselves and the Gestapo, Savage and Fontaine returned Little Benny to The Montclair. Traveling on foot through side streets and alleys to avoid detection, they arrived at Fontaine's apartment.

Fontaine was easy, but she wasn't that easy. Savage was convinced it was his charm, mystery, and sense of danger women were attracted to. Some people need a steaming hot cup of delusion to get out of bed in the morning.

Savage and Fontaine had a thing. They knew it the moment their eyes met. It was an all-consuming recipe of curiosity, passion and lust that drew them together. At 38, Fontaine had been around the block more than a few times. She put up a good front as the tough Chicago broad who could take care of herself, but she was getting weary. Something had to change. She needed a man she could lean on, someone to listen to her fume, then take control and convince her everything was going to be ok.

What Savage wanted was simple. He wanted to wake up to a beautiful woman... who wasn't annoying. An impossible dream? A wild fantasy? That's when Savage met Joslyn. He figured if he was going to be tortured for not being attentive to their every little sigh and coded whim, the least he could do was wake up to beautiful—or, more specifically, the thing that turned his motor on. Savage had a history of choosing the wrong women, but who could fault him for trying?

Fontaine was a 1940s knockout, but what they were doing together was all kinds of wrong. Savage didn't exist in 1942. He had no past or future. It could be debated if he existed in 2023. Was running from the FBI a life?

Savage was falling hard for Fontaine. Their lips met for a brief moment in the hallway on the way to her apartment. The smell of her perfume and whiskey filled his nostrils—pure intoxication.

Her second-floor apartment just two blocks from The Montclair was small but tidy. It displayed the barest of amenities of a woman focused on career, but it had all the right feminine touches. Savage wandered around her apartment, taking in clues.

"Who are you, stranger?" Fontaine asked.

"I'm your best nightmare."

"You handled yourself pretty well back there. Do you always blow up anybody who stands in your way?"

"Never bring a knife to a grenade fight."

"Where's the wife and kids?"

"No wife, no kids. I'd like to think I dodged a bullet. I'm a lucky guy."

"Is that what you tell yourself?"

"All day long."

"We're doomed, aren't we?"

"If there's a hell below, we're all gonna go."

"Man in his 50s appears from out of thin air, no wife, no kids? What's your angle?"

"Who me?"

"Yeah, you."

"If I *had* a wife and kids, you'd be complaining that I had a wife and kids."

"Smarty pants."

"What's your excuse?"

"Touché'. I'm a career girl."

"If making things more difficult than they need to be gets you excited, I can talk about a woman's place being in the home and shit like that."

"Sarcastic, aren't you? A little dark. There's a hole inside you, isn't there?"

"Is that a fact?"

"It's a little drafty."

"So, let me get this straight. You spend the better part of your life in a gin-stained booze club with sticky floors entertaining chain-smoking alcoholics, and you're asking if there's a hole inside *me*?"

"Listen, big boy..."

"I accept you as is, dents and all. Why can't you do the same for me?"

"I'm particular about the company I keep. I know a grifter when I see one."

"Right, I'm a low-rent grifter with a hole inside me, and you're the high-yella singer who gets to say whatever she thinks."

"You're a heel."

"I get that a lot."

"You have an answer for everything, don't you?"

"You're a dream."

"I get *that* a lot," Fontaine reflected. The words stopped coming. They looked into each other's eyes like it was the most natural thing in the world. They fell deep in the throes of the moment and the whole world went away.

He drew her close to him. He held her in his arms and kissed her sweetly on the mouth. He could taste her. She moaned. They clung together tightly as he tasted her neck. She tore his shirt off. After getting his pants off he picked her up, cupping her buttocks, and positioned her so she was sitting on top of him. He could feel her full weight as they kissed ravenously. She pulled him onto the bed. Savage leaned over her and removed her dress. Even in low light, he could see a tight stomach and plump breasts.

She looked like a pin-up girl with her lacy bra and panties. When Fontaine unhooked her bra, heaven was revealed with just the right amount of pendulous hang. Savage was so aroused he could hardly control himself as he slid her panties past her knees. A perfectly sculpted mound of pubic hair lay centered between luscious thighs and curvaceous hips. Fontaine was a fresh page in his fantasy file.

He lowered himself on top of her. They kissed and rolled together on her soft bed. He was poised to enter her when he noticed someone was sitting in a chair directly in front of them.

#

"Sorry to interrupt," said Stewart represented as a two-dimensional holographic image smoking a cigarette. Savage's body recoiled in alarm. Everything else in the room was still like a photograph, including Fontaine. Stewart continued. "My name is Dr. Stewart. I'm the one who brought you here."

"Who... What?" Savage said in a state of confusion.

"I'm responsible for all of this. I apologize for the interruption, but I need your help. This world needs you. This is life and death, and you know that."

"And you felt the need to share this with me at this precise moment?"

"This is very important work," Stewart continued. "I take my job very seriously and I need you to do the same. You're distracted. I need you to get focused on the task at hand."

"How did you..."

"Shut up." She inhaled deeply from her cigarette. An ashtray sat on the floor beside her booted foot. She leaned over and flicked the ashes into it, then crossed her legs.

"Stop fucking around," Stewart said with pointed seriousness. "You're thinking with your dick. I need you to aspire to a higher calling—a higher purpose. You're being called upon to do extraordinary things. Get those people out of Paris before you run out of options."

"This doesn't make any sense. Who are you?"

"I'm a designer."

"What does that mean?"

"I design things. What do you think it means? She who designs.

Look, we don't have time for this. I know you have it in you. You and Santiago have all the tools. Save those people, and I'll save you—focus."

Suddenly, Fontaine's front door burst inward with murderous rage.

Thirty-Five

Stewart grimaced inside her diving mask as she took in the salty ocean. As the water trickled in, the pressure inside her skull increased. Light from the surface diminished as she swam deeper. Stewart shivered involuntarily as the frigid depths consumed her. Thoughts of the ocean ruining her perfectly straightened hairdo made her feel stupid. Her new reason to be concerned was this impulsive plan of hers. It tormented her. The stupid idea of swimming so deep underwater using an antiquated breathing apparatus from the 1940s was suddenly all she could think about. And then there was the claustrophobia.

"What was I thinking? Am I going crazy?"

Stewart kicked harder as her fins propelled her downward. She clawed through the abyss as she descended into darkness. The realization that her extremities were freezing made her swim that much harder. Her fingers and toes went numb as her eyes darted from left to right. There was nothing but emptiness.

Tingling sensations increased as her paranoia grew. She felt eerie. Little creatures were brushing up against her. An amphibian tail brushed across the front of her diving mask. She spun around abruptly. It was gone.

There were scary things down there—lurking, watching, with glowing eyes and cruel teeth. Shadowy creatures inhaled her scent to inspect their dinner, then disappeared. Stewart spun around in terror. "Girl, what are you doing?"

This was their world—a world of predators and prey. Her only light source was the pulsating direction signal from her device. She double-checked her position. It was down there alright—somewhere. She swam harder to fight off the anxiety. Visions of sea creatures chewing her lifeless carcass consumed her. "Oh, God—oh, God."

Bizarre, nightmarish creatures could tear her to pieces before she knew it was happening. She would be helpless. What if her air tanks exploded? She could be critically injured, sink to the bottom of the ocean with God knows what kind of internal injuries. And the blood—her blood would attract everything with teeth within a seven-mile radius. Anything could happen in this undersea house of horrors, and there wouldn't be a soul to witness it. She would die alone.

Delusion and reality were becoming harder to distinguish. She was tripping on panic, and her erratic breathing wasn't helping.

"Was all this worth it? Should I have taken the money, had a Coke and a smile, and shut the fuck up? Corporate espionage happens every day of the week. Intellectual property is stolen all the time. The perpetrators are caught, they go to court, and settlements are negotiated. You receive a form letter apology, lawyers get rich, rinse and repeat. It's the way of the world."

Stewart's mind attacked her as she fought off self-induced terrors. She wondered if her annoying Type A personality had been the harbinger of her own demise. Maybe her colleagues were right about her all along. Perhaps she was finally getting what she deserved.

#

"She thinks she's so fucking smart," said the corporate ice blonde to the sharp featured brunette. She checked her face in the mirror as she wiped lipstick off her teeth.

"Always with the bright fucking ideas—always pushing. Would it kill her to take her fat ass home at a reasonable hour? Give the rest of us a fucking break? Fucking bitch. Is she really that clueless? Is she purposely trying to shame everybody? Fuck. Every time I turn around, she's either offering suggestions or making everybody look lazy. I hope that back-stabbing black bitch gets what she deserves in the worst god-damn way. Fuck her. Fuck that bitch."

#

Stewart had hallucinated her way back to eavesdropping on that little tête-à-tête between her colleagues from work. She remembered sitting in the stall of the corporate ladies' room with her feet up, hold-ing her breath. That memory cut deep.

"Bitch ass bitches."

But that flashback suddenly went up in a burst of bubbles. Stewart's reality was so intense, not even the effects of oxygen deprivation could mask what was rushing toward her. In the distance, Stewart could see a large nebulous shape coming right for her. It came swooping through the water at a tremendous speed. It was big, it was frightening, and it was vicious.

Thirty-Six

"The weakest link is the knuckle on the thumb," Santiago said as she sat on a stool in The Montclair's kitchen. She was showing Little Benny how to escape a wristlock. "Always work against the weakest link," she said with firm compassion. "Ok, your turn. You try it." Santiago grabbed Little Benny's right wrist, but he couldn't break her grip. "Jerk your hand downward, then circle up," Santiago said. "Turn against the thumb. That's the weakest link."

Little Benny did it and broke her grip. "I did it!"

"See?"

"That's the stuff!"

"One more time," Santiago said. She grabbed Little Benny's wrist again. He got it right this time, easily breaking her grip.

"Always aim for the weakest link in the chain," Santiago said.

"Well, I'll be a monkey's uncle! Thanks, Miss Dolores."

"Keep that in your brain. You might need it someday."

"You bet."

"One last thing. Once you're free, you strike. You always strike. It's not over until you decide it's over." She touched his Adam's apple. "Feel that?"

"Yep."

"It feels funny, right? Punch them right there with your fist as hard as you can. Break free—Adam's apple. Got it?"

"Break free—Adam's apple."

"How about showing *me* a trick," Buster said, staggering into the kitchen after a long night on the bandstand. "You gotta few tricks for me?"

"I could teach you a lot."

"You don't say? Little Benny, run on to your room. We got grown people stuff to discuss."

"Run along," Santiago said. "I'll show you a new escape tomorrow."

"You promise?"

"Run along."

Benny took off as Buster sized up Santiago. "Explain to me how somebody travels here from the 21st century? More importantly, Why here? Why not the Civil War? You allergic to slave plantations?"

"That's a good question."

"Somethin's fishy. Think about how all this sounds. Do I look stupid to you?"

"Well, you're no Rhodes scholar, but I think academia is overrated."

"You ain't funny."

"It's complicated and not very believable."

"What kind of scam ya'll runnin' here?"

"It's not a scam; we were hit by something. We're here, and we don't know why."

"You could wind up in a straight-jacket for talkin' like that."

"How we arrived here is beside the point. We know what the Nazis are capable of. None of it is good."

"So, we're supposed to pack up and run?"

"I would strongly advise it."

"Pack up and run..."

"Don't bother to pack. Just run, unless of course you feel the need to lose 160lbs before they blow your brains out."

Buster sighed like the life had been sucked out of him.

"All my life I been runnin'."

"You can stick around if you want."

"I been runnin' my whole life. There's nowhere else to run. Everywhere I go, I got somebody's knee in my back—The Mafia, the Klan, Nazis..."

"Maybe you'll find a new Montclair in England—maybe not. But at least you'll be alive. Maybe you can return after the war."

"Please tell me this is some kinda gag."

"We'd be the last people I'd pick to rescue you from the Nazis," Santiago said. "But if beating the shit out of Nazis somehow earns me the right to see my daughter again, then their ass is grass."

Buster shook his head.

"Yeah, I know it sounds crazy," Santiago continued. "But it's true."

"This is *all* messed up."

"Severely."

"I was going to ask Lorraine to marry me. I found a house for us."

Buster reached into his pocket and pulled out a ring box. He opened it. Inside was a shimmering diamond ring.

Santiago was bewildered. "Does Lorraine know how you feel?"

"Oh, *she* knows. Actions speak louder than words."

"Not with women."

"I never felt this way about a girl. I want to take care of her."

"If I were you, I'd become a heroin addict and forget the whole thing."

"Come again?"

"How do they say it? 'Don't hate the player, hate the game?'"

"In English."

"Lorenzo Savage."

"That son of a bitch. I told him to stay away from her."

Unexpectedly, Little Benny rushed in out of breath with a fearful expression on his face. "The krauts caught Boucher!"

#

Fontaine's front door burst inward with murderous rage. Savage and Fontaine were violently startled. Fontaine lurched backward, bumping her head on the wall. They watched Buster calmly stroll into the bedroom amidst broken door fragments as they regained their senses. Carrying a pearl-handled revolver in his right hand and a straight razor in his left, Buster's face was a canvas of pain. He was a shattered man.

His speech was soft but intense. His deadpan stare sliced right through Fontaine.

"When it's cold outside—when the world has gone crazy—when you're alone, and nothing makes sense. If there was one person who would come to your rescue, who would lay down his life for you. It was me. It's always been me."

Fontaine burst into tears. "I had no idea," she whimpered.

Savage jumped off the bed, covering himself as he sized up the situation. Savage and Buster squared off. Savage grabbed a towel and wrapped it around his wrist. Buster moved in closer, slashing with the straight razor with a crazed look in his eye. Even in darkness, Savage could sense that Buster was out of his mind with inconsolable pain.

"Buster!" Savage yelled. "Let's talk!"

"I warned you!"

Fontaine covered herself with bed sheets as Savage and Buster maneuvered around furniture. Buster slashed through the air. Savage backed up. Buster aimed his pistol as Savage charged. They fell backward, knocking over a lamp and desk settings. Savage beat the gun out of his hand with his fist.

Buster over-committed with a wild slash to Savage's exposed ribs. Buster moved in close, but the straight razor was pointing off to the side. Savage sprang forward and grabbed Buster's wrist. He used the momentum and his weight to force Buster backward against the wall. They hit hard, breaking a trio of photographs in glass frames.

They struggled as Buster tried to gain control of the straight razor. Buster was the bigger man but at a disadvantage with no way to use the straight razor.

Savage lifted his arms overhead as he jammed Buster's body against the wall. He used his knee to pummel Buster in the ribcage. His rib cracked as he doubled over in pain.

Still holding Buster's arm wielding the straight razor, Savage twisted Buster's wrist until he screamed. He dropped the straight razor. With blood-curdling rage, Buster yelled and used his body as a battering ram while lifting Savage off his feet. Buster charged forward with all his strength ramming Savage's body into the wall. Savage let out a loud groan as they bounced off the wall and went flying in bed next to Fontaine.

She screamed hysterically. "Oh, my God! Stop! Stop!"

Buster climbed on top of Savage as they traded punches next to Fontaine. Buster's weight pressed down heavily on Savage. The soft bed was no help in giving Savage leverage to roll out from under him. Buster grabbed Savage by the throat and choked him with all his might. His face grimaced in anguish.

"I was going to ask her to marry me, you son of a bitch!"

Fontaine looked on, now fully comprehending the gravity of the moment. "Stop!" Fontaine cried. She leaped off the bed and grabbed the pistol off the floor. "Stop!" She fired two shots into the ceiling. "Stop it, goddamn it!"

Still choking Savage, Buster stared eyeball to eyeball with him. Buster had lost his mind. Behind those eyes was a man in pain—a man whose last chance at love had been crushed to nothingness. "She was the only thing I ever cared about!"

Fontaine cried, "I'm sorry! I'm so sorry!"

Savage strained to roll Buster over to no avail. With as much force as he could muster, he head-butted Buster. Buster didn't move an inch. With no other recourse, Savage repeatedly head-butted Buster in rapid-fire succession. After the fifth strike, Buster's nose was a bloody mess.

He climbed off Savage in a dazed stupor. Savage brought both knees up to his chest and kicked Buster in the stomach, sending him flying backward through an open window. There was silence, then a muted crunch.

Astonishment washed over the faces of Savage and Fontaine as they covered themselves with blood-spattered sheets. They rushed to the window. They looked down to see Buster spread out on the sidewalk one floor below. He moaned softly.

"Jumpin' Jesus!" Savage shouted.

Santiago and Little Benny burst into the room past the splintered doorway.

"What the hell is going on here!?" Santiago yelled.

Savage and Fontaine turned to Santiago.

"He fell out the window," Savage explained, as he caught his breath.

"Lorraine, call an ambulance," Santiago ordered. Fontaine rushed to the phone.

Santiago turned her attention to Savage. "What's your major malfunction?" she asked with disappointment. "Get your clothes on. Schüller's on the rampage."

Thirty-Seven

Before Stewart could command her legs to kick like hell, she was overwhelmed. A massive swarm of giant blood-engorged leeches attached themselves to her body with surreal velocity. Stewart screamed so hard her mask turned sideways. It instantly flooded with water. The impact sent her flying backward. Her mask came off as dozens of slime-covered leeches covered her from head to toe.

Stewart's eyes bulged as she sucked oxygen from her regulator. She blinked spastically to clear her vision. She reached down to her device and typed. She couldn't see what she was typing. Everything was blurred. Her vision was utterly fucked. Amidst the onslaught, she typed code from memory and pressed ENTER—nothing. Everything she typed came up wrong. She could type without seeing the keypad, but the device was failing her again. "Fuck!"

Stewart was helpless. The leeches had attached themselves to her entire body. They drank deeply from her. Stewart's arms flailed as they drove her to the ocean floor. She clawed and kicked. Her terror-fueled screams sent bubbles to the ocean's surface. It took two hands to pry a leech from her face. Once removed, two more would take its place. Blood spread in a rust-colored cloud around her as she fought with every ounce of her being.

Other creatures smelled blood; that's when the frenzy began. Stewart's movements dissipated as other sea creatures came to feast. Her regulator was ripped from her mouth as her wet suit and air tanks were torn away piece by piece. She was helpless. She stepped outside of her body like an apparition to bear witness to her gruesome demise. So much blood, so much sea life, so much for revenge.

Her eyes shifted left and right for anything that could save her—there was nothing. She was alone in the misty forest feeding the eco-system—a gift she never offered.

"This is it?" Stewart said as she faded from consciousness. "This? Everything I've done. Everything I've worked so hard for has come to this?"

Stewart's body drifted. She floated within a cloud of her own blood as sea creatures picked away at her. There was nothing more to do. Nothing to do but shut the fuck up and die.

Thirty-Eight

"You're going to sneak into a concentration camp?!" Ernestine blurted with a stunned look on her face.

"Technically, it's an internment camp," Santiago replied. Savage and Ernestine reacted, equally annoyed with her specificity.

Ernestine, Santiago, Savage, and Charles climbed out of the car. It was the early morning hours. They were parked on the side of the road next to a forest of dense trees. Ernestine opened the trunk to reveal a cache of pistols, hand grenades, and submachine guns. Savage wore a prisoner's shirt and pants, while Santiago wore a German officer's uniform with a skirt, matching blazer, and a Garrison cap. Charles wore Burnhoffer's uniform and a turban.

"It's the only way to get Boucher out of there," Savage replied.

"Are you outta yo' damn mind?" Ernestine blurted. "Poor no luck havin' motherfuckas' are trying to escape concentration camps, and you wanna sneak into one?"

"That's the idea," Santiago replied.

"Concentration camps were built to keep people in," Savage explained. "They're not set up to keep people out."

"That's ridiculous," Charles protested.

"Holy Jesus on the cross," Ernestine remarked.

"Ask Holy Jesus on the cross who tipped Schüller off about Boucher's meeting with the Maquis," Santiago snapped back. "Boucher was trying to arrange an airplane."

"I know you don't think it was me," Ernestine replied.

"Then, who was it?" Savage pressed.

"How the hell should I know?"

"We have to get Boucher out of there," Savage explained as he handed Santiago a Walther P38. "He's our ticket."

"You keep it," replied Santiago. "You'll need it."

"It's the standard German sidearm. Goes with the uniform. We don't want to arouse suspicion for bad historical accessorizing."

Santiago took the pistol.

Ernestine broke in, "Oh, I see—so once you find him, you're just gonna walk right out the front gate?"

"Something like that," Savage replied. He noticed his clothes smelled. "Damn, you couldn't wash these first?"

"It was short notice," Ernestine replied. "Most people say, 'Thank you,' when someone spends money they don't have to get uniforms and guns off the black market."

"Thank you, but these clothes smell like cat piss."

"Schüller ordered the owner of the local dry-cleanin' establishment to be hanged just before you got here—so we're a little behind on the laundry. I apologize for the inconvenience. You can take this up with his wife at his funeral if you'd like."

"What's the idea with the uniform and the turban?" Charles interrupted. "This ain't gonna fool nobody."

"It will," replied Savage. "See, if you were just a nigga' in a Nazi uniform, you'd be shot immediately. Add a turban and you're exotic. You're an exotic Indian Nazi from the Indian Legion. 950th Infantry Regiment —Tiger Legion. For white people, exotic is preferable to being black."

"For cryin' out loud," Charles bellowed. "I don't speak no Indian."

"Make up any mumbo-jumbo Pig Latin you want. Nobody speaks Hindi here."

"Boucher is our only contact with the Resistance," Santiago explained to Ernestine as she holstered her pistol. "We need the Resistance to contact the British. They're the only ones that can help us get everybody out of Paris."

"This plan of yours is nuts," Ernestine said with her hands on her hips.

"There's no other way," Savage said as he stuck a .45 automatic inside the back of his pants. "Boucher is the key. Without him, we're all dead."

"All right," Ernestine relented, shaking her head.

"Take the car back to The Montclair and stay put," Savage ordered. "If you don't hear from us by noon, get yourself and everyone out of town any way you can. You better pray to black baby Jesus; we make it back."

Ernestine blinked, "Black baby Jesus? Jesus is colored?"

"We don't have time for this," Santiago replied.

"Listen, I just wanna say that I... I don't want you to think I'm ungrateful," Ernestine continued. "I... thank you."

"You can put me in your will," Savage replied. "Get out of here."

Putting aside her emotions, Ernestine maneuvered herself into the car, started the engine, and took off down the road. They watched her drive off.

"We need to move fast and get out clean," Savage said. "Get inside the compound and steal a car," he said to Charles. "Keep your eyes focused straight ahead and don't talk to anyone. Your uniform will do the talking. Get behind the wheel and be ready to rumble. You're our exit strategy."

"Put me in a car, and can't nobody catch me," Charles replied. "I once drove a race car for a rich white lady."

"Good to know. Just make sure you have that car ready to go with the engine running," Santiago ordered. "We'll be coming out hot."

"What's the signal?" Charles asked.

"We'll be blowing shit up," Santiago replied

"It's what we do," Savage added.

#

Drancy internment camp located in the northeastern part of Paris was a temporary holding pen for undesirables who would later be sent to a separate camp—one with lots of gas chambers. It was a large, high-rise complex constructed like a rectangular horseshoe centered around a large courtyard.

Originally designed to hold 700 prisoners, it now held thousands including military personnel. Human traffic was in constant flow as prisoners arrived through the front gate and departed to their deaths via conveniently located trains in the rear.

Swarms of Parisian Jews, gypsies, and undesirables disembarked buses and were checked through the front gate. Savage and Santiago blended in easily, walking through the crowd past the guards. Savage strode slightly ahead of Santiago, giving the appearance that Savage was Santiago's prisoner.

Leisurely strolling past the guards, not making eye contact, they marched deeper into the compound. Santiago moved just behind Savage and to his right. "We're in. Two o'clock. Thinks long term staring is socially acceptable even in 1942."

"Maybe he's Armenian."

"Please, shut the fuck up."

#

Charles stood inside the compound paralyzed as an Indian soldier from the Tiger Legion spoke to him excitedly in Hindi. Charles looked as if he was having a stroke. His face was frozen with surprise. The soldier continued to talk uninterrupted when his expression changed. He could see something wasn't right with Charles.

#

Suddenly, Savage and Santiago were startled by an abrupt command from behind them.

"Lieutenant!"

Savage and Santiago stopped in their tracks. They turned to see a greasy German guard walking toward them. He saluted Santiago.

"Excuse me, Lieutenant. What is your business here?"

"This is one of Major Schüller's tap-dancing darkies from The Montclair," Santiago responded. "He is to be held here until the major can question him."

"He is a tap dancer?"

"Yes. Major Schüller has special plans for this one. If you'll excuse me, we'll be on our way."

"I like tap dancing. I would like to see this tap dancing."

Savage gave Santiago a nervous look. The guard turned to his two fellow soldiers who were moving toward them from behind.

"Klaus! Heinrich! He is a tap dancer!"

Klaus and Heinrich stopped in front of Savage and Santiago.

"You are a tap dancer?" Heinrich asked in broken English.

"Nein," Savage replied. He turned Santiago. "I am not tap dancing."

The first guard gave Santiago a strange look. "You said he was a tap dancer. Did you not say he was a tap dancer?"

"He's a *shy* tap dancer. I don't think he feels like tap dancing right now. His wife was shot in front of the Eiffel Tower this morning. You know how sensitive artists can be."

Savage shook his head, not believing she just said that.

"We want to see tap dancing," said the first guard. "Give us a show!"

"Yes, I love the schwarzes and their tap dancing," Klaus said with excitement.

"I don't give a shit what you love," Savage replied. "I'm not tap dancing."

The first guard looked at Santiago curiously. "Excuse me. I have never seen you here before. May I see your orders?"

Santiago turned to Savage. "So, you couldn't have done a little step-ball-change so we could avoid this, right?"

"Tap dancing darkies? Really? Why bring up tap dancing? There was no need to bring up tap dancing. Sorry, I don't do jazz hands."

"But, you *do* tap dance; you just won't?"

"You think all black people can tap dance?"

"I didn't say that. You're implying you can tap dance but won't."

"Just because I'm black doesn't mean I can tap dance."

"I didn't say that."

"That's what you inferred."

"You mean 'imply.' 'Inferred' means to extract meaning from some kind of evidence."

"Are you fucking serious?"

Heinrich butted in. "Something is not right here. Lieutenant, show me your orders."

"I want to see some tap dancing," Klaus said with a joyous laugh.

"Ich tanze nicht Stepptanz," Savage snarled.

"Show me your orders, Lieutenant," Heinrich repeated.

They all stared at each other for a long beat waiting for someone to make the first move. Savage matter-of-factly reached back under his waistband, pulled out his .45, and shot Heinrich in the chest. Heinrich flew backward and fell on the ground with a stunned expression on his face.

"Oh, for crying out loud," Santiago yelled.

She grabbed the front of the first guard's helmet and twisted his head around with a quick jerking motion and a loud pop. He went down with a thud.

Savage shot Klaus in the throat, driving him backward. He dropped his machine gun and fell to the ground as a geyser of blood sprayed upward. An alarm went off in the compound. Guards and prisoners began rushing into the courtyard in all directions.

"Now you've done it," Santiago said.

"We needed a distraction," Savage said as he picked up the sub-machine gun. "We're finding Boucher and getting the fuck out of here. I hate France."

Savage and Santiago took off toward the apartment complex as guards and prisoners swarmed everywhere.

"Boucher!" Savage called out looking around frantically as prisoners ran by.

Shots were fired at Savage and Santiago as they ducked into the hallway of the building. The compound had escalated into violent chaos.

"I'll go upstairs and work my way around," said Savage. "You take the lower level. We'll meet back in the courtyard with Boucher."

"Great plan," replied Santiago. Savage gave Santiago the middle finger then ran up a stairwell. Santiago moved down the garbage-lined hallway. "Boucher! Boucher!"

She passed open doorways and looked inside to see huddled families. She pushed forward, calling Boucher's name. She turned down a hallway when she saw three French guards making their way toward her.

"I'm looking for a prisoner," Santiago said with her best ball-busting German tone. "A dwarf named Boucher. Where can I find him?"

"He is downstairs in the interrogation room," one of the officers said in German with a French accent. "We heard gunshots. What is happening?"

"There was a problem with a prisoner. It's been taken care of. Return to your posts."

"I am afraid I do not recognize your authority," the guard said. "Who are you?"

"I am an officer of The Third Reich, simpleton. I'll have you cleaning gas chambers for the rest of the war if you don't show me the proper respect!"

"A thousand pardons, ma'am. We do not see many female officers— especially one so... *magnifique*. We meant no disrespect. Perhaps we can offer you a drink before we escort you to the interrogation room?"

"Return to your posts at once!"

One of the other guards stepped forward. He took off his helmet to reveal a baldhead with a scar that ran down the middle of his face. "There is a room nearby with a bed. Would you like to relax a bit before you return to duty? We have good French wine. Unlike German men, the French know how to please a woman."

Santiago broke from speaking German. "Get the fuck outta here!"

The three guards grabbed Santiago and dragged her to a nearby apartment. As she struggled, they kicked in the door. A Jewish peasant woman and her young daughter were startled and ran out of the apartment past them. The guards dragged Santiago kicking and screaming and threw her on a stained mattress. The first guard looked down at her.

"They told us there would be benefits to Germany's occupation of Paris, but I had no idea we would meet a woman such as you." He began to take his clothes off. "You can take it rough or rougher, whichever you prefer."

"You guys want to rape me? Really? I could have sworn you guys were cock gobbling homos."

The guards gave each other a perplexed look.

"No," the bald man with the scar said. "We *love* women. We hold them in the highest regard."

They pounced on her together. Santiago spun her legs in a circle and kicked one of the men in the face, altering his course. It sent him crashing into a dresser. The other guard landed on top of her. Her legs were crouched beneath him. She sprung him upward and back, propelling him into the wall. He slammed hard and fell to the floor. The guard with the scar mounted her and grabbed her by the throat as he tore off her jacket.

"Welcome to Paris."

She drew her legs up and scissored his ribs with her thighs. Santiago snapped her thighs together in a quick jerking motion producing a loud pop. Santiago had crushed the guard's ribs. A tortured expression on his face preceded his relaxed grip on her. She punched him hard in the jaw sending him rolling off in agonizing pain.

Santiago jumped to her feet. She grabbed two empty wine bottles and broke off the bottom ends against each other. She pointed the jagged bottles in their direction with savagery in her eyes.

"Get up, pendejos! Take your punishment."

The guards regained their senses. They were in serious trouble. Santiago realized someone was standing behind her in the doorway.

"Don't let *me* interrupt," said a familiar voice. "Please continue. This is highly entertaining."

Santiago turned to see Major Schüller aiming a pistol at her.

#

Savage cautiously moved down the garbage-lined hallway holding an MP40. "Boucher!"

A German soldier turned a corner down the hall and saw him. Savage mowed him down with a burst of bullets. "Boucher!"

Savage continued forward, rounding the corner and walked directly into two armed German soldiers. One of them knocked the machine gun from Savage's hands. Savage recovered and punched the closest German in the jaw. The blow sent the soldier backward, leaving the previous soldier to grab Savage in a bear hug. He lifted Savage off the floor. Savage squirmed in pain as he felt his spine being crushed.

The other soldier regained his senses. He aimed his rifle at Savage, who was being lifted off his feet. Before he fired, Savage jerked the soldier's body in a semi-circle. The bullet hit Savage's attacker in the back of the head. His brains exploded on to Savage's chest. Savage was released and fell to the floor.

The other soldier froze, realizing his mistake. Taking advantage of the pause in the action, Savage rushed the soldier tackling him to the floor. He climbed on top of the soldier, but the soldier was stronger and rolled on top of him. He choked Savage with both hands around his neck. Savage strained to release the pressure.

He grabbed the soldier's right thumb and twisted it multiple times with a jerking motion until it broke. The soldier screamed as Savage rolled on top of him. Savage immobilized his arm with his armpit. Rising, Savage used his elbow to crash violently down into his face. The soldier went limp.

Savage panted with exhaustion. He took a moment to regain his senses. He saw stars and tried to clear his head. He looked up and was hit on the side of the head with a rifle butt. The stars disappeared.

Thirty-Nine

Stewart was out like a light stretched out on the cold floor of a decompression chamber. Although unconscious, she was aware of the pulsating vibrations of a vast mechanized behemoth. Advanced generators hummed beneath her like a purring monolith. Soaking wet and sore, she could have stayed there forever. After the horror she had experienced, she had no problem surrendering to the floor's warm comforting pulse. Her serenity was broken when she heard a voice.

"Baby girl."

Stewart opened her eyes to see Palmer's smiling face. He was dressed in a wet suit with a diving mask fixed on his forehead. "How you doin', baby girl?"

Stewart struggled to pull her thoughts together. "Why do you call me baby girl? I'm a grown woman."

"I'm from New Orleans," he said as he affectionately caressed her cheek. "It's a term of endearment."

"What happened?" Stewart asked as she took in her surroundings. "Where are we? Are we..."

"You're alive."

Stewart struggled to sit up but found it too difficult. She collapsed back on the floor. She noticed a giant leech lying next to her. She reacted by kicking it away violently. Palmer tried to calm her. "It's dead. Now, rest yourself," Palmer ordered with southern compassion. He touched her hair. "You're safe. For now, anyway."

"I feel awful."

"We need to talk."

"I'm sick."

"Yeah, you don't look too good, but you're still a dish."

"Thanks. It's good to know that being physically attractive is important even after being eaten by giant predatory worms."

"Some people got it; some people don't."

"Thank you. That's nice of you to say. I've taught myself to take a compliment without qualifying it. Let's move on."

"It was pretty wicked out there. You want some dope weed? It'll make you feel better. Gets rid of the nausea."

"You brought marijuana?"

"You smoke reefers, right?"

"You want to light up a joint right now?"

"Now is as good a time as any."

"You brought marijuana with you on a scuba diving mission?!"

"If you don't want none, just say so. This is good shit—not easy to get with the Übermensch runnin' around."

"I'd love a shot of bourbon."

"Sorry."

"Indica or Sativa?"

"What?"

"I can't smoke Sativa. It makes me flip out. Paranoid delusions, panic attacks, night terrors. It's bad, real bad."

"I call that Tuesday. You mind if *I* light up?"

"Light that bitch up."

Palmer unzipped the front of his wet suit. He took out a fat joint and a lighter. He immediately lit it up and took a hit.

"You saved my life," Stewart said.

"This is true."

"Thank you. But how? You said you couldn't swim."

"I said I *don't* swim. I didn't say I *couldn't* swim. I'm an excellent swimmer. I don't like things touchin' me underwater. Gives me the heebie-jeebies. I'm a pool swimmer."

That made Stewart smile. "A Pool swimmer?"

"That means…"

"I know what a pool swimmer is."

"That must have been pretty scary," Palmer continued. "I can't think of anything more terrifying than being eaten alive. That was one of yo' simulations, right?"

Stewart thought about that. "I never designed any giant underwater sea leeches." She looked around the chamber. "This was part of my father's terraforming infrastructure."

"Where did the leeches come from?"

"It came from the bastard who sabotaged my game."

"You scared the shit outta me floatin' out there." He offered her a hit of the joint. She declined.

"I appreciate what you did," Stewart said.

"Good. Let's get on up outta here. Lucky I found this place. There was no way I coulda' swam back to the boat with you."

Stewart's body jerked in fear as she realized something was very wrong—something was missing. "My device! Where is it?!" Stewart looked all around in a panic.

"You lookin' for this?" Palmer said calmly. He produced the device with a smile and handed it to her.

"Goddamn it!" Stewart bellowed in relief.

"Good thing it lights up. I chased it and caught it before it hit bottom." Palmer gave her a coquettish wink. "I figured you might find it useful."

"You figured goddamn right I'd find it useful! Without this I… It would be over. It would be all over."

She grabbed the device and turned it on. It seemed to be working perfectly. She exhaled in relief. "Thank you. Everything is working fine."

"That squares us, right?"

"What do you mean?"

"You saved my life, I saved yours. Even Steven."

"We're square. Even Steven."

They kissed without compunction. Stewart was surprised by her impulsiveness.

"Now, let's get on up outta here," Palmer said as he helped Stewart to her feet. Stewart was still light-headed as she tried to find her balance on spaghetti legs.

Palmer put Stewart's arm over his shoulder as he guided her along the nautical corridor. His arm was around her waist. They opened a hatch door and stepped into the next passage. They staggered forward as the vibrations grew louder and more intense.

They were bathed in a flashing red light that reflected off the pipe-lined corridor. The vibrations and the lights gave off an eerie subterranean ambiance.

Coming to a fork in the passageway, Stewart checked the tracking field on her device. "We're close. We're almost there."

They stepped through another chamber that led to a different passageway. Stewart checked the device as Palmer kept his eyes peeled. Stewart led them forward. Suddenly, she realized they were right on top of the signal. Stewart was puzzled. There was nothing in the corridor, just more passageway.

"End of the line?" Palmer inquired anxiously.

"Seems that way," Stewart said as she looked around. "There's nothing here. It must be on a different level."

"That means up. We're already on the bottom. This place is huge."

Palmer opened the door and walked through the next portal. It was an enclosed area.

"Look, we need to talk," Palmer said. "There's something I need to tell you."

Suddenly, a fist came slamming into Palmer's face. He went down hard.

Stewart recoiled. Mordecai stood in the doorway wearing a jade-colored flight suit. The wicked grin on his grizzled face was that of a serial killer's serial killer.

Forty

Two Weeks Earlier — 2023

"I found your money," Joslyn said nervously with a utilitarian smile. Savage knew this was coming. She nosed through his belongings when he left her alone at his place. He knew she wouldn't be able to help herself. She didn't have the attention to detail to return things exactly the way she found them.

"Money?" Savage replied as he nursed a gin and tonic.

"In the closet in the back."

"You were in my closet?"

"I wasn't snooping."

"You found four million dollars in cash in a locked trunk underneath the complete Marshall Cavendish Illustrated Encyclopedia Of World War II, and you weren't snooping?"

"I was curious."

Joslyn and Savage sat across from one another inside a booth at Corky's Diner. Joslyn always made Savage feel like she was doing him a favor coming to his favorite diner. Corky's reminded her of her 89-year-old father with its red leather tuck and roll booths and vintage photography. Savage loved old photographs. In his mind they were a doorway to another time.

"That's a lot of money," Joslyn said. "Where did it come from?"

"It's ours."

"Did you kill someone?"

"Be careful what you think you need to know."

"Where did you get it?"

"I can't tell you that."

"You're a criminal."

"I'm a professional."

"What does that mean?"

"You paid your roommate to take your college final exam because you couldn't be bothered to study for it. Does that make *you* a criminal?"

"That's not fair."

"You bribed a university official to help your daughter get into Yale. Does that make *you* a criminal?"

"You take personal things I share with you and throw it back in my face. You fight dirty."

"Let's discuss reality."

"I don't feel safe. I can't trust you."

"Trust? You searched me on the Internet. In the old days, you'd hire a PI to follow me around to find out who I am and what I do. Nowadays, you type my name into a search engine. But that's different, right?"

"Right. It *is* different. You're living in the past."

"That money is for us. We can do anything we want. We can have a life together."

"You want me to go on the run with you? Is that what you're asking me?"

"I'm off the grid—I'm clean. We can travel wherever we want, we can *be* whatever we want." Savage stared back at her as a young waitress with a 50s hair-do appeared. "You guys doin' ok?"

"We're fine. Thank you." Savage replied calmly. Sensing her intrusion, the waitress skirted away.

"We can do what we want," said Savage. "I want to marry you. That's what I want more than anything in the world."

Joslyn paused as her face flushed with emotion.

"I want to spend the rest of my life with you," Savage continued.

This was the moment of truth. Joslyn had been on the fence for months. Each day she didn't take control of her life and break it off with Savage made things more difficult.

"Lorenzo, you're a wonderful man. But..."

"What? What's the problem? Don't I make you happy?"

"I can't see it. I don't see us growing old together. I don't see us together when we're 80. I watch my father and his wife. I watch elderly couples in love walking in the park together. They look content—happy. We'll never be those people."

"How could you possibly know that?"

"You have a darkness inside you—secrets. Something happened to you. I don't know what it is, and I can't... I'm not saying you're a bad person. I love you, but I choose to walk in the light. I want to be happy. I want to be around happiness and light."

"Who doesn't? I do too. I changed my life for you. I got out of the business so we could be together. I don't want to walk in the darkness. I want to walk in the light—with you. I want to be happy—with you."

"My therapist says I have the right to break up with you."

"You told your therapist about me?"

"I've been struggling. When I found the money, I..."

That was the moment when Savage realized all the happiness they ever had would be lost to eternity like piss in the rain.

"Joslyn, I stood by you—your kidney transplant, the car accident, your kids, when your mother died, I... I was there for all of that. For you. I..."

"I know. Thank you. I'm grateful for all of that."

"I adore you."

"I can't live the way you live, Lorenzo. The way you dress. The first time I saw where you lived, I wanted to run right out the door. You don't cook. You don't eat clean. You don't even recycle. I want to live authentically."

"What the fuck are you talking about? Is this that Tony Robbins shit again? How important is that in the grand scheme of things? We can live however we want. Look at what we have."

"I'm sorry," Joslyn said as her eyes watered.

She picked up a napkin off the table and wiped her tears.

"You can't do this," Savage said as hope drained from his soul. His mind sought the words that would turn things around. "We laugh."

"Lorenzo..."

"Joslyn, I love you. I want to be with you for the rest of my life."

"Lorenzo..."

"I was better to you than anybody in my whole life."

"I'm sorry. I'm sorry, Lorenzo."

She reached into her purse and pulled out a gold pendant attached to a thin chain. Engraved on it was written:

Joslyn + Lorenzo Forever

She pushed it toward him across the table. Savage could hardly get the words out. "You've made the biggest mistake of your life."

Forty-One

"You, again!" Stewart bellowed.

"Yes, me again," Mordecai replied in his mellifluous Mid-Atlantic accent. "You couldn't do as you were told, could you? You couldn't follow simple instructions."

"No, I couldn't," Stewart replied as she casually swung the device behind her back.

"I'm sure you know what's next," Mordecai said.

"You're going to destroy the virus and apologize to me for ruining my father's life's work?"

"I find your sarcasm off-putting."

"If you destroy the virus, I'll vouch for you back home. They'll go easy on you and your maker. I give you my word."

"Go easy on us?" Mordecai laughed. "I love to laugh. Unfortunately, you're too late. The coordinates are set. The virus will be unleashed upon impact. You can't stop us. This little happy accident of genius has become far too lucrative. The Organization isn't going to turn their backs on billions of dollars in revenue just because you feel funny inside. What you created was wildly innovative, but like all innovations, someone comes along and does it better. Why can't you see the big picture?"

"It's a terrible picture. Who's behind this?"

"A plan of this magnitude could only come from a visionary. A scientific auteur, a genius—and a loyal facilitator like myself to ensure its success."

"Can you be more specific?"

"Every knee shall bow; every tongue shall confess."

"If you love him so much, why don't you marry him?"

"You're going to die at the bottom of the ocean."

Palmer butted in holding his sore jaw. "Look man, we visited that crazy-ass simulation of yours. Ain't you got better things to do? I would be more than happy to help you find another hobby."

"Where you see death and destruction, we see reconstruction and resurrection," Mordecai replied. "You have to tear down a building before you can rebuild it."

"And sometimes buildings become ruins," Stewart replied. "We're talking about an extinction-level event. If that virus makes its way back home, we're dead—we're all dead.

"I disagree."

"You're on the wrong side of this."

"Is that your opinion?"

"*Your* opinion is incorrect."

"An opinion cannot be correct or incorrect. It is a view, a perspective, a judgment."

"No, there are incorrect opinions, and yours smacks of insanity."

"What are you going to do about it?"

"Make your move, robot."

Mordecai winced and was overcome with emotion.

"I would appreciate it if you wouldn't call me that. Robot is an offensive and inappropriate slur. Especially to *my* series."

"You're an expensive appliance created by someone with extremely low self-esteem."

"It will bring me great pleasure to watch you die."

Stewart whipped the device from around her back and pointed it at him. She pressed a button—nothing happened. They stood for a moment looking at one another.

"Shit!" Stewart cried as she retyped the code.

Mordecai slammed the door and locked it from the outside. He looked through the porthole and frowned. Stewart and Palmer tried to open the door. It was sealed tight.

"I'd like to say it was a pleasure meeting you, but it wasn't," Mordecai said. "You said hurtful things. Enjoy the afterlife—if there is one."

Mordecai flipped a switch outside the door. Suddenly, a door slammed shut behind them. Thick black sewage rushed into the chamber. Before they knew it, they were waist-deep in slime.

"Oh, hell no!" Palmer blurted.

Mordecai was overcome with emotion from behind the door, then walked away. Stewart furiously typed away on the device.

"What do we do?!" Palmer yelled.

"Hold on; I'm trying! Give me a second," Stewart replied. Stewart had to hold the device high above the muck to see what she was doing. The compartment filled up rapidly with a whirlpool of black liquid goo. Stewart and Palmer stood on their toes to keep their heads above it.

"We're not going to make it!" Palmer screamed as the liquid rose over their heads.

Beneath the goo, Stewart and Palmer held their breath. Palmer searched in vain for a way out.

Stewart grew frustrated as the device refused to work. She continued typing as Palmer's movements slowed. Stewart grew light-headed as she fought to stay conscious. Palmer convulsed, then went limp. Stewart couldn't see, and her eyes burned. She slammed her eyes shut. She sucked in a large gulp of the black substance. Her body jerked involuntarily. Her eyes bulged open in terror. Stewart and Palmer vanished.

#

Stewart and Palmer materialized 47,000 feet above *Simulated Earth*—then dropped through the atmosphere. Still unconscious, they plummeted through the cloud cover, spiraling at an incredible rate of speed. Still soaked in black liquid, a shock of cold air slapped them awake. Their eyes opened. They tumbled and rolled as they dropped through thick billowy clouds and fierce winds.

The Earth became visible beneath them. A vast landmass grew more prominent as it rushed up beneath them. Stewart and Palmer heard screaming. They looked at one another and realized that *both* of them were doing the screaming.

"Oh my God, oh my God, oh my God!" Palmer yelled as Stewart fought back crippling panic and tried to type on her device.

"I... I... I can fix this! I can fix this!" Stewart screamed.

"I don't want to die!?" Palmer screamed.

"I'm trying!" Stewart replied as she fought fierce winds while typing. "Hold on!"

They tumbled downward as the landmass grew closer. Below them was a mountain. Details of the mountain came into view as their descent quickened. They were heading straight for the side of a jagged cliff. Palmer's face winced in terror as he struggled to process their predicament.

Stewart wept with frustration. Her tears and the wind clouded her vision as the device failed to work. She kept typing as the mountain sped up beneath them.

Palmer closed his eyes. He was paralyzed with fear. "Make this go away," he whispered.

Stewart stopped typing as her body went numb. There was nothing to do. She was consumed in paralyzing fear, but so what? It was all going to be over soon. She stared upward into the empty sky as she pondered the days that led to this moment. She saw her father's face. He smiled at her lovingly.

"You do good work, but there's always a tiny speck of shit on it, isn't there?"

-Dr. Aloysius Stewart

Stewart recoiled in anguish. She looked down at the craggy rocks below. The mountain came shooting up right under them. They were going to smash into a rocky crevasse at 120 miles per hour. They wouldn't feel a thing. At that speed, they would break every bone in their bodies and die instantly. Stewart passed out. Just before they smashed into the mountain, they were gone.

\#

Stewart and Palmer woke instantly. They materialized just below the surface of the ocean. The shock of finding themselves submerged in below-freezing temperatures stunned the fuck out of them. Palmer pissed on himself. The freezing cold produced involuntary muscle spasms and a searing chill that coursed inside their bones. It was painful agony.

Chunks of ice floated by as they watched helplessly. Behind them in the distance, a massive ocean liner was sinking and headed to the ocean floor. On the bow of the ship was written RMS TITANIC. Hundreds of dead bodies floated around them. Palmer turned his head and suddenly found himself face-to-face with the ghostly white corpse of an ensign from the ship. He panicked and kicked it away, recoiling from the shock.

The blurry blue-green water enveloped them as their brain functions struggled to comprehend what was happening. Stewart and Palmer were freezing to death. They kicked frantically in heart-bursting panic as they craved oxygen.

Palmer looked to Stewart for help. His face was contorted and ugly. He was freezing so severely he couldn't keep his mouth closed to hold his breath. Stewart typed on her device furiously. "Too slow, too slow."

She thought she'd found the trick to hacking around the damaged device, but it was useless. "Fuck!"

The coordinates she typed weren't locking into the system. It was rejecting her code. Stewart screamed. Oxygen expelled from her mouth in the form of bubbles as she turned to notice a big black shape. It was soaring through the water right toward them. It was a massive shark. Stewart and Palmer were floating right in its path.

"Too cold, too cold," Stewart murmured. Her eyeballs froze solid.

Palmer inhaled water. The shark's mouth opened. Freakishly massive jaws opened to reveal a gigantic flesh tunnel with rows of jagged teeth.

Just before the shark's jaws slammed shut, Stewart and Palmer disappeared in a blizzard of bubbles.

Forty-Two

Summer — 1942

By the early 21st century, you'd be hard-pressed to find anybody who wasn't taking the sleep medication Ambien to turn off their brains to get some shut eye. Savage considered it a wonder drug. But there was something better than Ambien. It was a tougher sell, but it got the job done—and you didn't wake up the next day to discover you bought a bunch of stupid shit on eBay.

Getting clocked in the head with a Gewehr 41 rifle butt is the best sleep you'll ever have. All your worries disappear into peaceful nothing-ness—complete darkness.

Everything you are, everything you ever were, and everything you think you are, become meaningless. R&D consultants would have to figure out a way around waking up with a bloody scalp, but if you've ever been strung out for 36 hours because of lack of sleep, you'll gladly take a smack to the head from the Wehrmacht.

For Savage, being knocked out allowed him to escape the velocity of his surroundings. But that was all coming to an end. He was waking up, and his head hurt like hell.

"Jumpin' Jesus," he thought to himself.

He could feel the dried blood tightening around his ear. Fortunately, he had the sagacity to wake up while still appearing unconscious. Hunched forward, sitting in a chair with his wrists tied behind him,

Savage peered through partially closed eyelids. He felt the clumsily tied knots that bound his wrists. "What is this, amateur hour?" he mumbled to himself.

He could have been out of those ropes in seconds but chose to wait. He gathered he was in an interrogation room. Originally a wine cellar, a tall wooden wine rack took up the length of the wall behind them. A dozen or so wine bottles sat among many empty slots. The floors and walls were filthy, with dark splotches of dirt and dried blood.

Boucher sat next to him tied up as well. His short legs dangled over the edge of the chair. He was wearing the same gray prison uniform Savage wore. He was conscious with a look of defiance scrawled across his lips. He had a black eye, a busted lip, and oozing black burn marks on his neck. He sat unfazed like he could take anything the Nazis had to dish out. Savage was impressed. Boucher was a tough little bastard.

Two massive, black-uniformed German soldiers stood near the exit carrying submachine guns. And there was Schüller in all his immaculate Nazi glory. He stood beside a grey-bearded doctor named Holzlöhner, who wore a lab coat and held a bloody scalpel.

Santiago sat tied to a chair between them. Like Boucher, she'd taken a severe beating. They'd torn off her uniform blazer, leaving only a ripped blouse exposing her bra. Her athletic body displayed welts and burns on her chest, thighs, and forearms. Her skirt was splattered with bits of blood that trickled down her bare legs. They smacked her around pretty good, but Santiago's obstinacy remained intact as she glared at them with a crooked grin.

Schüller moved close to Santiago. He looked at her like a child looking at a bug through a magnifying glass. "American women are so arrogant, so spoiled. I've seen your American films—thin, fast-talking, with your annoying little quips. American women act as if they're too good for anyone. You turn your nose up—so entitled, so infuriating. Men like myself simply aren't up to your standards, are we? You treat us like servants. I'd trade seven of you undernourished harpies for one wide-hipped Bavarian hausfrau!"

Schüller paced in front of Santiago, revealing the depths of his whacked-out mind. Santiago sat expressionless following him with her eyes. Savage, still feigning unconsciousness, turned his head ever so slightly to make eye contact with Boucher. Their eyes met with a look of recognition.

"I could never stomach the touch of a man," Santiago said to Schüller with a bloody lip.

"I like pussy. No, I *love* pussy. No dick for me, thank you very much. The thought of a dick disgusts me. Dildos are fine. There's no man attached. Men are pigs. Have you ever had a dick shoved up your ass?"

Schüller and everyone else in the room reacted to her audacity. She'd managed to loosen the ropes that bound her wrists, but they weren't loose enough for a clean attack.

Santiago wasn't worried. Now was the time to stall so she could recharge and slip out of her ropes. She could kick the McNuggets out of both Schüller and the doctor, but it was the two soldiers and their MP40s she was worried about. She would have the element of surprise, but it could all go up in a hail of bullets if she underestimated these death-dealing murderers. Without her arms free, she'd get killed right alongside Savage and Boucher—an amateur's move.

"Here's a question," Santiago asked. "Which sounds more appealing to you? The soft touch of smooth, beautifully manicured nails gently caressing your face? Or perhaps the fresh smell of a woman's hair after she's washed it. It tickles your nose and fills your senses. How about the taste of a firm nipple between your lips? And can anyone truly resist the irresistible aroma of a vagina?"

Schüller and the doctor gave each other a look of uneasiness while the two soldiers did the same. Savage turned his head slightly to Boucher to see his reaction. Everyone thought to themselves, "What the fuck?"

"That scent will make you whine like a puppy," Santiago continued. "You'd slap your own mother to have another whiff of that. The pungent aroma of vagina just inches from your face. You can taste her even before your lips touch it. It's a narcotic. It's the kind of drug that will put you in a trance. Blood rushes between your legs, and you become an animal. An animal ready to plunge into that vagina with the power of a human juggernaut."

Schüller and the doctor were speechless, hypnotically seduced by the imagery. And then...

"Now imagine a *man* touching you," Santiago continued. "A crude, putrid-smelling human—a man who never learned to wipe his ass properly. A man whose hands smell like piss and sardines. A man who lacks the most basic sense of intimacy. A man who wants to smear your face with his feces-stained beard and ram his ugly excuse for a penis in your ass. Now tell me which one of those scenarios sounds more appealing?"

Schüller and the doctor stared at her blankly.

"I'll stick to girls, thank you very much," Santiago continued. "Then again, if you prefer a filthy fat fuck's cock in your mouth, so be it. Who am I to judge?"

"Lesbisch," Schüller said, laughing with an insulting tone. "When you put it that way, I can't blame you. Still, it will be satisfying to break you. I'm looking forward to hearing you beg me to stop hurting you."

"Kann ich eine zigarette haben?" Santiago asked, as she surreptitiously continued to loosen her ropes.

"You speak German. Excellent. I'll torture you in two languages."

Schüller leisurely walked over to the table and picked up a pack of cigarettes. He took one out of the package and put it between his lips. He took a wooden match off the table and struck it off Savage's ear. Savage didn't move a muscle. Schüller watched Santiago curiously. He inhaled deeply from the cigarette, then took it out of his mouth and put it into hers. Santiago took a drag and blew the smoke out of her nostrils.

"Soften her up good for me," Schüller told the doctor. "I want her purring like a kitten."

"Please hurry back," Santiago pleaded with deadpan sarcasm.

"Make her beg," Schüller ordered.

#

Ernestine's car pulled off the road and into the trees. The darkness and foliage provided excellent cover from the main road. Charles, who was still wearing the turban and Nazi uniform, was sitting in the passenger seat. Little Benny crouched in the back seat with his eyes peeled as he clutched an MP40.

Ernestine had a bee in her bonnet, and she was running out of options. The overwhelming pressure was causing her to make hasty decisions.

"Ok, I need you Johnny-on-the-spot," Ernestine said to Charles. "Grab a rifle and walk me in. As soon as we find out where they're bein' held, we make a beeline out of there—pronto. We tell the Resistance, and they bust everybody out."

"Ernestine, I was just in there. I barely got out. Who knew they had a real Indian in there?"

"You' goin' back!"

"If that Indian sees me again, I'm dead."

"We're gettin' Boucher and those two weirdos outta there—we need their help to get that plane."

"Ernestine, I came to Europe to play guitar. I'm not cut out for spyin'."

"You think I wanna do this? My feet hurt, my bra is too tight, and I'm outta time. I gave The Montclair everything... but it's over. Right now, I just wanna get my husband, and get the hell out of this God-forsaken country."

"Ok! Ok! This getup should get us through the side entrance. Once we're inside, it shouldn't be too hard to find where they're being held. Getting out is another story."

"I'll cover you when you come out," Little Benny said. "Any monkey business and I'll let 'em have it." He locked a clip into the MP40. "They'll get what's comin'."

"You' stayin' in the car," cautioned Ernestine.

"Rats," Little Benny replied.

"If you see white people, shoot first and ask questions later."

"Solid."

"When we get in," Charles cautioned. "We have to stay close together. There's too many people. It's easy to get split up. We enter together; we leave together."

"How the hell did we get here?" Ernestine sighed.

"Bad luck."

"I'll say."

"Some people get dumb luck, some people get bad luck, and some people get the short end of the stick."

From out of nowhere, 11 German soldiers surrounded the car with their rifles trained on them. A symphony of chambered rounds filled their ears. Ernestine, Charles, and Little Benny froze.

"Is this dumb luck or bad luck?" Ernestine asked.

"It's the short end of the stick," Charles replied.

#

Doctor Holzlöhner had his work cut out for him. He thought, "Who was this woman? Where did she come from?" She had the kind of obstinate courage he had never witnessed before. She wielded a stoic countenance that betrayed nothing. She was excellent–a perfect specimen. She was obviously a highly trained spy. It would be an honor to break her until she was no more than a sobbing pile of flesh.

Eventually, she would tell him everything they wanted to know. Holzlöhner would take his time working slowly and meticulously. He recalled how well dismemberment worked and how the subjects quickly changed their tune. They were so eager to comply.

He knew working on the American would be tedious at first. He believed this was all valid research in the service of Der Führer. But deep down, he would be taking his sweet time to savor her torment. Breaking down this bitch would be a pleasure, and eventually, she would beg him to become his willing slave.

Holzlöhner was exactly three centimeters away from cutting into Santiago's left eyeball with a filthy scalpel. Then he heard something that broke his concentration. It was the sound of two faint explosions coming from outside the door. He looked over at the two soldiers who also heard it. They tensed with concern.

Suddenly, a barrage of gunfire erupted from a great distance. Everyone's head turned to look in the same direction. They froze for a full three seconds. They heard a loud explosion and screaming. All hell was breaking loose somewhere in the compound.

This was the distraction Santiago had been waiting for. She made eye contact with Savage. Suddenly, there was a teeth-rattling explosion that was too close for comfort. Like a jaguar, she sprang into action. Savage stood up and kicked one of the distracted soldiers in the testicles. Santiago's knee shot up like a missile into Holzlöhner's solar plexus. It sent him flying backward into a nearby table and into the wall. The table collapsed under his weight. He landed on the floor covered in broken wood and surgical tools.

The remaining soldier was slow to react and fumbled with his machine gun. He moved forward as Boucher stuck his leg out, tripping him while still tied to the chair. The first soldier retrieved his weapon as Savage and Santiago tackled him. They launched themselves at him while leaping over the second soldier. The force of the collision sent the first soldier slamming backward into the wine rack. Santiago's chair broke beneath her. They slammed into the shelves as the towering wine rack fell forward on top of everyone. There was a loud crash as wine bottles burst and wooden shelves splintered around them.

Santiago was entangled in the broken chair and ropes. Rising up through the debris, she head-butted Holzlöhner on the bridge of his nose as he staggered to his feet. He fell backward, holding his smashed nose.

The second soldier picked up his machine gun and fired a short burst at Santiago. She sidestepped then kicked the machine gun up and out of his hands. It sent a long spray of bullets over everyone's head.

Savage struggled to get to his feet. Boucher lay on his side, still tied to the chair. The soldier struck Santiago with a solid punch to her jaw. The punch sent her reeling backward into the wall.

The first soldier was back on his feet. He charged Santiago with the intent to grab her by the throat.

The second soldier attacked Savage with a knife, wrestling him to the floor. Savage rolled to the side and punched him in the throat. Santiago grabbed the soldier by the wrist, spun him around, and flipped him into the wall headfirst. She used the tangled rope and wrapped it around Holzlöhner's neck, then used her momentum to whip him into a circle and crash him into the first soldier.

Holzlöhner bounced off the first soldier then went after Savage throwing a wild right-handed punch. Holzlöhner's punch landed on the side of a wooden beam as he folded over in pain. The result was a broken wrist bent at an odd angle.

The second soldier charged Santiago. She jerked the rope and whipped Holzlöhner at him. Holzlöhner and the second soldier hit hard. Their faces slapped against each other with a loud, meaty pop. Both of them released an audible gasp of air and a painful groan.

Savage rushed over to Boucher and began untying him. "Shoot them!" Boucher said.

"Oh, hell no," Savage replied. "This is payback. Santiago would never forgive me if I shot'em. You see, these Nazis must learn that payback is a motherfucker, and school is in session."

As Holzlöhner and the soldier fell to the floor, Santiago grabbed two broken table legs off the floor and wielded them in each hand as weapons. Holzlöhner and both soldiers ignored their pain as adrenaline coursed through their veins. They charged Santiago, but she was prepared. She struck with pinpoint accuracy as their clawing hands were broken and made useless with circular figure-eight windmills of strikes and counterstrikes.

Holzlöhner and the two soldiers charged at her in intervals with the ferocity of everything they had. As one was struck and kicked backward, the other moved in to receive multiple strikes with the table legs. Fractured hands and broken wrists were followed by a dizzying array of painful blows to their heads and knees. The three men recoiled in agony. Their fear of dying was the only thing keeping them from giving up. Savage and Boucher watched in awe as Santiago humiliated them with advanced strikes, kicking, and punching combinations.

Santiago delivered a hard Muay Thai kick to Holzlöhner's floating rib sending him flying sideways. The first soldier, who was on his knees, violently pulled up a carpet Santiago was standing on. This whipped her legs up into the air. She fell on her back with a hard thud as the soldier leaped on top of her. Before he could land, she rolled sharply to the right as he landed on the floor with a grunt. She retaliated by moving back in his direction and stabbed him in the back of his head with the table leg.

The second soldier dove on top of her with a badly mangled arm. He screamed like a mad man. Santiago shifted with the momentum guiding him into a full roll with her on top of him. He reached for her face with his good arm. She struck him in the side of the bicep with the table leg as he screamed in agony. She struck again, snapping his arm at the elbow with a cringe inducing pop. The soldier screamed as Santiago forced the table leg into his eye socket. He died instantly.

The severely beaten Holzlöhner reached over and picked up a discarded submachine gun. Before he fired, Savage threw a bottle of wine at him. The bottle hit him on the side of the head with a loud crash and an explosion. The broken bottle covered his head with wine, blood, and glass. His machine gun went off, spraying a filthy still life painting hanging above Santiago's head. Holzlöhner collapsed into unconsciousness. His head was covered in blood with a huge gaping gash ripped across his face.

"You alright?" Savage asked Santiago.

"I got dibs on Schüller," she said with a wrecked face. Savage nodded and helped Boucher to his feet.

"You cool?" asked Savage.

"I have good news, and I have bad news," Boucher said.

"What's the good news?"

"The Maquis is here. They are outside right now."

"What's the bad news?" asked Santiago.

"Hitler is here."

"Can we meet him?" Savage asked.

"This means Schüller has to move faster. He has negroes to kill."

"He concocted a story for Ernestine about Hitler wanting Buster Pete's band to perform for POWs," Santiago added.

"That's a good way to get a bunch of surly musicians to load themselves on to a truck and travel to a killing field," Savage replied.

"My thoughts exactly," Santiago added.

"Anything else?" Savage asked Boucher.

"I have acquired an aeroplane."

Forty-Three

Stewart came to silently. She was carried across an airfield to a twin-engine cargo plane.

"Fuck this!" Palmer cried, wiping his face with a towel.

Stewart's vision was blurred as she tried to focus through the darkness and the blinding runway lights. Four workers in overalls were loading a large, ominous torpedo-shaped device into the belly of the plane. Someone wearing a grey flight suit was walking ahead of them. She couldn't see his face—too much glare. Seeing glimpses of the back of his head burned a hole in her chest. Stewart tilted her head. Mordecai was carrying her in his arms.

Palmer was walking just ahead. He was livid. "The fuck!" Palmer barked. The fuckity, fuck, fuck, fuck! You didn't tell me *anything* about this shit!"

Stewart blacked out.

Forty-Four

Savage and Santiago arrived at The Montclair too late. The club was dark and deserted. They crept through a ghostly stillness, veiled in rays of shadows and light. On the bandstand, the drum kit was in disarray alongside overturned chairs and music stands. Savage and Santiago walked around the club in silence. Schüller and his men had arrived, rounded up everyone, and carried them off on a one-way ticket to a cold, shallow grave. Savage and Santiago had failed.

"They came and went," a voice said from the shadows. "So much for your 21st-century *edjamacation*." With his pearl handled revolver in hand, Buster limped out from the shadows with his arm in a sling, a bruise on his face, and Fontaine on his good arm. "Ernestine talked up a storm, but Schüller has a way of gettin' his way. They're playin' a gig for the POWs. I heard Schüller say they'd be back tomorrow."

"How did you get away?" Savage asked.

"One of the soldiers found us hiding. I killed his ass."

"Bravo," Savage replied.

"There is no gig," Santiago said. "You'll never see Ernestine and the others again. Here's a tip: The next time someone from the future shows up to warn you about being murdered, give it some serious consideration."

Savage turned to Buster. "How long ago did they leave?"

"You just missed them," Buster replied.

"Schüller has Ernestine's husband Theotis in a concentration camp," Santiago said. "She'll do anything to save him."

"We know about it," Fontaine replied.

Savage noticed that Fontaine was wearing a large engagement ring on her finger. It sparkled even in the low light.

"And what about you?" Savage asked Fontaine.

"I'm with Buster. He loves me, and life is short."

"Right. *You're* the important one. We're just here for kicks."

Santiago touched Savage's shoulder. "Savage, we need transportation."

"You're lucky to be alive, motherfucka'," Buster sniped.

"Shut it." Santiago barked.

Savage stared at Fontaine incredulously. "You chose *him* over me?"

"I'm sorry," Fontaine said. "Sometimes, it's not the people who are bad; it's the timing."

"Clock is ticking," Santiago said to Savage.

"Just like that?" Savage replied as sadness washed over him.

"We need Boucher," Santiago said, trying to re-direct his focus. "He should be back by now."

"Even if he has a plane, it's too late," Savage replied. "How would we catch up to them?"

"If Boucher found a plane, we best figure out a way to get on it," Buster said.

"Perhaps what you need is superior German engineering," said a familiar German-accented voice. A German officer staggered through the rays of darkness. The group turned in his direction. Savage drew his pistol. In walked an inebriated Lieutenant Reiner wearing a disheveled uniform and an open bottle of cognac in his hand.

"Tick tock, tick tock. Time is of the essence," he said, drunkenly slurring his words. "My time is up, your time is up. Swiss time is running out. But perhaps I have a solution to your little dilemma."

"Who are you?" asked Savage.

"Lieutenant Franz Reiner at your service."

"What are you babbling about?" Santiago demanded.

"Our technology is world-famous, innovative, a work of pure GENIUS but... we do not treat people very well. That will be our legacy. Brilliant engineering, not so good with people."

"What's your point," Santiago demanded.

"I was Major Schüller's assistant. He is what you Americans call a son of a bitch bastard."

#

Schüller and Reiner were standing in the living room of a Jewish family of five. Soldiers were detaining the family as they sobbed in terror. As their home was being ransacked, a brown and white puppy was barking incessantly amidst the chaos. Schüller attempted to ignore the barking, but it wasn't long before he'd had enough. Aggravated, he casually walked across the room, picked up the puppy, and tossed it out of the window.

"Now, was that so difficult?!"

Reiner witnessed this as his soul turned barren and dark. Something inside of him died.

#

Reiner shook himself from his disturbing repose. "Der Führer has arrived in Paris to inspect Major Schüller's handy work. I am unable to continue my duties in good conscious."

"Where is Schüller taking the band?" Savage pressed.

"How do you Americans say, 'You scratch my ass, and I will scratch yours?'"

"That's not what we say," Santiago replied.

"Well, I need my ass scratched. I help you save your friends, and you help me escape to the land of the free."

"If you don't start talking, you're going wind up in the land of the dead," Savage said, aiming his .45 at his face. Reiner ignored him.

"Have you heard of Anton Flettner?" They all looked at him dumbfounded. "No? You have never heard of Anton Flettner? Well, I'm quite surprised. You see, he really is quite a genius."

"We don't have the time to discuss the life of Anton Flettner," Santiago pressed.

"Surely you have heard of the Flettner FL 282? No? Of course not! But I know about it! German engineering at it's finest!"

"Spill it!" Savage yelled.

"It's a hubschrauber!" Reiner replied, "A helicopter!"

Boucher abruptly burst into the club out of breath.

"We have exactly three hours to get everyone to the airfield."

"Tick tock," Reiner quipped.

Forty-Five

Cargo Plane — 30,000 Feet

"Was it so important that I be a part of all that?!" Palmer yelled, trying to contain himself. "Goddamn!"

"Blame *her*," said a male voice coming from the cockpit. *She* did it," he said, referring to Stewart. Stewart was unconscious stretched out on a bed of cargo netting.

"I'm done," Palmer continued. "I don't know what I'm doing anymore. A deal is a deal, but..."

"You are correct; a deal *is* a deal. You made good on your part of our contract, and I've made good on mine. The money is in your account. Spend it well."

"You were a little stingy with the details," Palmer said as he changed into a white suit. "You didn't tell me about... Well, you *know*, don't you?"

"Stingy?"

"Not telling me the whole story is the same as lyin'. You lied to me. Lyin' wasn't in the contract. I have been deceived and inconvenienced! And don't get me started on how all this looks! You're sick as hell!"

"That was on a need-to-know basis, and motherfucker, you didn't need-to-know."

"You knew I wouldn't go through with it if I knew everything. Your mistake was letting Stewart take me through the simulation. I didn't sign up for that. Getting the shit kicked out of me by Nazis is one thing—but that simulation... That's some depraved end of the world shit. What the fuck is wrong with you?!"

"When did you become little miss love & light? You're a third-rate actor, a Fine Arts major who pissed his life away. You don't get to be the whore with a heart of gold. You were paid to spy. Now suddenly, you're on a high horse with this virtue signaling bullshit. Shut up and spend your fucking money."

"I was over a barrel. I needed the bread. You hired me to keep an eye on her—not watch you turn everybody into brain dead savages."

Sabastian Ritenour stepped out from the cockpit area. He was wearing a grey flight suit, and his patience was wearing thin.

"You fucked my wife and got paid for it. Go home and keep your mouth shut. I'm sure you'll have fond memories of this little adventure, and you'll probably jerk off many times thinking about her. Take the money. Blow it on oxy, chronic, Mountain Dew, or whatever. I don't care. But if you mention one word of this, you're going to wake up in that little shithole apartment of yours dead. If you like, I can have Mordecai kill you right now. We can get this whole thing over with quickly. Would you like me to ask Mordecai if he has time to kill you?"

Palmer stared down at his hands trying to figure out how he got into this mess.

"Hey, Mordecai," Ritenour called turning toward the cockpit. "Do you have time to kill Palmer right now?"

Mordecai's head popped outside the doorway of the cockpit.

"Sure. I would be delighted. I could tear his head from his body and throw the parts out of the plane. It would only take a second."

"Mordecai has never had a come-to-Jesus moment," Ritenour explained to Palmer.

Mordecai smiled as his head popped back into the cockpit. Palmer was defeated. "Alright."

"This circumstantial morality crap is bullshit. People have whored themselves out for a lot worse than money—reap the rewards and shut the fuck up."

"You can call me a dog, but it won't make me bark. And if I bark, it don't make me a dog."

"Very pithy. A year from now, when you're in Jamaica sucking down Mai Tais and banging over-the-hill, divorced plumpers on vacation, you'll thank me. Forget everything you did here. Keep your fucking mouth shut."

Mordecai stepped out from the cabin door of the cockpit. Stewart's device was tucked inside his web belt. A pilot and co-pilot were at the controls wearing parachutes.

"We'll reach the city in a few minutes, sir," Mordecai said to Ritenour. He turned to Palmer and winked as he ducked back into the cockpit.

Palmer bit his lip. "Look, man, this is bigger than money or you being cucked. This goes against nature, mankind. This is *Fantasy Island* for psychopathic murderers. This is no game."

"It *is* a game. It literally *is* a game. Why can't you understand that?"

"You've been down there. Those people are real—that world is real. You created a fucked-up world, but at least give those people a chance. Give them a chance to fight back. If you unpack that virus, there's no coming back."

"I'm sorry you feel that way. Actually, I'm not sorry."

"Why are you doing this? Why do you want to burn this world down?"

"To get back at *me*." Stewart no longer needed to feign unconsciousness.

Forty-Six

Anton Flettner was a German aviation engineer and inventor. He was a genius whose concepts regarding counter-rotating intermeshing twin rotors became a tremendous technological breakthrough. The Flettner FL 282 was one of the first production model helicopters ever created for the German military. Used primarily by the Navy, it flew above gun turrets of convoy escort vessels in extreme weather. Originally built to carry one crewmember, it evolved to seat two, which became the Flettner FL 282B-2.

A newer experimental prototype of the Flettner FL 282B-2 called the Flettner FL 282B-3 (Stormbringer) was parked in Paris. It was waiting to be unveiled for a demonstration for Adolph Hitler and the German high command. This experimental prototype could seat five and fly faster than previous models. It was the latest in German flight technology.

As a flight enthusiast with access to top secret information from Berlin, Lieutenant Reiner knew precisely how to get his hands on it. They were running out time, and every moment doing nothing made everybody feel more anxious.

#

Little Benny leaned in with his ear close to the body of the beat-up guitar as Charles strummed a chord. It was hard to hear anything amidst the bouncing and rumbling inside the back of the covered truck.

It didn't help that Charles, Fats, and Benny were squashed together with 15 other people. Ten men and eight women, including Ernestine, were sandwiched together, still wearing their nightclub eveningwear.

Charles sat in Burnhoffer's uniform, worried and distraught. He, Little Benny, and Ernestine had been rounded up by Schüller's men and brought to The Montclair so they could be whisked away in one shot.

Ernestine knew everybody on the truck was going to be murdered. She had two choices; she could tell everyone what was going on. Then, everyone would panic, and things would go from bad to extremely bad. Or she could keep her mouth shut and bide her time until she had an opportunity she could use to their advantage.

In her mind, Savage, Santiago, and Boucher were most likely dead. Ernestine had no plan, no means of escape, and no sassy quips.

She clutched her purse, sitting atypically silent during the truck ride. The band sat along both sides of the back of the truck, smoking and talking nervously. A few people were standing closest to the front of the truck. The standing passengers held on for dear life as they were tossed from left to right.

The well-dressed couple Clyde and Pat sat close together. Clyde attempted to calm his fiancé's anxiety.

Charles took out a match, struck it on his thumbnail, and lit his cigarette. Deeply engaged in his thoughts, he inhaled deeply.

Sauce looked worried too. "Somethin' ain't right," he confessed in his gravelly baritone. "It just ain't right." Sauce was scared shitless, and everybody knew it.

"I'm wit' Sauce," said Spencer, who sucked on a toothpick while clinging to his saxophone. "Why would they drive us to a gig in the middle of the night? We ain't got nothin' but the clothes on our backs! What about my hair? I need my pomade!"

"We need to get the hell off this truck," Sauce interjected with a quiver in his voice. The rest of the group erupted into a cacophony of heated comments directed at Ernestine. Her silence spoke volumes.

"Ernestine!" Fats called out. "Ernestine?"

Ernestine stood up and found her balance. She stared at the other captives. A draft of cold air shot through the back of the truck. It chilled everyone to their core. Charles stood up to offer her support. Holding on to the side of the truck, and with a face devastated by sadness she said, "We're all goin' to die in the most horrible way imaginable, and it's all my fault. Sorry about that, folks. I really made a mess of things."

Forty-Seven

"He did all of this to get back at me," Stewart said. She was stretched out on a bed of cargo netting looking beat to shit. Ritenour and Palmer turned in her direction. Mordecai leaned in and took notice.

"Hello, sweetie," Ritenour said. "Did you get some rest?"

"It was you this whole time."

"Well, yes. I had a kerfuffle or two, so I had to improvise—but yes, I take full responsibility. *I* did this. Took you a while, didn't it? You're very smart... on paper."

"I had a feeling it was you when you showed up at the brothel. I was praying I was wrong. What did I do? What did I do to hurt you?"

"Seriously? Wow. You don't know?

"No. Why don't you tell me."

"You want me to believe the way you treated me was all in my imagination? Ok, I'll play. I did it to create a problem only I could solve."

"That doesn't make any sense."

"Allow me to explain. I thought if I implanted a Bio-mechanical nano-virus on *Simulated Earth*, you'd come to me for help. Then I would get rid of the virus. I'd be a hero, I'd get funding for my research, your game would go back to being *Up with People*, and you and I could finally be together, have a real marriage—be a family. I had no idea my virus would transform your game into the most popular franchise in the history of gaming."

"You're a stupid man, Rit."

That hit Ritenour hard. "No, I'm not. I'm a very smart man. I had no idea this would happen. Nobody did, or they would have done it first. I did all this so we could be together. As everything started spinning out of control, I realized we would *never* be together. You're not cut out for marriage, or anything resembling human relationships for that matter."

"I'm not perfect."

"Not the point. Here's the thing, you didn't come to me for help. You *never* want my help. You never want anything from anyone."

"So, if only I would have been a little more helpless, none of this would have happened?"

Ritenour took her in with a full gaze.

"I see who you really are."

"Rit, I'm smarter than anyone I've ever known with the exception of my father. You knew who I was when you married me."

"True, but I didn't count on falling in love with you."

"This was my father's dream! It was his dying wish! Not only did you destroy his life's work, but you also created the worst contagion in history! When this virus spreads to the colonies..."

"Have you been listening to me?"

"Do you know what it does to people who consume this garbage?"

"It's a game."

"It's not a game," Palmer said, cutting in. "It's real, and if we don't do something, it's going to wind up back home."

"And you were in on it," Stewart replied with distain. "*Godspell*? *Jesus Christ Superstar*? There was no way you could have known about those plays."

"You knew?!"

"I needed you to lead me here. To find *him*," she said looking at Ritenour.

"I was supposed to keep an eye on you," Palmer continued. "But things... changed. I started having feelings for you. At first, it was about the money. I wasn't thinking straight."

"I shared with you the most intimate..."

"I fucked up. I was the one who sabotaged your device. I did it back at my hotel room while you were asleep. You were moving too fast. We had to slow you down."

"Asshole."

"I'm sorry."

"Shut up."

"I'm truly sorry. Really, I am."

"Shut the fuck up!"

Stewart stared at Palmer with disappointment, then turned her attention to Ritenour. "Don't you get it? You didn't just ruin my game; you pissed on my father's grave. Worst of all, you brought out the absolute worst in people—the lowest, darkest part of humanity."

"It's a game, a simulation," Ritenour retorted. "Nobody back home is stupid enough to imitate this kind of behavior. They live vicariously through *this* world, so they don't have to act it out on in the colonies. Why can't you understand that?"

"But why even offer it? Even if they're living vicariously through the game, it's still in their minds; it's in their hearts."

"It's entertainment! Fantasy!"

"No, it's much more than that. There's a lot you don't see in the colonies. But I see it. People of color see it. Morons are looping violent acts in their minds, hyper-realistic simulations—torture, subjugation, murder. They're becoming numb to violence and horrible atrocities. Soon, they'll lose the capacity to distinguish fantasy from reality. And you're responsible. You did this."

"I had no way of knowing things would turn out the way it did, but at least it gives Joe Sixpack an outlet. It's already inside them. It gives them a chance to let off some steam, so they won't act on those impulses. Believe it or not, people like it. In fact, they love it. The numbers don't lie."

"Those numbers represent the worst and the weakest minds in our society. You're enabling legions of dumbass, racist human time bombs. They'll be riots just because somebody got a pizza order wrong. Simple disagreements escalate—stupid fights. And who do you think the victims will be? It won't be people who look like you. It'll be people like me. Loyalties will shift and they'll turn on you. That's what you created. A hate-filled world of bed-wetting idiots."

"You gotta stop this," Palmer begged, pleading with Ritenour. "You can keep your money—we gotta stop this before there's no way to turn back."

"It's too late for that," said Mordecai, sticking his head through the cockpit doorway.

"He's right," Ritenour said.

"Why?" asked Stewart?

A digital clock was situated in the center of the instrument panel. The minutes clicked backward. A computer-generated female voice announced the time left on the clock.

"16 MINUTES UNTIL IGNITION."

Forty-Eight

In the pitch-black sky, an indistinguishable object moved slowly and erratically into focus. It crested over the city rooftops with a blinking light that pierced the night. As the object dipped and ascended, a faint sound could be heard. It was the sound of a helicopter.

The Flettner FL 282-3 (Stormbringer) Prototype bounced and swerved through the summer night. A German Balkenkreuz cross was printed on both sides of its fuselage over a grey exterior. Inside the cockpit, Lieutenant Reiner flew the helicopter in drunken ecstasy. He smiled from ear to ear. Savage had changed back into his blazer and white shirt. He hung on tight in the co-pilot's chair.

"I thought you said you knew how to fly this thing?" Savage yelled to Reiner over the sound of the rotors.

"I lied. I have flown before but nothing like this. It is a prototype! How would I know how to fly something that isn't in production yet?"

Savage wanted to strangle him. "Land this thing! You're going to kill us!"

"I will never have the opportunity to do this again," Reiner replied with a mischievous grin. Savage held on with a concerned expression on his face. Santiago was wearing her suit, while Boucher still wore his prisoner's uniform. They sat in the back seat, terrified.

"Land this thing right now, pendejo!" Santiago yelled as both she and Boucher hung on with white knuckles.

"I do not feel well," Boucher said, looking pale.

"Do not worry," Reiner responded, laughing. "I think I have got the hang of this. I was the 13th best Luftwaffe pilot in the Hitler Youth Air Corps."

Savage looked at him, incredulously. "13th?!" he shouted.

"It was a large class. I also have the instruction manual." He held up the instruction manual so that Savage could see it.

Unexpectedly, the manual was sucked out of the window with a loud flapping sound. "Oops," Reiner said with a goofy grin.

The helicopter leveled off. Reiner finessed control of the helicopter as the passengers relaxed into a smoother ride. "We will arrive at the location soon," Reiner commented.

"Wait," said Savage. "Boucher, how much time do we have until the plane takes off?"

Boucher checked his watch.

"We have exactly two hours, 13 minutes, and 27 seconds."

"But we have less than an hour to get to the killing field to stop Schüller," Reiner added.

"Ok, put us down over there on top of the government building," Savage ordered. "I have something I need to do."

Santiago looked at him, curiously. "What?" she yelled over the sound of the rotors.

"Land on that roof," Savage ordered. "I'll be in and out in 10 minutes."

"Savage, we don't have time for this."

"Land it right now!" Savage demanded.

The helicopter banked to the right. Within seconds it landed on top of the government building as Nazi flags flailed from the wind of the spinning rotors.

Savage ducked out of the helicopter and ran to the building's roof entrance as Santiago followed. Once inside, they walked down a stairway leading into the building.

They stealthily moved down the stairs when Santiago stopped him. "You want to tell me what's going on?"

"Schüller has a safe in his office."

"And?"

"It's full of money, and I'm going to get it."

"You want to steal Schüller's money?!"

"It's not his money. It's money he extorted from The Montclair."

"A truckload of people are on their way to being murdered, and you want to break into a safe?"

"It's on the way. We have time."

"No, we don't! This is bad judgement, Savage!"

"I'm getting that money."

"You're a kleptomaniac!"

"Ernestine and the band are going to need money to make a fresh start. So will we. Wherever we end up, we're going to need cash and lots of it."

"That money will be worthless if those people end up dead."

"We can make it. The sooner we grab the money, the sooner we can get back in the air."

"We're going back to the helicopter!"

"We need that money!"

"Get back on the helicopter! Now!"

Savage tried to pass by Santiago. She spun him around and smashed his face into the wall. Maneuvering behind him and placing her forearm against his throat, she put him in a sleeper hold. Savage squirmed but couldn't break free.

"You must have forgotten you're my prisoner," Santiago whispered. "Here's a gentle reminder."

Savage's eyes rolled back in his head as he began to lose consciousness. Santiago lowered him to the floor as his body went limp.

Voices—Santiago released Savage as they listened to the sound of two Germans around the corner. Savage shook off his stupor. He groggily pointed to a sign above a door marked AUSFAHRT. He shook off the effects of oxygen deprivation and motioned for her to follow him.

They quietly crossed the hallway and exited through the door. They raced down the steps until they reached the first floor.

"I told you what would happen if you crossed me," Santiago whispered.

"Help me or stay out of the way."

Savage stopped and listened before entering the first-floor hallway. Santiago reluctantly waited with him. They heard silence, then quietly opened the door and stepped out into the main hall.

"This way," he told Santiago.

They continued down the hallway when Savage stopped, then backed up. They heard voices and footsteps coming their way. Savage and Santiago looked at one another, thinking they would be caught. Santiago noticed a closet. She tapped him on the shoulder, motioning him to follow her. They entered the small confines of a janitor's closet. Savage and Santiago stood inches apart as they waited in silence. The footsteps continued, accompanied by a conversation in German that grew louder, then dissipated as the sound of the voices moved further away.

Savage and Santiago waited an extra beat, then opened the door and looked out. Savage saw the hallway was clear.

"This is bullshit," Santiago protested. "If we get captured, you better hope they kill me first."

"This way," Savage said.

"How do you know where we're going?"

"I memorized the floor plan."

"Floor plan?"

"Shhh."

Savage saw Schüller's office and motioned for Santiago to follow. "This is it."

They heard more voices. Savage and Santiago raced a few yards ahead to Schüller's office. The door was locked. Savage examined the lock then pulled out two toothpicks from the inside of his breast pocket. Without missing a beat, he inserted the toothpicks into the lock and wiggled them around.

"You're breaking into Schüller's office with toothpicks?" Santiago asked.

"It's not the arrow; it's the Indian," Savage replied.

After picking around inside the lock, Savage opened the door. They moved inside the office and closed the door as footsteps and voices passed them in the hallway.

Savage turned on the light and immediately stepped behind Schüller's desk. "And Bingo was his name-O."

He kneeled and opened the double doors of the wooden liquor cabinet. To Savage's surprise, there was liquor inside. "Jumpin' Jesus."

"What?" Santiago asked as she listened for footsteps.

"There's supposed to be a safe here. She said it was here."

"Who?"

"Ernestine. The money's supposed to be here! Shit!"

"Savage, we don't have time for this."

"Ya' think?"

Savage looked around the office frantically.

"Where would he put it?"

"Savage."

"She said it was here."

"Savage."

"I want that money."

"Savage!"

"Fuck!"

He reached inside the liquor cabinet and tossed out all the bottles of liquor onto the floor. He felt the inside back of the cabinet and discovered the rear of the panel was false. He found a small catch on the inside right corner. He opened it with a soft clicking sound. Savage pushed open a false back revealing a gray metal safe with a combination lock.

"Found it," Savage said with a look of relief.

"Great. Do you know the combination?" Santiago asked.

"That would be cheating."

"What?!"

"This is a lost art. I learned this from an old box man in the joint."

"What's a box man?"

"Safecracker."

"Are you for real?

"Do bears shit in the woods?"

"Yes, bears do shit in the woods! And if you don't get that safe open right now, I'm leaving you for Dr. Mengele!"

Savage pressed his ear against the safe and began turning the dial. He heard the tumblers click into place as he gingerly turned the dial left then right.

Santiago's ear was to the door, she heard something in the distance.

"Savage!" Santiago yelled in a hostile whisper.

"Almost there."

Santiago had a strained expression on her face as the sounds behind the door grew louder. On the other side of the door, a soldier walked by Schüller's office and stopped. He noticed a light shining out from under the door. He knocked.

"Hallo? Herr Major? Bist du da?"

Santiago looked back at Savage.

"Savage!" she whispered.

"Almost," Savage replied as he listened intently to the tumblers inside the safe.

The soldier looked confused. He took out a ring of keys and tried to open the door as Santiago quietly slid the deadbolt into place.

The soldier was surprised the door wouldn't open and began banging on it. "Hallo? Wer ist da drin?"

The soldier took a beat to figure out what to do, then walked off toward the sound of voices down the hallway. Santiago was not happy.

"Savage, I refuse to be gang-raped by Nazis because of you. We have to move. We're going to be trapped."

"Almost..."

He heard the clicking sound of tumblers falling into place then waited a beat. He grabbed the handle and turned it. The door opened. The safe was packed with stacks of French currency and documents.

Savage turned to Santiago. "Merry Christmas, baby."

"Get it! Let's go!"

Savage rushed to the other side of the office, looking for something he could put the money in. He opened a closet and discovered an infantry backpack on the floor. He grabbed it and began stuffing money into it.

Santiago heard the sound of the doorknob turning. Before she could move, the door burst open, breaking the deadbolt. Two soldiers forced their way into the office, pushing Santiago backward. Santiago instinctively went into action with kicks and punches as the two soldiers were overwhelmed by Santiago's ferocious attack.

With multiple blows to the head and throat, the soldiers were dispatched as Savage continued stuffing money into the backpack. "This is a good score," Savage said.

"You get off on this shit!"

The backpack was soon full as Savage tied it off at the top and strapped it to his back. "Let's go."

They left the office and ran off down the hallway, stopping at the corner. Savage peaked around it. Two German officers and three soldiers with rifles were briskly walking toward them. Savage popped back around the corner, unseen. "We've got company."

Savage pulled the .45 from the back of his pants and silently cocked the weapon. He turned to Santiago.

"I'll take care of them. I need you to get back on the roof and have the helicopter meet me down on the street.

"Negatory, you'll never make it," replied Santiago. "We'll have a better chance if we stick together."

Savage turned the corner and began firing at the oncoming Germans. He took all five of them down with pin-point accurate headshots. Each soldier fell to the floor.

"That was a bad idea," Santiago said.

"Misdirection," Savage replied. "The shots will bring soldiers to this area. By the time they get here, we'll be long gone."

A blaring alarm went off as Savage and Santiago ran back into Schüller's office. Savage pushed a panel on the side of the wall. A sliding door opened. Savage and Santiago ran inside the passageway.

#

"They are taking too long," Boucher said nervously, reacting to the sound of the alarm.

Reiner, feeling the negative after-effects of the alcohol, leaned back in the pilot's chair with his head up, and closed his eyes. "I think it might be a good idea if you got out and told them to hurry. If the soldiers swarm us, it will be impossible to take off."

"Damn Americans," Boucher said with an annoyed tone. "All right—I am going to look for them. Stay alert. Be ready to take off. We will be leaving in a hurry."

"How will I know when to take off?

"You will hear screaming, lots of screaming—in German."

"Jawohl."

"And no sleeping!"

Boucher grabbed a rifle and climbed out of the helicopter. He sprinted across the rooftop to the entrance of the building. Reiner watched him run. His head fell back with his eyes closed.

#

Savage and Santiago reached the street level. It let out into an alley with cobblestones running the length of the building. The sound of French police sirens joined the security alarm in a cacophony of noise. Arriving at the corner near the main street, they looked in all directions.

"Which way?" asked Santiago.

"The alarm will lead them inside the building to search for us. We'll walk away out front in plain sight."

"Let's move," Santiago said impatiently.

With Savage wearing the backpack, they walked briskly toward the front of the building. They slowed down as they reached the street. In front of the building, a large civilian crowd gathered as French police and German soldiers conspired at the front of the entrance. Soldiers carrying submachine guns rushed into the building. Savage and Santiago cautiously weaved their way through the crowd as police sirens were heard in all directions. As the chaos escalated, Savage and

Santiago made their way to the rear of the crowd making sure not to draw attention to themselves.

"We need that helicopter," Savage said.

"You think?"

Savage and Santiago stood in front of the building across the street. Savage looked up.

"If we could get on top of this roof, Reiner could see us," Savage said.

Santiago looked for a way to get into the building. She turned abruptly and was shocked to find herself face-to-face with a ferret-faced French police officer. He looked at her curiously. "What do you think you are doing?"

Santiago was caught off guard. "I beg your pardon."

"A woman as beautiful as you should never wear trousers."

Savage looked down at her pants. Santiago looked at him, thinking, "Now what?"

"Why are you wearing trousers? A woman is like a flower. A woman's legs are like God's flower petals. A woman as attractive as you should reveal her legs for the benefit of admirers."

Santiago couldn't believe she was hearing this.

"Sorry, my chiffon dress is at the cleaners."

"Ah, of course. You are an American. You are too captivating to be a spy. Otherwise, I would have to shoot you," he said, laughing at his own joke.

"I'm not a spy."

"Of that, I am certain. I have a nose for spies. Perhaps we could have a drink, or I could show you the sights of Paris."

He noticed Savage standing next to her. "Are you two together?"

"This is my personal slave."

Savage mustered an imitation of a smile.

"Ah, I see. He is in your employ. Be sure to leave the nègre at home during our excursions," He laughed.

"Oh, I will," Santiago replied. "We should be moving along now. We're in a hurry. Nice chatting with you."

"I'd be happy to escort you."

"No need but thank you for the offer. Goodbye now."

"Oh, but allow me. A beautiful creature such as you needs police protection. If the wrong people were to see you walking with a nègre, there would be talk. And in Paris, reputation is everything." He moved in close to whisper in Santiago's ear. "It is said the nègre have tails like monkeys."

Savage looked at the police officer, imagining choking him so hard his head exploded like a zit. "I don't have a tail."

"I believe that you do."

"I believe you're retarded."

"We're going away now," Santiago said. "Thank you for your concern."

The police officer was focused on Savage. "You are an American as well. May I see your papers?"

"No, you may not."

"I demand to see your papers!"

"I demand you get the fuck out of my face," Savage replied.

The police officer noticed the backpack. "What do you have in the backpack?" he asked as his suspicion grew.

The police officer reached for the backpack. Savage slapped his hand. The officer recoiled then reached in again more aggressively. Savage slugged him in the side of the head with an overhand right. The policeman spat out a tooth and twitched as if he was having a neurological disorder, then fell to the ground unconscious.

"So much for peaceful conflict resolution," Santiago said.

"You should talk. You choked me out. I can't feel the left side of my face."

Very few people in the crowd noticed this except for the wrong people. Another policeman saw the scuffle and blew a whistle as other police officers rushed in. They began running toward them as Santiago intercepted them with sophisticated kicks, close-quarter Wing Chun strikes, and painful arm trapping. Three police officers fell hard on to the cobblestones.

"We won't be able to handle all of them," Santiago said as another police officer grabbed her around the neck. Santiago elbowed the officer in the ribs with a loud crunch. The police officer went down holding his ribs, as Savage kicked him in the face.

Savage and Santiago noticed a group of Gestapo and French police running toward them. As they grew closer, Savage and Santiago stood back-to-back, prepared for a death match.

They fought off 14 soldiers in quick succession with pistol shots from Savage and Martial Arts from Santiago. Brutal punches and kicks mingled with precision gunfire destroying their attackers. The wounded men groaned in agony.

Santiago picked up a submachine gun and sprayed the remaining soldiers. "Vámonos!"

Suddenly, they heard a gunshot and a loud explosion that rocked the entire block. A truck exploded, distracting everyone from Savage and Santiago. A half-block away, a gasoline truck was in flames as its contents burned white hot with pieces of debris flying everywhere. Savage and Santiago crouched to take cover. The situation made sense as they heard the sound of helicopter rotors.

They saw the helicopter as it swerved low and around the government building. It flew above the heads of the crowd and glided ahead of Savage and Santiago. It finally stopped and hovered eight feet above the ground. The crowd, along with the soldiers, were stunned seeing a helicopter for the first time. Shots were fired as it pulled away.

Savage and Santiago ran toward the helicopter. Santiago climbed aboard. A soldier hit Savage in the back of the head with his rifle. As the helicopter pulled away, Savage saw stars. He fought to stay conscious as he engaged the soldier in a manic boxing match. He pulled the rifle away from the soldier, turned it around, and shot him in the chest at point-blank range. Savage dropped the rifle.

He reached for the backpack. A young blonde woman in a brown Nazi uniform snatched it away before he could grab it. Savage chased after her, but the woman was too fast. Savage stopped, pulled out his .45, and shot her in the back of the head. Her skull exploded into chunks of meat, bone, and hair, splattering the faces of onlookers. Her body went tumbling into the crowd.

Savage ran over to the woman's body, picked up the backpack, and addressed the onlookers. "Excuse the mess."

He took off running back to the helicopter, dodging a hail of bullets. He threw the backpack up toward the aircraft. Santiago leaned out and narrowly caught it with one hand.

More shooting erupted as the helicopter gained altitude. Reiner and Boucher looked panicked as bullets ricocheted around their faces. Sparks exploded too close to their heads.

Savage sprinted toward the helicopter. He leaped into the air, barely managing to grab the aircraft's landing gear with one hand. He hung on as the helicopter continued to climb upward into the night sky.

Bullets whizzed by as Santiago leaned out, offering her outstretched hand. Savage hung on as he dangled over the city. Santiago strained to reach him. Their hands were mere inches apart as they stretched to bridge the distance. Savage grabbed her hand.

The helicopter banked sharply, forcing them to lose their grip. Savage fell, hitting his chest on the landing gear. He bounced off but managed to grab hold of the strut with the inside of his elbow.

Santiago leaned outside the door as she fought the wind and erratic movements of the aircraft.

"Keep it steady, dammit!" she cried. She reached down and grabbed Savage's hand firmly. They shared a sliver of meaningful eye contact. She pulled him up so he could steady himself on the landing gear. He leaned into the doorway and battled the wind. "You had to wear pants, didn't you?" he said with a straight face.

"You're wearing pants too, cabrón. Get in here."

Savage climbed into the helicopter. The rotors roared with difficulty as smoke trailed across the sky, then evaporated into the pitch black heavens.

Forty-Nine

"In the belly of this aircraft is the last virus in the chain," Ritenour continued. "I'm crashing this plane into the Eiffel Tower. The bomb will deploy the virus at the moment of impact. This will spread the virus over a large-populated area. The more chaos and panic, the better. The ratings will be insane."

"*You're* insane," Stewart retorted. "You're going to commit suicide?"

"Oh no. I have parachutes. But there's been a change in plans. We won't need *all* the parachutes."

Ritenour tossed Mordecai a pile of parachutes. Mordecai caught them, opened the fuselage door, and threw them outside as he battled gusts of wind. Ritenour held up two remaining parachutes.

"Four passengers, two parachutes. What do you do? It's must-see-TV. Does anybody want to take a stab at a solution to this little quandary? Stewart, you've always been a mathlete. Oh, and Palmer—I'm voiding our contract."

Stewart and Palmer stared at one another and then at Ritenour. Visions of their mangled corpses chopped by a blender of body parts and plane wreckage strewn across the city of Paris consumed their thoughts.

Suddenly, an explosion and a blast of heat singed their faces. The rear of the aircraft exploded into flying metal, smoke and fire.

Fifty

There would be no POW concert. There would be no photo ops with Mickey Rooney and Errol Flynn. No newspaper reporters or publicity. Everybody in the truck had to get on the same page or perish. The group hadn't been privy to the atrocities captured on film for future generations, but they knew the Nazis were up to some heinous, graduate school level murder.

Ernestine stood up. Clyde and Pat helped to steady her as she clutched her handbag.

"Schüller is holding Theotis hostage in a concentration camp," Ernestine said with a dead-eyed gaze. "He's been bleedin' The Montclair dry since he got here. He's going to kill him if I don't do what he asks. Schüller has been using me in the worst ways. He's been using all of us. And now, Hitler wants us all dead."

The pieces to the puzzle had fallen into place. A cold blanket of fear fell over the group. They were going to die like everyone else in Europe.

"I have a plan," Ernestine said. "If we stick together, it might work. When they take us off the truck, keep your eyes on me. Follow my lead, be brave, and fight like the devil. With a little luck, we might be able to walk away from this." Ernestine turned to Charles. "I need you to do exactly what I tell you."

#

The truck came to a stop accompanied by the sound of screeching breaks. The tension was thick as a brick. They waited in heart-pounding silence as they heard the sound of doors opening from the front of the cab and jackboots on dirt. The brakes from the other vehicles screeched behind them. The canvas covering the rear of the truck violently whipped back, revealing six German soldiers carrying rifles.

"Raus! Raus!" ordered the lead soldier.

The captives piled out of the back of the truck, illuminated by the early morning light. They were somewhere in the middle of the French countryside. Grass, trees, and hills were as far as the eye could see.

"I want to speak to Major Schüller," Ernestine demanded. She fearlessly walked up to a soldier and ignored his rifle. Shovels were brought out and dropped on the ground.

"We're supposed to be puttin' on a show for the POWs. What the hell are we doin' out here?! Where's the camp?! Where's the motherfuckin' camp?!"

Schüller stepped out from the passenger side of a German staff car. His boots gleamed in the moonlight as he walked toward the group. Ernestine turned away from the soldier and urgently ran up to Schüller, demanding an explanation.

"Ernst, you said you were takin' us to a POW camp. What are we doin' out here?! You wanna tell me what the hell's goin' on?! Where's Mickey Rooney!?"

Schüller smiled at Ernestine dismissively. He pulled out a Walther P38 from his holster, cocked it, and pointed it at her head.

#

Twilight kissed the French countryside. A vast expanse of verdant grass and trees stretched across the bright summer horizon. The wind blew across the panoramic landscape like a living postcard. Savage stared out across the tree line holding a rifle. Behind him, the helicopter sat motionless as Reiner busied himself, refueling the aircraft with containers of petrol. Boucher loaded a sniper rifle and stuffed extra ammunition into a bandolier hanging across his chest. Santiago checked her MP40 and shoved additional ammunition clips into an ammo pouch clipped around her waist.

Savage stared out into the distance. He leaned forward and jogged—slowly at first, then picked up speed. He jogged out into the distance away from the helicopter. Boucher, Santiago, and Reiner took notice. Santiago and Boucher picked up their weapons and took off after him.

#

Schüller placed the barrel of his sidearm against Ernestine's forehead. The group reacted with audible terror. Fats drew Little Benny close. Ernestine spit on the ground. Charles stepped out from behind Sauce, drawing attention to himself. "Wait. Hold it. Can we discuss this for a second?"

Schüller casually looked at his watch. "Of course. We have a few minutes before I kill all of you. What would you like to discuss?" He asked, fascinated by his query.

"Look what you're doing. Do you want this on your conscience?"

"I don't understand your question."

"Where's your humanity?"

"Where is *your* humanity?"

"My humanity is fine and dandy."

"Is it? Who was the previous owner of the uniform you're wearing?"

Charles stared back in silence.

"His name was Colonel Jürgen Burnhoffer. He was my superior officer—an annoying, tiresome dull waste of life, but still my superior officer. I disliked him, but he was still a human being. You Americans are so self-righteous when it suits your needs, yet you disavow any responsibility. Colonel Burnhoffer is of course, dead. It's likely you know something about it. He was left out in the middle of nowhere with a bullet in his head before woodland creatures feasted upon him.

"He had a homely wife and an effeminate son. Did Burnhoffer plead for his life before he died? Did he ask you about your conscience? Did he beg you to consider your humanity?"

"I didn't kill that Nazi."

"Ah, but you know who did, and yet you say nothing—you're an accessory to murder."

"I'm sure he was a swell, upstanding, God-fearing pillar of the community—that is if you leave out all the mass murderin' and racist shit. So, he had it comin'—but I didn't kill him."

"In case you hadn't realized it, we are at war. Not only are you an accessory to murder, but you're also impersonating an officer in the German Army. Do you know what happens to those who impersonate military personnel during wartime?"

"I can guess."

"They are shot by a firing squad. Oh, look—we just so happen to have a firing squad right here. Now, if there are no further questions, I shall carry on with the execution."

"We had nothing to do with killing that Nazi. Please! Let's talk about this! I know we can work something out!"

"You are mistaken. There is nothing to work out. I have the authority to do whatever I wish. Now pick up a shovel and dig. Consider yourself fortunate that I have enough *humanity* not to leave you to be eaten by wild animals as you did with Burnhoffer and the Freytags. Now dig!"

"There ain't gonna be no diggin'," Ernestine said with a blunt force stare.

#

Savage picked up speed until he was running full bore through the tall grass. After a few minutes, his breathing became labored. He was focused on something ahead in the distance. Santiago was running a few yards behind as Boucher picked up the rear. Savage breathed heavily as he maintained a firm grip on his rifle.

Soon the effort of running took its toll. Savage's breathing became difficult. His heart was about to explode. His joints felt the weight of gravity and age. He started to pant and slowed down to a limp. Was he having a heart attack?

"Jumpin' Jesus." He stopped and bent over, exhausted. He spat in the grass. "Fuck!" He kept jogging one step at a time as he fought through the pain.

Santiago caught up to him. She put his arm over her shoulder and helped him to keep going at a slower pace.

"I need a minute," Savage gasped.

"Cry me a river!" barked Santiago. "We don't have a minute!"

#

"There ain't gonna be no diggin'," Ernestine said, ignoring the pistol pointing at her head. "When I was a little girl, all I ever wanted was to be a part of somethin' bigger than myself. I wanted to do somethin' good in the world. Who'd have thought that a little colored girl from Harlem would wind up in the middle of a war in Europe?"

She looked directly at Schüller. "You hurt people. You murder people. You kill dreams. It says a lot about somebody who has to push people down so they can feel tall."

"Do all negroes deliver such long-winded tales of woe before they die?" Schüller interrupted. "The Jews are much more considerate when it comes to that. Perhaps this is a trait of the negro—long-term talking. Here's a tip: Shut your fucking mouth and die quietly. There's no need for tear-soaked soliloquies. You've had a hard and tragic life—understood. Perhaps in the next life, you'll return as Ginger Rogers. But for now, pick up a shovel and start digging!"

"You don't believe fat meats greasy," Ernestine said, staring Schüller down. She reached into her purse and pulled out a hand grenade. She pulled the pin while holding down the striker lever. Everyone recoiled in shock. She turned to Schüller. "I ain't diggin' a goddamn thang."

Everyone flinched, reacting to the threat of being blown to pieces. The soldiers tensed and aimed their rifles at Ernestine as the group clustered together in fear.

"I may not live through this, but you ain't either," Ernestine said.

"You took my husband. He's probably dead. Lord only knows how he suffered. I got nothin' left to lose. How 'bout you?"

"Throw the grenade away, and I'll free your husband!"

"You sound like a broken record. You tried to take away my dignity, and for that, I'm gonna take *you* away. I'm gonna make sure I'll be the last person you ever see. Tell your men to drop those guns, or I'll blow us all to bits."

"You black whore!"

"That's right, I'm a whore." She turned to her group. "I slept with Schüller to save Theotis' life—to save The Montclair. But what do I have to show for it? Everythin' I worked so hard for..." She turned to Schüller. "And now, you want me to dig my own grave? Drop that pistol, or I'll blow us all to Kingdom Come!"

#

Savage continued a heart-bursting trot as Santiago ran beside him. He slowed down to a complete stop. "I can't make it."

"We're almost there," Santiago said, also out of breath.

Savage looked up into the sky. His thighs ached. His face was covered in sweat as he grimaced. Boucher ran past them carrying his sniper rifle.

"We can't stop now!" Santiago yelled. "We're close!"

Savage fell to his knees in exhaustion.

"Get up!" Santiago yelled.

"I can't," said Savage, who was so spent he was delirious. "I just..."

"C'mon!"

"What are we doing? Why are we doing this?"

"Get up! We're running out of time!"

"What's the point?"

"The point is if those people die, then all of *this* was for nothing!"

Savage was in bad shape. He was sweating profusely. He felt severely weakened and started hallucinating. "I loved her more than anything."

"What?!"

"I would have done anything for her."

"Send in the clowns!"

"Nothing I did was ever good enough..."

"Get up!" Santiago was frantic. She slapped him. "On your feet, god-damit! I swear to God I am going to make it back home. If it's the last thing I do, I'm going to see my child again—but I can't do it without you! On your feet you son of a bitch!"

#

Savage was delirious. Suddenly everything stopped. He recoiled in delirious confusion. His surroundings looked strange, surreal—the faded color of burnt orange.

He saw himself as a teenager talking to his Uncle Benjamin. "How does one endure the cruelty of life without love's intoxicating distraction?"

Savage looked around. Everything was still. His surroundings were frozen like a photograph. The tall grass that once waved in the summer breeze now stood motionless.

Santiago was kneeling beside him, frozen in time. She'd stopped talking mid-sentence.

A two-dimensional hologram of Stewart stood before him with a concerned look on her face. "Savage, you need to forget Joslyn. I know this is hard to hear, but she believed you weren't good enough for her. You were a weekend treat that lasted longer than the expiration date. The entire time you were together she believed she would meet a handsome and sophisticated Ken doll with a large bank account, who would elevate her status and treat her like a princess. Someone to match the high standards she believed she deserved. Someone better than you. She was delusional. Ultimately, she ran out of time, her looks faded, and her choices with it. Hypergamy is a bitch — a curse.

"Everyone has baggage that affects their worldview and choices. She had steamer trunks of psychological baggage. In an alternate timeline you married her, and she beat you down until there was nothing left but a miserable old man — dead inside. No dreams, no ambitions. I've seen it with my own eyes."

Savage was dumbfounded. He stood motionless with his mouth open.

"Savage, Joslyn was lucky to have you — she discovered that too late. She was a one-way ticket to a wretched existence."

"I thought she loved me."

"No. You were a phase, an experiment. Like spoiled white girls who sow their wild oats fucking black guys in college to defy their parents. In her case she was getting back at her ex-husband. In her later years she would become a smelly old lady, a hoarder, a cat lady with 12 cats who goes to bed every night at 7pm. Is that how you wanted to end up—with this so-called love of your life? A ball-busting, dry pussy desiccated bitch covered in cat hair? You deserved better, much better. Savage, you're a rare professional whose destiny is nothing short of greatness. I need you. *Here*, right now. *This* is what's important."

Savage struggled to process. Stewart continued, "Savage, this is your moment to shine — this is your time. Work with me and your life will have more meaning than you could ever imagine. But I need you to dig — dig deep. Fight! Save Ernestine and those musicians and you'll save yourself... and the world."

#

Savage felt revitalized as he processed his return to reality. He saw Boucher running farther away — a masterclass in annoying athleticism. He turned to Santiago, who was animated again. "Did you see any of that?"

"What?"

"I dodged another bullet."

"What the hell are you talking about?"

"There's a woman — a woman named Stewart — she's behind all this."

"What the fuck is wrong with you?"

"We're running out of time."

Savage forced himself to his feet and started jogging again. His thighs pumped harder, moving smoothly up an elevated ridge. Santiago was right beside him. They came upon the crest of a hill and ducked down as they moved closer. Low crawling up to the top, they stopped short. They peered over the other side from a high position.

In the distance, there was more French countryside. A single dirt road snaked off to the far right. Two military troop trucks were parked off the main road with a staff car in close proximity.

Ernestine was clutching a grenade as Schüller and his soldiers trained their weapons on her. Charles, the captives, and the soldiers were in the throes of a Mexican standoff.

Savage and Santiago were too far away to hear what was being said. Savage checked his rifle. He'd never felt better.

"Let's kill every last one of those cocksuckers."

#

"Drop that pistol, or I'll blow everyone to Kingdom Come," Ernestine said.

"Please, be my guest," Schüller said with a confident grin. "Please, kill us all. If I hear one more story of hardship, I'll turn this gun on myself."

As Boucher aimed at Schüller from his elevated perch, a glimmer of light reflected from his rifle's scope. One of the soldiers noticed it.

"Herr Major!" one of the soldiers yelled, pointing to the grassy incline in the distance.

Schüller and Ernestine took notice. The distraction was enough for Schüller to reach over and smack the grenade from Ernestine's hand. The grenade went flying directly at the captives, who inhaled in fear.

Little Benny's eyes grew large as the grenade came speeding toward him. He caught the grenade as a reflex and stared at it in shock. He looked around, not knowing what to do.

"Over here!" Charles yelled.

Little Benny tossed the grenade to Charles. Charles caught the grenade, got down on one knee, and threw it like a fastball toward home plate. The grenade flew across the distance and exploded in front of a group of soldiers. The blast sent blood and body parts up in the air like a red tornado. Everyone dropped to the ground to take cover.

With a cruel frown, Schüller aimed his pistol at Ernestine's head. A shot rang out. A bullet hit Schüller in the hand. An explosion erupted with pieces of his hand, fingers, and blood bursting in his face. Schüller fell to his knees. He stared at his destroyed hand in disbelief. Bits of fingers lay on the grass in front of him.

The bullet came from Savage. Boucher looked over and gave Savage the thumbs up and a wink.

"Now!" Ernestine screamed.

"Light'em up!" Yelled Savage. Santiago, Savage, and Boucher opened fire on the soldiers.

Charles attacked Schüller, braced for the fight of his life. The captives attacked the remaining guards. Charles wrestled Schüller to the ground. Ernestine picked up a submachine gun and began shooting soldiers. All hell was breaking loose. The captives fought the soldiers with fists and feet. Schüller dodged punches from Charles while barking orders in German.

"Töte sie alle! (Kill them all!)

A canvas flap covering the second troop truck's side opened to reveal the barrel of an MG42 machine gun on a tripod. Two soldiers sat behind the butt of the machine gun with a case of ammo close by.

"Jumpin' Jesus." blurted Savage.

One soldier fed a belt of ammo into the machine gun. The other soldier pushed down on the receiver and aimed. The soldier squeezed the trigger. Savage hastily fired his rifle at the soldier behind the MG42. He missed—the bullet ricocheted off the side of the soldier's helmet. Just as the soldier was resetting to fire the machine gun, another bullet found its target in his right eye. His head popped backward as dark blood oozed from his eye socket. He slumped forward.

The shot came from Boucher. He smiled, looked over at Savage, and laughed. "Boucher's Black Eye!"

Santiago raced down the ridge into the melee as she shot soldiers with bursts of machine gunfire. Boucher and Savage picked off soldiers one by one as the fight continued.

Schüller and Charles were engaged in a life and death fist fight. Schüller was punched multiple times with devastating combinations that left him disoriented. Schüller picked up his pistol with his remaining hand and shot blindly in Charles' direction. He grabbed Ernestine by the hair as she was reloading. He struggled with her as she fought back, using her as a human shield.

The soldiers returned fire as Boucher, Savage, and Santiago took cover. Schüller crouched behind the truck as he threw Ernestine to the ground and ran in the direction of the staff car. Bullets whizzed by, knocking soldiers to the ground. Spencer cut a soldier's throat open with a switchblade knife.

"Get behind the truck!" Ernestine screamed, motioning for the group to move quickly.

Fats dragged Little Benny along as everyone ran for their lives.

Millicent picked up a rifle and shot a soldier in the chest. "How do you like them apples?!"

Little Benny split off and ran toward the back of the staff car. He ducked down by the rear spare tire then climbed into the back seat as bullets flew by.

Savage and Boucher were on automatic pilot, shooting the remaining soldiers as they ran for cover. Two soldiers attacked Santiago as she swapped ammo magazines. She retaliated with a volley of brutal Muay Thai kicks and vicious elbow strikes that took them both down.

The second soldier behind the MG42 shifted behind the butt of the machine gun and prepared to fire. Savage and Boucher fired at the same time, riddling the soldier with bullets. A burst from the MG42 fired harmlessly into the air.

Savage and Boucher raced down the ridge into the field. Schüller inserted himself behind the staff car's steering wheel and sped off down the road in a swerving frenzy. He winced in pain as his right hand bled all over the front seat.

Ernestine fired a rifle at Schüller and blew the top of his right ear off. Blood streamed down the side of his neck and face. Little Benny's head popped up from the back seat.

Ernestine stopped herself. She watched helplessly as Little Benny's sad face drew further away. "Little Benny!"

Little Benny looked fearful as he disappeared into the distance.

"Polecat!" Ernestine yelled.

Schüller drove intensely with his eyes forward, oblivious to his back seat passenger.

#

"Schüller got away! He's got Little Benny!" Ernestine screamed with a helpless wail.

"We'll need one of these trucks," Savage told everyone. "Collect as many weapons as you can."

"I'll see if the trucks are ok," said Spencer.

Santiago finished off a soldier breaking his neck with a triangle leg lock. Traumatized and disheveled, the group rounded up around Ernestine. Clyde and Pat were toting submachine guns. Boucher and Santiago closed in.

"Check the perimeter for hostiles," Santiago barked. "We don't need any surprises."

"Is everyone ok?" Ernestine asked the group.

Clyde and Pat helped the others collect themselves. They nodded in the affirmative.

"I been better, and I been worse," said Fats.

A lone soldier was seen running away in the distance. He breathed heavily in fear for his life. He was about to escape beyond the next ridge. A shot rang out. The solider tumbled to his death. It was Boucher who fired the shot.

"Last one," Boucher said.

That's when everyone noticed Charles laying sprawled in the grass. He was dead.

"Heavens to Betsy," Ernestine said.

The group was stunned. Fats tried to speak. There were no words.

"We need to get to the airfield," Savage commanded delicately. "We don't have much time. Schüller will figure out where we're headed, and he's going to use the entire German Army to stop us."

Fifty-One

The cargo plane was thick with smoke and fire. The plane's tail was blown off. Pieces of cargo were sucked out of its ragged hole and into the atmosphere. Everyone hung on for dear life as they fought the sudden change in cabin pressure and flying debris.

The co-pilot's head was pulverized with a large, jagged piece of metal that crashed through the cockpit window. The force knocked his body through the center of the airplane. Blood and brains splattered everywhere as he was sucked out the back of the plane like a rag doll.

The pilot screamed in a high-pitched wail as he tried to maintain control of the aircraft. Warning lights on the instrument panel lit up like Christmas.

The timer located in the cockpit's console continued to tick backward. The female computer-generated voice announced the time left on the clock. "8 MINUTES AND 13 SECONDS UNTIL IGNITION."

"German anti-aircraft weapons!" the pilot screamed as flak peppered holes throughout the plane.

Stewart stared at Ritenour, perplexed. "*This* was your plan?! Flying a plane over German anti-aircraft weapons?!"

"Oh, shut up!" Ritenour barked.

Stewart turned to Palmer. "Parachutes!"

Mordecai punched Palmer in the chest, knocking him across the cabin. Palmer struggled to recover and dove on top of the two remaining parachutes. Mordecai pounced, lifting Palmer by the throat with one hand. The plane twisted and turned as everyone fought to maintain their balance.

Ritenour fell into Stewart as he tried to restrain her amidst the confusion. Stewart bit him on the hand. Ritenour cried out and kicked her in the chest, knocking her across the cabin.

Mordecai was punching Palmer into a bloody pulp. A large, jagged, chunk of flak pierced through the cockpit window and cut the pilot in half. He stared into oblivion as the top of his torso fell to the floor. This pushed the yoke forward, sending the plane into a radical nose-dive.

Everyone tumbled toward the front of the airplane. Ritenour picked up a metal rod and began swinging it at Stewart. She tried to protect herself by holding up her arms. Ritenour smashed her shoulder. Stewart screamed in agony.

Palmer was taking brutal blows to the face. His nose and mouth gushed blood splattering his white suit. Peering through swollen eyes, Palmer saw Stewart's device tucked in Mordecai's web belt.

Stewart rolled in the direction of the rotating aircraft to get away from Ritenour. She landed on her feet a few yards from Palmer.

Mordecai swung a haymaker toward Palmer's head that would have knocked his head clean off. Palmer ducked under the punch and swiped Stewart's device from his belt.

Palmer yelled to Stewart, "Here!" Palmer tossed the device to Stewart. "It's fixed! Get us the fuck on up outta here!"

While registering a look of surprise, Stewart caught it.

Mordecai punched Palmer so hard he was knocked to the rear of the plane. Palmer's foot became caught in cargo netting. It was the only thing that saved him from being sucked out of the aircraft.

"6 MINUTES AND 27 SECONDS UNTIL IGNITION."

Stewart began typing. "Hercules punch!" She pointed the device at Mordecai. An invisible punch knocked him upward. Mordecai hit the roof of the plane hard, then dropped, crashing to the floor.

Ritenour leaped across the aisle to wrestle the device away from Stewart. She jerked it away and aimed the device at him. Ritenour was punched off his feet with a loud, hard, meaty slap to the jaw. He landed in a massive tangle of cargo netting.

Mordecai leisurely walked up behind Stewart and ripped the device from her hand. He lifted her up by the waist, walked her over to the fuselage doorway, and threw her outside into the wild blue yonder. Palmer looked on in horror.

Fifty-Two

Things were getting out of hand. It was becoming messy, and Schüller craved order. He wanted this to be over. He sped along in his staff car so consumed with his thoughts he forgot most of his right hand had been blown off. Half of his right ear was missing too. Thankfully he had two fingers and part of a thumb left.

Schüller was a half glass full kind of guy. His missing ear and fingers were the least of his worries. He had lesbians, niggers, and midgets to worry about—oh, and Hitler.

Blood was leaking everywhere. He was covered in it, and his hand started to throb. It occurred to him he should get himself to a hospital before he blacked out. "I should have killed that midget and those spies when I had the chance."

He pressed down hard on the accelerator consumed with retribution. The troublemakers were becoming a worrisome pain at the worst possible time. Hitler was in Paris, and those pests were going to make him look incompetent. "Why now? The Jews had been less trouble." He'd been shipping them off by the bushel without incident. "What did they want? Why were they here?"

It didn't matter. They had to be dealt with, and it had to be done before Hitler got wind of it.

Schüller was suffering from shock, but he refused to let that be an obstacle. "What was the spies' objective? What was their next move?" He surmised they would attempt to escape Paris. "Would they use the Bidasoa River into Spain? Their best escape route would be by air."

He reasoned that they planned on fleeing by plane—the airfield. "They're headed for the airfield. Where would they get an airplane?" It didn't matter. What mattered was he had to wipe them off the face of the earth. Everything he'd worked for depended on it. He needed to get to a phone, and he knew just the person to call.

#

Schüller looked in the rearview mirror. A Luger was pointing at the back of his head. Little Benny was doing the pointing. "Alright, Heinie. It's the end of the line. Turn this jalopy around, and no tricks."

"You're a brave boy. You obviously didn't inherit such bravery from your father."

"You don't know nothin' about my daddy."

"I know a little. A group of prisoners broke into the camp warehouse and stole food. The commandant offered a running start to freedom to anyone who could expose the thieves. Your father took it upon himself to expose the criminals."

"What happened?"

"Your father was a very fast runner."

"And?"

"Well, he was no Jesse Owens, unfortunately. He was shot in the back with a Panzerfaust. Ka-boom. Bits and pieces of him exploded everywhere."

Little Benny broke down. "Nazi bastard!"

Schüller slammed on the breaks. The car came to a sudden stop and skidded in a semi-circle. The pistol fired. The bullet grazed the back of Schüller's head. Little Benny went flying forward and down on the floor of the front passenger seat. The Luger fell on the floor of the back seat. Schüller struggled to maintain control of the vehicle. The car tilted, rolled over twice, then righted itself facing in the opposite direction.

Schüller and Little Benny were violently tossed around. Smoke billowed from the engine. Little Benny stared up at Schüller from the floor. Schüller looked down at him with a blood-soaked grin. "The game is afoot."

#

The Messerschmitt Bf 109 was the backbone of the German air force. It was a flying death machine that shot down more planes than any other fighter in World War Two. Schüller's whoring buddy, Captain Helmut Weber had access to one.

Schüller sat on the edge of the hospital bed pointing a gun at Little Benny with his good ear to the phone. His head and hand were bandaged. Schüller counted the telephone rings as he and Little Benny were locked in a staring match. Schüller's phone call early that morning woke Helmut up from a deep slumber. By the time he picked up the phone, he was livid. "Who is it?"

"Good morning."

"Who is this?"

"It's your friend, Ernst."

"Do you know what time it is?"

"No rest for the wicked."

"What do you want?"

"How are you, my friend?"

"What the hell do you want?"

"I need a small favor."

"No, Ernst. I am all out of favors. Go back to bed. It is too early."

"I wouldn't call you this early in the morning if it wasn't important."

"Ernst."

"This is a grave matter."

"What do you want?" Helmut asked, not believing this was happening again.

"I'm sure you're aware that Der Führer has arrived in Paris."

"Yes, what of it?"

"I need you to take care of a tiny situation."

"What kind of a tiny situation?"

"It will involve one of your fighter planes."

"No."

"It is of the utmost importance."

"No."

"It's a matter of national security."

"Ernst, it is so early. Send one of your men to take care of this."

"It's too late for that now. Black niggers are headed to the old airfield. They must not escape."

"Ernst."

"I need you to kill every one of those spooks before they reach the airfield."

"Ernst, as much as I would love to help you, I am afraid I cannot do that. My in-laws are in town. I am driving them on a sightseeing tour of Paris in a few hours. I could recommend someone else."

"My dear Helmut. Please don't make me do this again."

"Do what again?

"You know."

"Ernst."

"Helmut."

"You cannot keep doing this."

"I wouldn't ask if it wasn't important."

"My in-laws…"

"You'll be done in no time. You are the finest pilot in the Luftwaffe. It won't take long."

"Dammit, Ernst."

"Do it for me. Do it for the Fatherland."

Schüller smiled at Little Benny. Little Benny stared back at him in stone-faced defiance.

"You son of a bitch!" Helmut screamed in a soft whisper.

"Put your wife on the phone."

Helmut took a breath and exhaled deeply with his eyes closed. He turned to gaze at his sleeping wife. "Fucker."

"I tried to make this pleasant."

"Pleasant isn't what comes to mind when I think of you."

"I thought we had a special bond."

"This is the last time."

"Of course."

"And then we are done."

"I won't bother you ever again."

"Stay out of my life."

"Oh, and one more thing. Tell your wife I said hello. Give her my love. Give her my sweet love."

"Fucker."

Helmut slammed the phone down, then suddenly realized he might wake his wife. He forced himself to control his breathing, then made a call. "This is Captain Weber. Have my Messerschmitt ready to fly at once. I want it fully armed right away. No! Do it now! Right now!"

Fifty-Three

Boucher sat behind the wheel of a speeding troop truck. Savage and Santiago sat beside him. With submachine guns tucked between their legs, they raced along the road with their eyes peeled. They had forty minutes to get to the airfield. They needed to travel the distance to the airfield and be on that plane, or it would leave without them.

The American expats in the rear of the truck sat in silence with a severe case of "We almost fucking died." Their minds were filled with thoughts of uncertainty, the death of Charles, and the fate of Little Benny.

Ernestine, Sauce, Spencer, Fats, and the rest of the group sat in dazed silence. The giant elephant in the room was what everyone learned about Ernestine and Schüller. They'd heard rumors and gossip, but it was still hard to believe. It made them all realize how much she'd sacrificed for them.

Ernestine protected them from the violent plague that terrorized millions of people throughout Europe. A price had to be paid for artistic freedom, and Ernestine paid with her self-respect, her money, and her pussy. Atrocities were happening at unimaginable levels. While the idea of Ernestine sleeping with Schüller turned their stomachs, it was only one of many sacrifices she made to keep her people from being sent to their deaths.

Ernestine sat quietly with her hands in her lap. Millicent sensing her sorrow, sat beside her. She put her arm around her as they rocked to the rhythm of the moving truck. Fats stood up and took off his blazer and handed it to Millicent. She took it and wrapped it around Ernestine's shoulders—a silent gesture of gratitude.

#

At the front of the truck, Savage and Santiago sat close together but occupied separate worlds. They survived a cosmic hijacking, traveled back in time 81 years, lost a comrade, and stole Nazi loot. The events of the last few days were a nightmare. What more would they have to endure? And after they arrived in England, what next? How would they live? What new forms of vintage racism would they have to face?

A surly negro and a belligerent lesbian were prime targets in a world of unfiltered oppression. The bulk of their existence meant having to endure ignorant mouth breathers with a penchant for stupidity. Would they be stuck in the past for the rest of their lives? Santiago thought about her daughter Kris. The idea of never seeing her again chewed her up from the inside out.

One Week Earlier — 2023

"Don't cry," Santiago said as she knelt to give nine-year-old Kris a big warm hug.

"You're going away forever. You're never coming back."

"Nope. When I get back, it's just going to be you and me. We're going places, big girl."

"Please don't go," Kris said. She had been abandoned as a baby, and those feelings left an ugly scar on her world.

"Mommy has to work, but I'll be back soon," Santiago said as she smoothed Kris' long black hair from her almond eyes.

"I'll be back in a few days."

"I don't believe you."

"I know."

Perhaps Kris knew something Santiago didn't. Once the band was safe, nothing would stop Santiago from doing everything she could to return home.

#

Savage was alone in the world. He was good at rationalizing the choices he made for his profession, but it took a cosmic event to give him pause. He despised all the suburban black teddy bear dads with their lawnmowers, flip-flops, and weekend barbeques. He wanted the exact opposite of a middle-register existence—an existence that would stretch his life to a thin film of small insignificance. He'd stayed at the finest hotels and had more tail than a toilet seat. He outran the police, survived shootouts in rush hour traffic, and masterminded skillful heists from the largest banking institutions in the world.

But in the end, those tubby fucks had won. They'd given in to societal engineering and Mother Nature. They raised families, paid mortgages, and earned a warm smile at the end of a hard day. Savage had none of that. No warm smile for Savage. He would never have that, and for the first time in his life he was filled with regret.

The life Savage chose meant he had to walk away from relationships at the first sign of the law. In the end he had nothing—only experiences and memories—but memories fade.

Savage had failed in the matrimonial sweepstakes. He thought Joslyn could make him whole, and when Stewart assured him that would have never happened, he felt empty and alone. But at least he finally knew the truth.

#

"Savage, forget Joslyn," Stewart said. "She was a one-way ticket to a wretched existence. Is that how you wanted to end up—with this so-called love of your life? "Savage, this is your moment to shine—this is your time. Work with me and your life will have more meaning than you could ever imagine. But I need you to dig—dig deep. Fight! Save Ernestine and those musicians and you'll save yourself... and the world."

#

Savage was lost somewhere along the infinite corridors of time—trapped in a world worse than the one he'd rejected. But his skillset was valuable, and it gave him purpose.

He stared blankly out the window as the truck breezed past pastoral vistas. He chuckled to himself as a thought sprang into his head. He'd wound up with the perfect mate—a woman who could kick his ass.

"There's no radio in this thing?" Savage said to Boucher.

"This is a military truck. If you wanted a radio, we should have stolen a staff car. Then you could listen to all the German opera your heart desires."

Savage turned to Santiago. "What kind of music do you like?"

"I like all kinds of music."

"Really?"

"Yeah."

"Do you like Hendrix?"

"Jimi Hendrix?"

"...Yeah."

"Sure, I love Jimi Hendrix," Santiago replied.

"Really? What's your favorite Hendrix album?"

"Uh, I don't know."

"You don't know?"

"I'm not familiar with all his albums."

"How about one?"

"I don't remember the names."

"You love Jimi Hendrix, but you can't name one album?"

"He has some good songs. I'm no expert or anything."

Boucher's head turned slowly to look at them. He gave them a strange bug-eyed expression having no idea what they were talking about.

"I'm not asking you to be an expert," Savage continued. "I'm asking if you have a favorite Hendrix album."

"Maybe "Love" was too strong a word. I like a few of his songs. Whatever, ok?"

"Whatever?"

"Yeah, whatever."

"Whatever."

"Yeah. Whatever. Can you handle that?"

"I'm handling it right now."

"It's ok to enjoy Jimi Hendrix without having an encyclopedic knowledge of every album he ever made."

"You seem a little defensive."

"Defensive? Me? Do you have a prized Hendrix lunch box collection at home or something?"

"No, but I bet you have a Hendrix t-shirt in your dresser drawer."

"You'd lose that bet."

"You can't name a single album?"

"This is super-duper important to you, isn't it?"

"He's *only* the greatest rock guitarist of his generation, that's all."

"Excuse me if I don't share your sense of wonder."

"Early Hendrix or late Hendrix?"

"You won't quit, will you?"

"The Experience or Band of Gypsys?"

"The Wind Cries Mary."

"Is that the name of an album?"

"Hey, I know. Let's play a game. It's called *Silent Mouth*. You start."

"Just making small talk."

"Well, you suck at it."

"You said you love Jimi Hendrix. You really can't name a single album?"

"No, I can't, pendejo!"

"It doesn't matter."

"Why do you care so much?"

"Whatever... Little Benny."

"...Yeah, Little Benny."

"Fucking Schüller," Boucher added.

"Fucking Schüller," Savage and Santiago replied.

And in the blink of an eye, all hell broke loose. There was machine-gun fire and an ear-shattering explosion. The inside of the truck spun around in circles like a laundry dryer. Their world twisted into a hurricane of swirling debris.

Fifty-Four

The first thing Santiago heard was a high-pitched ringing in her ears. The ringing grew to a crescendo, then silence. There was moaning and the sound of destruction. The smell: burning rubber, gasoline, and fear. When Santiago opened her eyes, she couldn't see. Everything was distorted—blurry. She had a piercing headache as she lay on the grass with her body twisted at an odd angle. She blinked to clear her vision until finally, things came into focus.

Everyone inside the truck had been tossed around like children's toys. The truck was on fire. There was a large debris field covering the road and the countryside. Burning truck parts were flung about mixed with musical instruments, clothing, and strips of burning canvas.

Savage and Boucher were beginning to stir as Santiago stood up and staggered around to get her bearings. Ernestine and Sauce were already on their feet helping Fats, who was dazed but in one piece. Millicent wandered around deliriously as Spencer searched frantically. "My sax! Where's my sax?!"

Santiago took Millicent by the arm and made her sit down in an attempt to clear her head. "You're ok. We're alive."

From out of nowhere, Helmut's Messerschmitt flew overhead fast and low to inspect his handiwork. Helmut loved his job. He enjoyed the sense of power coupled with anonymity. He could kill tens of people at a time at will. He experienced all the power and the glory of a kill, with none of the unpleasant aftertaste of being there. Being a fighter pilot was cool as hell.

"It is a Messerschmitt!" Boucher yelled. "Take cover!"

There was nowhere to hide except to jump down into a shallow gorge next to the road. Connected to the gorge was a drainage tunnel and a piping system just large enough for human beings.

The group ran in desperation to get there. They helped each other along the way. Fats' massive form was light as a feather when his life depended on it.

Spencer and Millicent were snapped back to reality as the Messerschmitt's distinctive roar tore through the sky.

They were sitting ducks. Something had to be done and fast. Savage ran out into the open, frantically searching for something. The truck's contents were flung everywhere. Savage raced around searching as Helmut flew overhead, unleashing a hellish barrage of machine gunfire. Savage rolled and took cover as torrents of bullets narrowly missed him.

"He's trying to commit suicide!" Ernestine yelled to Santiago.

After each pass, Savage made a run for it. He scanned the debris field. Finally, he saw it. The butt of the MG42 machine gun was sticking out of the corner of a piece of canvas. Santiago and Boucher kneeled, looking out from the drainage tunnel. Everyone else from the group crouched behind them.

"What is he doing?" Santiago yelled.

"He is doing something stupid," Boucher said. "And he is going to need help."

Savage grabbed the MG42 and ran for cover as Boucher sprinted out of the gorge. He grabbed an ammunition belt lying on the grass. He ran toward Savage. The truck was turned over on its side. Savage was using it for cover as he set up the MG42 on the top of the wheel of the truck to point upwards. The Messerschmitt made another pass firing at Boucher as he ran toward the truck.

A hail of bullets peppered the air near Boucher as the ground ripped up around him. He barely made it to Savage as the plane circled for another run.

Savage grabbed the ammunition belt from Boucher and realized he didn't know how to load an MG42. Boucher shoved him aside. He took the ammunition belt and began loading the weapon. "Silly Americans," he said with exasperation.

Loading the MG42, he finished it off by slapping down the receiver assembly with a loud metallic click. The Messerschmitt was right on top of them firing non-stop. It nearly shot off Savage's foot. Boucher dove for cover.

As the plane circled, Savage balanced the machine gun up against the top of the upturned wheel and aimed. The Messerschmitt was too fast as it strafed the entire area including the truck. The destruction was so overwhelming Savage and Boucher ran back to the drainage tunnel.

"We're dead meat," Ernestine yelled.

"What we need is a miracle," Boucher replied.

"A miracle," Savage said. "That's exactly what we need." Suddenly, something occurred to him. "Jumpin' Jesus! What's today?"

"What?" Boucher replied.

Santiago sensed something was up. "The date!" she barked. What's today's date?!"

"It's Wednesday, July 15th," Ernestine blurted.

Savage checked his watch.

"This is perfect!" Savage responded.

"What's up?" Santiago inquired.

"We need a miracle, and we got it," Savage replied.

"What the hell you talkin' about?" Ernestine asked.

The Messerschmitt strafed the area again, nearly killing them all. They huddled together in fear for their lives as the plane arced overhead. Savage looked at his watch.

"Five seconds. Get ready."

"Five seconds?! Get ready for what?!" yelled Boucher.

"Do you know what a solar eclipse is?"

Suddenly, darkness fell in a blanket of pitch black. Helmut was startled into blindness. He panicked and fought to regain control of his senses. Savage patted Boucher on the back, then ran back to the machine gun perched on the truck's front wheel.

As the Messerschmitt banked overhead, Helmut turned a light on in the cockpit. Savage saw the light and let loose with a hail of machine-gun fire that ripped into the airplane.

Helmut was stunned. He'd been hit and realized his legs were covered in blood. Seething with anger, Helmut was determined to finish them off once and for all.

He pointed the nose of the plane straight down and fired. Bullets sprayed the area as Boucher and Savage took cover. A bullet tore through the shoulder of Savage's blazer, missing flesh.

Helmut heard a clicking sound. His guns were jammed. Frustration consumed him as he cursed under his breath. He steered the airplane to plummet at a downward angle. Savage stood up from his concealed position and fired at the Messerschmitt until he ran out of ammunition. An onslaught of bullets had passed through the plane, hitting Helmut's upper torso. He screamed like an old white lady.

Flames flickered inside the cockpit as Helmut thought about his wife and in-laws waiting for him in Paris. They would wait for hours, but he would never arrive. He would never see his wife's face again. Smoke and flames filled the cockpit. The plane arced upward, then dove straight down into a cluster of trees and exploded into a giant fireball.

As the eclipse faded back to normal daylight, Boucher turned to Savage. "How did you know that was going to happen?"

"Let's just say I got an A in history."

Savage and Boucher slowly emerged from around the overturned truck to inspect the carnage. Two of the passengers from the group's entourage lay dead. A man and a woman lay sprawled upon the grass with bullet holes raked across their backs.

"Tough break," Savage said, attempting to produce the correct amount of compassion.

The rest of the group emerged from the drainage tunnel. Ernestine and Santiago trotted over to get a closer look at the bodies.

"For crying out loud," said Ernestine, who was weak with distraught. "Clyde and Pat. They were gonna get hitched." She turned to Savage. "We ain't leavin' them out here like this."

"I know," said Savage. He turned to Boucher. "How far away are we from the airfield?"

"We are very close."

"How close?"

"It is right there."

And there it was, three-quarters of a mile away. The road led right to it. A torched and mangled chain-link fence stretched out around it. The torched control tower could be seen standing tall in the distance.

Fifty-Five

The shock of seeing Stewart thrown out of the cargo plane shattered Palmer. Then he got angry, piss mad angry. He saw a flare gun slide across the floor. Palmer instinctively grabbed it and fired it at Mordecai. Mordecai's chest exploded. Sparks and fire burst throughout the cabin. Palmer stumbled toward Mordecai. He ripped the device from his hand and kicked him out of the doorway and into the sky.

The out-of-control plane banked hard to the left and upward. Everything in the aircraft shifted to one side. Debris spun everywhere. Ritenour struggled in frustration. He was severely entangled in cargo netting.

Palmer heard a tortured scream and crawled across the floor to the doorway. He peered outside to see Stewart hanging onto the side of the airplane by a handhold. She was screaming bloody murder.

"Sweet Jesus!" Palmer cried.

He looked down and realized that Mordecai was hanging on to Stewart's ankle with one hand. They dangled on the side of the burning aircraft like ribbons in the wind. Mordecai sprang upward, climbed over Stewart, and worked his way back into the airplane. He stood upright before Palmer with visions of horrific murder in his blood shot eyes. Palmer was defenseless.

"Get me out of here!" Ritenour yelled.

Mordecai reluctantly diverted his attention from Palmer and rushed over to free Ritenour. Flak continued to explode around the airplane.

"3 MINUTES AND 26 SECONDS UNTIL IGNITION."

"We won't make it!" Ritenour ordered. "Deploy the virus now!"

But the pilot was long dead. The top half of his torso fell to the floor like a sack of apples. His death grip pulled the yoke back, spiraling the plane upward into a brain-crushing ascent. The sudden incline swung Stewart's body up near the doorway, where she found another handhold.

Mordecai lost his footing and leaned forward to maintain his balance. He had nothing to hold on to. For a few brief seconds, Mordecai teetered helplessly off balance. He looked into Ritenour's eyes like a loving boy to his father. "I shall avenge your death."

Ritenour bristled and extended his hand. Mordecai reached toward him. Before their fingers touched, Stewart stepped in with a metal rod and swung it like a baseball bat. She hit Mordecai across the face so hard, a cacophony of flesh and metal could be heard. Mordecai was knocked backward off his feet through the rear of the aircraft. His flailing body met the void.

#

The burning airplane rose upward then banked downward into a twisting death spiral. The plane's contents spun around violently. Everything turned topsy-turvy as it suddenly banked upward again. Palmer clung to the inside of the aircraft. He tossed Stewart the device. "Please get us the fuck on up outta here!"

"2 MINUTES UNTIL IGNITION."

Ritenour was a fly caught in a spider's web. Stewart turned to Palmer. "Put on the parachute and jump. Do it now."

Palmer paused. "You still mad?"

"Jump."

"I'll make it up to you."

"It will never be enough."

"It never is." Palmer struggled to get to his feet and grabbed the parachute. "I ain't no paratrooper."

"Shut up and jump," Stewart replied with contempt.

Running on pure trauma, Palmer put on the parachute and buckled up. "I feel like we coulda' been somethin'."

"Jump, or I'll knock your ass off this airplane!"

Palmer crossed himself. He took a final look at Stewart. "I fucked up. I'm really sorry."

Palmer flung himself through the open door. A gust of fire and smoke shot up after him.

"1 MINUTE 13 SECONDS UNTIL IGNITION."

Stewart watched Ritenour struggle. She fought back the tears as her shoulder throbbed in agony. It was finally over. She should have been apoplectic. Instead, she was overcome with sadness. The man she loved, the man she married, had created the dumbest evil in history. "Was I that bad?"

Ritenour was in the throes of a compressed tantrum. "Get me out of this."

"What were you thinking?"

"You think I'm stupid," Ritenour said as he coughed from the smoke. "Goddamn it, I was in love with you. But I guess I was only destined to be the guy who shows up at award shows with you."

"We never talked about this."

"I'm not your wife! You're *my* wife!"

"Rit..."

"I deserved better."

"Goddamn, you..."

"What about *my* dreams? What about *my* career—*my* aspirations?"

"Rit, I'm sorry. We talked about your work. I know we did. I..."

"Oh no—I can't discuss anything about myself because ultimately, there will always be a tangent. A tangent that leads right back to you. It's your world, and we're all just pom-pom girls cheering your success."

"I'm so sorry."

"I offered to test my research on *Simulated Earth*. Did you support that idea? Did you offer to help? Put in a good word for me at The Organization? Sure, you did. But then something came up. Something always came up."

"I guess we're way beyond that now."

"36 SECONDS UNTIL IGNITION."

The engines of the airplane sputtered. The wind slammed against the fuselage as the airplane dove, then banked upward with a groaning moan. The sound of flak explosions grew silent. The engines died—silence—the wind.

"I guess I should blame myself for tolerating you this long," Ritenour continued. "The drinking... the cheating... see? Once again, you're off the hook. It's all *my* fault. *I* chose you. All this happened because I married an overeducated narcissist."

Ritenour's anger escalated. "Know this about me, Marianne. I am not a Beta Male. I am a visionary! I am an Alpha Male, not your chauffeur!"

"13 SECONDS UNTIL IGNITION."

Stewart stared at him in a sad trance. What was left of the plane continued to soar upward toward the Mesosphere.

"I'm sorry, Rit. I fucked up our marriage. I thought I was doing the right thing."

"There is no right thing. It's *your* thing."

Stewart struggled to keep her balance as she maneuvered toward the open door. Flames rushed through the fuselage. Stewart tucked her device into her pocket and strapped on the last parachute.

Ritenour stared back at her, expressionless. "My self-worth doesn't come from my usefulness to you!"

Stewart jumped out of the aircraft.

"No one will ever love you as much as I do," Ritenour muttered.

Stewart fell fast as she tumbled through the air. Visions of their wedding, dinner parties, and family gatherings flooded her thoughts. Stewart flattened out to control her descent as she soared downward through the atmosphere. She twisted around to look upward. The airplane disappeared into the heavens.

"IGNITION."

A loud, fiery explosion cracked the sky. An intense fireball followed. The force of the blast sent shock waves that slammed into Stewart.

Pieces of airplane rained down around her. She covered her face from the explosion, curling herself into a ball as she plummeted.

From the ground, Savage noticed a tiny black dot falling from the sky. Stewart felt the wind blast her from every direction. The green expanse rushed upward. She reached for the ripcord.

Fifty-Six

When the Germans took over Villeneuve-Orly Airport during the Battle of France, they used it to launch Luftwaffe bombers and fighter units. Because of this, it became a prime military target for Allied forces. The Royal Air Force and the US Air Force had destroyed much of the airport's infrastructure with precision bombing. With German military personnel needed elsewhere, a small skeleton crew was left to repurpose what was left.

The runways were pockmarked with craters and debris, making it unfit for the Germans to use as a launching site. There was not one runway that could be used for takeoffs or landings—except one. While this last runway suffered damage and was unfit for larger aircraft, a skilled pilot could maneuver a takeoff and land with the knowledge of what to avoid. While the Germans declared Villeneuve-Orly Airport unusable for military operations, it was still suitable for clandestine use.

#

Ernestine and the rest of the group arrived at the airfield under Savage, Santiago, and Boucher's protection. Savage and Santiago were expecting another fight as they cautiously trekked across the debris-littered landing area.

"We made it," Boucher said as they trotted toward the runway. "This airfield has been abandoned since the Germans gave up trying to repair it. The Allies use it for target practice."

With the control tower still intact, there was destruction of airplane hangars, airplanes, and mechanical equipment as far as the eye could see.

"Must have been some party," Savage said as he got a whiff of burning rubber and corpses. The group clustered together as they avoided broken wheel assemblies, propellers, and a decapitated arm still in its sleeve.

"Eyes forward," Santiago cautioned to everyone. "We're almost there."

"How is an airplane supposed to land in this?" asked Savage.

"Very carefully," replied Boucher. "Hurry. We are running out of time."

"Where the hell is it?" Savage asked.

"Right over there," replied Boucher.

He pointed to a section of debris with twisted beams. Visible through the arch of a bent metal support, a large silver twin-engine passenger airplane sat on the runway.

"Hurry! There is very little time," Boucher said with urgency.

The pilot sat nervously in the cockpit, checking his watch. He saw the group running toward him and straightened up in his seat with excitement. He started the engine. The propellers spun and gathered speed as the engine roared. The group moved briskly through an obstacle course of rubble.

Millicent tripped. Savage helped her to her feet. She sprained her ankle and was now limping forward in pain. Savage swept her up in his arms as the group ran toward the aircraft. The airplane turned down the runway as it prepared for takeoff with the fuselage passenger door wide open.

Then they heard a familiar sound. It grew louder, stopping Savage and Santiago in their tracks. It was the sound of a helicopter. It was coming in for a landing.

"It's Reiner!" Santiago yelled.

As the group boarded the plane, Ernestine, Santiago, Boucher, and Savage waited outside the plane's door to watch the helicopter touch down. As the helicopter's engine was turned off, Reiner, Buster, and

Fontaine climbed out. Overjoyed, Ernestine ran over to them to give them a big hug. Savage, Santiago, and Boucher followed.

"Heavens to Betsy!" Ernestine cried. "I never thought I'd see ya'll again. Come on now. Let's get on the plane."

Reiner, Fontaine, and Buster were strangely silent.

Savage sensed something was wrong. After a beat, Little Benny stepped off the back of the helicopter.

Ernestine screamed. "Little Benny!"

Schüller stepped out after him holding a pistol. His head and right hand were still wrapped in bandages. Two bloody fingers poked through the dressing. "How could you leave without saying goodbye?" He inquired with a disturbed grin. "Don't you think that's a little rude?"

"Where's Theotis, you son of a bitch?" asked Ernestine.

"Theotis? Oh, you mean your husband? Oh, he's long dead."

Ernestine's entire world died.

"His defiance was admirable," Schüller continued. "You would have been proud. Over time he grew weaker, but he never lost that niggery insubordination. We did our best to break him. Eventually, I grew weary of his insolence, so I blew his brains out."

Ernestine's legs lost all their strength. All the oxygen left her body. She began to lose consciousness as she sank. Savage propped her up. The realization that the love of her life was truly dead made her want to disappear. With all the strength she could muster, she maintained her balance and confronted her husband's killer.

"You've been lyin' to me as long as I've known you," Ernestine replied.

"You whored yourself for a dead nigger."

"You…"

"I still remember the look in his blood-shot eyes when his brains splattered on my boots."

Ernestine lunged forward with rage. The barrel of Schüller's pistol touched the back of Little Benny's head.

"Drop your weapons, or the chimp dies."

Boucher, Santiago, and Savage reluctantly tossed down their weapons.

"Put your hands up," Schüller said as they slowly complied.

"You don't know when to quit, do you?" Savage said.

"You think you can humiliate me, then ride off into the sunset and live happily ever after? You don't know who you're dealing with."

"Actually, we do," Savage replied. "You're a depraved Nazi war criminal. If we don't kill you, the Americans will. If the Americans don't get you, the Russians will. The Russians will murder you, rape you, rape you again, then hang you upside down naked from a church steeple."

"Raped by men," Santiago added. "Filthy *Russian* men."

"Very funny," Schüller replied. "We have a score to settle, and it involves all of you dying an excruciating death."

Reiner broke into the conversation, unable to contain himself. "He captured us at The Montclair while I was trying to help Buster and Lorraine to escape," he said apologetically. "We had no choice."

Schüller struck Reiner in the back of the head with his pistol. "Mewling simp," he snarled.

Reiner touched the blood on the back of his head as his eyes watered.

"You'll get yours soon enough," Reiner whimpered under his breath.

Little Benny stood like a little gangster with a scowl on his face.

"Let us go, Schüller," Savage demanded. "We'll leave Paris like Hitler wanted. You'll never see us again."

Schüller laughed. "Which one of you shot my hand?"

"It was not I, but I wish it were," Boucher replied.

"I missed," said Savage defiantly. "I was aiming at your head."

"Still, a remarkable shot," Schüller said. "Black nigger bastard."

"Nazi cuck bitch," Savage replied.

"You and I have unfinished business," Santiago said cutting in. "Let's not forget you tortured me. You're a malignant bastard and I demand recompense."

"Malignant bastard?" Schüller said in mock confusion. Reiner chuckled. Schüller noticed Reiner's amusement, then turned back to Santiago. "I don't think I've ever been called that before. But as much as I would like to continue this conversation, first things first."

Schüller turned and shot Reiner in the chest. The force of the bullet sent him stumbling backward like a broken marionette. He died instantly with his eyes bulging out of his head.

"Son of a bitch!" Santiago yelled as the group backed up in horror.

"You're such a dick," Savage remarked.

"Sorry to interrupt. You were saying?" Schüller said to Santiago.

Santiago moved toward him, prepared to take a bullet as long as she got her hands on him. Schüller dragged Little Benny close to him by the wrist.

"Make one false move, and I'll kill this little nigglet."

Santiago looked into Little Benny's eyes. She gave him a subtle nod of the head.

Suddenly, Little Benny performed the wristlock escape as Santiago had taught him. As a big finish, he punched Schüller in the throat as hard as he could then kicked him in the balls for dessert. Schüller's body curled over in debilitating agony.

Santiago kicked Schüller's pistol upward. It hit him in the face as the gun went off. Schüller backed up red-faced as he coughed violently. He fled toward a nearby building. Santiago ran after him. Schüller spun around awkwardly, fired a shot, and barely missed Santiago as she ducked.

Ernestine picked up a rifle.

"Run motherfucka', run!"

She took careful aim and fired. The bullet hit Schüller in the buttocks. The force sent him tumbling. He screamed as he toppled to the ground. He got up and kept running with a severe limp. A burned-out airplane hanger was just ahead of him.

Boucher picked up his rifle and ran after Schüller. Ernestine ran toward Little Benny and the rest of the group with a teary-eyed embrace.

"Get on the plane!" Santiago yelled.

"She's right," said Savage. "We're running out of time!"

"You ain't gotta tell me twice," Buster replied as he helped everyone edge closer to the plane.

"Let's go!" Ernestine yelled as she trotted toward the rumbling aircraft. She passed Savage then stopped. "You did all right."

"We got lucky."

"I thought we could call Paris home."

"Fuck Paris. You made The Montclair home—a home for jazz. A home for black virtuosos. *You* did that."

She gave him a hug. "You're a piece of work."

Santiago joined them.

"Thank you," Ernestine said to Savage and Santiago.

The pilot leaned outside the cockpit window, frantically waving his arms. "WE ARE LEAVING!" he said as he pointed to his watch. Their time was up.

Savage turned to Buster and Fontaine. "Time to go!"

"What about Boucher?" Santiago said.

"There's no time!"

They ran to the plane and climbed through the fuselage door. In the distance, they heard a loud explosion. A German troop truck crashed through the gates and was barreling toward them at breakneck speed.

"Rats!" Little Benny yelled.

"Fucking Schüller!" Santiago blurted. "Take off!" she ordered the pilot.

"We're not going to make it," Savage replied. "If we don't stall that truck, the plane won't make it out of here."

"What about us?"

"I know."

"I have a daughter."

Savage processed. "Stay on the plane. I'll hold them off."

"Shit!" Santiago said, realizing she couldn't let Savage fight the Nazis alone. "God, dammit. Ok. Let's end this."

Savage noticed Fontaine giving him a last look. Then something suddenly occurred to him. "Wait!" Savage jumped out of the airplane and sprinted to the helicopter.

"Savage!" Santiago yelled.

Savage reached behind the back seat and pulled out the backpack with the stolen money. He sprinted back to the plane.

"You'll need this," Savage said to Ernestine, as he handed her the backpack. "It's the money Schüller stole from you. Don't spend it all in one place."

Ernestine's eyes grew wide. "Heavens to Betsy, you did *real* damn good."

"It's less than you deserve."

Fontaine looked at the bills poking through the seams of the backpack. "You're a hero," she said to Savage. "You're one of the good ones."

"I'm not so sure about that," Savage replied as a recent memory suddenly popped into his brain.

Three Weeks Earlier — 2023

Savage looked down into a freshly dug grave. Perspiring heavily, moonlight illuminated the outline of his glistening torso covered in a dago tee. He breathed heavily. He shoved the sharp end of the shovel into the ground, making it stand straight up.

Taking a moment to catch his breath, he turned and walked out of sight. He returned with a body wrapped in plastic and duct tape. Carrying it over his shoulder, he threw the corpse into the grave. He looked down at the body then disappeared again. He returned with another body wrapped in plastic and duct tape and threw it into the grave next to the first. Taking a handkerchief from his pocket, he wiped the sweat from his face as his breathing stabilized.

He kneeled, looking into the grave. His face showed a combination of sorrow and detachment as he spoke to the corpses. "This isn't me. I'm not even here. I'm still in bed. This is the Ambien talking. This is what they call an Ambien blackout. But I'm not blaming the Ambien. You did this. We could have been so happy together. But no—you like to blow things up so you can feel like you're in control of your life. And everyone else is just... background." Savage's face contorted in sadness. "I would have taken a bullet for you."

He tossed a gold pendant attached to a thin chain into the grave. He shoveled a patch of dirt in after it. The pendant read:

Joslyn + Lorenzo Forever

"I brought along your therapist for company. I'm sure you two will have a lot to talk about."

The second pile of dirt covered the pendant. The third pile of dirt turned everything to black.

\#

"Thank you," Fontaine said as her eyes filled with tears. Buster pulled Fontaine to her seat and gave Savage the stink eye as the sounds of seatbelts clicked into place.

"Hey," Savage said to Buster. "The next time you make a record, get a good entertainment lawyer. You're a goddamn music legend for Christ sakes."

Buster didn't know what to make of that, but he had an inkling Savage knew something he didn't. "You a' motherfucka' on that guitar," he replied begrudgingly.

Savage let that sink in. It meant a hell of a lot coming from a jazz legend.

"See you in the funny papers," Ernestine cut in.

Savage smiled.

Little Benny hugged Santiago. "I love you, Miss Delores."

Santiago waved goodbye as she and Savage exited the plane.

"Savage!" Little Benny yelled.

Savage poked his head back through the doorway of the plane. Little Benny looked like an old soul. "Keep that pop in your collar."

That's when the pieces fell into place. Savage recognized his old Uncle Benjamin in those youthful eyes. "Yessiree," Savage replied wistfully.

Savage slapped the side of the fuselage twice and slammed the airplane door shut. The plane moved down the runway. Savage and Santiago checked their weapons.

"One of these days I'm gonna get the girl," Savage said.

"Not if I get her first," Santiago replied. "Which would you rather be? The chump holding his wife's purse at the mall, or the bad motherfucker saving the world from evil?"

Savage smiled. Boucher ran up to them out of breath.

"Schüller escaped. He took off on a motorcycle."

"We know," Savage said. "He brought company." Savage pointed to the truck speeding toward them. They heard gunshots coming from the truck.

"I hate Nazis," Boucher said.

"If you run, you can catch the plane," Santiago told him. "Your call."

Another gunshot was heard as it whizzed past them.

"We must delay the Germans so that the plane can take off safely," Boucher argued.

"We'll handle it. Get out of here," Savage said. "This is your last chance to escape. Santiago and I will keep them busy."

"You need to get back to The Resistance and continue the fight," explained Santiago. "The French will have their revenge."

"Of that, I am certain," Boucher replied, chambering a round in his rifle.

"You can tell your grandchildren that you stood for something bigger than yourself," Savage said.

"Everything is bigger than myself," Boucher replied with a wink. "You Americans and your melodrama."

They watched the truck move closer. They heard more gunshots.

"You are good fighters," Boucher said. "We could use more like you. Bonne chance." He winked and sprinted off toward the control tower.

Suddenly, hell rained down in the form of hot Nazi lead. Savage and Santiago took cover.

The airplane continued to taxi down the runway, swerving to avoid obstacles and craters. Bullets punctured the airplane's fuselage.

"They're not going to make it!" Santiago screamed. "Aim for the tires!"

Savage and Santiago returned fire. Their aim was true as bullets pelted the front tires of the speeding troop truck.

The plane gained altitude then dropped back down on the runway. The pilot, bathed in sweat, bit his lip as he pulled back on the yoke. "We're too heavy!"

Hysterical screams of panic filled the passenger cabin.

Savage and Santiago hunkered down amidst the hellish onslaught of German firepower. The airplane ascended—its landing gear ripped to shreds by enemy fire. Savage shot one of the soldiers in the head as his body tumbled from the side of the truck and on to the tarmac.

A Panzerfaust round detonated near Savage and Santiago. Their bodies were thrown in a heap as they clung to consciousness. The plane ascended.

Savage and Santiago lay dazed with their ears ringing as they watched the plane gain altitude. It flew higher and higher, disappearing into the heavens.

#

"We did it," Savage said, still recovering from the explosion.

"How about that," Santiago replied weakly.

The troop truck screeched to a halt with the sound of blubbering flat tires. Nine, heavily armed soldiers jumped out of the vehicle and surrounded Savage and Santiago.

Schüller climbed out of the passenger cab of the truck with difficulty. His blood trickled onto the tarmac.

"Ernestine had a tight little box. I'll miss her." He moved closer to Savage, speaking in confidence. "You know what I find a terrible curse?"

Savage stared back at him.

"Large women with small breasts. It's God's practical joke!" he said with a maniacal laugh.

"It's over," Savage said.

"Oh, really?" Schüller turned to his men. "You see? It's over! These two American spies have single-handedly defeated the German Army," Schüller said, laughing. He turned back to Savage and Santiago. "Explain that to me. Explain to me how it's over while my trained killers have you surrounded. This should be interesting."

"The Buster Pete Band escaped. The score is: Negroes 1, Nazis 0. You've failed. And you know how old uncle Adolph is about failure."

"Please continue. This is fascinating."

"In a couple of years, the war will be over. You and these poor saps will either be dead or in prison for war crimes. You're already losing the war. It doesn't take an Einstein to calculate Germany's dwindling resources won't keep your tanks and planes running."

"Is that so?"

"It is so. Your armies will be reduced to old men and boys fighting against hardened Allied soldiers. Give yourself up and I'll try to talk Santiago out of killing you with her bare hands."

"That's very kind of you."

"Surrender to us, and we'll turn you over to the Americans," Santiago added. "But this deal is only for your men, not you. I'm going to kill *you*, and I'm going to take my sweet time doing it." She turned to Savage, "It's the right thing to do."

Schüller found this all very amusing and looked back at his men as they chuckled in amusement.

"Insanity obviously runs in your families," Schüller said. "You believe this is a win for the negroes? You think they'll find refuge? If you believe life is difficult under German law, wait until they return to the United States. Are you naïve enough to believe they'll be celebrated as heroes for their dramatic escape? Parades in the streets of New York? A key to the city? A national holiday?

"You Americans and your delusional patriotism is a mental illness. You claim to stand for peace and fairness in the world. Your countrymen have committed far greater crimes against spooks, injuns, prairie niggers, coolies, and everyone else living in your little cesspool of a melting pot. And you call *me* a criminal?"

Savage turned to Santiago. "Prairie niggers?"

"What? You're suddenly offended?"

"I'm triggered."

Savage and Santiago felt dispassionate revenge. Schüller had a point, but they weren't going to give him the satisfaction.

"Everybody's hands are dirty," Schüller continued. "So don't point your filthy finger at me. I guarantee you if the Americans capture me, I shall be treated far better than any of your negro colleagues."

Suddenly a Nazi staff car with a pair of motorcycle escorts drove up in front of them. The armed bodyguards were dressed in black military uniforms with swastikas and armed with submachine guns. The driver stepped out and ran around the front of the car and opened the passenger door.

Out stepped Adolf Hitler. Exiting from the back seat was Joseph Goebbels, Albert Speer, and Heinrich Himmler. The escorts dismounted and stood beside them. Schüller's men parted like the Red Sea and snapped to attention. Hitler walked up to Schüller with a look of pure menace.

Santiago gave Savage a deadpan look. "I thought he'd be taller."

Schüller clicked his heels and gave Hitler the Nazi salute. "Mein Führer! You are just in time!"

"You were ordered to remove the Untermensch from Paris. Why are these vermin standing in my presence?"

"Mein Führer, I have at this very moment captured these two American spies. The woman is a lesbian!

"Wow. Really?" said Santiago.

Hitler took note of Santiago's response.

Schüller continued. "As you have ordered, mein Führer, I have rid Paris of the negroes. Instead of degenerate jazz music, the sounds of Wagner shall echo in the streets, cafes, and restaurants of Paris. Our greatest composer shall herald the victory of the German people. These two, of course, will be hanged in public and displayed as an example. The French shall know that The Third Reich is not to be trifled with!"

"Nein! They shall be shot by a firing squad with you beside them,"

Hitler replied, spitting with anger. "You have failed me for the last time! I believed you were a superior officer! I was warned about you, but I would not believe it! I humiliated myself, defending you! A true son of Germany would never disgrace the Fatherland! I believed in my heart, the blood running through your veins was pure and righteous, yet you defile yourself by lying with vermin!"

Goebbels handed Schüller five enlarged black & white photographs. Hitler turned away in disgust. Schüller looked at them, stunned. Oxygen evacuated his lungs.

Candid black and white photographs depicted Schüller, forcing himself on Ernestine in a variety of sexual positions in his office.

Blood drained from Schüller's face as nervous anxiety exploded throughout his body. "Reiner."

"This is the last time you will betray me," Hitler continued. "This is the last time you shall make me look foolish! You have failed the German people for the last time!"

Fifty-Seven

Ernestine sank down in her seat and exhaled as the sound of weapons fire faded. The airplane engines moaned like a vibrating death machine. She turned around, checking to see if everyone was safe. Out of the corner of her eye, she noticed two people sitting together in the rear of the airplane. They weren't part of the group. She couldn't see them clearly in the low light. Ernestine squinted her eyes trying to get a better look. One of them was a strangely dressed colored woman. That woman was Stewart. She was sitting next to a colored man wearing prisoner's garb. That man was Ernestine's husband Theotis.

Stewart noticed Ernestine looking at them and smiled. She tapped Theotis on the knee and pointed toward her. Theotis caught Ernestine's eye. He smiled and gave her the OK sign. Ernestine's eyes grew big with excitement. Her face looked like it was about ready to explode.

Fifty-Eight

Inside a brick courtyard, a Wehrmacht captain stood with a pensive expression on his weathered face. He took out a cigarette, lit it with a brass cigarette lighter, and inhaled deeply. After a beat, he dropped the cigarette on the ground and stepped on it with his boot.

"Achtung!"

Twelve German soldiers with rifles sprang to attention. Savage, Santiago, and Schüller were tied to separate poles in front of a brick wall riddled with bullet holes and human splatter.

Santiago was panicked and lost control. "Everything you did was for nothing," Santiago fumed at Schüller. "It was a waste! A waste!"

"Fertig!" said the captain.

The soldiers readied their rifles. Schüller's complexion was chalk white. "This is wrong. This is all wrong. This wasn't supposed to happen this way," he said, trembling uncontrollably. "I'm good looking. I was supposed to retire as a wealthy man and open a little coffee shop in Innsbruck."

"Zielen!"

The soldiers aimed their rifles.

Savage turned to Schüller. "In what fairy tale do you murder millions of innocent people and live happily ever after?"

"Go to hell!"

"I'll be there waiting," Savage replied. "Don't be late."

"Feuer!"

The soldiers fired. Bullets perforated Schüller's torso dozens of times. Geysers of blood gushed from his wounds. His eyes bugged out from their sockets as he took his final breath. Dark clumps of blood and bile poured from his mouth and ears. Schüller stared into oblivion as he slumped forward. Savage and Santiago were gone.

Fifty-Nine

Savage's eyes opened to reveal the night sky and the sounds of musket fire and screaming. He was weak and disoriented. Blurred images of people rushed by like ghosts. He could feel the earth on his face and smell burning gunpowder in the cool air. His brain was telling his body to move, but his body wasn't responding. Santiago was lying next to him, unconscious.

Tiny pinholes of light dotted the pitch-black heavens. A large bonfire burned nearby. It bathed teepees in a warm flickering glow.

"Happy first Thanksgiving," Stewart said kneeling over Savage. She was dressed in Native American buckskin holding a tomahawk. There was a splash of blood across the front of her tunic.

"Savage, you did it. I'm very proud of you. I'm very proud of both of you."

"Why? Why are you doing this?" Savage asked in delirium.

"I was once lost, but now I am found. Savage, we are both found."

"What?"

"Each of us have our... *issues* within our respective worlds. We're outliers, misfits, renegades, living outside our insipid societal rituals—but we have a gift—a calling. My father may have been a patronizing piece of shit, but he was *my* patronizing piece of shit. But he had the right idea. We teach through example. Savage, we have a purpose and a job to do."

"What's that?"

"We make things right."

"I... I have... so many questions."

"You're the hero of the most popular lifestyle simulation game in the colonies."

"Game?"

"It's more real than reality."

"This is a game?"

"It's open season on evil, and we're going to deliver justice."

"This is all a fucking game?"

"Get some rest. I need you at your best."

"I..."

"Nighty, night."

"Noooo," Savage fought to stay conscious but gave in and passed out.

Epilogue

Savage felt the cold as his eyes opened slowly. He was lying on the freezing floor of a hallway. He was confused, blurry-eyed, and shocked to discover he was still alive. He fought to regain his equilibrium and realized he was freezing to death. He couldn't feel his fingers. Santiago was unconscious lying next to him. They were wearing the same clothes from moments before. He struggled to clear his head and realized he was in some kind of passageway.

"Santiago. Wake up," he said, shaking her.

She started to come around still groggy. She woke up startled with an involuntary jerking motion. Savage held her in his arms to calm her. "We're alive."

Her brain fought disorientation as the freezing cold enveloped her.

Savage released her. "We're on some kind of a ship."

Santiago looked around frantically, trying to get her bearings. Savage helped her stand up.

"It's fucking freezing!" Santiago blurted as the crisp cold cut through her.

Wobbly and rising to their feet, they pulled themselves up against the ornate walls of a wooden railing that ran down the length of a corridor. Thirty feet in one direction of the hall was a nautical doorway with a porthole.

"This way," Savage said as he helped her get her balance.

They stumbled along the length of the passageway to the door and peered through the porthole. They saw the deck of a ship with a railing in the foreground and the ocean behind it. They opened the door and stepped out to reveal they were on an ocean liner. They shivered uncontrollably as they impulsively backed up towards the hallway. They slammed the door behind them.

"We're at sea," Santiago announced. "Goddamn it. But where? Where are we?"

"The better question is, when are we?" Savage replied.

"It isn't 2023; that's for damn sure," Santiago answered. "This passage-way looks ancient."

They peered through the porthole and saw the deck of the ship. Savage and Santiago saw couples wearing heavy coats walking by in early 20th-century winter apparel. They appeared to be wealthy tourists on vacation, taking in the view of the ocean. Large chunks of ice floated by like little islands.

Suddenly the door burst open. They stepped backward as a large, well-dressed man stepped in. All three were startled to see each other. "What's all this then?" The man said. "Oh, a thousand pardons."

He was bundled up in an early 20th-century heavy coat, scarf, and top hat. He had a long grey-speckled beard and spoke with a posh upper-class British accent.

"Excuse us," announced Santiago. "Ugh... My name is Dolores Santi-ago. This is my faithful negro companion, Lorenzo Savage."

"Charles Hayes at your service," he said, ignoring Savage. "Lost your way, have you? It's a big ship."

He got a good look at them and realized they were inappropriately dressed for the weather. "I wouldn't go out there if I were you. A bit nippy would be putting it mildly." Hayes' eyes locked in on Santiago with a flirtatious grin.

"Where are we?" Savage interjected as his teeth chattered. Hayes ignored him.

"We left our coats back in our room," Santiago continued. "We didn't think it would be so cold today, but boy were we wrong," she said as she tried to control the involuntary chills that took over her body.

"Don't worry your pretty little head. We British are known for our resourcefulness. Here's a little something I learned about this ship a few days ago."

He looked both ways down the corridor to make sure no one was watching. He gingerly stepped past them and behind them. With a finger motioning for Santiago to follow him, he led them to a narrow closet marked CREW ONLY. He opened the closet. In it were two dark blue heavy overcoats.

"You can wear these for now, but you'll have to return them before the crew finds out."

"Thank you. We certainly will," Santiago said as she put on the coat. Savage did the same.

"Glad to be of service," Hayes said with a smile.

"Much appreciated," Savage said in relief as he buttoned up the coat. He shivered with numb fingertips.

"I can tell by your accents you're American. Returning home, are you?"

"Yes. Going home," Savage answered. "Home sweet home."

Offended that Savage was speaking to him, Hayes frowned and ignored him. Savage noticed this but decided to press his luck anyway. "Listen, guv'nor, we've lost track of time on the ship. What's today's date?"

"I beg your pardon?"

"What's today's date?"

Hayes turned his attention to Santiago. "My humble apologies, but I'm not in the habit of conversing with jungle bunnies. I served the Queen in Africa. Surely you understand."

Savage smiled, suppressing the urge to collapse his skull.

"I understand," Santiago replied. "Please forgive my manservant. We just need to know what today is."

"It's been four days, but I can see how that happens. I often lose track of time myself—there's so much to see and do. This ship is truly a modern marvel of technology. Perhaps you'd like a personal tour?"

"What day is today?" Santiago asked again.

"It's Monday," Hayes replied.

"The date. What's the date?" Savage asked again, pressing harder.

"Its April 15th, you black ape!" Hayes replied, not able to contain himself.

"Not this shit again," Savage said under his breath.

"I beg your pardon?!"

"I apologize for my valet," Santiago said, attempting to pacify Hayes. "We need your help."

"I refuse to be addressed by this darkie," Hayes retorted.

"Motherfucker," Savage said under his breath.

"What did you say?" Hayes replied.

"Nothing," Santiago said, giving Savage a look of caution.

"This may seem like an odd question," Santiago continued apologetically. "What year is this?"

Hayes gave them both a strange look. "Who are you?"

"We need to know what year it is," Santiago asked again.

"You're not supposed to be here," Hayes said with suspicion. "You're stowaways. I won't be a party to this!"

As he turned to leave, Savage grabbed him by the arm. "What year is it?"

"Get your niggery hands off me!"

Hayes jerked his arm away and threw a punch at Savage's head and missed. Savage grabbed his arm and wheeled him around in a semi-circle, slamming him into the wall. Savage pressed against him.

"What did you call me? Say it again!"

Hayes head-butted Savage sending him back into the opposite wall. Savage bounced off the wall in pain and fell to his knees in front of Santiago. Hayes ran out through the door escaping outside to the deck.

"Help! Stowaway! Stowaway!"

"Great!" Santiago said as she helped Savage to his feet. "Thank you for your help," she said with angry sarcasm.

Savage held his bruised forehead, trying to maintain his equilibrium. "We've got to get out of here!"

Savage and Santiago took off, running in the opposite direction down the passageway. They stopped at a corner and listened before they turned. They heard voices from a distance.

Hayes was telling a group of crewmembers about Savage and Santiago. "This way! They're down the next passageway!"

"They're coming this way," Savage said.

Santiago looked around the corner and darted her head back.

"There's five of them. I need to take care of those clowns before more of them show up and overtake us."

"Ok. I got your back."

"You've done plenty. I'll handle this."

Santiago calmly stepped around the corner and walked toward the group with an innocent expression on her face. "What's going on, fellas?"

"That's her!" Hayes shouted, bringing up the rear behind four of the ship's crewmembers. "She's one of the stowaways!"

Instantly they were upon her. As the first crewmember reached out to restrain her, she grabbed his wrist and jerked his arm downward. She broke his nose with a solid punch using the heel of her hand. As he sank to the floor, she had already intercepted the next crewmember with a brutal front kick to his groin and a double front kick to his face.

The third crewmember threw a punch Santiago easily evaded. She re-directed it into the face of another crewmember. The sound of the punch echoed through the corridor. The crewmembers recoiled in pain. She finished them with double elbow strikes sending them into unconsciousness.

The last crewmember froze. Santiago side kicked him in the face. This sent his head backward, slamming into Hayes' face. They both dropped to the floor, unconscious. Santiago heard a sound and turned to see Savage finishing off the first crewmember with a hard overhand punch to his chin. The crewmember dropped to the floor with a heavy thud.

"Let's go!" Savage barked.

They ran past the unconscious crewmembers and turned another corner. Another crew of nine, including the captain holding a pistol, blocked their exit.

"Stop right there! Don't go any further!"

Savage and Santiago froze and put their hands up. Their eyes darted around for options, but there was nowhere to run. They were trapped.

"Put the woman in the brig," the captain ordered. "Throw the nigger overboard. This is how we deal with stowaways."

Savage noticed an ornate brass emblem on a closet door that read RMS TITANIC. Blood pounded through his temples. His eyes widened with recognition. "What year is this?"

"Shut your nigger hole," the captain ordered. "Take him away."

"Captain Smith! You're Captain Edward Smith!"

"Who are you? I doubt I have met your acquaintance."

"It's Monday, April 15, 1912!"

Santiago looked at him like he was a ghost. "What are you talking about?"

"We're on the Titanic! We're going to hit an iceberg!"

"Silence the nigger," Captain Smith ordered. A crewmember slapped Savage across the face with a pistol.

Savage fell to his knees. "A lot of people are going to die!"

"The darkie is clearly touched," Captain Smith chuckled. "Take him on deck and toss him overboard.

"Listen to me," Savage pleaded. "You have to change course. We're going to hit an iceberg!"

They grabbed Savage and Santiago roughly, moving them out onto the deck of the ship.

"You have to believe me," Savage said forcefully. "We're going to hit an iceberg. This ship won't be able to withstand the impact."

"Stop the fucking ship!" Santiago yelled.

"If you don't do something, we're all dead," Savage continued.

Ignoring them, the crew and Captain Smith dragged Savage and Santiago next to the deck's railing.

"Do you have any last words?" Captain Smith inquired.

"You don't have enough lifeboats for the crew and passengers!"

"He's right!" added Santiago. "Change course! Do it! Do it now!"

"They're obviously opium addicts," Captain Smith said jokingly. The crew laughed.

"The Titanic is unsinkable. But you're not. Monkeys don't swim very well. Toss him over," he ordered.

They lifted Savage in the air, moving him close to the edge of the railing. Large chunks of ice drifted by in the frigid waters.

Suddenly they heard a loud, frightening BOOM. The ship shuttered violently. The crew put Savage down. They listened to the eerie creaking sounds of huge metal structures folding inward. Everyone froze.

A terrified young ensign ran up to Captain Smith, barely able to contain himself. "Sir, we've hit an iceberg! We're taking on water!"

A cacophony of screams erupted from all areas of the ship as passengers ran past them in hysteria. The captain and his crew turned to Savage. Their sunken eyes filled with debilitating fear.

"Sweet Moses, how did you know?" The captain asked.

"Oh, so *now* you're inquisitive!? Motherfucker, you pistol whipped me and called me a monkey not two minutes ago!"

Savage tortured them with his silence. The eerie sounds of buckling support beams and shrieking metal were so terrifying it made their skin crawl. Crippling fear raced down the spines of the captain and crew.

"For God sakes man, help us!" Blurted the captain.

Savage got back on the clock. "Alright, listen up. This is what I need you to do."

The End

Printed in the USA
CPSIA information can be obtained
at www.ICGtesting.com
LVHW020913010324
773138LV00012B/311